How to Fix a
Flubbed Summon

L. N. Clarke

NAUGHTOBELUS

How to Fix a Flubbed Summon

Published by Naughtobelus Books LLC

www.naughtobelus.com

Copy Editor: Chelsea Beam

Cover Font: Hophus Roghus by Bombastype
Chapter Number Font: Ivory by FaceType

ISBN 979-8-9862466-0-4 (paperback)
ISBN 979-8-9862466-1-1 (hardcover - case laminate)
ISBN 979-8-9862466-2-8 (hardcover - dust jacket)
ISBN 979-8-9862466-3-5 (ebook)
ISBN 979-8-9862466-4-2 (audio book)

First Edition 2023

Library of Congress Control Number: 2023920370

*To my dad,
who began every story on a dark and stormy night.*

HOW TO FIX A
FLUBBED SUMMON

One

Bottles and Bed Imps

GROWINA CROWE WAS—technically speaking—an ageless beauty.

Despite her baby cheeks and smiling eyes, her premature gray had made her appear middle-aged before her twentieth birthday. She had looked fifty in her thirties, fifty in her forties, and, if the trend continued, would look fifty until her skeleton joined the remains of the Wontmoil dancing band in the local cemetery.

Luckily, they were desperate for an accordionist.

Bodies were, in Growina's opinion, little more than a great place to display potato-print fabrics and crocheted shawls. However, as she fidgeted in the entryway to Pollywog's Pampering Powders, she got the distinct impression it was her face—not her butter-kitten print—that would be factored into the owner's forthcoming decision.

"Do you know what I sell here?" Jacqueline Pollywog asked, while holding a bottle between two manicured fingernails like it was a dead cockroach.

Growina glanced around the store. "Face dust, lip ink, and charcoal for the eyes?"

"It's makeup, Growina. Do you know what makeup is for?"

"Personally, or historically?"

Pollywog released the bottle into Growina's outstretched hands. "It's for making young people look older and old people look younger. It's what I do for a living. So, I'm unsure why you think I'd be interested in cross-promoting *literal* de-aging serum."

Growina beamed, sales pitch already prepared. "I'm offering sixty percent of every purchase, plus ten copper fudgels for each customer who enters my apothecary shop—even if they don't buy. *And* the serum will help with your store's stated goal of making everyone in Wontmoil feel beautiful!"

"I see. Do you, by any chance, recall what the owner of the fitness center said when you asked her to promote your strength-boosting potions?"

"That she'd go broke if the wannabe warriors in this town discovered they could gain muscle from a bottle rather than honest exercise?"

"Right. And what about when you dragged that bubbling cauldron to the tellers at the bank?"

Growina scrunched up her nose in thought. "Turning silver fudgels into gold fudgels will devalue the currency and the labor required to earn it, eventually resulting in widespread economic collapse and the end of society as we know it."

Pollywog shook her head. "That one was a bad example, but the point is made. If everyone in Wontmoil purchases your serum, no one will require my makeup. I can't accept your offer."

Growina's eyes grew wide. She nodded sagely. "Because I'd rob you of the joy of helping others yourself!"

"Right. Yes. What you said."

Something outside caught Pollywog's eye, and she pursed her lips. It was the same look that crossed every local's face when a particular sort of outsider wandered into town . . . specifically, the sort that made the bell jingle on the door to

Growina's apothecary shop.

Growina spun in time to see a mobile heap of apparently-distressed black fabric skitter into an alley beside the butchers. "Oh, bother. That looks like Margaret. Everything's always 'end of the world' this and 'eternal doom' that with her. I'd better head back before she blasts my door down."

She stuffed her hands into one of the several dozen pockets in her puffy skirts and retrieved a handful of glowing pink marbles. Each was as large as a thimble and full of glittering nectar.

Pollywog raised her hands in protest. "Wait. Stop. I don't want to clean—"

Growina dropped a marble and smashed it under her feet, releasing a puff of smoke and an expanding pool of dark liquid. Thorny vines shot upward, wrapped around her buckled boots, and yanked her into the pool.

Pollywog gritted her teeth as the liquid evaporated. "—the glass."

* * *

An excerpt from the Lazy Botanist's Guide to Naughtobelus.

Solus Floribunda BLASTED GLASSFLOWER

Habitat: Unknown

Appearance: A woody plant with vine-like growths, thorny armature, and vibrant flowers.

Characteristics: Plant is aggressively stingy. Cuttings only removable inside sealed glass orbs with no exposure to atmosphere. Do not drop, or parent plant will reclaim cuttings and surrounding objects. Consumption of fruit is not advised.

Author's note: Only known plant is located at Herbs and Vices in downtown Wontmoil. If a specimen shatters, lost valuables and pets can be retrieved at the counter.

* * *

"Let go, you silly bramble," Growina ordered as she tugged her cat-paw shawl free of a trellis.

Even with her instantaneous (if undignified) teleportation into her backyard herbary, someone was already pounding on the shop's entrance. She scurried inside, danced around jars of seldom-dusted backstock, and burst through a wispy curtain into the storefront.

"Just a moment!"

The apothecary shop had five bolts and a heavy bar on its double doors, which was excessively paranoid for the dull town and doubly so for her merchandise. Few fences could move a pile of potions, and most were already her customers. But Growina discovered early on that illiterate burglars could cause more harm to themselves than her bottom line. Decades after her worst break-in, she still received soggy correspondence from two darling young men who had confused myrrh and mer.

"Margaret!" Growina wrenched the doors open to reveal a wide-eyed witch with both fists in the air. "Lovely to—"

"Imps," Margaret said between ragged breaths. "The wretched, tiny, bitey kind." The witch shoved her way into the shop and glanced from shelf to shelf as if tracking a fly. Her head jerked about and caused the constellation-shaped jewelry in her braids to jangle.

Growina tugged the doors shut to block out sunlight and waited for the shop's cozy lighting and woody fragrance to take effect. Within moments, Margaret's shoulders sagged, and her breathing slowed enough to explain her previous outburst.

"The head of the barding school hired me to sort out a bed imp infestation," she said. "They're gnawing holes in his boot leather in the night."

"We have a boarding school?"

"No. Barding. You know . . ." Margaret flailed her hands to indicate something large and curvy. "Horse armor."

"Ah. That makes more sense. Why is he wearing his boots to bed?"

"Please." The witch moaned. "Have you got something?"

Growina nodded and hustled to a small wooden rack. Her powders and potions were labeled, but she was familiar enough to identify them by appearance. In under a second, she had a vial of pea-green powder plucked and set onto her cluttered counter. "Sprinkle this between his sheets and leave it a week. The imps will mistake the odor for flatulence and search for an uncontaminated nest. Anything else?"

Margaret's mouth opened and closed again before she said, "No, just the imp dust."

Alarm bells rang in Growina's head. Margaret was a talented witch, and the head of a coven with an entry in every adventuring journal in Naughtobelus. She had more positive qualities than a lizard had scales. Frugality, however, was not one of them.

And who hired the famous Bograven Sisters for *bed imps*?

Growina crossed her arms and scowled. "Okay. Out with it. What's going on?"

"Nothing! Lots and lots of nothing. Honestly, I *am* a bit low on insta-stake and bandage-in-a-bottle. Also, the ingredients required to change the weather and transmute objects.

Oh, and those tiny candles that discreetly freshen a powder room. But funds are tight."

"Since when?"

Despite the stated lack of funds, Growina searched behind her counter for an unused basket, placed the imp vial into it, and collected the woman's necessities as she listened.

"Since Theo put a protective barrier around the howling woods. Don't get me wrong, it was the right thing to do and a clever bit of engineering. But—oh. Not those. The pink ones."

Growina replaced the blue candles she had selected and picked up a bundle in baby pink. "Now that you mention it, it has been quiet."

"Exactly. We've banished every bloodthirsty beast in the penta-city conurbation. Now, we're squabbling over house pests and undead horseflies. It's the end of adventuring as we know it."

"Oh, rubbish," Growina said. "Something nasty will pop up soon. It always does."

"Easy for you to say! You provide vital services. You don't know what it's like to be unneeded."

Growina's smile faltered, and she glanced toward a brand-new display rack packed with tiny bottles of anti-aging serum. Above it hung a hooded cloak from a party she attended solo and a bottle bandolier she crafted *just in case* someone invited her on an adventure.

She shook her head and handed the basket to Margaret. "To hold you over till the next doomsday."

Margaret feigned shock, even as she gripped the handle. "What? I can't accept this!"

"Shush. You're one of my best customers, and it'll do me no good if you go out of business."

After a quarter second of pretend-pondering, Margaret replied, "Fine. I see your logic. But not for free." She flicked a hand in the air, and a thick book appeared. It floated like a poplar seed into her open palm, and she shoved it into Growina's hands. "Hold on to this until I pay every fudgel."

Growina examined the symbols scorched into the book's leather binding. "A grimoire? But won't you need it for your work?"

She hoped Margret would change her mind and accept the goods as a personal gift. Better to receive nothing in return than have an awkward sense of debt between them. Still, she did not protest, because something in the witch's posture indicated the grimoire was meant to preserve her dignity, not satisfy a financial contract.

"I rarely require *that* one," Margaret said in a tone reminiscent of a bully discussing their victim among peers.

Growina's eyes narrowed. "Why's that? Are the spells impractical, or—"

"Er, as much as I'd love to stick around and talk shop in your shop, I can't keep my client waiting."

"It's half-past breakfast. What time does that man go to bed?"

"Growina, please."

"But—"

"Imps!" Margaret hoisted the basket, spun on her heels, and snapped her fingers at the doors as if they were disobedient puppies. They flew open with a squeal and knocked the doorbell around so violently it jangled like a fire alarm.

Impressive magic, but hardly necessary for someone with a free hand to turn a knob.

The witch inhaled and steadied herself before she stepped into the sunshine. "Good seeing you!"

"But—"

"Ta!"

She strode out and slammed the doors with a twist of her

hand, leaving Growina alone in the dim storefront with a heavy grimoire and a half-dozen imp-related questions. Still, the interaction had gone well for an early morning encounter with Margaret. Perhaps a dry spell had done the persistently pessimistic witch some good.

Growina took a moment to gather her thoughts and plan the rest of her morning. She had a display to dismantle, but not before she brewed a pot of home-grown tea. Every effort deserved a reward, and what better to pair with a steaming cup of tea than a brand-new book?

TWO

The Captain and the Thespian

FAR FROM WONTMOIL and the penta-city conurbation, deep within the prosperous city of Leechleif, there existed a woman who was everything Growina Crowe was not. She was youthful and brawny, skilled with a sword, and could fell a pine while reciting poetry backward in a ballgown. Many said the woman was the most desirable in Naughtobelus.

Or, at least, she would be if she were a real person.

Florian Honeybeard, the male actor who strapped on two bags of rice to star in her theatrical production, commanded less respect than the character. Without his scripts, feminine makeup, or gorgeous costumes, he was exceptionally average in appearance and ability—so much so that he found himself a victim of mistaken identity more often than any man deserved.

That appeared to be the case again as he stood in the home office of Leechleif's wealthiest mercenary company. Based on his reception when he arrived, he suspected their captain had confused him with someone unsavory. Specifically, an unsavory person who owed her a great deal of money.

"I think there's been some confusion," he explained, careful to maintain an air of professionalism despite a growing urge to leap out a window and skitter down the street like a spooked kitten. "I'm a thespian. From the Spherule Theater. I've come on behalf of my management to discuss the renewal of your annual membership."

Captain Beatrix Bodkins gripped the armrests of her spider-like chair—an impressive device propelled by the reanimated limbs of horrific monsters she had conquered—and walked it right up to his legs. She bared her fangs as she jabbed a finger that might as well have been a dagger toward his face. "Do you think this is a good time to get funny with me?"

Florian grimaced. He spent most of his adult life in heavy robes and thick makeup, but never realized until this moment how much sweat his face could produce on command. "No?"

"Good." She leaned back and shouted to someone in another room. "Wardric! You're not gonna believe this. Peterman's back!"

"No kidding?" a rumbling voice replied from somewhere within the house. A barrel-chested man with a long goatee stumbled downstairs three steps at a time.

At first glance, Wardric the merc appeared to be decorated head to toe in narrow blades. However, once Florian finished swallowing his tongue in shock, he realized the items strapped to the man's torso and legs were pencils and paintbrushes, not daggers and knives.

"Woof," the enormous artist said. "I don't know if it's wise or foolish to come back after you skipped out on Bodkins, but I'm impressed by your guts, man."

As discretely as he could, Florian performed a breathing exercise meant to relieve stage fright. This was not what he agreed to when management asked him to visit the theater's wealthiest patrons. But he was an actor, dang it, and a famous one—technically. Whoever this Peterman was, he had seemingly done nothing horrible enough to warrant arrest or execution. That was a good sign.

With luck and a bit of improvisation, it might be possible to—

"Foolish," Bodkins confirmed. "But well-timed. We're suffering a shortage of contracts this month, and I'm *starved* for action."

She slammed her fist into her armrest to punctuate her words. The impact made her curls bob and inspired three of the severed limbs supporting her chair to tremble. She leaned over and growled at them.

"Action?" Florian asked.

Her head snapped up. "You owe me fourteen gold fudgels' worth of adventure. 'The quest of a lifetime,' you said. And you're not running off again till I get what I paid for, with interest."

Florian struggled to come up with an intelligent response and failed miserably—a distressing phenomenon, as he was an expert ad-libber with prompts and context. Without knowing who Peterman was before he took the mercenaries' money and ran, it was impossible to build a character in his mind.

Was the man a charlatan? A boat captain down on his luck? A party planner? What exactly had he promised?

"Adventure," he said eventually. "Of course. Where to, then?"

Bodkins' brows arched. "What? To lunch, of course!"

"Eh?"

Wardric perked up. "Oh yeah! I've still got the thingy somewhere. I'll go find it."

He rushed down a hallway and Bodkins slowly urged her chair after him.

Florian muttered, "Thingy?" under his breath, then glanced back at the front door.

"You lookin' to find out how fast I can skewer a rat?" Bodkins asked, seeing the movement.

He straightened and shook his head. "Me? No. I'm just . . . admiring the architecture."

Admiring the architecture. Yuck. When Florian returned to the theater, he would sign up for improv night. No excuses.

Bodkins was equally unimpressed. "Hmph. Come on. Food's this way."

When they finally got settled, Florian grimaced. Food was a generous description for the tin pan of mush Wardric slapped onto the dining table in front of him. Globs of unidentifiable beige sloshed onto the gnarled tabletop, making Florian recoil to avoid stains on his trousers.

It was impossible not to notice that Bodkins and Wardric's dishes were more stew than goo, and that they had spoons where Florian had none. Even stranger was the fact that they stared expectantly at him rather than digging into their lunch.

"Oh!" Bodkins said as if she suddenly remembered her kettle was on. "Do we need to shut the drapes? Set the mood?"

He searched her face for a hint of sarcasm but found none. Was Peterman a performer, perhaps?

"We've got some candles in the silver drawer," Wardric added. "And we can get close and hold hands or whatever."

Florian tilted his head. The setup sounded familiar, but the only thing that came to mind was a scene from a romantic comedy, which did not fit the narrative.

"I'm not holding hands with *anyone* unless it's necessary for the visions," Bodkins declared.

Oh, fudge.

Icy goosebumps ran up Florian's arms and made the hair on the back of his neck stand on end. Drapes? Candles? Visions? Peterman was a soothsayer!

And Florian was in big trouble.

With the right motive and backstory, he could imitate any living being on Naughtobelus. But how did one fake a vision of the future and make it come true?

Fortunately, in understanding his predicament, he also gained a secret weapon. He finally knew how to play Peterman's character.

It was time for the show to begin.

"I have to be honest with you," he said with a conspiratorial air. "The problem isn't the ambiance or physical contact. It's my supplies. I don't have them with me, and I can't perform without them. If you like, I can head back and—"

"I knew it!" Wardric shouted.

Bodkins hushed him. "I gave you three times as many fudgels as you requested to pay your debts and purchase supplies. What did you do with my money?"

Florian mentally kicked himself for the mistake, but remained in character. "The money was fine. It's the supplies themselves. Unfortunately, I haven't found everything I need. But I can go back out and look."

Wardric raised a hand and bounced around like a child in need of a toilet, but Bodkins ignored him and continued her interrogation. "What happened to your great connections? Your smuggler friends?"

Florian tried to remember the props his crew gave soothsayers, but it seemed like random junk to him, as if the prop masters knew the audience was as clueless as they were. There were reflective rocks, sticks suspended by strings, and colorful glass jars. But what was meant to be *in* them? What were they made of that required smuggling?

"They were liars," he said. "Terrible friends. They didn't have the stuff after all."

"I was right!" Wardric blurted, despite the nasty glare he received for it. "That's why you didn't come back. You couldn't get ahold of the banned plant!"

Bodkins sighed, reached into a pouch on her shoulder,

and produced a copper coin. "Fine. You were right, and I was wrong. He's not complete scum. Happy?"

Wardric snatched the coin and nodded.

Finally, things were looking up.

Florian cleared his throat. "So, you see, I can't predict an adventure for you yet. But if you give me a bit more time, I can find the plant."

"Time's up," Wardric said with a grin before he reached beneath his chair and retrieved a tiny bottle of what looked like emerald eels engaging in a game of tug-of-war. He set it before Florian and leaned back like he had produced a lost script from the suspiciously obliterated rival theater in Mooncalf-Pale.

"Ah," Florian said with all the enthusiasm he could muster. "You found it."

He inspected the bottle as if impressed. It seemed like the right thing to do, and it gave him time to stop his brain from screaming and form a new plan. The mercenaries would not let him out of their sight until he predicted an adventure. So, that was what he would do.

The only question was *how*.

Bodkins gestured at the plate in front of him. "Well? You've got the weeds. You've got the salt paste. What next? Do you eat it?"

That answered part of Florian's question. If the mercenaries knew the ingredients and not the ritual, it gave him more room for creativity.

"Eat this?" He held up the bottle of thrashing weeds. "Not a chance. Wardric, was it? I've changed my mind. I would love the curtains drawn and some candles lit. Also, do you have something I could cover this pan with?"

Light was one of the most powerful tools in an actor's kit, and dim lighting did more than set a mood. It hid the fine details and sleight of hand, leaving more to an audience's imagination. That was precisely what he needed to convincingly fake a fortune.

Wardric whistled as he prepped the room and wandered off to fetch a lid. It took him less than a minute, but it seemed like ten under Bodkins' constant scrutiny.

"This do?" Wardric asked as he set a lid down.

Florian grinned. "Perfect. Now, I need you both to think very hard about the sort of adventure you want. Clear your mind of everything else and keep thinking about your desire as I perform the ritual."

With a flourish, he reached for the stopper on the bottle. The weeds inside struggled against the glass, each leaf pulling against the others where they connected at the roots. With any luck, they would continue to do so—at least temporarily—when dropped in a pan of salt.

"Here we go," he said as he plucked the stopper out, dumped the weeds into the paste, and slammed the lid down.

If he were on stage, he would shout some kind of incantation. Maybe call to the moon and stars for assistance or beg the local spirits for inspiration. Unfortunately, he needed realism, not showmanship.

He closed his eyes and muttered, "Please let this work," several times at a volume only a dog could hear.

As he mumbled, he gripped the edge of the lidded pan and swirled it about on the table for good measure. The more texture in the result, the more convincing his "visions" could be. A couple of triangles could be a fanged beast. Ripples could be ocean waves. Maybe he would see an army of slime monsters. Who could say?

When he felt enough time had passed, he stopped swirling and gripped the lid. "Let's see what we have."

Bodkins bit her lip. Wardric trembled in his seat.

Florian lifted the lid.

"Well, that's not good," he said before he could stop himself.

Bodkins leaned toward him and squinted into the darkness. "What? What do you see?"

"It's . . ." Florian was at a total loss for words as he stared down into his bowl of mush—and the perfectly illustrated human skull within it. The image was not an abstract shape, like a fluffy cloud bunny.

It was a *skull*.

The blackened weeds, finally free of their roots, wriggled from its eye sockets toward the edges of the pan.

"It's bad," he said. "Something creepy and cursed that shouldn't be here. Huge and skeletal with hollow eyes." He squinted at the shapes left behind by the weeds as they attempted to escape their salty doom. "And tentacles."

Bodkins gasped. "It's *perfect*. Where is it?"

Florian's brows knit. Most of the weeds reached the edge of the pan before they stopped moving. But one escaped and took off across the tabletop.

"It's pretty far away."

Wardric threw out an excited guess. "Mooncalf-Pale?"

The weed dropped off the edge of the table, determined to escape despite its withered appearance. Florian left his chair and sank to his knees to watch it more closely.

"I think much further than that."

"Picaroon Pelf?" Bodkins asked. She waited only a moment before she gasped and changed her guess. "The penta-city conurbation?"

The shriveled weed struggled toward a crack in the floorboards where it might escape into the foundation, but each wiggle was wobblier than the last. Finally, the whole leaf gave up and fell flat.

"Yes," Florian said once he was sure it would not move.

"That's the spot."

Wardric grumbled. "I hate that place."

Florian's pounding heart slowed. Far away was good. It meant he would be long gone when they realized there was no tentacled monster awaiting them. Next time a mercenary was late on a yearly subscription to the theater, management could drop by themselves.

Still, he could not resist asking, "Why is that?"

Bodkins leaned back in her chair and closed her eyes. "They call themselves adventurers there, and we call ourselves mercs, so they think they're better than us. But they take fudgels to fight evil, same as we do. We're just more honest about it."

"Oh. Does that mean you won't be going?"

"Don't be ridiculous!" she said. "The rest of us are ready to go as soon as you get some lunch."

And scene.

Florian exhaled and let his shoulders sag—as if the curtain had closed on his performance—before he processed her words and tensed up again.

"What do you mean, 'the rest of us?'"

THREE

Thumps in the Night

An excerpt from the Lazy Botanist's Guide to Naughtobelus.

Dendrolycopodium Motus Wriggleweed

Habitat: Any place at all, if you allow it.

Appearance: Flat-branched plant with scale-like leaves and short stems.

Characteristics: Plant cannot stand its own kind. Mature branches tear free of parent and wander to new soil to start anew (much like my relatives).

Author's note: Wriggleweed is dangerously invasive due to its rapid reproduction and spread. Possession of live specimens is illegal in most cities without conservationist permit. No excuses.

* * *

Growina tapped the end of her pen against a glass enclosure to silence the squabbling plants inside, then returned her attention to the book on her potting bench. From a professional perspective, Margaret's seldom-used grimoire was as informative as it was entertaining; the hand-scribbled notes among the cryptic instructions offered a window into the witch's more bizarre purchasing habits.

They came in three flavors: clarifications (*pugnut-sized ball of grave dirt refers to western pugnuts, not eastern!*), corrections (*recipe is outdated. Do not wrestle crows for their spit. Insult them instead.*), and substitutions (*this stinky flower is extinct. Use shrews' droppings for similar effect.*)

The final category excited Growina the most. It offered an opportunity to surprise Margaret with ingredients that were not as extinct—or *flipping impossible to find*—as the witch supposed. She was only halfway through the grimoire and already had a half-page list of impossible items she could pluck from her herbary at a moment's notice if Margaret needed them.

Unfortunately, the spells in the book were borrowed from witches much older than the Bograven Sisters, and although the ingredients they called for were not extinct, the nasty beasties they banished probably were. Of the non-beastie spells that remained, many felt behind-the-times or oddly specific, which explained why Margaret rarely required them.

"A charm to seduce the last of the snow river sprites?" Growina read with a giggle. "Good luck with *that* ancient spell. He's been happily married for fifty—oh. Oh!" She flushed and turned the page. "Naughty witches."

Based on the inverted graphite on the following page, the next spell was even older than the last. Margaret must have taken a rubbing from a stone tablet or monument.

"To summon an otherworldly companion," Growina read. "Hm. That doesn't sound so bad."

The instructions themselves were a mess of scribbled substitutions, forming a list that ultimately ended in a scrawled, "not enough supplies." Between Margaret's handiwork and the faded graphite, Growina was forced to flip her paper over and copy the original by hand to read it clearly.

"I have that!" she said as she put a check next to the first ingredient. "And that. And the berries. Oh, come on now, everyone has that! Where did she look?"

Growina finished her review and leaned back, pleased with her progress. Every line with a listed ingredient had a check mark beside it. That made one entire ancient spell Margaret could pull off from this grimoire without substitutions. She would be so excited!

Growina's smile faded the more she stared at the page. Unlike the newer spells, the companion one was not only meant for experienced witches. It read more like a potion recipe with accompanying mental exercises: the sort of thing a child might invent when playing make-believe. There was no finger-twirling, fluid-smearing, or secret bargain with a dead-eyed monster that rose from a bog in the dead of night.

Weird.

"Bets on if this summons anything?" she asked her garden.

Plants were excellent listeners and always appreciated a conversation. However, the wriggleweed on her potting bench thrashed, opposed to the concept of company entirely. She rolled her eyes and tapped her pen against the enclosure again.

"Shush. I'll prune you tomorrow."

The plant had a point, though. Constant engagement was exhausting, especially when you couldn't choose your company. Small bursts of activity were much preferred, with adequate downtime in between.

Unfortunately, the sort of person with room in their life for an unmarried friend with too many plants rarely respected her need to recharge. That did not mean the right person was not out there somewhere. Perhaps, in another world, there was someone else who longed for a quiet existence with brief bouts of excitement—on their own terms.

She chewed her lip, then reached for an empty basket. And why not find out? The spell wouldn't likely work, anyway.

The sun slid behind her garden's brick walls while she gathered ingredients. Glowing mushrooms took over from there, lighting her way with bioluminescence. The air was a tad cold after dark, but that was fine. She had everything she needed at that point, anyway, save candles and a cauldron.

"Kitchen, kitchen," she muttered as she made her way inside. "And maybe a snack. Oh! My future friend may be hungry, too!"

Growina grabbed a heavy sweater, put the kettle on, and dug beneath her counter for a cast-iron cauldron. She set out some cookies, just in case, and searched the cabinets for candles in black. The spell also called for a protective circle made of anything one could sprinkle or set, so she grabbed the first thing that made any sense: a bowl of cinnamon potpourri.

No reason a spell shouldn't also smell great.

The location she chose in the center of the herbary had a thin layer of dust from a thousand ground potions, but it was the only space clear enough to set up her circle. She swept the ground, sprinkled the cinnamon, placed the cauldron, and lit the candles and fire. Then she lifted her copied page of instructions.

"Three whiskerroot petals, freshly picked."

She dropped the petals into the cauldron, then flinched as if they might ignite in a puff of sparkling smoke. Instead, they drifted into the simmering liquid and sat, soggy and pathetic, on the water's surface. She stuck out her bottom lip. It would be disappointing if, after everything was done, she ended up with a batch of herb and berry soup.

"Oh, bother," she said as her eyes returned to the page. "I was supposed to think about my companion while I did that. Hmm."

She closed her eyes and imagined a cozy weekend with a friend, both lounging in puffy armchairs and reading the gazette. Maybe they shared a funny cartoon or put their heads together on a puzzle. Or perhaps they noticed an ad for adventure and agreed upon a spontaneous outing. The important thing was the comfort they shared in the same relative space.

Growina squinted at the subsequent recipe lines, tossed more ingredients into the cauldron, and raised a brow. When she copied the instructions from the grimoire, her focus had been on the plants, not the mental exercises. But now that she was midway through, the phrase, "Imagine an ideal physical form," struck her as strange.

Her limbs went cold and prickly, even as her cheeks heated. Either the witch who wrote the instruction was choosy about their friends, or Growina misjudged the spell entirely.

"Is this meant to be a *romantic* companion?" she asked the flowers that bloomed in moonlight.

They had no clue.

Something told her she should stop, but then the spell soup turned a bubbly green, and the air smelled more of licorice than cinnamon. The companion spell was working, for better or for worse, despite its childish steps and her inexperience. That was wild!

"Okay, well. I'm skipping that part. What's next, hm?"

She added more herbs and the liquid turned mauve. Then she thought of her companion's interests—which really meant her own—and held the final ingredient aloft. The only steps left were to drop it in and focus on her companion until the candles burned down.

Easy peasy.

Based on the length of the wicks, she had a good twenty

minutes beneath the stars before she met a new friend or cleaned up her mess, which was good because her nerves were prickly, and her hands shook. The combination of low visibility, spooky effects, and the thrill of the unknown made it hard to focus. But Growina was determined to get the spell right, so she sucked in a breath of chilly night air and settled in her circle.

Something, somewhere, screamed.

It was a high-pitched shriek that went on and on, like an opera singer with massive lungs. Or a teapot left alone on a stove beside a tin of shortbread cookies, entirely forgotten by a nervous apothecary in her haste to prepare her very first spell.

"The tea!" Growina shouted and jumped to her feet.

The hem of her dress bumped the nearest candle, and it toppled and splattered the cauldron with wax. Its flame ignited the potpourri circle, which went up like dead grass in a months-long drought.

What should have been a relaxing wait became a frantic fire dance with skirts in the air and a screaming kettle to add extra anxiety.

And yet, through the chaos, Growina heard something new. First, a rustle, then thumps like a few heavy footsteps.

Her heart thudded.

The ritual was incomplete, so nothing should have happened. Yet, she could not shake the feeling that someone was watching. Somewhere in a bush or behind a tree, someone slunk ever closer. Someone who did not care that the soup glowed red and the circle she sprinkled to keep evil away was naught but a scorched black ring in her garden.

Again, something crunched, and her heartbeat sped up. No friend of hers would sneak up in the dark. Perhaps an intruder was drawn by the lights, or her clumsiness changed the spell's parameters. Either way, she had seconds left to react.

Growina dropped to her knees and snuffed the lit candles. Then she kicked the fallen one so it rolled itself out. The herb soup faded to a slimy gray, and its scent was replaced with the smell of burned cinnamon. Most importantly, though, the footsteps stopped. Her garden was silent—save for the still screaming kettle—and Growina was alone in the dark.

Almost.

Before she could relax and regret her actions, something leapt from a tree and scurried straight for her. She shrieked and dodged, but it sped right past and into a bush on the far side of her circle. Growina clutched her sweater and tried to decide between laughter and tears, as both felt equally appropriate.

It had been a squirrel.

FOUR

It Ate the What?

"APOTHECARY!"

Growina raised her cheek from her pillow, blinked at her blurry grandfather clock, and whimpered. The shop would not open for another three hours, but customers routinely ignored her signage. To them, every job was time-sensitive, yet none ever thought to pre-purchase supplies.

It was terribly frustrating each and every time.

"*Apothecary!*" the voice wailed again. Knuckles rapped rhythmically on the store counter.

. . . On the store counter?

Growina leapt up, fully awake, and flung her quilt like it was covered in spiders. There was only one customer with the audacity and ability to let himself through the bolted doors: Theo.

"Be right there!" she called as she wriggled out of her nightgown and into a snake-pattern dress and scaled shawl. She stumbled downstairs and smoothed her hair with her fingers before she pushed through the storefront curtains and said, "Theo!"

The bearded wizard's eyes widened, even as his hands withdrew from the counter. "Oh, good! You're still here."

Growina wanted to ask him where he thought shopkeeps

went in the night. Folded up in a storage shed, perhaps, or carted off in a box to the bank with the profits? Or—

Something outdoors snagged her attention. Two figures darted past her stained-glass windows, whispering in the excited tones of secret lovers . . . or children returning from a night of mischief. It seemed the wizard was not the only person in Wontmoil up before the sun.

"Or, perhaps not," Theo said, and snapped his fingers. "Hello! Customer here! I need that purple potion that helps you see residual magic. Also, three bundles of Fang Lock, two pouches of Leadfeather, and a bag of footprint powder. Fast. It's an emergency."

"Oh!" she said with a flush. "Sorry. Footprint powder isn't a product. It's baking flour people sprinkle on the floor to spot mischievous spooks."

"Wonderful. Give me that."

Her brow creased. "You . . . want me to sell you my baking flour?"

"Yes."

"From my cupboard?"

He rubbed his eyes and groaned—a demonstration of the condescension that made most wizards unbearable—but Growina had a hard time taking him seriously. Theo rejected wizard's robes in favor of suits and embroidered coats, but he could not resist a curly felt hat. And though his selection fit his profession, it stood out like a dollop of burgundy frosting plopped atop his noggin.

"It's an emergency," he repeated, "meaning I don't have time to hit every store. I'll take what you have."

Growina shrugged and retrieved the flour but paused when she got to the Fang Lock jar. "Looks like I only have one bundle left."

"Oh, no, that won't do. My aim isn't what it used to be.

Tossed bundles end up all over the place." Theo's eyes took on a dreamy appearance. "Last one hit a hen and made her lay kumquats. Would it take long to gather a few fresh bundles?"

Her stomach did somersaults at the thought of the wizard in her herbary, since it was still a disaster from the night before. Theo was respectful (for a wizard), but even he would have questions. What would he think of a career apothecary attempting an advanced witch's spell?

"Not a good idea, I'm afraid," she said. "The sentry shrubs are testy today."

That was technically true. The sentry shrubs were *always* upset, though they hadn't attacked in at least a decade. The walled herbary had few regular guests and even fewer visiting strangers, so there was not much around for a guard bush to bark at.

Fortunately, Theo's face betrayed his botanical ignorance even before he opened his mouth to say, "Ah. Sounds bad."

Growina gathered his potion and Leadfeather pouches, then set the products on the counter. "What kind of creature has magic, wings, and massive fangs, but also requires flour to spot?"

Theo reached into his pocket for coins. "The kind I haven't identified yet."

She smiled, unsure what he meant, then looked up to see another figure run past her window. "You mean you haven't seen it?"

He handed her fudgels and grabbed his supplies. "No one has. There were no witnesses when it broke into the bank."

"The *bank*?"

Someone else ran past the windows, but now Growina knew where to.

"Wait!" she called before Theo could phase through the still-locked doors. "If there were no witnesses, how do you know it wasn't a person?"

He turned with a smirk. "Because it didn't steal any fudgels. It ate the locks."

* * *

An excerpt from the Lazy Botanist's Guide to Naughtobelus.

Rhamnus Irascibilis Sentry Shrubs

Habitat: The deadly maze by Picaroon Pelf

Appearance: Woody plant with thorny stems, compound leaf blades, and purple foliage.

Characteristics: Plant is hostile, territorial, and over-protective. Establish pecking order within its pack before attempting sample collection.

Author's note: Harvested stems in the hands of a mage can seal the maw of a massive monster . . . or a gossip who won't leave a botanist be. Keep jabbering, Gary. See where it gets you.

* * *

Growina skidded to a stop at the edge of a crowd that huddled around the Wontmoil bank. Half of the business owners were there, some still in bonnets and fuzzy slippers. They encircled a cowering teller in front of the newly chained door—one that now had jagged gouges torn from the front.

"And how do I know my money is safe?" Jacqueline Pollywog asked as she gestured toward the hole where the enchanted lock once sat. "Am I supposed to just take your word for it, alien? Show me proof!"

"Not a chance," replied a familiar child with four dark eyes and emerald short-pants.

"Nobody's touching anything till management arrives!" the child's twin, who hovered five feet off the ground, agreed.

The sight of the "kids" made Growina grin, as she had not seen the alien twins in years. Zizel and Zemni moved to Naughtobelus from a fantastic world where anything imagined would simply appear from thin air. And since they retained their magical gifts in Growina's world, they adventured for giggles rather than coins. That made them the perfect choice to defend the carts that moved fudgels between different banks.

. . .Or close enough to perfect, at least, since neither one had a vivid mind's eye.

"Don't make me hit you with a bat!" Zemni shouted at a red-faced butcher who dared to creep close to the door.

Three steel letters appeared in the sky directly above the butcher's head. Each one thudded—B. A. T.—into the grass and forced him to dance back into the crowd.

That left room for Theo to emerge and wave his hands at the hovering kids. "Give way," he said, "and I'll have this mystery solved in a jiff."

"It's the silly hat man!" Zizel cried as if she had spotted a rainbow septicorn. "Scram, silly man! We don't need your help."

Zemni squinted with all four eyes at once. "Has he got a bag of baking—"

"Observe!"

Theo downed the purple potion in a single gulp, then spun in place with one arm held out like he had misplaced some matches in a darkened room. His legs wobbled as he repeatedly turned and glanced around in all directions—which was not the reaction Growina expected.

"Wha—?" was all he managed to say before he pitched to one knee, spilling his flour all over the grass.

Growina nudged her way through the crowd. "Theo! Theo, are you okay?"

Zemni perked up. "Plant lady! Did you poison the wizard?"

"You didn't have to do that for us," Zizel said.

"Yeah, we can poison him ourselves!" Zemni added.

Theo looked up long enough to glare, then lowered his head again.

Growina crouched by his side. "I don't understand. I tested that batch myself this weekend."

"It's fine," Theo said with a croak. "The potion works fine. It's the residual magic that's wrong. It's too bright. Too much."

Zemni floated closer. "Explain."

"The magic is *everywhere*. I expected some on the doors and perhaps a trail to the monster's lair. But, instead, there's a cloud. A layer of fog that encompasses every inch of the town. And the colors! Ugh! Lime green and puce? I'm going to be sick."

"You sure that isn't normal?" Zizel asked. "Some places are more cursed than others."

Theo glared again. "A woman sent for me this weekend because her pooch pooed a slimy hankie, and she thought it had excreted ectoplasm."

Zemni scrunched up his nose. "Was it haunted?"

"Well, it's haunting *me*, but no. No ghost. The dog ate a snotty rag. And yet, I went there anyway."

"To care for the dog?" Growina asked.

"Because I was *bored*. My point is: this town isn't cursed. It's so flipping dull that dog squat is news! But now, it seems our boring town is drenched in foul magic. I just don't know why, or from what. . . or who would have brought something like this here."

The questions made Growina's stomach flop. She picked at her fingernails as she asked, "What about when? We still don't know *when* it came here, right?"

Theo shook his head and climbed to his feet, already less green than before. "I'm positive the creature arrived last night."

 FIVE
The Haunted Tour

"WELCOME TO THE Indited Castle, home of the wretched wizard Sigeric Slugbeard," a tour guide announced in a manner so dry it was in danger of crumbling to dust. "Normally, we'd call it the *former* home—seeing as he's deceased and whatnot—but we haven't yet convinced him to leave."

Florian leaned close to Wardric and whispered, "*The* Wizard Slugbeard?"

"Yeah," Wardric said with a dismissive wave.

"The one responsible for the Gart Splagosion? Where the sky erupted in flames, inanimate objects revolted, and everyone lost the ability to spell?"

"That's the one."

"And we're walking into his castle? Where he still lives?"

"Naw. He's been dead for like . . ." Wardric chewed his lip in thought. "A lotta years."

"You know what I mean," Florian snapped. "Where he *is* residing."

"Shh. I wanna hear."

The deadpan guide ushered them into the historic castle and past a sign that advertised both admission and room rates at the entrance. Tours were pricy, but Bodkins had a seemingly infinite number of fudgels . . . which was a shame because a payment dispute would have been an opportunity for Florian to remain outside (and head for the hills) while his semi-kidnappers enjoyed the tour.

The guide, who wore a purple-and-black striped dress that could not have looked less comfortable, said, "To your right is the game room where Slugbeard hosted countless board game sessions and spontaneous executions." She gestured with an exaggerated (yet sluggish) movement of her arm to a room with a gorgeous gaming table and a single overnight guest passed out on a couch.

Florian mouthed, "Executions?" to Wardric but got only a thumbs-up in response. He scowled at the bearded merc, then at the castle's dusty floor, which crunched like sand beneath his boots. Mooncalf-Pale seemed sandier overall than he remembered, but a long time had passed since his last visit.

"To your left is the waiting room, where Slugbeard entertained guests before meals. And where he hosted spontaneous executions."

"Ha!" Bodkins shouted while two of her chair's monster legs—one tan and furry, and the other scaly and salmon pink—stomped the floor in amusement.

The guide bared her front teeth as if genuine smiles were painful, then turned around to resume her scripted routine.

Florian interrupted, struck by a sudden idea. "Excuse me! Sorry. Where can I find the toilet?"

Bodkins and Wardric exchanged a look before Bodkins asked, "You gotta pee?"

Florian flushed, mainly because the conversation was humiliating as a mature adult. But also, because, in hindsight, the move he attempted could not have been more transparent. How many plays had he starred in that contained an escape plan from a restroom?

"Toilets are down the hall and through the double doors,"

the guide said. "They are marked 'toilets,' unlike the kitchen, which is marked 'kitchen.' Do not mistake the two unless you want us to add your bones to the tour. The head chef is very handy with a knife, you know." The guide's expression didn't change as she continued to say, "Just kidding, of course. The head chef is lovely. Just a bit of execution humor for you folks."

Nobody laughed.

Bodkins shrugged and addressed Wardric. "Make sure he can't get out."

Wardric deflated. "But I wanted to see the tour!"

"Don't worry, you won't miss anything exciting," the guide said. It was, technically, reassuring, but not in any way her bosses would approve of.

Wardric followed Florian to the double doors at the end of the hallway like a depressed puppy, then reached out a hand to stop him from entering. "Hold on. I gotta do my thing."

Florian's brows raised, but he waited by the doors while Wardric retrieved a paintbrush, went inside, did goodness knew what, and re-emerged. The merc tucked the paintbrush into a loop on his jacket and nodded in Florian's direction.

"Come find us when you're done."

Florian blinked. "You mean you're not going in with me?"

"No way. I'm not your dad."

The mercenary stomped off and shook his head while Florian stood dumbfounded. That was not how any of the plays he starred in went. The mercs were supposed to watch him as they had the previous night when they camped out in the woods, not abandon him beside a castle loo. Still, he was not about to turn down an opportunity for escape.

Florian shoved his way into the narrow service hall. He ignored the door that said 'toilets'—Wardric likely checked it for windows, anyway—and went straight for the one labeled 'kitchen.'

A bedraggled pastry chef jumped when he burst in.

"Hello!" Florian said with his biggest smile. "Sorry to interrupt your work, but I was wondering if you had a note bat I could borrow to send a message to a colleague."

The pastry chef's expression shifted from wide-eyed surprise to a look that said, "This is not in my job description." But he had an answer prepared, nonetheless. "Overnight guests can request a note bat from reception, which is located in the gift shop-slash-spontaneous execution room on the first floor. Are you an overnight guest?"

Florian considered fibbing but decided the point was moot. "Not exactly. I'm here with a tour group. What if I give *you* the message, though? Can you send it on my behalf? I can pay you next time I'm in town."

The pastry chef shook his head. "Sorry. Against the rules." He returned to a tray of fruit-topped puff pastries.

Florian waved a hand to get his attention again. "Wait. I really do need your help. The people I'm here with forced me to come against my will. I need a rescue."

"Oh, I see now. There's one like you in every group. Look, the tour is only two hours long. It's a slog, I know, but it's over before you know it. And, if you're lucky, you won't even get to meet the wizard. He sets up ridiculous gimmicks to make guests think he's haunting the place when, really, he's out back feeding my signature sweets to squirrels."

Florian grimaced as his foot slid through another pile of dusty grit. The castle staff clearly seemed more committed to their haunted house aesthetic than maintaining a sanitary space for food preparation.

"I'm not talking about the tour itself. I'm not even supposed to be in Mooncalf-Pale. I've been kidnapped . . . more or less."

The pastry chef frowned and set down a cup of fresh blackberries. "Have they hurt you?"

"Well, no, not yet. But they're making me go on a dangerous adventure against my will, and—"

"Sounds nice." The man shrugged. "Wish somebody would force me to go on vacation. I haven't had a day off to see the theater in six months."

Florian perked up. "Ah! The theater! You like the theater? Do you go often?"

"Used to go a bunch, back before the local one got hit by an asteroid. Funny how it landed on the building and missed everything around it, right after a critic said our performances were better than ones in Leechleif."

"Right. Huh. Funny, that. Have you been to the Spherule in Leechleif?"

"Not me, but the head chef's gone a bunch. She loves that one lady—Ida Trumpet or something. Seen maybe a dozen of her shows."

"Ava Triumphant! That's me!"

"What? No."

"Yes! I'm her. Well, I play her. I'm an actor from the Spherule Theater, and I need to get them a message, fast."

"No kidding? Hold that thought." The pastry chef cleared his throat and shouted, "Hey, chef!"

A tall woman in a crisp uniform stormed into the kitchen and barked, "What?"

Florian could hardly contain his excitement. What luck! He had a genuine fan in the castle—and in a position of authority, no less. If he read a script with the same scenario, he would tell the bard that the coincidence was unrealistic. And yet, here it was, playing out before him.

"Remember that Ava Trumpet character you're always going on about?" the pastry chef asked.

Florian bit his lip, ready for the big reveal.

"Ava Triumphant," the head chef corrected. "Show some respect. That woman's strategies shaped my career. Face your enemies head on, she taught me. Never go around what you can go through! Can't wait till I save up enough for a backstage pass so I can pick her brain for hours. So, why is a guest in my kitchen?"

The pastry chef grinned. "Apparently, that guy is—"

"Desperately looking for a note bat," Florian said, then immediately hated himself.

He had minutes, at best, before the mercs got suspicious. Not hours to spend discussing Ava's mottoes with a fan. But it was not the ticking clock that stopped him in his tracks. It was something else—a weird twisting in his chest when the chef described her idol. What was that?

The head chef's expression mirrored her colleague's from a moment before. She sighed and broke out the rehearsed response. "Overnight guests can request a note bat from reception."

"Down the hall in the gift shop?" Florian asked, much to the surprise of the poor pastry chef. "I'll head right there. Thanks so much!"

He darted from the room before either could respond, then across the hall to the toilets. Despite Wardric's assurance that he couldn't escape, he scanned the perimeter for a potential exit. None existed, as expected, but one wall had a rectangle of pink bricks that clashed with the castle's decor. He pondered the window-shaped patch for a moment, then used the room for its intended purpose.

A scowling Beatrix Bodkins awaited him upon his exit. "Get lost?" she asked without a hint of humor.

"I wasn't feeling well," Florian replied.

Technically, it was the truth. Spherule management had

prepared him for encounters with fans who could not distinguish between characters and performers. But the conversation in the kitchen made him physically ill. Was it guilt at the thought of letting a fan down, perhaps? Or self-loathing for his failure to embody any of the qualities he projected on stage?

"Right," Bodkins replied. But she got only a few steps past the double doors before she added, "Okay, you got me. I never show my hand this early, but I'm deadly curious." She turned—but not to grill Florian. Instead, her gaze drifted to his still-crunching boots, which she addressed with a smirk. "Well, Eddie? What did Peterman do?"

To Florian's horror, the dust on the floor drifted toward Bodkins. It moved slowly, as if caught in a draft at first, then picked up speed and volume until it formed a sandy tornado. He stepped back as it coalesced into the form of a man with more swagger than human bones should allow. Then, the semi-transparent fellow grinned with a mouth that was short several teeth.

"You're never gonna believe this, boss."

Six

Collywobbles

BODKINS LEANED FORWARD to peer into a dingy display case, getting close enough that her chair's legs bumped against the glass. She squinted at the artifacts inside as if they were glittering treasures and not rusty bits of ruined rubbish. One item in particular—a tattered book with a hole burned through the center—held her fascination more than the crumbling swords or dented helmets.

"I vote we let him try," she said. She pressed her face so close to the glass it left a puff of condensation on the surface.

Eddie, the walking sand sculpture, guffawed. Which was impressive for a man with no lungs.

Wardric, on the other hand, wrinkled his brow. "Whaddya mean? Just let him contact his friends? What good will that do?"

The tour guide stepped forward to interrupt. "For your own safety, please keep off the displays. I should warn you that smudging the glass will anger the resident ghosts, who might follow you home to exact revenge. I should say that, but I won't because it's the cleaning staff you really have to worry about. Anyone who can keep dead folks tidy should scare you more than ghosts."

Bodkins pulled her face away from the glass with haste and

lowered her chair to Wardric's level. "It'll do no good at all. That's the point."

Florian crossed his arms but struggled to come up with a rebuttal. Even after catching him red-handed, the mercenaries refused to accept that they had the wrong man. It was just ol' Peterman, up to his shady tricks, trying to pull one over on the poor castle chefs. But they were convinced he would never fool *them*! Oh no.

At least, not if he wanted to keep his head attached.

"What the boss is trying to say," Eddie said, despite a glare from Bodkins that made it clear she needed no assistance, "is that it's moot either way. If he's tipping off his cohorts about the monster in the penta-whatsa-contrabobble—"

"Penta-city conurbation," Bodkins corrected. "It's how snooty people pronounce *suburbs*."

"If he's telling them where the monster is, we already have a head start. And if he really is calling someone to bail him out, they won't show. Anybody who cared enough about him to chase mercenaries across the countryside would've come looking for him already."

Florian opened his mouth to object but closed it again and frowned. Unfortunately, the stuck-up sandcastle had a point. Not one, but *two*, rehearsals had passed while he followed the mercs through miles of wooded countryside toward the penta-city conurbation. Surely, in all that time, *someone* had alerted management to his absence? He was the star of the show!

The Spherule management team knew where he lived, and they knew where he had been the day before. It was not like a burly painter and a woman in a chair made from monster legs could march through Leechleif without drawing attention. Someone, somewhere must have seen which way they went.

So why had no one come?

"I need to sit down," he muttered.

"Funny you should say so," the tour guide said, "because we've reached Slugbeard's famous torture seat. No spikes or clamps on that one, but I'm told it gets uncomfortably cold, what with its proximity to all the ghosts . . . and the stained-glass window, of course. Hah. But really, the rest of the chairs are fine. Just avoid the one in the center."

Wardric perked up. "I smell cider!"

He was right. The air in the conference-style room smelled of tangy apples and hot spice. It was a pleasant change from the other rooms, which stank like a linen skirt left for months at the bottom of a costume chest.

The tour guide nodded. "Please enjoy a complimentary beverage as we transition from the historical tour to the legendary *haunted hallway*. Unless, of course, you're allergic to dairy, citrus, tree nuts, ectoplasm, mint, cinnamon, collywobbles, nutmeg, brown sugar, apples, cobwebs, bone dust—"

"I'll take one," Florian said and grabbed a mug from the conference table.

The cider was blessedly warm and smooth, despite the unusual additives. Florian fell into a chair and gulped it down, then closed his eyes and tried not to imagine what his management might have done between discovering their star performer was missing and deciding—for whatever reason—that it was fine.

"Peterman!" Bodkins called. "Come on. Wardric's gonna explode if we don't get to the haunted stuff today."

"I wanna see the ghosts!" Wardric begged.

"I haunted you for ages!" Eddie said. "Wish I'd known you'd pay five fudgels a day for it. I'd have charged."

Wardric rolled his eyes. "It's not the same. You were a jerk."

"You're only saying that because you haven't met Slugbeard."

"Wait." Florian rose from his chair to re-examine Eddie's

sandy face. "You're a ghost? I thought you were a construct of some kind."

The swashbuckling sandman feigned offense. "*Former* ghost, thank you. The boss put me back together."

Florian spun on Bodkins. "You're a *necromancer?*"

The tour guide's expression said she was not paid enough to deal with a necromancer in a haunted castle.

Bodkins shook her head. "That's such a nasty term. Makes it sound like I dig up corpses and make them march about. No. I'm a *spirit stitcher*. I stitch spirits to . . . well . . . anything that doesn't already have one. Eddie here wanted his old body back, but it deteriorated ages before I found him. We tried to make him a wooden body that looked the same, but, let's just say it's hard to craft a face based on someone's distant memory of themselves. So, I stitched tiny bits of him to grains of sand and let him build himself. Pretty clever, eh?"

"Ghosts!" Wardric wailed, prompting the tour guide to usher them all into a dimly lit hallway.

Sorrowful music drifted in and out of earshot with no apparent source and candles flickered in a nonexistent breeze. Wardric sucked in an excited breath, but Florian merely shook his head. He had seen better special effects in grade school performances.

Nevertheless, he lowered his voice to avoid spoiling Wardric's experience as he asked, "Whose spirits are in the chair?"

Bodkins tilted her head. "What's that?"

"Your chair. I've been trying to figure out how it works, and I think I get it now. You've stitched spirits to the monster limbs to make the chair walk. But . . . whose? Are they the original monsters? Or human enemies you've defeated?" He shuddered at the thought.

Bodkins laughed. Not a wicked laugh, like one might

expect from a mercenary who fused ghosts to severed monster limbs, but a delighted giggle as if he had asked her how to fasten a bra with one hand.

"A merc's gotta keep some secrets."

Goosebumps ran up Florian's arms, and it took him a second to realize it was because a chilly breeze had blown through the haunted hallway. Perhaps there were staff members in another room with billows and tubes for ambiance, or maybe the hall was naturally drafty. Either way, it didn't help the uneasiness he felt while looking at Bodkins' chair up close.

One of the hand-like limbs repeatedly balled itself into a fist, as if trying its best not to punch a crater into the floor. Another tapped out a rhythm, as if bored.

"Ghosts!" Wardric cried again, but with a hint of alarm rather than impatience.

Florian looked up from the chair in time to see a pale-blue skeleton, translucent as a sheet of stained-glass, swoop toward him from the ceiling. He shrieked and toppled backward onto the dusty floor with both arms flung up to protect his face.

It wasn't until he pulled his hands away and saw the tour guide's weary expression that he realized the skeleton must have been one of the "wizardly illusions" the pastry chef warned him about. It was not, as Wardric apparently believed, a real ghost.

Embarrassed, Florian picked himself up off the floor. His heartbeat continued to thud in his ears even as he dusted his trousers and examined the ceiling for markings that might indicate the source of a magical projection.

As a victim of mistaken identity accidentally kidnapped by a band of adventure-seeking mercenaries, it did not surprise him that his nerves were shot. But as a professional thespian accustomed to jump scares, prop monsters, and stage fright, it bothered him a great deal that he could not get his emotions under control. Even after a moment of meditation, his heart would not stop pounding.

And was it his imagination, or was his face getting prickly as well?

"Ooh! Another one!" Wardric shouted.

Florian refused to flinch a second time. He stepped forward to see the new specter, which soared down the hall with a cutlass in hand. Unlike the shoddy skeleton, the new illusion was remarkably detailed, with a realistic face, unkempt hair, and brows that flared upward in a look of permanent concern despite the bloodthirsty glint in its ghostly eyes.

"Look out!" Wardric said, but Florian held his ground.

No two-fudgel parlor trick was going to fool *him*. If he squinted, he could almost see the strings holding the cutlass in the air. He could smell the herbs the wizard burned to cast the illusion. It was a fantastic job, but not the best he had ever seen.

The ghost swung its cutlass in a comical arc and severed Eddie's head from his sandy body.

Eddie screamed. Florian screamed. Eddie's head thudded to the ground, bounced like a melon, and rolled into the far wall. Then he burst into laughter.

"Edward!" the apparently real ghost exclaimed. "How long has it been since I last executed you?"

"Not long enough, you stinky sack of slugs!" Eddie replied. His head reverted to dust, drifted toward his body, and re-formed atop his shoulders. "How's the wife?"

"Still not speaking to me," the ghost said with a shrug. "Can't say I blame her."

Eddie made to nudge the ghost, but his fist passed straight through the fellow's shoulder. "You *did* try to destroy Naughtobelus. She's right to hold a grudge. How were you stopped, by the way? I was dead for that part."

Wardric squealed. "Is that Slugbeard? Are you Slugbeard? For real?" He turned excitedly toward Bodkins, then frowned. "What's wrong with Peterman?"

That was a good question. Florian was not at all sure what was wrong with him. Both of his arms trembled like he had been lugging sandbags for hours, and his legs were literally letting him down. He sank to the ground, unable to stop himself or catch a breath, and tried to blink away an inky blackness oozing into his vision.

"I—" he tried, but that was all he got out before the room went black and pain shot through his gut.

Florian had never felt so hungry in his life. He was ravenous, unable to think of anything but his empty stomach as he slithered around the darkness in his mind. A faint purple light drew his attention and he rushed toward it, reaching for the glowing object with smoky, tendril-like fingers. He sank his teeth into it, ignoring screams of panic as he gnawed through metal and stone, spraying shards and shavings in the air until he consumed every morsel.

It wasn't enough. He needed more. He—

Something cold passed under his nose.

"There ya go," the tour guide said.

He shot up to a seated position and blinked into the candlelight, which was far brighter than he remembered. Everyone—including the wretched wizard Sigeric Slugbeard, creator of the Gart Splagosion—huddled around him with concerned expressions.

"What did you see?" Bodkins demanded.

"He said he was hungry," Wardric offered. "Want me to get those chefs?"

"No!" Florian said, surprising even himself. "I'm fine."

"It's the collywobbles," the tour guide explained. "We get one or two bad reactions a month, but the chef insists on adding it to the cider. Says it heightens the excitement in the hallway. No offense."

Slugbeard shrugged. "Heightens my excitement when they drop. Let's up the dosage."

Bodkins cleared her throat. "We're cutting this tour short. Time to go."

"He said he was fine!" Wardric protested

"I know he's fine. But you forget one thing. Peterman is a soothsayer. Which means *that*—" She pointed to Florian where he still sat on the dusty floor. "—was not an allergic reaction."

Wardric frowned. "It wasn't?"

"No. It was a premonition."

SEVEN

Dangerous Demands

AN EXCERPT FROM the Lazy Botanist's Guide to Naughtobelus.

Coffea Coccinea COLLYWOBBLES

Habitat: Warm, dry environments free of thrill-seeking wildlife.

Appearance: Woody shrub with compound leaflets, crimson flowers, and clustered berries.

Characteristics: Powdered berry pits are effective as a mild stimulant when consumed in small quantities. Allergy or excessive consumption can lead to heart palpitations, skin irritation, and stomach distress. Not yet regulated, but some busybodies with nothing better to do have considered it.

Author's note: Do not feed to goats. Do not feed to goats. Do. Not. Feed. To. Goats.

***

Growina chewed her lip and contemplated her choice of afternoon beverage. The bit of her subconscious accustomed to solving daily frustrations with a quick pick-me-up urged her toward a second pot of black tea. But the last thing she needed on top of the morning's excitement was a fresh cup of artificial anxiety.

"Peppermint, then," she compromised before she put the kettle on.

Unlike the night before, she was painfully aware of the lit stove and impending whistle as she bundled her shawl around her shoulders and made her way out the back door. If something more sinister than a squirrel made its way through her garden, the aftermath would be easy to spot in the afternoon sun. She made her way toward the ritual site but paused before her sentry shrubs.

"Oh! The Fang Lock! I almost forgot. May I have a few twigs for potions, please? Great. Sorry if this stings a bit."

It was wise to ask *any* plant permission before harvesting, but with sentry shrubs, it was essential. However, despite her polite request, the shrub gave her hands a good smack when she snapped off some twigs. She tucked them into one of her many pockets, and rubbed her sore knuckles.

"I can't grow mine back, you know."

The ritual site beyond was as she left it, unfortunately. The scent of singed cinnamon still lingered in the chilly breeze, and the scorched circle stood out like a painted target in the soil. However, the rest of the herbary looked as it should. Even the over-dramatic plants that regularly wilted at the brush of a finger stood crisp and healthy in the afternoon sun. Except—

Growina sighed, then crouched to inspect the soil. "Weeds? In *my* herbary?"

Weeds were not unheard of, all squirrels considered, but the season was wrong for a new infestation. Fortunately, she had just the thing to deal with them. She hurried inside to grab the kettle, which was already sputtering, and returned to drizzle a bit of hot water onto the unwelcome plant.

"That sneaky little thing won't be back next—oh!"

The sneaky little thing had friends. A whole trail of them, in fact.

Growina scootched along the path with her steaming kettle in hand until she doused every weed from the ritual site to the garden wall. Then she sat back to mourn her peppermint tea.

"Where have you been?" a shrill voice demanded.

Growina jumped a foot in the air.

"We told you, we had to get the bank manager," a child replied.

"Yeah! An' we did!"

Growina scrabbled onto an overturned tree pot and hoisted herself up high enough to see over the top edge of the wall. Sure enough, several shop owners had the childish Zizel and Zemni cornered on the sidewalk behind the herbary wall. (If one could corner aliens capable of instantaneous travel.)

"Good," Lora, Wontmoil's most popular tailor, said. "Because we have a list of demands for them."

A tall figure in a sharp suit stepped forward. Between the unusual clothing and a pair of copper spectacles welded to its dome-like noggin, it took Growina a moment to realize it was a clockwork construct and not a gawky businessperson.

"The bank does not respond to demands," the construct said without a hint of emotion.

Lora glanced at a carpenter, who shrugged. "Well, you'll respond to this if you want to continue doing business in this town." She held up a sheet of paper covered in scribbles of different colors. "It's signed by every merchant in Wontmoil."

"I didn't sign it," Growina said, to the surprise of everyone below.

Only the carpenter seemed embarrassed. "We couldn't find you."

"I was in my shop."

"Ah."

"The bank does not respond to demands," the clockwork construct repeated.

Growina tried not to giggle at the exasperated expressions on the shopkeepers' faces. Perhaps it was their first interaction with a construct created for a specific purpose. But anyone who bothered to befriend one knew most struggled with nuance. Or, to put it another way: to get the answer you wanted, you first had to ask the right question.

"I think," Growina said while she wriggled about in a poor attempt to remain upright on her elbows, "they wish to file a formal complaint."

The construct froze in thought, gears turning inside its clear, dome head. It gave a single nod. "The bank values customer feedback."

Lora's metaphorical gears were invisible but just as slow. "Er, we, the merchants of Wontmoil—" She looked up at the fence for a moment and added, "Crowe included, I presume—no longer feel our money is safe in the local bank."

Growina shrugged. As someone whose money grew on trees, her income far exceeded her expenses. If some fudgels were to walk out the door in the pockets of someone who needed them more, that would not be the worst thing to happen.

The construct's shiny head gave a few more rattles and clicks. "Before the recent incident, your money was ninety-nine-point-seven percent safer in the bank than your personal safe. Currently, your money is ninety-eight-point-two percent safer in the bank."

"Well, that's not true, is it?" a grocer asked. "What if the thing that broke the door comes back?"

"Preliminary investigations indicate the locks were the exclusive target of the attack."

"We gathered that the thing eats locks," Lora said to regain control of the conversation. "What we de—I mean—to feel secure, we need to know that the bank-lock-eating-thing won't be back to chew more holes in the doors. And we don't feel it's our responsibility to pay for the creature's removal, either."

"Your feedback has been noted," the construct said with another mechanical nod of its head. "The bank will advertise a bounty for the capture of the perpetrator."

"A bounty?" Zemni shrieked. "Why not use us? We're free!"

"It is against bank policy to knowingly put employees in mortal danger."

"We're security," the child said and rolled his top two eyes while his lower ones remained fixed and glaring. "Danger is what we *do*."

"Preliminary investigations indicate the perpetrator was drawn to the magical properties of the door locks. You are visitors from a magic-based planet. The bank calculates the odds of your deaths at eighty-seven-point—"

"Poo," Zizel said. A piece of dog excrement materialized in the air between the twins and their mechanical employer, then splattered to the street.

The construct tilted its head with a creak to inspect the splatter, then raised it to stare. Technically, the poo was impressive, as Zizel's visual imagination was almost as foggy as her brother's. But it was the unpredictability of the twins' spells that made them threatening, so their boss was indifferent.

Zemni levitated to Growina's level and gestured at the construct as if he wanted her to step in and reason with it. She shook her head. Wontmoil merchant business was one thing, but she was not about to meddle in bank affairs.

"I know where you live, plant lady," the boy grumbled as

he drifted to the ground and shoved his hands in the pockets of his adorable short-pants.

Growina smiled. "That's nice. Could you remind the big fellow there?"

She pointed to the carpenter, who turned a lovely shade of red. Zemni grumbled and shot a look at his sister. Then, before anyone could say another word, both vanished in puffs of lime green glitter.

Satisfied with the results of her bank-bullying, Lora ushered her companions back to work.

Growina had one last question for the construct. "Has the bank calculated the odds that those twins will get into trouble anyway?"

The bank manager did not have the disposition for laughter, but it made a series of clicks Growina recognized as amusement before it said, "One-hundred percent."

Growina did have the disposition, so she snorted out a giggle and waved farewell before she let go of the wall and slid down. Her elbows ached from leaning against brick and she gave them a rub. Then she turned her forearms around to examine black scuffs on the puffy sleeves.

"Oh, no!"

Her gaze traveled from the sleeves to the front of her dress, which was also a smudged mess. Thankfully, several seconds of rigorous slapping removed most of the dust from the filthy fabric. But her relief was short-lived.

Growina stepped back to take in the entirety of the pattern smudged on the wall. Under normal circumstances, she might assume it was nothing more than soot from her ritual fire that the wind blew against the brick. But in context, it took on the appearance of a shadowy creature with spindly limbs and dozens of appendages that twisted around like vines.

Or, perhaps, if she squinted her eyes—like tentacles.

$\mathscr{E}$IGHT

Smooshy Stone

GROWINA WRESTLED HER way into an orange dress with an autumn leaf pattern and tossed her dirtied outfit into a basket. As much as she loved her pumpkin clothes, the mid-day change was good for her health. Soot was soot and lock-chomping monsters were lock-chomping monsters, she figured.

Until she had proof that one was evidence of the other, there was no point ruining a lovely day with worry.

Still, it was long past time to clean up the ritual mess. If *she* suspected her fumbled spell, goodness knew what conclusion an over-zealous adventurer might jump to. She smoothed her skirts, skipped down the stairs to her storefront, and dug beneath the counter for the sponges she used to clean spills and shattered bottles.

"Apothecary!" Theo shouted, far too close for comfort, and then, "Oop!"

Growina leapt to her feet to see the wizard topple into a spinning rack of embroidered drawstring bags. Somehow, miraculously, the display held his weight, but he seemed unable to right himself while it turned beneath his hands.

"What are you doing here?" she asked as she hurried over to help. "You're supposed to be in bed until the potion wears off."

"I was! I mean—I meant to be. But I had an epiphany! I need more of that potion. And a small favor." Theo crouched and felt along the floor. His wandering hands brushed a large bag embroidered with honeybees, which he grabbed and slapped onto his head.

Growina bit her lip to hold in a giggle. "More potion? But you said yourself the whole town was covered in fog."

"That's what I thought at first, but as I was making my way through the streets, I stumbled upon a patch of fog that was brighter than the rest. Needless to say, I never made it home."

She frowned and searched the floor for his hat. "I don't know that it's needless to say. You could have gone home for a rest and returned to—"

"The question is," he said, "if it isn't fog, what is it? And I have a theory. I suspect it's off-gassing."

"What's that? Monster flatulence?"

Theo sighed in the way only wizards could and said, "No. Well, somewhat. Maybe. But no. I suspect the creature is excreting the fog—by evaporation, perhaps—and it's consuming magic to replace what it's lost."

Growina stood on her toes to swap the bag on his head with his (only slightly less silly) hat. "The creature is eating its own flatulence?"

"No, that's the acting board of the local wizard's association. The creature is eating magic like you would drink water if you were sweating in summer heat." Theo held out a hand and stumbled in the general direction of the rack that held the purple potion he required.

Growina darted out in front of him. "Hold still. I've got it." She plucked the potion and set it in his hand. "But I still don't understand what you plan to do in your current state. You can't face a monster like this."

"Ah, well, that's a good segue into the small favor I wish to ask of you. Would you mind being my eyes while I search for its lair? Be my eyes on this plane, I mean—I'll be using mine to follow the creature's gaseous trail."

A funny sensation rippled across Growina's cheeks and settled, heavy, in the back of her throat. She had waited for *decades* for someone to invite her on an adventure, but Theo was the last person she would expect to offer. Did he even know her name?

She resisted the urge to accept on the spot and instead asked, "Me?"

"You're the only person I can trust to understand my instructions and *not* try to steal this capture from under me."

"Ah." That made more sense. "What do you need me to do?"

Theo fumbled to retrieve her payment, then tugged the cork from the purple potion and took a small sip. His eyes narrowed as if he was staring into the sun. "Follow me, and make sure I don't fall in a ditch."

He wobbled in the general direction of the shop entrance, muttered something beneath his breath, and stepped straight through the closed door.

Growina sighed and turned the doorknob. Keeping him safe was going to be a challenge if he continued to walk straight through solid objects. At least witches had the decency to open doors first.

"One moment," she called as she set the sign on her door to "Out for Lunch" and latched it. "Okay. Where to?"

Theo's head swiveled, then he pointed down the street to the right. "That way."

His pace was brisk for a person who could not see where his feet landed, but his posture had enough wobble to draw tight-lipped stares from several shop windows. Growina gave each of them an apologetic smile and wave.

Thankfully, Theo's magic trail eventually took a sharp turn into an alleyway—there, the only obstacles around were literal.

"Step to the left," she said. "Someone left out a bucket of—you know what? It's best I don't say."

"Looks like the creature avoided it, too. The trail raises off the ground here as if the creature crawled sideways along the wall. And the colors are getting worse. We must be close."

He directed Growina out of the alley and onto a narrow street she could not identify to save her life. They walked a block to the left and turned off the road again. It was strange how buildings one passed every day felt completely unfamiliar from the rear.

She grabbed his elbow to prevent him from strolling straight into a brick wall and asked, "Why is it taking this zigzag route?"

"Because it either knows we can hurt it, or it doesn't."

"Huh?"

Theo bit his lip, took another sip of the potion, and led her toward a stone wall she recognized despite their abnormal approach; they were nearing the cemetery.

It was one of her favorite haunts (pun intended) when she was desperate for a conversation. Skeletons were better listeners than most living people, since they were eager for updates from the outside world and had no personal stake in current affairs.

"Either the monster knows people can harm it and is taking measures to evade us, *or* it doesn't know if we can harm it and it's evading just in case. Wait . . . is that . . .?"

He pointed toward a patch of wall where the shadow of a tree swayed across the surface . . . except there was no breeze to make a tree sway and no tree of the right shape to cast the shadow.

"Got you!" Theo said and ran toward the wall.

He reached into his pockets for his Fang Lock and Lead-feather, as if preparing for battle. Growina winced. At his current velocity, that battle would likely be between his face and a rock.

The shadow twirled as if startled and darted over the wall at a speed spooked cats could only dream of.

Unfortunately, Theo did not seem to register the change.

"Wait!" Growina called. "You're headed straight for a—"

He passed through the wall like a ghost and left Growina behind. Her shoes crunched in a patch of gravel as she skid-ded to a stop.

"Help!" he called on the other side of the wall. "There's stuff all over, and the creature is getting away!"

"Those are gravestones. You're in the graveyard!"

She took a step back to get her bearings, then froze. The wall looked odd where the shadow was, and it stank of mil-dew and candle smoke.

"Get in here!" Theo shouted.

"I think you'd better get back out here," she replied.

"What?" Theo shrieked.

Growina barely registered the cry. She lifted a hand and brushed the stone wall, which rippled like the surface of a bubble. The stone felt as solid as pumpkin pie filling, and her fingers smooshed straight through.

"There's something inside the wall! It feels like . . ." Her hands moved through the pudding-like illusion and bumped into a metal knob. "It's a door!"

"Okay, I'm coming back. But whatever you do, don't—"

Growina turned the knob and wrenched the door open, revealing a stairwell which Theo immediately appeared in—and tumbled down. It was hard to tell if he was screaming or swearing as she chased his rolling body down the steps. Fortunately, the way was both cushioned and lit by a blanket of bioluminescent moss.

"Are you okay?" she asked as she ran to him.

"No, I'm not okay! I let the creature escape, fell down a hole, and lost my hat—again! And what in Naughtobelus are you doing instead of helping me?"

She paused with both hands buried in the moss beside him. "Gathering spores?"

"Gathering spores!" he spat.

She shrugged, pulled a few clumps of moss from the step, and stuffed them in a pocket. "I'll help look for your hat."

Theo rolled to a seated position and said, "Thanks."

"Oh! There it is! Looks like it rolled over next to that chest."

"Chest? What chest? Take me to the chest."

Growina helped him up and walked him to the far side of the short tunnel, where a chest-like shape sat, also covered in moss. He felt the object, set his hands against it, and muttered something that sounded like a sneeze. The lid of the chest shot open and sprayed clumps of moss everywhere.

She leaned forward to see what was inside. "There's a rock."

Theo groaned and threw his hands in the air. But Growina was not ready to dismiss the shiny river rock. It must have been locked in a chest for a reason. She carefully lifted it out and turned it over.

"There's something written on the underside. Wud mapl orng ruk beneet str."

"Are you illiterate?" Theo asked with an air of annoyance that reminded her he was still a wizard, despite his disdain for the local association.

"I'm not, but it's possible the person who wrote this was."

Theo snatched the rock away, realized it was too large for his suit pockets, and held out his empty hand. It took her a moment to realize he was waiting for his hat. "Why do you assume a person wrote that?" he asked as he stuffed the rock into his hat and pulled it close to his chest. "We don't yet know what we're chasing. The creature could be a thousand years old and unbelievably intelligent. This message may be encoded."

Growina pondered the possibility while he made his way up the fluffy steps. On the one hand, based on the mossy growth, the little cave felt single-purpose and undisturbed. On the other, it would be a relief to discover the monster was an ancient creature recently awakened instead of a misman-aged summon by an inexperienced apothecary.

If only there was a way to find out for sure . . .

"What am I hearing?" Theo shouted down the stairs.

She hurried to catch up and stepped out into the fading sunlight beside him. Sure enough, there was a low murmur, like the hubbub at the bank. Had there been another incident?

"Follow me," she said.

For once, Theo listened. She guided him around the cem-etery until she found the gate, then followed a familiar path back toward the shops on her street, where the chattering was emanating from.

"Aren't we right by your shop?" Theo asked when she brought him to a stop. "Why are there so many people here?"

Growina gaped at the crowd waiting less-than-patiently outside her closed door. There were familiar customers from Wontmoil—the Bograven Sisters, the wizard's association, and a handful of independent adventurers—as well as some shady characters she had never seen in her life. Her cheeks prickled with embarrassment when she realized what it meant.

"It's possible I forgot to mention something important before we left," she said.

Theo's eyes narrowed, but he held his tongue.

"The monster you're chasing . . . It seems the bank has put a teeny tiny . . . bounty on it."

NINE
The Forest of Lightening

FLORIAN'S EYES BURNED like he had shoved his face in campfire smoke. It took serious effort to drag them open and, even then, the shapes bobbing around him were fuzzy. He licked his dry lips and tried to recall how he had ended up flat on his back in what felt like the most uncomfortable horse cart in Leechleif.

Something had gone wrong. That much he knew right away. He recognized the stomach pain that typically accompanied a botched production with forgotten lines and misplaced props. And yet, the sensation was comforting, because it meant the lovely woman who came into focus was probably not a fan who had lured him into a compromising situation.

He would never forgive himself for such a dastardly breach of professionalism should that happen.

"What?" he croaked, then coughed and attempted to re-moisten his mouth.

The woman, who had big brown eyes and ringlets that cascaded around her face, smiled. His cheeks prickled with embarrassment as he tried and failed to return the expression. The lady looked familiar, but her name was out of reach . . . as was much of the vocabulary he prided himself on. Nevertheless, her presence was comforting, even as loose branches in the cart dug into his back and crushed his sides like massive hands.

"Sorry about the Skrabblin's Dagger," she said. "'It was all we had to help you sleep off the effects of the collywobbles. We usually only use the stuff when hunting and—you know—*hunting*."

Comfort gone.

Florian shot up as everything came flooding back at once. Or, at least, he tried to shoot up. The monstrous arms carrying him like a baby in front of Bodkins' magical chair had a tight grip on his shoulders and legs, and a piece of rope bound his torso to it.

"What's going on?" he demanded. "Where are we going and why am I tied up?"

She laughed. "You're not tied *up*. You're tied *down*. We're taking a shortcut through the Forest of Lightening."

"Forest of lightning?" he said as he struggled out of the clawed hands and tackled the knot at his waist. "And you're standing beneath a tree?"

Wardric called from ahead. "I wouldn't do that if I were you!"

Florian glanced toward him, but Bodkins waved a hand to draw his attention back. "Before you get distracted, tell me everything you remember from before we knocked you out. It's important."

He released the rope, took a deep breath, and tried to recall the events that led up to his unexpected nap. After a moment, his eyes widened. "Eddie is a baddie!"

Bodkins raised a brow. "Eddie was in your premonition?"

"That's a lie!" Eddie's disembodied voice shouted. It echoed like an announcer in an empty theater.

Florian shook his head. "Not a premonition. A deduction. Did you notice the wretched wizard Sigeric Slugbeard knew him by *first name?*"

"Did you also notice," the voice said, "when he mentioned executing me? That wasn't a euphemism, you hollow-headed charlatan. I knew him *before* he caused the Gart Splagosion. Don't lump me in with those weirdos."

"Oh, so I suppose in the days before he set the sky aflame and executed random citizens, he was a really decent guy, eh?"

"Yes!"

Florian sneered and searched for the source of the voice. "Well, *excuse me* for not spending my precious free time reading the early biography of Naughtobelus' most despicable wizard."

"Not my fault you're uneducated."

Bodkins rapped her knuckles against a heavy wooden box strapped to her chair. "Stop bickering and tell me about the premonition!"

Florian frowned. "Is the sand man in the box? Why is the sand man in a box?"

"Because if he drifts away here, we may never retrieve every piece of him. He gets fussy when a single grain of sand is wedged in a floorboard."

The boxed-up Eddie muttered, "I'm willing to lose a few someplace uncomfortable for the soothsayer."

Florian pulled a horrified face, but Bodkins rapped on the box again. "Quiet. Premonition."

"Oh, right. The dream. Um . . . I remember being quite hungry. Then I saw something glowing and rushed for it with these . . . shadowy protuberances. They scrabbled like hands and wriggled like snakes all at the same time. Someone screamed, and I couldn't tell if they were yelling at me or something else, but I remember being scared. Then I came to and got sick."

"All over the floor!" Wardric said with a laugh.

Florian glanced over again. For some reason, the bearded artist was clinging to a tree as if his life depended on it. Like Florian, he had a rope harness around his waist that led to Bodkins' chair, as if both were in danger of falling from a cliff. Perhaps, had the three of them been scaling a mountain—even a prop one—the whole setup would have been impressive.

Laid out horizontally, however, it was ridiculous.

Bodkins grunted. "Okay, I think I've got enough to chew on. Hold tight, Wardric!"

Her chair took off and dragged Florian after. He yelped as his toes snagged on rocks and roots, much to the amusement of the annoying sandbox. When Bodkins finally reached the tree beyond Wardric's and clung to it with her chair's arms, Florian collapsed into the grass, exhausted.

"Why are you doing the thing with the ropes?" he asked her between gulps of air.

"Because we're in the Forest of Lightening. What would you do instead?"

"I don't know. Avoid the trees? Spread out? Make ourselves less of a target?"

She frowned. "I think you're confused."

"No, you're the one who's—"

"Storm's coming!" Wardric interrupted. "Hold on!"

Bodkins' chair squeezed the tree like it might burrow into the bark. "Come on, Peterman. Grab a claw!"

Florian was not sure how the real Peterman would respond to such an offer, but he shook his head and backed up. There was no way he was getting himself fried to a crisp while clinging to the tallest tree in the forest. Instead, he resumed his battle with the knot at his waist, stopping only when a pebble smacked him in the forehead.

"Hey!" he shouted as another rock whizzed by his ear—from below.

He risked a glance downward. It seemed everything on the forest floor not secured by roots was drifting slowly skyward as if weightless.

Including him.

Florian spun forward on frictionless feet, sure he was about to smash his award-winning face straight into the dirt, but he hovered above the ground instead.

"Peterman's loose!" Wardric shouted.

"Yes, I can see that," Bodkins replied. Then, to Florian, she shouted, "Pull yourself closer."

Florian's ascént dramatically accelerated. Before he could process Bodkins' instruction, he flew halfway up the side of the tree and came to an abrupt halt at the end of his rope. The sudden tug caused him to swing toward the trunk, and he balled himself up like a baby to brace for impact.

"Pull closer," she repeated. "Don't try to hold the tree!"

His hands and arms shook, and his heart felt like it was continuing upward without him, but he was surprised to find he was not afraid.

He was *flying*. Weightless as a bird, as if in a dream. It was kind of neat.

"I'm okay!" he shouted to the mercenaries.

"Of course you're okay," Bodkins replied. "It's not the lightening you need to worry about."

"Yeah," Wardric agreed. "It's the sudden re-heavying that'll get ya!"

Florian pulled himself closer to Bodkins with the rope. Nothing about "sudden re-heavying" sounded enjoyable. That assessment proved accurate when he reached for Bodkins' hand and instead plummeted at non-bird speed toward the ground in front of her chair.

Fortunately, he was prepared. He rolled shoulder-first, saving himself some broken bones, and leapt to his feet as if expecting applause.

"Rocks!" Wardric shouted.

Bodkins made a canopy with her monster limbs, and Florian had just enough time to scurry beneath it before every pebble, leaf, and clump of mud came tumbling back onto them from the sky. He listened as the pebble-rain bounced off thick scales and fur, clinging to the chair and inhaling the pleasant aroma of Bodkins' citrus perfume. Or perhaps it was bug repellant?

When she pulled the canopy of limbs away, the forest looked as it had before . . . which said a lot about the frequency of the lightening storms.

Florian crept around to the side of the chair and sank to the ground. "I'm just gonna . . . sit a second."

"Bodkins laughed. "Peterman's a clown, but he accidentally made a good point. There must be a better way to cross."

Wardric released his tree and ran to join them. The enormous artist stared into the distance for a moment, then said, "I've got an idea. But I don't want him watching me."

She nodded. "No problem. Peterman, turn around and close your eyes. Wardric's a little shy about his process."

"His process?" Florian asked, but did as he was told, anyway.

Behind him, fabric rustled and pouches snapped. Something with a marble inside rattled. There was a swish, a splat, an "Ooh!" from Bodkins, and it was done.

"Okay, you're good," Bodkins said.

Florian turned back around to see a rope fastened with iron loops to the tree beside them. It led to a tree beyond with similar fasteners and one beyond that. The same rope connected every tree in a line from where they stood to the limit of his vision—which was impossible unless Wardric could run and fasten iron hoops faster than Florian could turn around.

Wardric pointed proudly to the seemingly infinite rope. "Now we attach our ropes to that one instead of each other and follow it straight through—bats!"

"Huh?" Florian asked.

Sure enough, an entire colony of bats blasted through the branches above their heads in a cacophony of wings and squeaks.

"Bats?" Eddie said. "In the Forest of Lightening? Never."

Wardric harumphed at the Eddie-in-a-box. "Was too. Looked like note bats."

"Bank bats," Bodkins corrected. "You missed the gold collars."

The two mercenaries shared a look and held it as if communicating silently until Florian sighed and asked, "So? What does it mean?"

"One of two things," Bodkins said. "Either today is a holiday and nobody told us, or someone's robbed an un-robbable bank in the exact direction we're heading. Which means, we need to get there before those bats deliver their notes."

TEN

The Penumbral Magwod

"STEP ASIDE, or I'll turn you into a newt!" Margaret shouted at a man who was approximately 70% robe, 20% hat, and 10% beard.

"How do you know I don't *like* being a newt?" the wizard replied far too quickly to claim it as a joke.

Margaret's eyes widened and her fists clenched in time with the ideas that were undoubtedly flying through her mind. Fortunately, she decided not leave salamanders squirming all over the cobblestones in front of Herbs and Vices.

"I have witnesses," she said, "who can confirm I was here first. And the first to arrive should be the first to enter. It's common sense."

Margaret pointed at the other two members of the famous Bograven Sisters as if their presence proved her point. Sylvie—a white-eyed witch who rarely spoke—tugged her cloak's hood over her face in response. She would make a terrible witness, in Growina's opinion, as she would sooner forfeit Margaret's position in line than open her mouth in public.

But she was definitely a better candidate than the third sister.

"Let's turn them all into newts," Vivienne, the pale witch, said. "We can turn them back when it's their turn. And if one or two get gobbled up by feral cats in the meantime, it'll teach the rest not to jump the queue!"

Fortunately, Vivienne was all talk. A threat from Margaret carried some weight, and a single word from Sylvie would send anyone with self-preservation scrambling for cover. But a thousand horrible threats from Vivienne were no more intimidating than the grumblings of a busybody who could not comprehend why the neighborhood children insisted upon playing beeveball so close to the decorative shrubberies.

Growina raised a hand. "As the owner of the shop, I think—"

"I, too, have witnesses!" the over-bundled wizard declared, as if he was presenting a case to a judge.

He pointed to the huddled mass of hats and beards that called themselves the wizard's association, and every one of them nodded emphatically.

"What?" Margaret cried. "That's preposterous! They only just arrived!"

"Actually—" Growina began before a grating voice cut her off again.

"The Penumbral Magwod demands immediate entry to this establishment!"

Everyone spun to determine the source of the outcry. A stranger clad head-to-toe in armor as black as a starless night stood behind the cluster of sneering wizards. He was a head taller than the tallest wizard (minus their felt hats) and he clutched a fat hen in one arm like it was a cat.

"Pardon us," the bundled wizard asked, "but was that . . . you?"

"No," the voice said. "And yes."

A considerably shorter young man with a plumed hat stepped from behind the silent giant. He bowed and held both hands up toward the stranger. "The Penumbral Magwod—"

"*Magwod*," one wizard repeated in a clipped, mocking fashion.

The young man frowned, but the stranger calmly scratched his chicken's feathers as if the teasing were inconsequential.

"The Penumbral Magwod insists upon his privacy. As such, I have been appointed his voice and face for the duration of this mission."

"And you are?" Margaret asked.

"Chip! Though that fact is irrelevant. Throughout this adventure, I am merely the vessel through which the Penumbral Magwod—"

"*Magwod!*"

" . . . shall communicate with you, his competitors."

"Competitors?" the bundled wizard asked with a snort. "Getting a little full of yoursel . . .ves there, eh, Chiperoo?"

Chip rolled his eyes. "Surely, you've heard tales of the Penumbral Magwod. He's the most effective adventurer in the penta-city conurbation."

"Not a peep."

"I've heard of him," Theo said.

Growina jumped. The stress of the crowd was enough to make her forget the smartly dressed wizard still wobbling beside her with his hat in his hands. For the first time in her life, she knew how it felt to be a florist on romance week or a chocolatier for the holidays. And if she had learned one thing from observing those vendors, it was that she *had* to bring order to the mess quickly, lest the arguments devolve into physical violence.

Theo continued, oblivious to her concern. "And by the look of the magic surrounding that big fellow, he's got more surprises stashed in his suit than ingredients in one of Pollywog's revolting pot pies."

The statement made Growina a little hungry, but it also

gave her an idea. She waved her hands in the air again. "I'm afraid Theo arrived before any of you by a matter of hours, which would, by your logic, place him first in line to enter the shop."

Witches and wizards alike groaned, but Theo perked up. "Indeed—"

Cutting him off, Growina added, "And since he's invited me to join his adventuring party, I'll allow him to complete his shopping before anyone else begins."

It was a tiny fib—okay, an enormous one—but if Growina played it off as an innocent misunderstanding, it might give her the leverage she needed to *finally* join one of her customers on an honest-to-goodness adventure. Not to mention it would be an opportunity to conduct her own investigation into the origin of the mysterious monster before she found out via a surprise visit from angry clockwork bankers.

Theo stumbled over his response. "That . . . well . . . it's . . . Apothecary, can we talk?"

"Growina," she said.

"Pardon?"

"My name's Growina Crowe. Ready to shop?"

"Wait!" Margaret shouted. She shot a glance at her sisters and added, "We want to join your party as well."

Theo puffed up like a dog defending his home from a postal worker. "Absolutely not!"

"You sure?" Growina asked. "You said you needed help navigating the streets in your current condition. And it's not like I would know how to capture the creature or fight off competition in an emergency."

Growina thought the alliance was a fun idea. What a delightful way to get to know her regulars!

Unfortunately, Theo was less keen. "The witches only want my place in line," he said with a scowl.

"Naw," Vivienne shot back. "We want to spend your fudg—oof!"

Margaret carefully removed her elbow from her sister's ribcage and said, "Team Wontmoil versus the lesser adventurers of Naughtobelus. We'll have this sorted in a day and split the bounty five ways."

"I'm not interested in the money," Growina corrected.

"We'll split the bounty four ways."

"And I suppose you'll defer to my leadership?" Theo asked.

The bundled wizard snorted. "Defer to a wizard who couldn't last three months in the association? Not unless they have a death wish."

Chip cleared his throat. "The Penumbral Magwod asks—"

"*Magwod.*"

"Oh, stuff it! The Penumbral Magwod asks that you hurry it up. He hasn't got all night."

Theo waved the young man off and glared at the bundled wizard, too absorbed in the conversation to remember his own warning about the silent, chicken-wielding competitor. "Remind me again, old friend . . . which of us built the protective barrier around the Howling Woods, and which of us merely *thought* about it for two years?"

For a moment, the bundled wizard's narrowed eyes and fluffy brows were visible beneath his beard. He stuck his nose in the air as if smelling something putrid and said, "Shoddy, irresponsible work. You failed to consider the placement of the pillars in relation to the division of property! We were developing plans to ensure an even distribution of pillars to parcels, so no landowner would lose an unfair share of their revenue from unusable farmland!"

"I placed the pillars according to the stars and moon phase at the time of the spell casting," Theo said. "If I had waited for the stars to move instead of the pillars, it would have taken

. . ." He paused to do the mental math. "Three hundred and twenty-eight years to build the barrier, during which time, the farmland would be used only by howling horrors. The parcel owners and their descendants would eventually perish from old age—if they survived that long."

"Adventurers!" someone called from up the street.

Theo again waved them off. "And who," he asked, "do you suppose would charge those parcel owners a hefty fee for the removal of each and every horror that wandered onto their land?"

"Adventurers!" the voice called again.

A person was running toward them. They were not familiar to Growina, but they dressed like a local. Possibly someone from the outskirts of Wontmoil or one of the surrounding towns, but whoever they were, they appeared to be in distress.

"Is it possible that it was your own loss of revenue you calculated into your plans?" Theo demanded of his former colleague before he turned to the source of the shouting and asked, "What?"

"It's the barrier around the Howling Woods," the stranger said between gasps. "Something's eating the pillars!"

* * *

An excerpt from the Lazy Botanist's Guide to Naughtobelus.

Dendrocnide Dormi Skrabblin's Dagger

Habitat: Outer rim of the Howling Woods to the west of Wontmoil.

Appearance: Woody plant with heart-shaped leaves, multiple stems, and fine stinging hairs.

Characteristics: Though not deadly on its own, the toxin delivered by the plant is famously used by Skrabblins (small, gerbil-like imps) to fell their prey.

Author's note: Skrabblins claim human flesh tastes of day-old diarrhea, and they will only attack in self-defense. *Do not give them reason to.* They will knock you out cold and fill your pockets with spiders. Lots and lots of spiders. Every pocket. So many spiders.

* * *

It was all gone. Every bottle, bundle, jar, and candle was stripped from the shelves of Herbs and Vices, save the lavender candles nobody liked, the Skrabblin's Dagger (which customers were too afraid to touch), and a large jar of fish sticks beside the cash box.

Growina grabbed a handful of the latter and offered them to her guests, who shook their heads in turn.

"Okie dokie," she said as she snapped the fish stick in two and watched a boneless baked tilapia expand from the stem like fungus.

The arti-fish-al snack came courtesy of Growina's mer-friends, who enjoyed the flavor of seafood despite their present anatomy, and she quite liked the concept of cruelty-free fishing. But it was hard to sell others on a protein product that oozed from the end of a stick.

No matter. It meant more for her.

Theo rocked in a chair with his hat in his fists. The destroyed barrier and subsequent mocking from his former colleagues had sapped all that remained of his earlier enthusiasm, but he was a problem solver by nature. He refused to allow a tiny thing like a defensive disaster that could unleash countless howling horrors on the town keep him down for long.

"There's nothing I can do right now, anyway. It took months to build and position those pillars. No point starting again until we have the culprit returned to whatever strange place it came from or crawled out of."

"Yeah, we got that the first three times you said it," Vivienne said. "So, what's next?"

Theo frowned and squeezed the hat. "I have made a few discoveries on my own, but what I say now must stay between the five of us."

"Seven!" a childish voice shouted before Zizel and Zemni appeared in puffs of green glitter like party poppers in short-pants. "We're joining Team Wontmoil."

Growina clapped her hands in delight, thought for a moment, and frowned. "I thought the bank said you weren't allowed to participate?"

Zizel smirked and leaned forward until she was horizontal in the air. "Said not to go near the creature, sure. Didn't say we can't help someone else do it."

"Clever, right?" Zemni added and tapped a finger against his temple. "So! Silly hat man! Do tell. What's in the silly hat?"

ELEVEN
The Welcoming Party

FLORIAN SLID HIS harness along the rope bridge toward what felt like the millionth copy of the same basic tree. His fingers were raw from fumbling with knots in diminishing light and his skull throbbed in spots from the debris that rained down with every lightening event.

Worse, he was out of ideas to coax the tight-lipped Wardric into disclosing how he managed to run a bridge across an entire forest in under three minutes.

Fortunately, the day's frustrating journey was nearing a visible end.

"The trees stop ahead," Bodkins said. "We'll head to the nearest valley and set up camp in a ditch. Stay low and slow out there if you can."

Florian made a sour face. "Not that I don't appreciate the crisp air and invasive wildlife, but can't we stay at an inn for once? Slimy pond water and borrowed razors disagree with my complexion."

"If you're worried about my old razor cutting you, I have bad news about the sort of people who frequent the inns in Picaroon Pelf," Wardric said with a chuckle.

Florian's eyes widened, and he strained to make out the grassy land beyond the edge of the forest. "Is *that* where we are? Picaroon Pelf? Really? I always imagined it was built on a swamp full of brambles and flesh-eating lizards."

Most everyone in Leechleif had a unique mental image of the forbidden city since every map and travel guide displayed only a blank space with the word "Avoid!" scribbled on the page. Perhaps it was a mountainous region with toxic plants and poisonous rocks. Maybe it was a plateau littered with roaming schools of flying piranhas in purple top hats. It was impossible to tell which first-hand accounts were legitimate and which were bogus when nobody was inclined to confirm their accuracy.

"Naw," Bodkins said. "The land's fine. The people, on the other hand . . . well. Let's just say not *everyone* prone to violent crime is interested in rehabilitation."

"And can you blame 'em?" Wardric asked as he scooted along the rope bridge. "Manipulative telekinetic therapy is spooky business. How can you be sure the person messing about in your head has their own on straight, eh? Docs should try more potion therapies and see if folks like that better, I think."

"Sounds like someone else's problem to me," Bodkins said with a shrug. "Our job is to stop the violence and collect fudgels. What happens out here only involves us if we get too close. Which reminds me—anyone who hasn't emptied their bladder yet should do so while we still have relative cover. That means you, Peterman."

Florian opened his mouth to argue that he had just used the facilities in the Indited Castle, before realizing how many hours had passed since. The one-two punch of collywobbles and Skrabblin's Dagger was still messing with his faculties.

"All right. I'll find a tree," he muttered and let out some of the rope on his harness.

Wardric continued toward the edge of the forest but

shouted over his shoulder, "Keep it quick! Remember, what goes down must come up! And then down again! Hah!"

Florian scowled. He could not understand why the mercenaries were in such good spirits. All day long, he had boiled in the sun, frozen in the wind, and battled swarms of biting bugs that had no right to be around after summer. Then again, the mercs anticipated an exciting monster hunt at the end of their journey, whereas he was dreading the repercussions for failing to produce said monster.

The thought of wearing his own filth for a hat was not particularly appealing, so he finished his business as quickly as possible and hustled to catch back up to the others. Unfortunately, the voices that greeted his ears upon his approach were not the ones he expected.

"Aww, lookit the lovely couple," a gravelly voice purred. "Out for a stroll in the woods?"

"Nobody *strolls* in the Forest of Lightening," another snapped. "They're couriers, clearly. Or art smugglers. You can tell by the paintbrushes on the larger one's jacket. Symbols of their trade, I figure. These two must be loaded."

"Thought you'd take a shortcut, eh?" a third voice asked. "Hope you didn't forget your toll money."

Florian weighed his options. He could continue forward into an ambush, but that seemed equal parts unwise and unhelpful. Likewise, staying put while tied to the rope bridge was akin to flipping a coin to decide his fate. A retreat into the woods would get him to the other end of the bridge, but not out of the forest. Should he go around the bandits, then? Find his own path through the 'Pelf?

He bit his lip and untied his harness, determined to size up the ambush before he made any rash decisions. The mercs were mercs, after all. For all he knew, it was the bandits who were in for a deadly surprise. And he was not sure if that was a good or bad thing where he was concerned.

Upon careful approach, he found the situation far from sorted. Two figures in woody camouflage pointed short swords at the mercenaries' throats, while two others in the trees aimed bows for backup. There was a non-zero chance Bodkins could still take them down between her own abilities and the massive monster limbs attached to her chair, but the unarmed Wardric would wind up a bearded pincushion if she tried.

"In case my associate wasn't clear," one of the two with swords said, "you'll be giving us all the money you have on you, immediately and without a fuss."

Bodkins glanced to Wardric. She seemed oddly calm, considering the circumstances. "I don't carry coin on my person."

"You think you're the first person to try that?" the bandit asked. "Just give me your purse."

She shrugged, untied the bag at her hip, and tossed it to the bandit, who shook it upside-down and frowned.

"Maybe she's telling the truth?" a tree-bandit asked, earning a deadly glare from the purse-holding one; he appeared to be the leader.

"Nobody travels this far without money. How would they pay for lodgings and food?"

"I said I don't carry coin," Bodkins explained in a tone one might expect from a schoolteacher, "not that I don't have money. The fudgels are in another world, and only I can retrieve them from the bag. While living, I should add. It's very clever magic."

"Pull them out, or I'll shoot the painter!" a tree-bandit shouted, but the bandit with the bag held up a finger.

"It's a ruse, fool. The fudgels are somewhere else."

Florian perked up, suddenly struck by an irresistible, if ill-advised, idea. Until now, he thought escape was his best option for survival. After all, he possessed no weapons or combat experience outside theatrical choreography.

What was he meant to do? *Act* his way out of danger?

But that was precisely what he could do.

He pressed his back against a tree and hummed. Vocal cords, like other muscles, had to warm up for professional use. Fortunately, a bit of mm hehe hoho was impossible to hear over the increasingly agitated shouts from bandits who were unused to dealing with women like Beatrix Bodkins. Perhaps she was telling the truth. Perhaps she was toying with them. Hopefully, they would never find out which.

Florian finished his vocal exercises, made himself as invisible as possible, and called out in a gravelly voice, "I bet the coins are in that big wooden box!"

After an agonizing silence in which he was sure they were sending someone to look for him, a bandit replied, "Well, what do you know? A big wooden box. We'll be taking this off your hands now."

Florian grinned and exhaled. A job well done.

But Bodkins was too honest for her own good. "You won't find fudgels in there," she said. "Let us pass, and I'll pull some coins from the bag for you. Keep messing with my stuff, and you'll get nothing."

"This thing feels like it's full of bricks!" the non-leader said with a grunt. "It's gotta be money. Nothing else is this heavy."

"It's human remains," Bodkins corrected as if discussing the weather. "There are zero fudgels on us. None. No money. Not even a voucher for ten percent off a dinner at Barnaby's Boar Buffet. You're wasting all of our time."

Technically, there *were* human remains in the box, but the last thing Florian wanted was for Bodkins to talk the bandits out of opening it. He gritted his teeth and searched his imagination for a way to signal his plan to her.

"You got sand in your ears?" he shouted in his best bandit voice. "The box is ours now. We're getting a load of it with our own eyes!"

Surely that was heavy-handed enough to plant an idea in her mind.

"Yeah!" the bandit with the box added. "You're not stopping—huh?"

There was a click of brass latches, a groan of heavy wood, and something similar to the sound of angry bees. Unable to help himself, Florian peeked around his tree to see the chaos unfold.

"Get it off!" someone shrieked from within a cyclone of swirling sand.

Both bandits on the ground desperately swatted at the air as if they could shoo the gritty onslaught away from their faces. It brought back memories of windy beach vacations with breezes that stripped layers from his skin. He shuddered even as swords emerged from the cyclone and deposited themselves before Bodkins' chair.

"Make it stop or you're done for!" a tree-bandit declared.

Florian thought fast and changed his pitch to match the leader. "No! Shoot the sand!"

"But I might hit you," the tree-bandit whined.

"Thafs na me! Pah! If in ma mouf!" the actual leader said, and even Florian raised a brow in confusion.

Wardric, who had thus far failed to assist in any way, plucked a couple of thin brushes from his jacket and daintily dabbed them in what looked like an open clamshell. Florian rolled his eyes so hard his sockets ached. What was the big guy planning to do? Paint himself out of danger?

As if he could hear Florian's thoughts, the bearded artist held both brushes forward and flicked them very deliberately in the air. Then he cleaned the brushes and returned them to their holsters. A second later, there was a frightening crack and shrieks of panic as both tree-bandits (and the branches they were tied to) came crashing down into the sand-cyclone.

That . . . was unexpected. But the bandits' reactions were not. All four were clever enough to register the loss of their advantage, and none were foolish enough to bet on the odds. They took off at a run and continued to flail even when far from the cyclone and mercenaries.

Florian whooped in celebration.

Bodkins tutted. "I was hoping to solve that peacefully," she said. "They had every right to charge a toll for access to their land."

Eddie reassembled himself and pointed a pale finger at her. "That wasn't a toll. That was a robbery. Just because you didn't feel threatened doesn't mean they weren't breaking the law."

"Whose law? This is Picaroon Pelf. You need to get back in your box before bits of you blow to every corner of Naughtobelus. What were you thinking, pulling a stunt like that in the Forest of Lightening?"

The sand man huffed. "The universal law of . . . you know . . . not being a complete bum face. And it wasn't my idea. It was his!"

Florian's elevated mood plummeted to the earth like a loose clump of mud in a lightening event as Eddie's finger swung his way. He sighed in resignation and stepped from behind his tree so Bodkins could get a look at him.

Her jaw dropped. "I figured you were halfway to Mooncalf-Pale by now."

Florian cursed himself. In his excitement to execute what he thought was a brilliant plan, he had accidentally done something worse than abandoning the mercenaries to certain death.

He had broken character.

Ava Triumphant might have rushed into danger while dual-wielding swords and singing falsetto, but the shady Peterman would have vanished like a hairpin dropped in grass. Drat.

"I, uh," he waffled. It was difficult to fire up his improvisational skills while coming down from a post-ambush rush. "I'm still not feeling well."

That would have to do. And it seemed to satisfy Bodkins because she chuckled and waved him back to the rope bridge. Eddie returned to his box with only a bit of snark, Wardric took his place in line, and everything seemed to be back on track.

At least, until Bodkins turned her head and eyed Florian with suspicion. "You really helped Eddie come up with that plan?"

He shrugged. "I guess."

"From behind a tree? While he was in a box?"

"It wasn't that difficult."

"How?"

Florian saw his chance and jumped. "First, tell me how Wardric broke those branches. I saw him do something with paintbrushes, and then the branches split. What did he do?"

She waited for Wardric to nod his approval, then said, "He painted cracks in them."

"He painted cracks on nothing, and it caused cracks in the branches?"

Wardric laughed. "I painted them on the trees as I saw them from my perspective."

"And that made it real? Like the rope bridge?" Florian tugged on the rope and felt its splintery surface in his hands. "You painted this into reality? That's incredible!"

Wardric flushed and examined his boots. "It's okay. I need more practice with color theory especially. And the effects fade after a day. I don't know how to make anything permanent."

Florian recalled the pink bricks where a window should have been in the Indited Castle. Had Wardric painted those as well?

"Wow," he said, unable to think of anything better.

Bodkins grinned. "Okay. Your turn. How did you do it?"

"Hmm." Florian took a deep breath, recalled the gravelly voice of the tree-bandit, and said, "I told ya, the box is ours! Don't make me use abrasive language!"

"Abrasive!" Eddie's voice said from within his sandbox. "Hah! I get it!"

"You're both children," Bodkins said.

Wardric was enraptured. The artist clapped his hands like a child at a party with an exceptionally competent stage magician and said, "Do it again!"

Florian switched to the lead bandit's voice. "Shoot the sand! Ignore the probability of stopping a dirt tornado with an arrow!"

Wardric clapped with delight again. "You're amazing!"

Florian beamed. Yes. Yes, he was. And perhaps, if the mercs saw that, they mght reconsider their earlier dismissal of his claim to be a professional thespian, rather than a soothsayer. "Thanks. You're very kind."

"No way," Wardric said with the toothiest smile. "I mean it. You're really good. I bet if you wanted to, you could do improv at the Slimy Salamander. It's five whole fudgels a night!"

Florian managed to hold his smile, though it slid into a grimace against his will. "Thanks."

TWELVE

Spitting Snakes

"Breakfast!" Growina sang. She backed through curtains and into her storefront with a tray of piping hot blueberry muffins.

The adventurers snoozing in her shop wriggled and moaned as if she had burst in with a bottle of artificial sunlight. Of the three witches resting head-to-stomach in a triangle on the still-filthy floor, only Margaret tried to sit up. Theo dragged his beard through a puddle of drool on the counter where he had passed out beside his rock. Only the two alien children, who hung upside-down from the ceiling like bats, seemed excited about the muffins.

"Mmmm! Smells sugary!" Zemni said and stretched himself into an inverted letter y.

The smell *was* delightful if Growina allowed herself to boast. Sweet, buttery, and not a whiff of burned edges. It had been ages since she'd baked for anyone other than herself, and she was terrified she would fill the entire house with smoke from splashed batter.

"There's only enough for two per person," she said. "I didn't have the ingredients for more."

Zemni floated over, snatched a muffin, and shot a nasty glare at Theo. "That better not have been my muffin flour you dumped all over the stones outside the bank!"

Theo said nothing.

Margaret carefully shifted Sylvie's head from her lap so she could stand. The quiet witch lasted about two seconds with her ear pressed to the cold floor before she, too, was up and shifting Vivienne.

"Anyone come up with a brilliant strategy in the night?" Margaret asked as she selected her muffin. "All I had was a dream that the children's heads spun around and then they vomited snakes on me."

"I could do that with the snakes!" Zizel declared through a large bite. "But *he* can only spit the word snake at you."

Zemni crossed his arms. "Not true! I can make the word snake out of snakes! Like—mmph!"

Everyone turned to see the wide-awake Vivienne pointing two fingers toward the boy, whose mouth was unexpectedly stuffed with muffin.

"I didn't want to see it," she said with a shrug, as if that was an excuse to attack a "child."

Technically, Naughtobelus age did not apply to the aliens, who did not age linearly and could have been anywhere from ten to seven hundred years old in local time. But Growina could not imagine them as anything but children due to their appearance and propensity for mischief.

She shook her head in disapproval, having no other method to shame a naughty witch. Attacking children! Honestly.

"Wait. Wait! I *do* want to see it!" Theo shouted at a volume inappropriate for both the location and hour.

Everyone winced.

"Sorry. Uh . . ." He grabbed the stone from the table, wiped his beard with his sleeve, and hurried to the aliens. "Can you read this?"

Zizel crossed her arms. "We both tried last night. 'Wud

mapl orng ruk beneet str,' isn't any language we've learned on any planet. It has to be encoded."

"Understood," Theo said before raising an impatient finger. "However, from what I gather, your skills will produce a physical representation of whatever word you speak, regardless of what you intend to produce. Correct?"

"Oh, way to go, ugly hat," Zemni spat through a mouthful of crumbs. "You know she's sensitive about that, right?"

Margaret snatched a second muffin from the tray and shook her head. "The wizard's idea is sound . . . and it's the only one we've got, what with all the newbies in town popping off spells and obscuring the monster's magic signature."

Growina tensed at the mention of the magical signature. The topic had sparked a vicious argument the night before. Theo insisted he should ask other adventurers to stop using magic, and the witches threatened to do many uncomfortable things if his loose lips cost Team Wontmoil the bounty.

"Fine," Zizel said. "Give me the rock."

The alien scrunched up her nose and opened her mouth to speak, but Growina interrupted. "One moment, please. Let me get a broom, just in case."

"Broom?" Theo asked. "What for? I have a spell to fix glass, should anything shatter."

"And it's not like you've got anything left to break. Other than those nasty fish sticks," Vivienne added.

Growina pouted. The fish sticks were good! But she acquiesced and stepped aside so Zizel could do her thing.

"Wud," Zizel said, and a wooden plank fell from nowhere at all. It clattered to the tiled floor and sat there uselessly as the party examined it for nonexistent clues.

"Maybe you pronounced it wrong," Theo offered.

"You tell me how to pronounce wud, genius," Zizel snapped, and another plank clattered into the first.

"Forget it. Just continue."

"Mapl orng ruk benneet str," Zizel said.

Before their eyes appeared: a map, an orange, a gorgeous throw rug, a single lima bean, and a metal star.

Theo scowled. "Maybe if we arrange them in order?"

"Give it up," Vivienne said. "The kid didn't decode the message. It's obvious she created items that sounded a bit like the words on the stone."

The naughty witch dropped to the floor in what was meant to be a huff, but the cobweb-like fabric of her layered dress turned the move into a graceful flutter like a panicked jellyfish. Even Theo looked ready to return to his drying drool-puddle and go back to sleep.

But Growina had an idea. "What if that's the answer?" she asked. "Not that I'm an expert like you are. But I do know a thing or two about moss, and the samples I collected yesterday are the fast-growing sort. This means the stone may not be as ancient as we think! And Theo and I already discussed the possibility that the author was illiterate. What if someone carved the stone during the Gart Splagosion when everyone lost the ability to spell?"

"I think people had more pressing problems during the Gart Splagosion," Margaret began, but a look at Sylvie silenced her.

Not one to participate in idle conversation, Sylvie had not bothered to emerge from her warm cloak. But now, one of her dainty hands extended from the fabric and pointed at Growina long enough to be uncomfortable. By their reactions, it seemed both Margaret and Vivienne interpreted the gesture as agreement with Growina's theory, if not irrefutable proof of its accuracy.

"All right, it's misspelled," Margaret said as if she had not been mid-argument. "How do we get from that to a message that makes sense? Wood, map, orange, rug, bean, star? What's that even mean?"

Theo was at the materialized pile in under a second. "If it's a sentence, it only makes sense that some of the words aren't nouns. So, of course, asking the alien—"

"Zizel," said Zemni.

"Asking Zizel to turn them all into objects produced some false results. Someone take notes."

Margaret rolled her eyes but nonetheless produced a leather-bound notebook and fountain pen. The wizard did not wait for her to confirm she was ready.

"Wud could mean a plank, a small forest, or maybe the word 'would.' As in, 'Would you write those in the notebook?'"

"Speak to me like I'm your assistant one more time, and you'll *eat* the notebook," Margaret snapped.

"Noted. Skipping mapl for now because it's hurting my head. Orng ruk could be orange rug? Or orange rock. And beneet str sounds like 'beneath star.' That gets us . . . wood mapl orange rock beneath star. Rocks are more common than rugs in the woods, I suspect."

"If it's in a wood, could mapl be maple?" Growina asked. It was worth a shot.

"Yes! Wood maple orange rock beneath star!"

"Sounds like directions by landmarks," Margaret said. "But I wouldn't know where to start. Any forest could have a maple tree and an orange rock."

Theo dropped one of the materialized clues that he had been fidgeting with. His face had the same expression Growina's had when she had realized she left the kettle on mid-summon. The classic "how could I forget something so obvious" stare.

"Not any forest." He licked his lips as if they had suddenly gone dry. "I know exactly where this is. But you're not going to like it."

* * *

An excerpt from the Lazy Botanist's Guide to Naughtobelus.

Glycine Piscosa FISH STICK / FALSE FISH / STENCH STICK

Habitat: The sandy floors of temperate shorelines and salt lakes.

Appearance: Brown to black seaweed with multiple axes from which thick branches of variable lengths grow. Branches dry thin, but pale core—with legume-like texture—re-expands upon breakage.

Characteristics: Edible core is a meat substitute known by experts for its heart health benefits, but fishy odor is repugnant to all but the most enthusiastic botanists.

Author's note: Do not pack these as a portable snack at work. This is a social faux pas. No one will tell you so directly, but you may later find yourself in an awkward conversation about the mystery jerk who popped stench sticks in the lunchroom. That guy. Pfft. Right? Who does that?

* * *

"You're right. I don't like it," Vivienne declared with her arms crossed.

The pale witch was rude, as always, but she was not the only one perturbed. The five members of Team Wontmoil who were permitted to hunt the magic-eater all stood at the edge of the Howling Woods with their respective cloaks, shawls, and ridiculous hats drawn snug against the chill.

"Doesn't look like a maple to me," Margaret agreed. "It's too big. Has to be an oak."

Theo furrowed his brow and re-examined the blackened stump before them. It was true that oak trees were typically larger than maples near Wontmoil. And, the stump he had selected was too old and charred to have telltale leaves, off-shoots, or seedlings that would help with identification.

But the party had a secret weapon that was as good as seedlings.

They had an apothecary.

Growina pointed to a patch of bark less charred than the rest. "It's definitely a maple. Or was one, rather."

"Yes!" Theo said. "It is. And ahead to the left is an orange rock as tall as my waist. I remember it well because it's impossible to move and located exactly where I wanted to place a pillar for my barrier."

"Your broken barrier," Vivienne reminded him with a snort.

He frowned so deeply his face seemed in danger of sinking into the crease between his eyes. "This is why I work alone."

"Nothing in there we haven't handled before," Margaret interjected as a peace offering. ". . .Well, except the creature we're pursuing."

Theo nodded, smoothed his unwrinkled suit, and directed them through thorny underbrush and hanging moss to a great orange boulder. It looked like it would be more at home in a desert than a haunted forest.

He patted the rock as if trying to sell it used at a discount. "One orange rock. Now what?"

Sylvie crouched and pointed to a crack near the base of the stone. It resembled a five-pointed star. She followed the crack downward with her finger to a spot that shimmered and wobbled like the cemetery wall.

Growina gave a giddy giggle as the white-eyed witch's hand slid through the puddling-like magical illusion, groped around, and emerged with yet another carved stone.

"Are you kidding me?" Theo whined. "Are we playing some kind of children's—"

"Silence!" Margaret snapped.

Growina jumped, worried the witch was about to start a fight, but Margaret set a finger to her lips instead. Everyone held their breath and listened for the telltale howl of approaching horrors. Leaves rustled to their left as if a dog or jungle cat paced just out of sight.

Theo slid Fang Lock from his sleeve, and the witches held their hands at the ready like conductors at the start of a concert. Lacking combat experience, Growina popped a random potion from her potion bandolier to feign readiness.

The rustling slid behind them, back to the left, and around to the right.

"The Penumbral Magwod—" a voice shrieked so suddenly they all yelped, "—demands to know what you're doing here!"

"Oh, for the love of . . . stop sneaking up on people!" Theo shouted with one hand to his chest. "You almost caught Fang Lock to the face!"

Chip, who honestly deserved more credit for surprising a vigilant adventuring party in the Howling Woods, responded with a rude gesture to the wizard until his armored friend stopped him. The two shared a look too brief to communicate anything meaningful, and yet, Chip relaxed.

"The Penumbral Magwod gathers you're following the same trail as he and commends you for your ingenuity. No other adventurers have noticed the creature's leavings thus far. However, he is disappointed that you spooked the creature and created a skunk cloud of magic in the process!"

"What skunk cloud? We haven't done anyth—ow!" Theo

turned to see Margaret holding her fingers up as if she had flicked him from several feet away. ". . . I mean, your friend is emitting as much magic as we are, if not more. It's a wonder the creature doesn't gobble him up."

It was not the smoothest move Theo had ever made—which was saying a lot for a wizard whose standards of etiquette were slightly above those of a crotchety miser in the giving season. But based on the young man's reaction, it had successfully distracted the pair enough to dampen any further curiosity they might have about the magic around the orange stone.

Chip glanced at the giant for guidance again, then nodded. "The Penumbral Magwod is willing to consider this incident a mutual misunderstanding and not deliberate sabotage. However, should your ineptitude cost him another opportunity to capture the creature . . ."

The armored giant lifted his hands as if gripping a ball, and a swirling mass of lava, orbited by glowing hornets, appeared between them.

" . . . you will learn why they say he's effective."

THIRTEEN

Picaroon Pelf

FLORIAN SLANK, head lowered, behind Bodkins' chair and tried to resemble one of its limbs.

It was not the least dignified role he had ever attempted. Once, when he was just a boy with stars in his eyes, he had played a rutabaga in a school performance of *The Pixie and the Hare*. Most children would have taken insult to such an assignment, but he gave his root vegetable a tragic backstory—a brilliant witch transformed by a jealous rival—and was subsequently transferred to set design.

"Peterman's weirding me out," Wardric complained. He was far too calm for an unarmed artist strolling through the scariest city in all Naughtobelus.

Bodkins turned to stare. "What are you doing? Quit walking so close."

"I'm trying to make myself invisible," Florian whispered. "This place is horrible. The streets are sticky and the buildings are moist. Everything smells of dog vomit laced with eggs and cabbage. And absolutely everyone is staring at us!"

"They're staring because you're wriggling," Eddie said. "Please act normal."

Florian straightened and glared. What, exactly, was "normal" supposed to look like when walking beside a paintbrush-covered giant and a sand man sitting atop a wooden box to avoid touching the sludge?

"I thought the whole point of camping in a ditch was to *avoid* Picaroon Pelf."

"To avoid sleeping in the 'Pelf, yes," Bodkins said. "They won't try anything while we're awake. Not unless they want their ghosts tied to gooey brooms for all eternity."

Florian shuddered and furrowed his brow to blend in and look like less of a tourist. However, despite his efforts, he could not stop staring at the barred and booby-trapped windows of the buildings they passed. There were six tripwire crossbows and a trap door on *one* shop entrance! If the Spherule Theater prop department put that many traps in a cave full of treasure, they would be booed out of town for their lack of authenticity.

"This is the place!" Bodkins declared and led them all down a stone ramp to a basement that was slightly less musty than the town itself.

Their destination was some sort of underground bazaar packed with tables that advertised wildly different products and services. Florian wrinkled his nose at one with several glass tanks and a sign that read, "Used newts for baking, pranking, and spellcasting! Most aren't transformed humans!"

The vendor behind the table was asleep with a hat over their face and, thus, did not witness Florian's disgusted gag. Unfortunately, the one at the adjacent table was wide-awake and painfully gregarious.

"Don't like newts, eh?" the nosy vendor asked. "Says a lot about a person when they can't stomach the innocent little creatures."

Florian blanched. "Oh, no, it's not the newts themselves that—"

A sandy hand gripped his wrist. "Don't talk to that one. He's a troublemaker."

The vendor crossed his arms and pouted as if insulted. "Troublemaker? For what? My observational skills? Intimate knowledge of the technical workings of the human mind? Bet you'd love to know what your newt-hating friend here really thinks of you, eh?"

Eddie turned his back without a word and Florian made to follow. But the crowd-pleaser in him could not walk away without an apologetic wince. The vendor was rude, conceited, and far too loud, but it was all a sales pitch for his . . . couple's therapy? Maybe?

Florian read the sign on the vendor's table.

"Mind-reading," the vendor announced before he finished reading the words. "10 fudgels a pop! Is she cheating? Where did he bury the stolen treasure? Is that really a diamond, or polished glass? No questions asked because I don't have to!"

No one replied.

"Oh, I see," the vendor called after them. "You're all in on something. Don't want me seeing it, even if it gets you stabbed in the back, eh? See? I can read you, too!"

Eddie sighed and drifted back to his perch atop the wooden box on the back of Bodkins' chair. "Some people, eh?"

"Quiet," Bodkins snapped. "Carl!"

A fellow with a white beard looked up from a table that only held a stained ledger. "Stabby! It's been ages!"

"Stabby?" Wardric asked.

Bodkins shook her head. "It's a long story, and not what we're here for. Carl, I couldn't help noticing a conspicuous event in the Forest of Lightening, and I suspect you might know something about it."

Carl's eyes widened. "Who? Me? I wasn't anywhere near the fool when—oh, you mean the bats."

If the man was joking, he was a better actor than Florian.

Bodkins was unbothered. "Exactly. Did you happen to get

a peek at the message they were carrying?"

Carl glanced around the room and leaned in close. "The penalty for intercepting a bank bat in transit is steep. I *might* know someone who would do a thing like that, but compensation for that sorta information would have to be worth the risk taken. If you get what I mean."

Bodkins reached into her bag, produced a fistful of . . . something, and deposited it into Carl's hand.

He moved the compensation beneath his table for examination and smiled. "That'll do. Just a moment."

The old man donned a pair of spectacles inlaid with colorful stained-glass and flipped through his ledger. Each page was a mess of multicolored scribbles. Florian squinted at the pages and tried, in vain, to make words from the scribbles.

Meanwhile, Carl seemed to have no trouble copying the hidden message to a spare sheet of paper.

Bodkins accepted the copied note, grinned like a child with a holiday pudding, and said, "We have our destination!"

A wave of relief passed over Florian as he realized he would not have to fake a monster to escape punishment—apparently, there was a live one they were heading towards. Relief then shifted to horror as he followed that logic to conclude he would soon face *an actual living creature.* Potentially one terrifying enough that the bank sent an entire colony of note bats to warn about it.

His original plan may have been preferable.

"Well?" Eddie asked. "Where are we headed?"

Bodkins smiled conspiratorially and slid the note into her bag. In a play, this would have been the signal to leave the deadly stench pit, but that was not the sort of luck fate had in store for Florian Honeybeard.

Once again, a hand grabbed his wrist, but this time, it did not belong to the sand man. Instead, it was large, rough, and held him in place while another ripped a chunk of hair from his head.

"Ow! Hey!" he shouted as the gregarious vendor giggled and backed away with the clump of hair held high.

Clearly intent upon making a break from the underground bazaar with the stolen strands, the man backed toward the door and dramatically stuffed the hair into his still-cackling mouth. Then he swallowed it with a grimace and froze as if stunned. His eyes bugged.

Florian rubbed the sore spot on his scalp and muttered obscenities, sure the vendor was unwell. But the man raised a shaky hand toward the group and shouted the one thing required to convince any of them he was telepathic.

"T-tentacles!"

"Oh?" Bodkins asked.

The man responded, "It's *eating pixies*! Pixies! Not even worrying about what they'll do! I can hear their tiny screams! I can see its claws and teeth! I'm going to be sick. What is this thing?"

Bodkins glanced at Eddie and shrugged. "We're hunting a monster. You figured it out. Congratulations. Happy now?"

The man was not happy. He was scared to an inch of his self-touted wits. "How have the pixies not killed it? What is it? Who are you people?"

"Wait a minute," Florian said. "I thought you said you're a mind reader. I'm not thinking about any of that. For the past twenty minutes, I've been preoccupied with your town's revolting odor. No offense."

The vendor shrugged as if to say it was no bother and went back to shaking. Bodkins shushed the trembling man and chewed her lip in thought.

"He saw something deeper than your conscious mind. You still have a connection with the creature, and we may need that to get ahead of the competition. Wardric, search the tables for wriggleweed, Collywobbles, and Skrabblin's Dagger. Lots."

"Hey," Florian objected. "Don't I get a say in this?"

It was one thing to have his allergy-induced nightmares misconstrued as fateful predictions, but he drew the line at deliberate and repeated poisoning to replicate the previous outcome.

Bodkins nodded and said, "Hey, Carl. You have somewhere private I can talk to my associate?"

Carl jerked his thumb toward a door behind him. "Break room's free."

"Thanks."

That was probably not a great sign. How many people came out of private discussions with mercenaries unharmed? But resistance was pointless, so he followed her into a small room with a smaller couch and tried not to jump when she slammed the door.

"You get five questions," she said and sat back in her chair.

Her brown eyes were piercing in the dim glow of a single enchanted candle, and Florian could not help but compare the encounter to some of his teenage experiences with young women raised on romance novels. Only, instead of planting an awkward kiss on his lips, Bodkins was more likely to bury a fist in his gut.

It spoiled the mood somewhat.

He shook his head. "I don't follow."

Bodkins sighed. "I want you to feel like a member of this team, but I get the impression you don't understand we're the good guys. So, I'm giving you five questions. Anything you want to know. I'll answer truthfully."

Florian's mind blanked as it always did when asked if he had questions. Questions were things you brought up in a moment of confusion. Not things you saved up like coupons to retrieve upon request.

"I don't suppose I can ask you to take me home?" he asked with a nervous laugh.

Bodkins smiled. "I'm going to refuse to answer that one, so you don't waste a question on something you already know the answer to."

Well, at least she was honest.

"Okay, then. Why do you need me to come along *with* you?"

"At first, it was for insurance. Wardric believed in you, but I was convinced you'd try to sell us on a false prophesy and vanish again. Now that I have proof you are what you say you are, I need your help to locate the creature before other mercenaries and adventurers swoop in to claim the bounty from the bank."

Florian perked up. A bank bounty was likely a considerable sum. Possibly ten or more times what he would have received from Bodkins' donation to the theater had she not mistaken his identity at her front door.

"And I'm one of the team," he began, "meaning I get a share of the bounty if we catch the thing?"

She laughed and, for once, it sounded like genuine humor instead of mockery. "Sure. You need it more than we do. Waste of a question, though."

"Drat. Um . . ." He paced in front of the couch and demanded his brain come up with something meaningful. Something that had been gnawing at him since day one. "Got it! Whose souls are in your chair's limbs?"

"My own. Each leg is a piece of me."

"But . . ." Florian's mouth opened and closed as he imagined ways to extract more information from her without asking a fourth question.

Fortunately, she obliged without his asking. "It's how I'm able to control them so easily. If the spirits belonged to other people or monsters, I'd have a chair that did whatever it wanted. That's not exactly independence. So, I put my fear of spiders in that leg. My social anxiety is in this arm. And that claw over there is my hatred of buttermilk dressing. Could never stand the stuff."

"That's . . . very specific."

And very interesting. But not what Florian needed to feel better about following the woman toward a monster that, according to his subconscious, ate pixies. Then again, he was still convinced his subconscious was full of nightmares, rather than a supernatural connection to a nasty beast.

"Why did you become a mercenary?" he asked.

Bodkins leaned further back in her chair and brushed her curls behind her ears. "When I was a child, adults often treated me like I was invisible. So much so that some men once had an argument right over my head about who was more worthy of a woman's affection. Of course, the argument turned to a display of physical superiority. They figured the one who was the tallest, strongest, and fastest was most worthy, because the *delicate* woman needed a *strong* man to survive in today's world. And that got me thinking. Humans aren't the strongest creatures in Naughtobelus, nor are they the tallest or fastest. Today's world wasn't made for us at all. We used our intellect and tools to shape it into what it is. And had we been smaller, slower, weaker creatures, we still would have found a way. We'd simply have engineered different tools. So, that's what I did. I learned spirit stitching and built tools that made me bigger, faster, and stronger than anyone I knew and I dedicated my life to protecting the vulnerable from bullies and monsters alike—at my discretion."

Florian stared, unblinking, then shook his head to snap out

of it. "That's, uh. That's not what I was expecting."

"Last question, quickly. Wardric's likely purchased half the contents of the tables by now."

Florian tried not to laugh but smirked despite himself. "All right. Last question, I guess. Where are we going?"

Bodkins grinned and gave him a thumbs-up, then moved her chair closer to whisper the answer. "We're going to Wontmoil."

 Fourteen

Forbidden Formula

GROWINA DABBED COLD water onto a muddy stain on her dress to avoid meeting her companions' eyes, lest she be drawn into their conversation. Usually, she would jump at an opportunity to help someone solve a problem, but it was better to be a vine on a wall than forced to pick a side in an argument well outside her area of expertise.

"We have to go back," Theo said for the fourth or fifth time that afternoon. "How many hours will you waste before you admit we missed the key?"

Margaret shot an icy glare in the wizard's direction. "If Sylvie says she didn't miss anything, she didn't miss anything."

"She hasn't said a word! See, this is why I work alone."

Theo whipped off his hat to wring it in frustration, but Margaret only scowled and returned to her ongoing analysis of the new stone. The three witches hovered around Growina's counter, scribbling on, crumpling, and discarding pieces of paper.

"You're right," Vivienne said to Margaret. "It can't be a coincidence that the numbers go exactly to twenty-six. There *must* be a way to convert them to letters. But I'm not getting anything from this."

Growina glanced up from the hem of her dress long enough

to review the latest page of inky scribbles. The witches had the text from the stone copied down—1 14 21 c 5 3 26 7 9 c 18 x o x—followed by another nonsensical set of characters.

"Anuceczgicrxox," Theo read (or, rather, attempted to read without accidental vulgarity). "Marvelous. You've decrypted a sneeze. Next, we might learn how to spell a hiccup."

Vivienne was undeterred. "It could be a misspelled message, like before. Maybe it says . . . a new see zig rocks? Hmm. Or the letters could be scrambled."

"Falls apart a bit at zgicrxox, yes," Theo said in a tone that was easy to mistake for agreement if used by anyone other than a wizard.

The pale witch kicked the counter so hard it made the stone jump. "What would you try, then?"

"I'd go back to the orange rock in the woods and find the key to this puzzle, which we *obviously missed* in our haste to depart."

"Our haste," Margaret reminded him, "was due to the presence of the pernicious mugwort. And the last thing we want is to lead him straight to that rock. It was lucky he thought we were chasing the creature, or we'd be out there fighting for this stone rather than here decoding it."

"Penumbral Magwod," Theo corrected, and then, when she rolled her eyes continued with, "I'm relieved you're the ones decrypting the stone since you clearly have the superior vocabulary."

Vivienne made a rude gesture. "Witches don't *need* to memorize a bunch of words to do magic. It's wizards and similar mages that started that weird practice."

"You want a word? I'll give you a word."

Theo muttered one that sounded even more like a sneeze than Vivienne's scribbles, slammed his hat onto his head, and walked straight through the front door without opening it.

That was Growina's cue to step in. She hustled to the shop's entrance and threw the bolts as fast as she could, lest the witches wreck her shop in their haste to pursue him.

Her concern was unnecessary. Instead of a rapid chase, there was a loud "yipe" from outside the shop, followed by an eerie silence in which the remaining team members weighed the potential risks and merit of checking on their companion.

Growina finally gave in to curiosity and cracked the door enough to watch the scene unfolding outside.

"Couldn't help but notice that you didn't go home last night," a tall wizard with a crumpled hat said. "Is this what you've been up to? Cowering in the shops?"

Theo straightened. For all his flaws, he was, without a doubt, the bravest person Growina had ever seen in the face of bullies.

"I kept myself busy. Hope it gave you enough time to visit my home under false pretense and fill it with bugs. Would be a terrible shame if you had to come up with your own ideas instead of stealing mine."

The tall wizard (and two shorter ones previously obscured by his billowing robe) gasped as if struck. "Are you accusing us of breaking rule number forty-dash-b in the official wizard's code of conduct set forth by our founding members in—"

"My partner's canceled your fake spellbook order and squashed the bugs by now."

"Blast!"

"What do you want?"

One of the smaller wizards scooted from behind the tall one, and Growina was delighted to see they wore a fake beard sculpted out of felted wool. It had little curls and everything.

"We need the other half of the formula," they said, then leaned forward and whispered, "I think you know why. Name your price."

Theo crossed his arms. "For the hundredth time, it's destroyed. You know it's destroyed. I know you know it's destroyed. You cannot buy, borrow, steal, demand, request, or stealthily copy something that *doesn't exist*. Stop trying."

The tall one smirked. Or, at least, Growina assumed he smirked based on how his mustache twitched. "We all know your ego won't allow you to sit back and watch while we replicate your work and take credit. You've got proof somewhere, and you're waiting to produce it and embarrass us with it the moment we succeed. It's in your nature."

"Wrong," Theo said. "And if you happen to succeed by exhaustion or pure luck, I'll thank you to keep my name out of it. I don't want my legacy tarnished by something so distasteful. Now, if you don't mind . . ."

Theo attempted to maneuver around the trio, but they moved to follow. A quick pivot in the other direction had the same result. He flexed his fingers and inhaled as if to cast something nasty.

Margaret interrupted. "Theo, get back. We need to talk."

Growina jumped, unaware the witch was beside her, and wondered how long she had been there.

The felted wizard also squinted into the cracked doorway to see who had spoken. "Your whole team in there?" they asked. "What are you up to?"

Theo shook his head. "Nothing of value. In fact, I was *just leaving*."

Vivienne whispered, "What are they talking about? What has he done?" but Margaret shushed her.

The wizards again blocked Theo's path. "We're close, you know. Almost ready to roll out a prototype to catch this creature. We'd give you a share of the bounty, as well. Like royalties."

Theo snarled. "Today, it's to catch the creature. Last month it was to build a pen for ghost chickens. This is . . . oh, how does that phrase go? A solution in search of a problem. You don't even have a good use for it, yet you're willing to risk the future of Naughtobelus to make it happen."

The one with the felted beard threw their arms in the air. "You're being overdramatic! Anything in excess could destroy Naughtobelus. Chipmunk overpopulation could destroy Naughtobelus. Too many rainstorms could destroy Naughtobelus. Everyone doing the wiggle-thump jig at the same moment could destroy Naughtobelus."

Theo tried and failed to dodge them again. "Have you ever watched wicked people use defensive tools to hurt innocent people and thought, 'I wonder if the inventor of that tool would have burned their design if they knew?'"

"Nope."

"Well, I have. And I did. Now, back off!"

Theo spat a series of words that made him sound like a cornered cat protesting pets, and the air around him shimmered. He parted the wizards like curtains and stormed off into the city.

That was enough to get the witches moving.

"Sylvie, can you trail the wizards to find out what they're building?" Margaret asked. "We'll keep Theo out of trouble."

Growina gave Margaret an awkward smile. "Anything I can do?"

"Actually, yes. One moment." The witch held her hands toward the door, palms flat, and closed her eyes in concentration. "You can keep the stones hidden until we return. I've set up a rudimentary barrier and soundproofing to keep you as safe as possible and to prevent eavesdropping."

Growina nodded, then furrowed her brow. "How will I know if a customer knocks?"

The witch shot her a look that made it clear she should

craft a "temporarily out of stock" sign, then waved the others toward the door. "Let's go before they get far."

And then there was silence.

Silence, and a shop in desperate need of cleaning. That should have been exciting. Powdered herbs produced enough dust to keep Growina's broom busy without the help of a stampeding crowd. But there was something unquestionably satisfying about a thorough spring cleaning, even if the opportunity presented itself in the fall.

But, after everything she had gone through over the past few days, the chore felt mundane and mechanical, even as she grabbed her trusty broom.

It was not that she had expected the adventuring party to hand her a spellbook and stick her in front of the monster. Those skills took years, if not decades, to master. But she had hoped to be of more use than as a security guard for chiseled rocks.

Not to mention that she was no closer to understanding her role in the disaster than she had been a day ago.

The creature and clues seemed to be connected. It was nearby when they discovered both, after all. And the clues were older than the mess in the garden—which still needed a tidying. But was that enough to conclude that the timing of her goof-up and the monster's appearance was a coincidence?

Growina shook her head and swept dust and dried mud into a pile. Out of concern that wizards were outside the front door, she nudged it all through the bottle-filled hallway and out the garden exit. Then she stopped to squint at the mess on the doorstep.

Something in the pile of debris glinted in the afternoon sun, and not in a shattered bottle or dropped vial way. It looked like a tiny, stained-glass window beneath the layer of dirt.

Growina crouched down and gently tugged the delicate thing free. "A pixie wing?"

It certainly looked like one. Or part of one, at least. Though Growina had never met a pixie in person. Any creature that used the Howling Woods as a hunting ground was too dangerous for the average apothecary. Or adventurer, for that matter.

Perhaps someone stepped on the wing in the woods and got it stuck to their shoe? Stranger things had happened in the past twenty-four hours.

She pocketed the wing for her companions to see and returned to the stones on the counter.

"I suppose I should hide you," she said. After decades of blathering on to plants, it seemed rude not to extend the courtesy to rocks.

There was a cabinet in the corner with a hidden compartment, but she owned nothing interesting enough to justify using it. This was as good a chance as any. Besides, the compartment was the perfect size for two stones to fit—with effort.

The first slid in without a problem, but the second was lumpy and took some maneuvering to cram into place. Maneuvering that forced Growina to put pressure on the letter O between two X's.

It popped loose.

Terrified that she broke the stone, Growina juggled the loose letter and made to press it back into the hole, but another glinting object inside the space stopped her. She dropped the O in her pocket alongside the wing and used her fingernails to jiggle the tiny thing free.

It was a key.

FIFTEEN

The AMMs

GROWINA CREPT OUT of her front door and scanned the street for lurking competitors. Technically, she was supposed to stay put and guard the shop from snoops while the other team members were away.

But that plan had fallen to pieces when she had asked herself what an apothecary could do to stop determined wizards or an armored giant after they passed through the witches' defenses.

Besides, Theo had stormed off in search of a key, and then Growina found one! The sooner she caught up to the wizard, the sooner everyone would quit bickering and work together. (Hopefully.) She *had* to abandon her post because the team needed her help. Not because waiting for everyone to return and witness her exciting discovery was mind-numbingly boring.

Truly!

Theo likely took a circuitous route to the orange rock since both the annoying wizards and perturbed witches were on his heels when he left. So Growina did the same, lest she arrive only to find the witches had intercepted him early. She made it only two blocks, however, before a slender hand reached out of the shadows and tugged her behind a pile of broken shipping crates.

"What—" she began, but Sylvie set a finger to her lips and gestured to an altercation outside Pollywog's Pampering Powders.

Someone was harassing Pollywog. Growina squinted through wooden slats at the heavily bundled wizard from the previous day. She made a mental note to ask his name; she was running out of ways to identify people by facial hair alone.

"Absolutely not!" Pollywog snapped at a volume that would have sent Growina scurrying away.

The wizard did not budge. "Perhaps you fail to grasp the miraculous opportunities presented by this discovery. Imagine, if you would, a scenario in which the creature currently haunting this city could be caged rather than driven out of town."

"I don't want it caged *or* driven out," Pollywog argued. "I want it neatly banished to another world so it and we can live our lives in peace."

"A world from which someone could easily re-summon it?" he asked with a twitch of his bushy brows, as if he had caught her in a logical fallacy.

"Someone like a wizard, you mean?"

The bundled man held up his hands. "We're getting off track. Just imagine, hypothetically, that the monster was caged. Your town could put it on display and charge admission to see it! Imagine the money that would flow into Wontmoil then."

"And all it would cost is every drop of tranquil tree oil in the town and surrounding forests."

"Exactly."

"The oil I use in all of my lotions and scrubs."

"Well—"

"Absolutely not."

The wizard groaned. "We're on the precipice of a revolutionary shift in the way Naughtobelus manages monsters and miscreants. On the cusp of cages and traps that can't be escaped with the flick of a wrist! The merchants of Wontmoil could be the first to join the movement. Believe me—if you refuse, some other town *will* accept, and you will regret your decision. AMMs are the future if you like it or not."

"AMMs?" Growina muttered to herself.

"Anti-Magic Machines," Sylvie whispered in response.

Growina turned to stare at the witch, who had never, as far as she could recall, uttered a single word in her presence. But Sylvie avoided eye contact and attempted a smile that barely shifted the corners of her mouth. It was a clear message to move on.

"I tell you what," the wizard said. "We'll re-plant all the trees when we collect the bounty. Every single one. How's that?"

Pollywog tapped her foot. "So I can re-open my business in ten years when the trees mature? No thanks. And you haven't yet mentioned what it costs to maintain a cage with a magic-eating monster inside."

"Ugh. We're working on the tree problem and the side effects, okay? Maybe, in a year or two, we won't need—"

"Side effects?"

The wizard set his hand to his forehead. Or, at least, to a spot on his oversized hat beneath which his forehead might reside. "We're off track again. Let's start over."

Growina suppressed a groan at the thought of the wizard restarting his sales pitch, as much as it delighted her to know she was not the worst negotiator Pollywog had ever encountered.

Fortunately, Pollywog was also done with the man's fruitless arguments. "I've told you twice that I'm not interested. If you make me tell you a third time, I'm calling the gatekeepers."

Everyone, including Growina, sucked in a breath. *Nobody* liked the gatekeepers. Primarily because the only gate in Wontmoil was easy to circumvent, with no walls built around it. But also, folks disliked the fact that the gatekeepers made every peacekeeping mission they participated in worse for their efforts.

Bullies hated them. Victims hated them. There was no way Pollywog would call them over a minor annoyance. But the wizard did not know that.

"Okay, okay. If that's your decision," he muttered. "But you know where to find me when you change your mind."

Without so much as a wave, he hobbled off to lick his wounds, thoroughly embarrassed by Pollywog's rebuttal. Growina expected Sylvie to follow, as per Margaret's earlier instruction, but Sylvie shook her head instead. It seemed the AMMs were 'what the wizards were building,' and Sylvie required no further information. The secret formula that Theo had invented and later destroyed must have been related to anti-magic.

Unfortunately, the conclusion of Sylvie's assignment left Growina with only one option herself, and it was one she desperately hoped to avoid.

Waiting.

* * *

An excerpt from the Lazy Botanist's Guide to Naughtobelus.

Schistostega Pennata DRAGON'S GOLD

Habitat: Dark, humid spaces such as leaky caves and the underside of wet logs.

Appearance: Luminous moss with feather-like, leafy texture.

Characteristics: Due to its ability to thrive in low-light conditions, this reflective moss is often mistaken for enchanted treasure by dungeon-delving adventurers. Unfortunately, it has no magical, medicinal, or monetary value. In fact, it's not even genuinely bioluminescent!

Author's note: Dragon's Gold cannot compete with any other plant on Naughtobelus. It may have originated in a less hostile world. Perhaps the summon on which the spores traveled also fell prey to our local wildlife. Unfortunate. But it wasn't a plant, so who cares, really?

* * *

When Theo finally stumbled through the door to Herbs and Vices, he looked as deflated as a popped puffball mushroom. The witches behind him also dragged themselves in as if they had spent the afternoon dancing in heels.

They were barely inside before Vivienne flopped to the floor and whined. "Surprising no one, there was no key. Just an ugly rock with a spell on it to hide the hole we already found."

"Actually—" Growina began, hardly able to contain her excitement.

"No Magwods either," Margaret said. "Penumbral or otherwise. We know this because he made us look everywhere for the guy."

"We can't discount the possibility that he found the key while we were away," Theo argued with little energy, as if he had made the same point ten times already.

"It turns out—" Growina said, but Vivienne interrupted her again.

"I'm not even sure we're on the right track. Like, I get you found the first stone near the creature, but how do you know they're both related? Eating locks and crafting puzzles are *slightly* different skill sets."

Theo harumphed. "Obviously, the puzzles are the work of the creature's summoner. Or a previous adventurer who successfully banished it. And I wouldn't discount the thing just yet. It's smart enough to evade us, after all."

"Shame they summoned it so long ago," Margaret said. "We'd get double the bounty if we turned in the summoner along with the summon."

"I have the key!" Growina shouted and held up the object she found in the stone.

After an uncomfortable silence, Theo crinkled his nose. "I don't get it."

"The key. I found it inside the second stone. Oh, and I looked up the moss we found in the cave. Apparently, it's not even from Naughtobelus. That supports your theory, right?"

Theo took the key from her hand and looked it over, but his expression did not change, which was more than a little disappointing.

Growina had expected celebration, not confusion.

"This isn't the type of key I meant," he finally said. "I was talking about an *encryption* key. Like a string of letters or mathematical formula we can use to translate the message. But this . . . you say you found it in the stone?"

Growina's smile drooped despite efforts to maintain it. "Yes. The O popped out from between the two X's, and the little key was behind it."

"Interesting. And where are the stones now?"

She hurried to her cabinet, opened the hidden drawer, and

slid a felt-covered panel to retrieve the stones inside.

Theo grabbed the second one and examined the hole. "Do you still have the letter O?"

She nodded, reached into her pocket, and produced the letter—along with the piece of pixie wing.

All three witches gasped.

"Where did you get that?" Margaret demanded. There was an urgency in her eyes that Growina had not seen since the morning she arrived in search of imp dust.

"I found it on the doorstep when I was sweeping the floors," Growina said. "Thought maybe one of us tracked it in on a shoe."

To her surprise, Margaret flicked her fingers toward the front door to throw the bolts and blast it open. Then she searched the cobblestones outside. Growina thought to correct the woman's assumption and send her to the back garden instead, but the singed circle and days-old cauldron still sat among the rows of plants. Best to not.

"Just the one wing," the witch said as she shut the door, "and no sign of a body. That's good. No blood for them to track."

It was Growina's turn to be confused. "Blood for who to track?"

"The pixies!" Vivienne shouted as if Growina had asked the color of grass. "Do you have any idea what they'd do if they found that here? We need to burn it, fast."

"Someone is threatening us," Margaret agreed. "This is a warning."

"Someone or some*thing*," Theo added. "It could be the creature itself."

Vivienne rolled her eyes. "The creature eats locks! It's not a strategic mastermind. This was planted by someone smart enough to send us a message and maintain plausible deniability. Someone who knows where we're meeting and wants us out of the way. It's got to be the wizards."

Theo pulled off his hat and sat behind the counter. "Preposterous. Frankly, I'd rank the entire lot of them behind the creature in terms of intelligence, even if it is a feral beast . . . which it isn't. The wizards can't reverse-engineer half a formula invented by a junior member decades ago."

"The AMMs, you mean?" Growina blurted before she could stop herself.

Theo grew painfully silent, and his face twisted into an expression usually used by school principals at the end of their patience. "Where did you hear that acronym?"

She flushed and glanced at Sylvie, but the silent witch sank further into her hooded robes.

"We, uh . . . we saw a wizard arguing with Jacqueline Pollywog about tranquil tree oil. Sounded like they needed a lot of it to power a cage for the creature, but she wasn't interested in sharing."

"Explain," Margaret said.

Thankfully, Theo took charge. "Anti-magic machines. I invented anti-magic when I was in the association. Well, re-invented it, I suppose, based on some artifacts left behind by Sigeric Slugbeard after the Gart Splagosion. But I quickly realized what I'd done and burned the formula to save Naughtobelus."

"Is that why you left the association?" Vivienne asked. "I always thought it was because they were, you know . . . you know."

He sighed. "Thank you for trying not to say wizards."

Growina stepped aside and fidgeted with the first stone, happy to have everyone's attention off her. She had been so excited to help when she thought she had Theo's key, but everything after that made her realize how naive and uneducated she was.

Perhaps she had no value to add, except as Sylvie's version of Chip. And nobody needed that.

"Sounds like they're doing it with or without you," Margaret said, "and will use up all the tranquil tree oil in the process. If your formula is less harmful, why not help them?"

Theo waved his arms around while he answered the question. "Today, it's a cage for a monster—which I already find distasteful. Tomorrow, it's a cage for a human. The day after that, well, maybe they'll decide it's the human they want to strip of magic. Or the Howling Woods. Or Wontmoil itself. The wizards could eliminate every competitive source of magic in Naughtobelus, one justification at a time."

Margaret grabbed one of his flailing arms and stilled it. "Okay, I feel like we need to take a step back before we get too worked up. We have a magic-eating monster on the loose, right? And someone or something is threatening us with a pixie wing. Plus, there are wizards on the verge of an anti-magic mistake with unknown consequences. Not to mention the unsolved puzzle etched into the stone on the counter. Which of these problems should we focus on first?"

"I vote the puzzle," Vivienne said. "Now that we know there's no key, we can get back to solving it properly."

"Actually . . ." Growina said, and for once, everyone quieted. "You said the encryption key could be another string of letters, right?"

She held up the first stone with the message they had decrypted. "What about this?"

Sixteen

Slugbeard's Spellbook

"Forgive my asking," Florian started as he scooted around a protruding chunk of marble, "but if we're in such a hurry to reach Wontmoil, why did we stop at a tourist attraction?"

Bodkins used two beastly arms—ones with terrifying claws—to lift her chair up and over a collapsed archway rather than squeeze through. "This isn't a tourist attraction. It's a historical site."

"I fail to see the difference."

Wardric, who was brawny enough to navigate crumbling ruins without breaking a sweat, hummed a cheery tune to himself as he shimmied through doorways and pawed at piles of rubble. Similarly, Eddie flowed through the crevices between stones, pleased to be somewhere that was not breezy, sticky, or confining.

Florian was less enthusiastic. The prospect of digging through a dilapidated building for anything short of a lost puppy felt like an enormous waste of time and energy.

"Tell me," Bodkins said as she lifted a cracked column in a single massive claw. "Do we look like a team that can banish a creature that eats pixies?"

"Uh . . . I guess?"

Florian nudged a rock with his foot, unsure what the others

were searching for or how he could help. The structure they stood in had the skeleton of an old schoolhouse or community center, which made it unlikely they were hunting for buried treasure.

Bodkins cackled. "For someone advertising grand adventure to mercenaries, you have limited knowledge of the subject matter."

Florian frowned as, once again, his ability to improvise failed him. Half of his brain screamed, "I'm not a soothsayer! I am a thespian, and I want to go home!" and the other half was desperate to play the role long enough to collect his share of the bounty. Truth be told, the Spherule Theater needed it. Despite fantastic reviews and a loyal fanbase, ticket sales were insufficient to cover the ever-increasing cost of materials and labor.

Sure, the theater could pay people less and cheapen their props to remain competitive with other, lesser-quality entertainment venues. But management at the Spherule cared for and believed in their employees . . . which was why it made no sense that they had not even tried to locate Florian when he—and their wealthiest donors—went missing.

Did they think he was taking the mercs on an extended tour of the countryside? Who would play Ava Triumphant in his absence?

"Don't worry, it's a good thing!" Bodkins said with a shrug. "If you seemed too savvy, I'd question your motives. But since you're confused and I'm bored, let's see what Wardric thinks. Hey, Wardric!"

The artist looked up from his pile of rocks and quirked an eyebrow.

"What do pixies do if you mess with them?"

He chewed his lip and answered, "Bite. Stab. Throw rocks. And if you really mess up, they curse you. Met a man once who kicked a pixie by mistake, and now he's got full-sized mushrooms growing outta his—"

"What attributes might our creature possess that it can devour pixies without fear?"

Wardric pondered the question for another few seconds. "Thick skin, I guess. Or big claws and teeth. And magic can't hurt it."

"Exactly," Bodkins said. "It's impervious to magic, but so far hasn't used any—that we're aware of. Which means we need to focus on physical offense. And that's fortunate because the tip I received about a powerful artifact in Slugbeard's castle was rubbish."

The grains of sand that made up Eddie's body drifted over and reformed in a manner that reminded Florian of water pouring into a human-shaped mold. If water could flow upward. And the mold could blink. And had only half a face.

The entire process was horribly disconcerting and likely deliberately so.

"What's this about a tip?" Eddie asked. "I thought we dropped in on Ol' Slug to make Wardric happy."

"Hey, me, too!" Wardric whined.

Bodkins scowled at the sand man, and it gave Florian the tiny twinge of satisfaction a rule-abiding child might experience when a teacher reprimanded a naughty classmate.

"You're supposed to be searching the ruins," she said.

"I am!" Eddie said and gestured to the missing half of his face, which was, presumably, still slipping through cracks in the rubble. Gross.

Bodkins sighed. "One of our customers in Leechleif was a gregarious collector of odd historical facts. Told me if I passed by the castle, I should check out Slugbeard's Spellbook. Apparently, there's a cult that thinks Sigeric Slugbeard was an average wizard blessed with a spellbook that gave him unlimited power and a warped conscience."

"Oh, yeah," Eddie said. "That fits my interactions with—*snake!*"

Bodkins tilted her head. "Snake?"

Eddie froze in fear, single eye wide and lips stuck in a half-grimace for an uncomfortably long time. "Sorry," he said when he finally relaxed, "there was a snake in the rubble. Not venomous, though. Just ugly."

"Why do you care?" Florian asked. "You're a ghost."

Eddie crossed his arms. "I don't have to justify my phobias to you."

"Anyway." Bodkins swished her hands as if she was shooing away the irrelevant chatter. "I saw a book in the castle, but it was toast. If that was Slugbeard's secret spellbook, it's no wonder he was defeated."

"*Assuming* he was defeated," Eddie corrected.

Wardric grunted as he shifted a stone slab that might have once been a tabletop. "Not this again. There are records of the guy's execution. We looked them up for you."

"Yeah. Seventeen records. From different people in different cities. Even I got a good poke in before he dusted me. And he won't tell anyone what finally did him in for good."

Bodkins waved her arms again. "Point is—the book in the castle won't help us and wouldn't have even if it was intact. But artifacts we find here, at the last known Battle of the Frost Spinners and Blaze Blasters, might."

"Frost what? Blaze who?" Florian asked. He'd memorized scripts full of sonnets that were easier to follow than their conversation.

"They were junior sports teams," she said, "back before schools banned magic-based sports."

He furrowed his brow. "You said magic won't help us."

"It won't. But these kids carried temperature-resistant

blades that held a permanent edge and sliced through steel."

"I see why they banned the sport," Florian muttered. "But let's say we do find an artifact of some ages-old sports battle. Isn't it our responsibility to hand it over to the owners of the property? You know, the nice old couple who let us in?"

She crossed her arms. "Sure! And we will. Eventually."

"Found another spoon," Eddie said. "There's a fortune in rusty spoons out here. Not a single fork, though. You'd think a school that let kids blast blazes and swing swords would trust them with basic cutlery."

Bodkins glanced over to where Eddie's missing eye was searching. "That's a promising sign, though. Means folks that came before us searched the site for magic but not metal."

"Or," Eddie countered, "they searched for metal and left the spoons because nobody needs this many—*spiders*! Spiders! Eee, spiders!"

The sand man's screech made Florian's heart pound like his orchestra's percussion section when Ava Triumphant faced off with a villain. Eddie flung himself backward, smashed into a wall, and dissolved into dust. When he finally reassembled himself in a fetal position on the ground, his entire face was intact.

"Sword's in there," he muttered and pointed a trembling finger. "And a skeleton."

"You're a ghost," Florian reminded him. "Nothing can hurt you. Calm down."

He half expected Bodkins to chastise him for making light of Eddie's fear, but she was busy wrangling a monster limb that was shaking like a puppy in a thunderstorm. The resulting vibration was severe enough to make her chair wobble comically, contrasting her stern expression.

"I'll get it," Wardric volunteered before he skipped to the fallen wall and tugged at chunks of stone and plaster. "Aww.

It's the fuzzy jumpy kind of spider! Hey, little buddies! Sorry, I gotta move your rocks. No hard feelings, eh?"

"Less talking. More sword-getting," Bodkins commanded as her chair continued to shake.

"Understood!" he said as he lifted the weapon. To its credit, the blade still gleamed in the sunlight despite a corroded scabbard and missing harness. "Aww. This poor skeleton. Looks like nobody found them under all the rocks."

Bodkins clicked her tongue. "He was the sports coach, and he's happy all the kids survived. Besides, it's quieter out here than the city graveyard, though he regrets never visiting the ocean."

Florian opened his mouth to ask how she could possibly know all that—but then he remembered her abilities. So instead, he nervously scanned the ruins for an invisible spirit and said, "Well, I suppose we have a sword for Wardric, now. Do we keep looking for more?"

"For me?" Wardric hopped out of the rocks and shoved the scabbard into Florian's hands. "No way. I don't know the first thing about swords."

Florian blinked in disbelief. "But . . . I figured . . . I mean. You're so tough."

"Believe it or not, muscles don't come with free swordsmanship. Though I've met folks who thought so and paid the price for it. Poor things."

"Give it to Eddie," Bodkins snapped, still frustrated with her disobedient chair limb. "Swords are his thing. Art is yours. Peterman communes with monsters and passes out in his own sick. We all have our talents."

"I can also be very irritating!" Eddie complained.

Florian held his tongue.

The guy did not look ready to receive a weapon, much less use one. Fortunately, a distraction arrived in the form of a wide-eyed woman with her hands in the air. It was the owner of the ruins and surrounding farmland.

She was definitely not popping 'round to invite them for tea and snacks.

"Hello! You there! Hello! Are you adventurers?"

Bodkins scowled and shimmied her chair around to face the woman. "We're mercenaries, yes."

The woman's face paled for a moment, but she caught herself and resumed her questions. "Wonderful! Are you available for hire right now? We have a situation."

Bodkins looked at Wardric, then back at the woman. "Normally, I'd say yes. But we're in a bit of a hurry to—"

"Did you dig that up here?"

Florian froze with the corroded scabbard in his hands as if caught pilfering, though they had not yet departed with the weapon.

Bodkins, meanwhile, did not miss a beat. "What can we help you with?"

The woman smiled, grateful. "Something's after our cows. We locked it out of the barn, but it won't leave. I think it's one of those howling horrors. Awful sounds coming from it."

Bodkins wrinkled her nose but exited the ruins, nonetheless. "Howling horrors? All the way out here? Seems odd, but we'll take a look. Eddie, grab the sword."

Eddie did not budge. Instead, he gripped his torso and whispered, "One crawled on my eyeball."

"Your eye is sand," Florian whispered back, but it was no use.

"All right, well, *someone* has to back me up," Bodkins said. "Volunteers?"

Florian slid the blade from the scabbard and felt its weight in his hand. Despite its age, the weapon was exquisite. Masterfully crafted from an unfamiliar metal that looked bright as steel in sunlight and dark as coal in shadow. Just holding it made Florian long for an evening of intense training. Or a week of choreography for a tricky scene. He could spend hours swinging the blade to feel it slice through the air.

But pre-production training and scripted combat were nothing like a proper battle with a howling horror. Whatever a howling horror was. Someone else would have to volunteer.

"Sold!" Bodkins shouted, and Florian jumped.

Before he could protest the apparent misunderstanding, she clapped her hands together and cracked her knuckles. Emerald light wove like threads between her fingers as she brought them together and apart. The light twisted in the space above her hands, eventually forming a tiny human figure that stood and tested the motion of its limbs.

It was incredible to behold, like nothing Florian had ever witnessed. A living doll of brilliant light that strolled in place between her palms as if trapped in a glass ball. He held his breath as it reached for the old woman with one fragile hand. Then he released his breath with a sudden scream as the sports team coach's skeletal hand slammed down on his shoulder.

"If you would," the skeleton said and nodded toward the sword.

Florian handed it over.

"We'll be taking the sword as payment," Bodkins told the old lady. "And the ghost requires passage to the beach. Oh, and if this is a howling horror, I need to know what direction it came from." She looked over her shoulder at the team before she added, "If it's where I think, our journey's about to get exciting."

Florian watched her dash toward the barn with a spirit-stitched skeleton in tow and forced his dropped jaw shut so he could squeak out his delayed response.

"Great."

SEVENTEEN
The Spoon of Glarblarkle

"You're sure about this?" Margaret asked.

Growina glanced at a scrap of paper in her hand that read, "Wrecid stacu xox," and took a deep breath. "Yes. I think so. I mean, if we're reading it correctly, I can't think of anything else it could be."

Theo slunk from a nearby bush, stood, and pressed his back against the wall they were hiding behind. "And you learned about this place from skeletons? What were the skeletons doing out here?"

"Well, I imagine they weren't skeletons at the time. The Wontmoil Dancing Band loves to tell stories from when they were alive. Especially the older members."

"Then how come we've never heard of it?" Vivienne demanded. "I've been here my whole life and never knew we had a statue of the wretched wizard. I mean, why would we? Slugbeard never set foot in our town."

Growina shrugged. "Not many people take the time to listen to the dead. Anyway, the band members told me the statue appeared before the end of the Gart Splagosion, when everything was chaotic. Nobody knew the sculptor. And when the dust settled, the town voted to destroy it. Then these folks came out of nowhere and ran off with the pieces."

"These are not folks. These are cultists," Theo said. "It's an important distinction. We're not dealing with normal, rational people here. This could get messy in ways we've never imagined."

"Agreed," Margaret said. "We can't knock on the door and expect them to let us in to examine their statue. We need a plan. Preferably one involving subterfuge."

"And magic!" Zemni said, prompting everyone to flinch and spin.

When—and how—had the twins shown up?

Five glittering letters that spelled the word 'magic' appeared in the air and fell to the grass. The boy giggled and nudged his sister for approval, but she was staring off into the distance with eyes as wide as fried eggs.

"Look at the sun!" she said. "I swear it was morning a minute ago. I must have lost a whole hour somewhere. If someone finds an hour, it's mine."

Zemni crossed his arms. "Hey, no fair!"

"Have you two been into some sugar?" Margaret asked.

"Boiled sweets!" Zizel said, a bit too loud. "The construct that runs the bank bribed us to stay put. Didn't work, but they were yummy. You have any?"

"No," Vivienne snapped. "And lower your voices. We're stalking a cult."

"Cult," Zemni repeated. Each letter appeared as gelatinous green goo and plopped onto the grass with a disgusting squelch. "Hehe."

Theo attempted to regain everyone's attention. "Ignore the children. We need a plan to get into this mansion without stirring up trouble. Spellbooks, everyone."

At once, all three witches produced grimoires from thin air. Being who he was, Theo instead plucked a pocket-sized book from his suit jacket. They pored through their books for a moment while Growina rocked on her heels and the twins pretended to paw at nonexistent texts.

"Invisibility," Margaret said finally. "It's the obvious choice."

Theo shook his head. "Not unless you have enough supplies for everyone. We don't know what kind of defenses they have in there. Sending someone alone would be too risky."

Margaret frowned.

Vivienne raised a finger. "Shapeshifting! Should take us ten minutes to brew up a cauldron and turn us all into cultists."

"Absolutely not," Theo replied. "Shapeshifting into other humans is banned in four of the five cities in the penta-city conurbation for a reason. It's on the psychological warfare list because it sows distrust not only between the wizard—or witch—and their victim, but between the victim and their social circle as well. Not to mention the witnesses . . ."

Vivienne jabbed a finger toward the wizard. "*This* is why you work alone."

"Chocolate!" Zizel shouted in the same tome Margaret and Vivienne had used. "Do you have any?"

The hovering children in short-pants snickered while the rest of the party grumbled. It seemed the adventurers had plenty of tricks up their sleeves for scary monsters and supernatural spooks, but few were designed for midday stealth missions.

No matter. Growina had a small arsenal of experimental potions strapped to her bandolier and could not wait to contribute.

"What about apathy?" she asked. "Not us, I mean. The cultists. I packed a bottle of concentrated whatever nectar. Figured if something attacked me with a big maw, I could just . . . you know . . . pop it in."

"Concentrated whatever nectar?" Theo asked in a tone that sounded far more cynical than he likely intended. "Pop it in?"

Growina flushed. "That's what the plant is called. Whatever. It makes you stop caring about everything. Short of bodily functions, I guess. It's a rare plant, but I have a conservationist permit."

Vivienne did not wait for Theo to complain about the potential physical or psychological ramifications of dosing an entire gated mansion full of cultists with a plant that made them apathetic.

"Sold!" she said. "Now how do we get it in them? Darts?"

"And where would we procure those?" Theo asked with his hands on his hips. "Have you seen a traveling merchant around?"

"I bet the kids can make tons of darts," she replied.

Zizel and Zemni grinned at each other and said, "Tons of farts!"

Theo pulled the collar of his shirt over his nose and whipped his hat off to fan the air. "No more candy for you two, ever. This is why I don't have children."

Margaret produced a tiny object from her pocket, set it on the ground, and waved a hand toward it. It expanded into a full-sized cauldron, already filled with bubbling water. Curious, Growina kneeled and checked underneath for a flame. There was none. She made a point to ask the witch about the spell later, as it would save her hours in the lab and kitchen.

"We'll put the potion in a soup and trick the cultists into eating it," the witch said. "Go on."

Growina wiggled the cork off the bottle, poured the contents into the cauldron, and stepped back to avoid the steam. The others followed her lead but wrinkled their noses as they stepped away from the apathy hazard and into the lingering alien toots.

"The soup has to be irresistible, or they won't take it," Margaret said. "I have a packet of dried pea soup with seasoning, but that may not be sufficient."

"I have carrots," Vivienne said. She produced baby carrots from a bag in her pocket and shrugged at everyone's confused stares. "Emergency snack."

Margaret took them and tossed them into the water. "A protein would be nice, too. Wizard, you have any jerky or beans on you?"

Theo shook his head. "Not in any form compatible with soup. Wizards carry vitamin-enriched bread on adventures. It's compact, durable, and—"

"Anyone else?"

Growina fumbled around in her pockets and produced three twigs. "I have fish sticks!"

"No. Not that. Please. No offense."

"Oh."

Sylvie waved to get everyone's attention, then wandered to a large bush. She set her fingers to the soil in front of it and waited. Less than a minute later, a plump bird emerged and hopped into her hands.

Growina gasped and turned away, unwilling to witness violence. But instead of squawking, the sound of cubed meat hitting liquid reached her ears. She turned to see no mess or feathers—and made a mental note to never anger Sylvie.

"Smells fantastic," Theo said. "But how do we know if it tastes good?"

"Hold on, everyone. Silence," Margaret whispered with a hand up. "I heard something."

Everyone quieted, just as they had in the Howling Woods, and listened once again to suspiciously rustling leaves. No one said a word, but their eyes asked the same questions. Was it the creature again? Magwod and Chip? Nosy wizards? Or something worse?

"We know you're there!" a nasally voice screamed from

within the cultists' mansion. "No one escapes the attention of the all-seeing one!"

"Thieves, we have you targeted!" another shouted. "Attempt to flee, and you will be eliminated!"

"Thieves?" Theo muttered. "All-seeing one? What are they on about?"

"Oh, that's me," a young man with a crossbow said as he emerged from the bush by Sylvie. He had a hunched posture and unblinking eyes. "I'm not really all-seeing, though. It's just . . . people never seem to notice me when I'm around."

"Oh, I hate that!" Growina said.

"Right?"

Theo harumphed and asked, "What are you planning to do with us?"

"Depends on how fast you turn over the Spoon of Glarblarkle."

"The what now?"

"The glowing spoon you stole from our safe."

"Glar-blarkle," Zizel said, and a shiny belt buckle struck the brim of Theo's hat, driving it over his eyes. Zemni found it hilarious.

Theo pushed his hat back up. "Please ignore them. We don't have any magic spoons."

"Look, guy. I really don't wanna argue with you. But I see a wizard, two floating weirdos, and a buncha witches around a potion. And you're telling me you *aren't* the ones who took our enchanted safe and the spoon in it? Like, who else would do that? Give me a break."

Margaret stepped forward. "Wait. The safe was also enchanted, and both are gone?"

"Yeah."

"And nothing else was taken?"

"Yeah. Why?"

"Have you heard about the incident at the Wontmoil Bank?"

The young man shrugged, glanced up at the mansion, and gave a thumbs-up to indicate he was fine.

"A monster ate their magic lock," Margaret said, "and we're one of the adventuring parties out hunting it. That's probably what got your spoon, too." After a nudge from Sylvie, she added, "Oh, and this isn't a potion. It's lunch."

The young man stepped closer to look at the cauldron. "Smells good. What is it?"

"Pheasant soup."

Growina bit her tongue and gripped her skirt to keep from blurting that the bird Sylvie added was not a pheasant or that the young man should not lean over the pot. The last thing they needed was for him to inhale the steam and act out of character while his cult watched.

"Poisoned?" the young man asked.

Theo's eyes widened. "Poisoned? Surely you jest. Poisoning is an extreme violation of the official Wizard's Code of Conduct, punishable by four hundred hours in the dungeon of—"

"Prove it."

Everyone shared a glance, and Margaret asked, "Prove it?"

"Yeah. One of you taste it. Right now."

Zemni bounced around in the air. "Ooh! Me! Me! I want to try it!"

"Me too!" Zizel said. "Ladle!"

A ridiculous ladle with fork-like prongs appeared, but the children were unconcerned with its proportions or appearance. They dipped it into the bubbling liquid and eagerly shared the resulting spoonful. Then they both exhaled and drifted to the ground.

"That was delicious," Zemni said.

"Yes, I believe it was the hint of basil that brought it all together," Zizel replied.

The adventuring party shared a concerned glance.

"Another spoonful?" Zemni asked, but before he could reach the cauldron, the young cultist held out a hand.

"Stop. That's enough. We'll be taking this stew in exchange for your lives."

Theo harumphed again. "Well, that's certainly great for my sense of self-worth."

The young man shrugged and waved someone over with a series of hand signals. "The Spoon of Glarblarkle magically produces a scoop of whatever the holder desires. If you were the ones who stole it, you wouldn't be making lunch."

Growina clapped her hands. "That's so fun! But wait . . . did all of you eat from the same spoon?"

"Back away from the food!" the nasally voice called as two men with muscular arms and tiny legs stomped into view.

The robed men grabbed the cauldron by its handles and carried it back around the wall as the all-seeing youth followed, crossbow still raised.

"Now, get out of here!" the nasally voice shouted.

Team Wontmoil complied. After all, there was nothing left to do but wait . . . again . . . while the monster and other adventuring parties did goodness knew what. At least Growina was not alone this time.

Eighteen

Apathy Soup

An excerpt from the Lazy Botanist's Guide to Naughtobelus.

Stapfiella Apathis Whatever Plant

Habitat: Hot places with, like, wet stuff.

Appearance: What's that color that's not gold? Amber? With pointy bits. Can't miss it.

Characteristics: Eat the leaves, and you won't care about anything at all. Clever plant.

Author's note: Forget it. I'll write this section later.

* * *

The gate to the cultists' mansion crashed open as subtly as a snapped pot rack in the middle of the night. No one emerged to investigate, which meant either the apathy soup had done its job, or Growina had made a grave miscalculation with the dosage. Hopefully, the first.

"Behind me," Margaret instructed, much to Theo's displeasure.

Despite grumbling from the wizard, who thought himself the leader, Team Wontmoil fell in behind the witch and crept like spooked cats through the gate and across the poorly maintained courtyard.

When they reached the mansion's front door, Growina expected Margaret to nudge it open and peek inside like a burglar. Instead, the witch flicked a finger and sent it crashing open, just like the front gate.

"Not criticizing your methods," Growina said, "but is there perhaps a quieter way to open locked doors? Seeing as we're breaking in and all."

Margaret snorted. "Probably."

The team scooted through the ruined doorframe and paused when they spotted the first cultist "guard" in the narrow foyer. The woman wore hand-me-down armor with a cartoon spellbook scratched across the chest. She had a sword, technically, but could not be bothered to reach for it. Or get off the floor.

"Hey . . . you. You should stop," the guard said.

"No, thank you," Theo replied. Then, to the group, "If I were a statue of Slugbeard, where would I be?"

"A courtyard?" Vivienne volunteered.

Theo rolled his eyes. "We're in a classic post-elemental mansion with no apparent alterations to the structure. *Everyone* knows these buildings are solid and self-contained. The very idea that one might have a courtyard is laughable."

Vivienne's eyes narrowed.

Zemni raised a hand as if holding an invisible goblet. "Hear, hear!" he said as if he had any clue what Theo meant.

Everyone shared a look. It was weird enough that the twins were on the ground. Agreeing with Theo, even if he was right, was wildly out of character.

"I really hope the effects of this soup aren't permanent,"

Margaret muttered as she headed for a corridor with doors on either side.

"Oh, no, no, no," Growina assured her. "In fact . . . hmm."

Theo stopped and turned to stare. "Hmm? What's hmm?"

"Nothing! But, maybe, perhaps, we should pick up the pace a bit."

Margaret groaned. "Statues are heavy. I propose we check for a cellar."

Before anyone could respond, however, Sylvie raised a hand and gestured toward a worn path in the aging carpet. The threadbare stripe followed the hallway and turned at a fork, as if the cultists took the same route every day.

"I propose we follow that path," Margaret corrected.

Several cultists stirred as Team Wontmoil wandered through a hallway to a great room, but none moved to stop them. One suggested that someone else might stop them, however, and another asked that they stop each other. Theo politely declined.

"This looks like the place," Margaret said when the doors swung open.

That was an understatement. The room looked like the home of a candle enthusiast who married a collector of rodent bones. It was impossible to walk toward the statue at the center without toppling a pile of tibias or sending a tiny skull skittering across the room. And the sculpture itself was equally unpleasant.

"Did they repair it with paste," Vivienne asked, "or sap?"

"Both, perhaps," Theo replied as he kicked a pile of melted candles to get a better look at the reassembled wizard. "The condition is a lot worse than I expected. I'm not sure where to begin."

"Hey, man, not okay," someone said, making them all jump.

A trio of cultists in embroidered robes sat in the corner doing not much of anything, although it looked like they had once been playing some sort of tabletop game that involved literally stabbing a game board with daggers. Not a great sign, should they find the motivation to get up.

"You can't just come in here and kick our stuff, you know," one of them said. He had spectacles that made his already wide eyes look enormous. "We've got rights."

Growina flushed with embarrassment. The cultist had a point. "Apologies. We're getting a look at your statue here, and then we'll be gone. Promise!"

Vivienne rolled her eyes. "You don't have to apologize to him. He's had the apathy soup."

"Naw, man," the bespectacled cultist said. "I didn't eat that garbage. Carrots are gross."

"Yeah," another added with a halfhearted chuckle. "He's always like this."

"Okay!" Margaret replied. "Back to the statue. I see no writing, and Sylvie can't find any obvious magic. But we have a key, so in theory, there is a keyhole."

"Try his mouth!" Growina blurted. She fidgeted when Theo raised his brow and tried to explain. "XOX reminded me of two dead eyes and an open mouth. Wretched statue, XOX. I thought it was funny."

"I thought it was kisses and hugs!" Zizel said.

Zemni chuckled. "Wretched statue, kisses and hugs?"

"I do see something," Margaret said as she stood on her toes and peered into the statue's beard-encircled mouth. "Hand me the key."

"Hey, man," the bespectacled cultist called again. "Don't touch that. It's, like, sacred or whatever."

"Sacred?" Theo spat. "Sigeric Slugbeard was a stain on history. His actions were murderous, chaotic, and extremely harmful to the environment. Why would anyone worship him?"

The cultist shook his head slowly, as if underwater. "Naw, you don't get it. It's not the man. It's the power. The man was only the vessel, you know? Not worthy. The power is the thing. It needs a better vessel, see?"

"I do not see. And I think I lost a portion of my intelligence just listening to—"

"Got it!" Margaret shouted. Then, "Oops!"

The witch stumbled backward with the statue's bearded jaw in her hands as two heavy objects slid from its throat and thudded to the floor. Vivienne hurried to scoop them up but held them as if they were week-old socks found under a bed.

"Is this a joke?" she asked as she gripped what appeared to be the sculptor's hammer and chisel.

"Hey!" the cultist with the spectacles shouted. "Stop that!"

He shifted to get up, and Theo took a casual defensive stance. Even with throwing daggers, one sluggish cultist was no match for a trained wizard. Three, however . . .

"The others are moving," he said. "I suspect the beard detachment has upset them enough to outweigh the benefits of the soup. Do we have what we need? Can you put it back?"

"It's a bit heavy!" Margaret replied with a grunt.

Both twins floated up to assist. Zemni hoisted the beard with surprising ease. "We'll help! But there's a cost."

"Yeah! Candy!" Zizel squealed, and a painful rain of hard candies skittered into the rat bone mess below.

"The twins are back to normal!" Margaret cried.

Theo adjusted his stance. "They're not the only ones."

All three cultists in the corner staggered to their feet, lackadaisical expressions replaced with scowls and hunched shoulders. Meanwhile, somewhere down the hall, someone far too alert shouted commands at a murmuring crowd.

"Time's up," Vivienne muttered.

"There!" the twins said as they snapped the beard in place. "Ta-da!"

For a moment, it looked as if the cultists might settle back into their corner. Then there was a pop, and the jaw hit the floor in a cacophony of shattered stone.

"That's it!" the formerly relaxed cultist said. "I'm mad."

Margaret held up her hands. "Wait! I can fix it. I have a spell for this!"

"No time!" Theo said as more cultists burst into the room.

Despite the danger, Growina could not help but grin at the sheer number of people who had stripped to their bloomers under the soup's influence and failed to correct the situation before they hurried to the great room. One was even in a cult-themed robe, brandishing a bath brush as a weapon.

"You have defiled the sacred statue of the first vessel!" a cultist in pastel undergarments and quilted slippers declared. "For that, you shall pay!"

Margaret waggled her fingers toward them. "Not today!"

"Obviously," Theo said with a snort. "Because you haven't got a fudgel to your name."

"Seriously? *Now*?"

Sylvie elbowed Margaret and pointed to a second doorway, through which more cultists poured. It was impressive that so many could live comfortably in the mansion. Unfortunately, it seemed the late arrivals had taken more time to prepare.

"New plan," Vivienne said. "Let's get out of here."

"Can't without a fight," Theo said. "We're surrounded."

"Not necessarily." Growina rifled through her pockets for a handful of marbles. "Everybody pair up and take one of these. When I say so, hug your partner and throw it as hard as you can at the ground. Trust me."

Every member of Team Wontmoil gave her a dubious look

but went along with her request for lack of better options. Even Margaret and Theo gripped each other awkwardly by the waist. Then Growina held her marble aloft and counted.

"Three, two, one, *now!*"

Cultists jumped back as the marbles shattered, smoke billowed, and inky pools of vine-filled nothingness opened beneath the adventurers' feet. Then every member other than Growina shrieked as the vines dragged them down into the darkness.

Growina was the first to wrestle free of the vines, mainly because the Blasted Glassflower was familiar with her unconventional means of travel. It took some coaxing for the plant to release her frustrated and cursing companions.

"Where are the twins?" she asked.

Visions of the children facing off with cultists alone because the vines failed to reach them flooded her imagination. Then she remembered the aliens could travel wherever they wished, relaxed, and immediately found something new to panic about.

The adventurers were in her garden!

"Never mind them. The door is this way. Come on!"

She ushered them quickly past trellises that blocked their view of the singed summoning circle and toward the shop door. Only Sylvie stopped to scowl at something in the circle's direction, but Growina quickly found a distraction.

"Look! It's the children!"

She pointed to a window as they approached, through which they could see the children holding up their un-smashed marble and guffawing at the disheveled state of the others. Vivienne gestured at them in a manner that was altogether inappropriate for children, alien or not.

They all poured into the rear hallway.

Growina let out a held breath. Her secret was safe, at least temporarily. She *had* to clean up the garden, though. No more excuses.

"My word," Theo exclaimed as the adventurers piled into the empty storefront. "That went poorly. Did we at least get what we needed?"

Vivienne set the hammer and chisel onto the shop counter as the twins tossed their marble back to Growina.

"It wasn't candy," Zizel said with a frown.

Growina's eyes widened. "Did you try to eat it?"

"Candy," Zemni muttered, but nothing appeared. It seemed the children were suffering from something even worse than apathy soup—a sugar crash.

"It's just the artists' tools," Vivienne said. "What are we supposed to do with that?"

"Decrypt them, I assume," Theo said, and pointed to a bunch of seemingly random squiggles carved into the metal. "Here we go again."

Vivienne whimpered like a puppy at a dinner table. "Can we go home and nap first? My brain is cabbage."

Sylvie nodded and opened the door, then stepped back with a start.

"I like that idea," Margaret agreed. "But we'll want to avoid that angry mob."

NINETEEN
Stage Fright

"You need a hand with that?" Eddie asked as he swung the newly-acquired enchanted sword from the historical site at a rusted plow.

The weapon sliced through the metal like cheese and sent the sand man stumbling through his target and into the grass. He righted himself and nodded approvingly before he returned it to its sheath.

Florian rattled a vial of dried leaves, unsure what Eddie could do to 'help' him ingest the collywobbles that Bodkins insisted he consume in order to re-start his visions. "No, thanks."

"You sure? I could brew a cup of tea for you. Might take the edge off."

"No, no. I need to do it my way."

"How about a snack when you're done?"

"I'm fine."

Eddie scowled and set his hands on his hips. "Why do I get the impression you don't like me?"

Florian froze, not because the guy was wrong, but because he was unsure how to answer. Truth be told, he had no idea why the sandy swashbuckler still set him off. Bodkins had worried him at first, but he had warmed to her quickly, and he had never had a problem with the chronically congenial Wardric.

What made Eddie any different?

"I dunno," he said. "I guess we got off on the wrong foot. I'll get over it."

"I see. It was the spying. I get that, truly. But the boss was right. You were trying to sneak off before you proved yourself. Makes me wonder why you came to the door in the first place."

"I've often wondered that myself."

Eddie chuckled. "If it helps, I'd have stepped in to save you if you angered that chef. Pretty sure she knew you weren't her favorite action hero."

Florian bristled. "What's that supposed to mean?"

"Ah. It's just . . . you know. You aren't the action hero sort. That's all."

"How dare you."

Eddie raised his hands in mock surrender. "Okay, tough guy. Forget I said anything."

"No, I will not. I'll have you know I studied under one of the best swordsmen in Leechleif."

"Which explains why you've spent most of this trip complaining about sticky shoes and mice in your tent?"

That was a low blow. Heroism and a desire for sanitary sleeping conditions were not mutually exclusive.

"I've carried my weight pretty well, considering the circumstances," Florian said.

The sand man shrugged and fidgeted with his sword. "The stunt you pulled in the forest took guts, I'll give you that. But you're no Eva Trumpets."

"Ava Triumphant! Why is that so difficult to—hey!"

Florian dodged just in time to avoid a jab from Eddie's rapidly produced sword. He staggered away, mouth agape.

"You're off-balance," Eddie said.

It was true. He *was* off-balance, but that was hardly the problem.

"You tried to stab me!"

Eddie shrugged. "You said you were trained."

"I *was* trained. But they also gave me a sword at the time."

"So, grab a stick."

"Against a blade that slices through plows?"

"Grab two sticks."

Florian grumbled but stomped over to the plow out of sheer spite and retrieved its splintered handles. He kept one for himself and tossed the other to the sand man's feet.

"You could not have picked a worse weapon," Eddie said with a chuckle. "But we'll make it work."

He re-sheathed his sword, lifted a wooden handle, and lunged.

"Hey!" Florian shouted as he attempted to parry. "Aren't you supposed to warn me first?"

Eddie shook his head. "How many fights have you been in? Actual fights with consequences."

"Counting this one?" Florian asked. "One. You?"

Eddie thrust again as he answered. "Hundreds. Maybe thousands. This isn't a fight, though. If it was, you'd be on the ground. This is horseplay. And you're still off-balance."

Florian scowled. "I know I am. Maybe you wouldn't get into so many fights if you had a better attitude. Ever think of that?"

"Hah! I suppose that's true. Plenty of wannabe kings woulda loved it if I'd shut up and left their hoards alone."

"Wait," Florian said as he dodged a swipe from Eddie's wooden handle. "Wait. Stop for a minute. Kings? There haven't been kings in ages. How old are you?"

Eddie lowered his weapon. "Old. Things have changed

a lot since I was flesh and blood. Pampered fella like you wouldn't've lasted ten minutes with my crew."

"I choose to ignore that comment because I'm too curious. Were you one of the Stealthy Eight? The folks who ran the old dictators off? My parents read me stories about them when I was little."

"More like stealthy thirty. The eight everyone knew about weren't all that stealthy. But, yeah, I was one of them. Sigeric, too, believe it or not."

Florian examined the sand man with newfound fascination. "That's unbelievable. Sorry, I guess I took you for a criminal of some sort."

"I *was* a criminal!" Eddie said with a laugh. "Back then, it was perfectly legal for an enterprising swindler to hoard all the food and starve his workers. We were the bad guys for breaking it up."

"Bad? For saving countless families?"

"The laws were made for those in power and changed daily at their whim. It was impossible to restore balance without breaking rules, but few back then understood. They thought we were crude and violent—and maybe they were right. The team named me Edward Inkfist since I once shoved a quill through a lawmaker's—"

"That isn't your real name, then?"

"Nope. We had to protect our families. You didn't think Slugbeard was a real name, did you? Slug beard?"

"I . . . I think it's fairly common to have a name that ends in beard," said Florian Honeybeard.

Eddie tilted his head back and guffawed, showing off his bafflingly sparse sand-teeth. "In some places, maybe. But not here. If you met someone with a name like that, chances are they're descendants of my crew."

"Oh. I see." Florian toed the grass while he weighed the

information against his pitiful memory of his genealogy. "I don't suppose you had actors in your crew? For political infiltration and what not?"

"No, nothing like that. We had a couple of soothsayers like you, though. Really nice people. I made them tea with honey to help with the aftertaste of the bitter collywobbles. They told me it helped. You *sure* you don't want any?"

Florian opened his mouth to decline, snapped it shut, and nodded. "You know what? Okay. I'll have some."

"Great! I'll get a fire started."

Eddie danced off to grab supplies, and Florian once again eyed his vial of leaves. The collywobbles in the castle cider had made him dizzy for hours, but he had no clue how much the tour guide had added. Should he set a little to his tongue at a time and wait for something to happen? Or did it take a whole spoonful to produce wild enough visions to satisfy his soothsayer role? The thought made him irrationally nervous.

"Just do it," he told himself. "Eat a pinch and get it over with."

It was no use. His nerves paid his mouth no mind, and his fingers refused to pull the cork from the vial. Strange how anticipation of discomfort was so much worse than the discomfort itself. But he often found company helped in such circumstances, so he wandered to a patch of grass where Wardric sat cross-legged with a brush.

"What are you up to?" he asked.

Wardric jumped, fumbled with his brush, and visibly blushed. "Oh, nothing. Practicing my craft. It's not at all what I pictured in my mind."

The response made no sense until Florian spotted a gorgeous lily growing in front of Wardric's feet. The brilliant flower was orange with garnet splotches and utterly indistinguishable from the real thing, aside from its unpainted underside.

"It's amazing," Florian said.

Wardric shrugged and looked away. "It's all right. The red's a bit thick. I meant for it to have more texture, but my brush was too wet."

"Well, I've seen a lot of fake flowers, and this is by far the best."

Wardric looked up and furrowed his brow. "Where have you seen a lot of fake flowers?"

"It's not important. Mind if I sit with you while I work up the courage to eat a leaf?"

"Umm . . ."

The big man glanced at his flower, his brush, and back at the grass. Then his brow furrowed further. It brought back memories of the rope bridge in the Forest of Lightening.

"Stage fright?" Florian asked as he settled beside the artist. "I used to have that, too. You know what helped?"

"Picturing everyone in silly trousers?" Wardric asked.

Florian shook his head. "What? No, that would never work. Who told you to do that?"

"A witch. But when she did it, the silly trousers appeared. So, it might be a witch thing."

"Must be. Well, I didn't materialize any clothing. All I did was put myself out there, over and over, until it felt normal."

"And that cured your anxiety?" Wardric asked. His eyes were as big as a puppy's.

"Absolutely not. But it made it easier to pretend I wasn't bothered. And after a while, I believed it, myself."

Wardric nodded and picked up his brush. "Okay. Then let's make a deal. I finish this flower, and you eat a leaf."

Florian gripped the vial, stomach already turning, and contemplated the agreement. It seemed fair enough. One fear for another.

A shout from Bodkins interrupted his thoughts. "Buzz

off!" she demanded. "I'm trying to concentrate!"

Both Wardric and Florian turned to see Eddie deftly swerve around a flailing monster arm. He gripped a metal cup in one hand like a cudgel and had a bundle of sticks tucked in the opposite armpit. It appeared he 'had touched a pack attached to Bodkins' chair and got a claw to the chest for his trouble.

"I need tea from the bag!" he whined as he dodged. "It's for Peterman!"

Served the guy right for his earlier antics and for interrupting what looked like a complicated spirit stitch. Despite the flailing from Eddie, Bodkins held tight to a brand-new limb removed from the expired howling horror. Ethereal thread stitched it to the chair beside her armrest while an emerald replica spun in midair.

"Incredible," Florian whispered.

Wardric leaned close. "She's pretty impressed by you as well."

"By me?" he asked, surprised by his own interest in the casual flattery. "Whatever for?"

"You predicted a bank attack six towns away, got into the monster's head, and hung onto that connection without even trying. That's expert-level stuff! Not what she expected from a squirrely guy peddling adventure for debt repayment."

"Squirrely?" Florian spat.

So much for flattery. He understood that, to the mercenaries, he was the same man who took their money and ran. But they had traveled by his side for days. Surely, they knew by now that he was not a swindler. He was Ava Triumphant! . . . Or, at least, the guy who played her. That distinction was bothering him now more than ever.

Wardric smiled, serene as a stagnant puddle. "Forget that. Watch this."

He produced a tiny palette—already smeared with warm

colors—and twirled his brush between red and yellow until he had a streaky orange. Then he hunched over the lily and delicately stroked the air in front of it. The underside changed from a smooth gray to a vibrant color with a velvety texture. Wardric added some reddish spots and leaned back to observe the work at a distance.

"It's half in the fingers and half in the mind," he said, "which is why I struggle when I'm observed."

Florian shrugged. "It turned out perfect. I don't see what the problem is."

"It's okay, I guess," Wardric said without making eye contact. "Your turn?"

"Yeah, okay."

Florian popped the cork from the vial with a tremor in his hands. He glared at the contents and muttered, "Squirrely," as he plucked out a leaf and held it in front of his face. It looked like something he would garnish a meal with, not a powerful plant that could knock him on his back.

"Worried about the taste?" Wardric asked.

"No," he said. "It's not the taste. It's the dizziness and dissociation. And the Skrabblin's Dagger. Please don't do that again."

Wardric gave a thumbs up as Florian held up his end of the bargain. The collywobble leaf felt like burned paper on his tongue. It crumbled to shards and made him gag as he struggled to get it down his throat. But that was not the worst thing about it.

"I was wrong!" Florian cried as he scraped his tongue against his teeth like a dog with a mouthful of medicine. "Tastes awful!"

"Hot tea on the way!" Eddie shouted.

The sand man darted over with a steaming mug of peppermint tea, and Florian grabbed it despite the heated handle.

He slugged the beverage as fast as he could and stopped only when he felt it burn his mouth.

"Gah! Thanks. That was—"

Florian froze. Either the undiluted collywobbles were faster than the ones in his castle cider, or the taste was so bad it was making him faint. Dark spots flickered at the edge of his vision, then coalesced into murky shapes laid atop the real world like double vision.

"Is it starting already?" Wardric asked.

Florian gripped the artist's arm to hold himself steady. As before, the hazy dream his companions called a link with the monster blotted out his vision. Unlike before, however, it was bright and colorful—not crisp enough to identify objects, but far from the tunnel vision he had in the castle.

The creature did not slither. It slunk. There was a subtle bounce to its vision, like the footsteps of an animal on the prowl. It was still hungry. Still searching. But the desperation was gone. The creature was no longer scrabbling toward every bright light it saw. It was plotting. Pacing.

Florian sucked in a breath and felt a squeeze from Wardric's hand.

"What's going on in there?" Eddie's voice asked from another world.

"It's the creature," Florian said as the vision darted from shadow to shadow, offering brief glimpses of orange sunlight broken up by shuffling shapes that could only be human legs. "I think . . . I think it's intelligent."

TWENTY

Pie Pants

Herbs and Vices stank of cornstarch and hot iron by the time the Bograven Sisters departed. The three women faded into the crowd outside, shrouded in pastel fabric that concealed their spiderweb fashion. The makeshift disguises would never hold up to a thorough inspection, but lace and tulips were out of character enough to get them home unnoticed.

Growina waited until the witches were safe, then stood on her toes to see what the hullabaloo was all about. Something had the neighborhood riled up and, based on passing conversations, it involved the recent influx of adventurers. Unfortunately, it was hard to tell if the town was angry about something the adventuring parties did or what they so far had failed to do.

"That charm was in my family for five generations before the monster ate it!" someone shouted across the street to a friend. "The original sage of Paltersnotter Pond made it to ward off evil spirits!"

"Sounds like it didn't do a very good job!" the friend replied, forcing Growina to hold in a snort of laughter as she passed.

Voices grew louder and tempers hotter as she nudged through furious locals to join her fellow merchants at the corner of Wychwood and Main. It seemed the citizens of

Wontmoil were just as tired of the "non-local beef-brained brutes who bought up all the baked goods" as they were the monster devouring their heirlooms. Which was fair, she supposed. The traveling adventurers were wealthier, on average, than Wontmoil citizens and consumed twice as much food to maintain energy. But the creature itself was quick and clever. It would take more than angry words and pointy sticks to scare it off.

Speaking of which . . .

"Explain yourselves!" screeched Lora, the tailor, as Growina reached her comrades at the corner.

The merchants surrounded three wizards—none of which were Theo, thank goodness—and they seemed intent upon violence. The wizards, meanwhile, bore smug expressions that suggested they could spin the dire situation to their advantage. One of them, a man with a ridiculously bulbous hat, cleared his throat.

"The wizard's association was founded to—"

"Not your organization, radish-head," a blacksmith snapped. "Your actions. Yesterday, you sent your people door-to-door asking for tranquil tree oil and an iron cage. Today, we're missing six barrels of oil and two shelves of ingots. Do you think us fools?"

The wizard harumphed. "Surely, you aren't suggesting our honorable association would stoop to petty thievery?"

"Stoop?" Jacqueline Pollywog asked. "Absolutely not. You'd have to leap to reach that bar."

All three wizards gasped in a manner that seemed rehearsed.

"Madam! There's no need for hostility. If you're convinced a wizard is responsible for your loss, we'll lodge your complaint with our internal investigations team when we return to the tower, simple as that. In the meantime, you're all welcome to witness our live capture of the creature tomorrow, free of charge!"

Pollywog crossed her arms. "Internal investigations? So you can find yourselves innocent of the crime? Rubbish."

"The association has over three hundred official members. Perhaps only one of which, *hypothetically*, nicked your property. Are you telling me you're able to identify the guilty party yourself?"

She glared in silence, and the radish-headed wizard took it as confirmation of his assumption.

"You see? Without an internal investigation, we'll never know who was responsible! But I assure you, we'll identify them, and you'll have your justice. In the meantime—"

"I don't want justice. I want my oil. What does it matter which bearded weirdo took it? Find it and return it at once, or else."

All the wizards set hands to their chests in mock offense—and no wonder. Mages with all of Theo's abilities and none of his scruples would naturally see a beauty shop owner as a harmless annoyance. It was a colossal error, but an understandable one.

Growina knew what Pollywog could accomplish with nothing but a sharp tongue and proper organization, and she would personally wrestle a Howling Horror in the buff before she gave the shopkeeper reason for vengeance.

"What's this about a live capture?" a cobbler interrupted, much to Pollywog's dismay.

The wizards perked up. "Ah! So glad you asked! I'm sure you've noticed by now that our competition is ill-equipped to stop the magic-eating beast."

Several bystanders muttered affirmations. They were accustomed to monsters that adventurers could drive away in an afternoon—clumsy creatures searching for food and obnoxious infestations with well-known deterrents. But the magic-eater was different. Wontmoil had seen nothing like it in ages.

Perhaps the radish-head man was about to clear that up—

"It's because the creature is a cursed spirit!" he shouted.

—Or not.

Growina raised a brow.

The wizard smirked as all eyes turned to him, thievery forgotten. "It's true! The ghostly creature can't be expelled by normal means because it isn't of this mortal plane. No potion can poison it, and no sword can scratch it. You will never dispose of it without our anti-magic machine!"

"Now, hang on a minute," Growina said, much to her own surprise. The town's immediate attention made her skin crawl, but she could not stand by while the wizard fibbed. "It's a bit wibbly looking, I'll give you, but it's no ghost."

She recalled how the shadowy monster moved when she spotted it gnawing on the door by the graveyard. It scurried over the wall when it fled, not through the stone like Theo. That was very un-spirit-like of it. According to the reanimated skeletons, ghosts could float through anything they chose—no matter how unpleasant the voyage. One had hopped through a live cow before their reanimation and still got queasy every time they heard a moo.

"Even as we speak," the wizard said, ignoring her objection, "my colleagues prepare a world-changing invention that will rid your lovely town of its magic-eating pest in minutes! Can the competition promise that?"

The crowd, which had grown more excited as the radish-headed wizard's voice raised in pitch, muttered in agreement, but Growina only tsked. Theo was right. The association wanted a reason to use their machine and did not care if it helped or hurt the people of Wontmoil.

Fortunately, Pollywog was not through with them. "You,"

she said as she pointed at the wizards, "just confessed to the theft of my oil. The fellows who harassed me yesterday swore they couldn't operate your machine without it. And you!" Her hand swung to point at a heavily muscled man with a broadsword and no shirt. "Drop those pies!"

The random adventurer, who was sharper of blade than wit, released his grip on four rectangular packages he had purchased from a baker. The boxes burst as they smashed into cobblestones, splattering everyone around with raspberry filling and causing further consternation. He stared down at the mess and stuck his lower lip out like a toddler.

"Hypothetically," the radish-head wizard said, "if we accidentally used your oil to power our prototype, we would compensate you for the loss."

"I don't want to be compensated. I'm not an oil vendor. My products require raw materials. And why did you say that in the past tense?"

Growina shook her head. "They haven't used it yet, I don't think. I think we'd know if they did."

"Are you defending them?" Pollywog snapped.

Growina's skin heated at the mere thought of assisting the slimy scoundrels, and she shut her mouth to avoid further misunderstandings.

The shopkeeper turned back to the wizards. "Give it back now, or I'll call the gatekeepers. I'm serious."

This time, the threat did not feel like a ruse. Tempers were high enough that merchants might involve the worst peacekeepers in the penta-city conurbation—and that did not bode well for Growina's predicament. Would her own neighbors call the gatekeepers on her if they thought she had summoned the monster? And what would the gatekeepers do, exactly? She made a mental note to broach the subject with Margaret later.

"I can't help but notice your associates don't share your sentiments," the wizard said with a smirk. "Perhaps we should ask their opinions? Who here thinks we should return the oil and leave the monster to gobble your property?"

Merchants looked everywhere but at Pollywog while other townsfolk mumbled something that ended in "monster."

"What was that?" the radish-head asked. "Return the oil? Let the monster chew through every magic trinket in town and move on to the next?"

"No," Lora said, with her head bowed in shame. "Trap the monster."

"Yeah," the crowd agreed. "Trap it."

"I don't believe this," Pollywog said with her hands on her hips.

Growina stepped forward again, nerves already shot. She would rather be anywhere else, but she would kick herself forever if she did not at least try to stop the launch of the AMMs.

"It's not that simple—" she began.

Pollywog cut her off. "That's enough out of you!"

Growina stepped back in shock as the woman reeled, face contorted with rage. "I'm sick to death of your lot creeping through this town, starving us out, and robbing us blind. We were better off with the monster."

"My . . . lot?"

Lora, spotting a chance to shift Pollywog's wrath to someone else, nodded. "Yes! All your customers, with their eye-sore outfits and weird behavior. They distract our children from their studies and charge us for magic when they know we're vulnerable."

"But . . ." Growina said. "But everyone here charges for professional services."

"Yeah!" The shirtless adventurer with pie-covered pants contributed.

"Stay out of this!" Pollywog snapped. "And unhand that pastry!"

The man whimpered and returned his new snack to the baker.

"Not like *them*," Lora continued with a wave toward pie-pants and the still-smug wizards. "They're not out here cleaning chimneys. They fly through the air and summon swarms of spiders and turn pigeons into puppies for laughs."

Growina furrowed her brow. "I think you made that last one up."

"That's not the point! The point is, they're *disruptive*. They don't fit in here, with honest folk who solve problems the hard way instead of . . . wiggling their fingers. Not that you'd understand. When you want something done, you cook up a bag of powder to do it for you."

"Ooh. No. I never store powders in bags. Fabric and leather are porous, so a jar is—"

"Still not the point! Forget it. I don't know why you chose this town to set up shop, but I wish you'd move along and take your creepy clients with you."

"Now, come on, Lora. That's too far," Pollywog said, but it was too late.

A stubborn frown tugged at the edges of Growina's mouth—the kind that, when combined with trembling arms, indicated an imminent breakdown no matter how many calming breaths she took. Nothing would save her from public embarrassment, and so, for the first time in her life, she puffed up her chest and summoned her inner Theo.

"You may not remember, but it was *you* who summoned all these adventurers here." She turned to the shirtless man and said, "No offense."

Pie-pants shrugged, and she continued.

"Check the signatures on the ultimatum you gave the bank.

You'll see mine isn't on it. But yours is. All of you. Because you left me out of the decision."

Once again, the merchants stared at their shoes while the rest of the town muttered. But Growina had more to say.

"And yes, my customers are different, but what's wrong with that? They studied hard to learn their craft, same as you, and hope to make a living from it, same as you. There's a lot worse a person could do with magic."

Lora folded her arms and shrank into herself. "Exactly. There's a lot they can do with magic. And what do the rest of us have? Nothing. We're helpless if we don't pay their fees."

"You had my offer for permanent pressing powder, for one thing," Growina said. Then, to the blacksmith, "And I tried to share potions that keep fires burning all day. I offered the cobbler a glue that works better than tacks, the baker a sweetener that won't rot teeth, and the carpenter a soak that lets you mold wood like clay. All of you turned me down because you didn't want to direct your ordinary customers to my shop. So, you have no right to complain about the ones I have."

"Crowe . . ." Pollywog said.

"Nuh-uh. I was *trying* to warn you that those scoundrels from the academy are building something that could wreck all of Naughtobelus. But you're too busy picking on people over fashion and raspberry tarts. No offense."

The shirtless adventurer swiftly hid a tart, and Growina turned her back on the gathering. Concerned townspeople moved aside to let her pass, but she stopped after a few steps.

"Oh! And another thing. Herbs and Vices has been in my family for four generations. It has more right to be here than you do."

So there.

Twenty-One

Cozy Up

FLORIAN DUCKED TO avoid decapitation, much to the frustration of his companions. Even Wardric, the most empathetic of the three mercenaries, sighed as he gripped Florian's shoulders to route him around a pothole.

Their annoyance was understandable.

"You sure you don't want a ride?" Bodkins asked, not for the first time since they started down the gravel road lined with quaint cottages and rustic wood cabins.

Florian shook his head, which was a terrible idea in hindsight, considering the collywobble-induced monster vision still laid over his own. Truth be told, he did not hate the idea of sharing a ride with the mercenary, at least until the visions faded enough for him to differentiate obstacles in his path from those the monster encountered.

The problem was . . . he did not hate the idea of sharing a ride with the mercenary.

Sure, Bodkins could stitch his spirit to the business end of a veterinarian's glove if he crossed her, but she was still a fascinating woman. After years of relationship avoidance thanks to confused and often aggressive fans, who knew how he would react to a cuddle on a chair built for one. Especially while vulnerable and somewhat—wait—was a fly buzzing around *his* head or the monster's?

Florian furrowed his brow and resisted the urge to flail at the insect, lest he give the team another reason to tease him— or worse, offer him Skrabblin's Dagger.

"So, what was it that time?" Wardric asked, as if he already knew the answer. "An unusually large rat? A pile of cow plop? Another view of an old lady's bloomers?"

Florian grunted. "No, nothing like that. And I still don't know how the creature got so close to that woman without her noticing. This was . . . um . . . what's that thing where you run up walls and do backflips?"

Wardric thought about it. "The spangled smew shuffle?"

"That's not it. Anyway, the creature scurried over a wall and picked a fight with a violent plant. I thought the shrub might whump its head off, but our monster is fine and currently gnawing on an enchanted clothes iron."

Eddie sauntered closer. "They've got sentry shrubs in Wontmoil? Huh. I heard it was a hoity-toity bureaucratic town full of councils and associations. Surprised they didn't pull up the nasty shrubs and plant busybodies with rulebooks in their place."

Florian frowned as Eddie elbowed his shoulder far too hard, but held his tongue. Between the bounty, the displaced howling horror, and the vividness of his visions, it was impossible to deny that he had a natural predisposition for prophecy. That should have been thrilling, or at least curious, as the skill in question took a lifetime to master. Nonetheless, he could not muster the slightest bit of enthusiasm.

A memory of a scrap-wood stage and the warmth of his parents' honest praise popped, unbidden, into his head. In that youthful moment, he was convinced that acting was his life's purpose. Why else would it come so effortlessly? Why else was he able to read an audience and deliver a performance that left them enraptured? Because he was secretly a soothsayer?

Rubbish.

He was born for theater.

He was the best.

"I think I'm having a crisis," he muttered.

"Well, no wonder," Wardric said with a pat on his back. "Must be spooky looking through a monster's eyes. Can you taste the metal, too? Gross."

"Fortunately, no. I don't receive all of its senses. Only vision and emotion. Though I have noticed a difference in clarity this time."

Difference in clarity was putting it lightly. The previous vision in the Indited Castle was akin to a search for colorful lanterns in a midnight fog. Formless limbs had thrashed in search of magical objects to fill his aching belly. This time, the fog was gone. There was still a haze at the edge of his vision and glowing rings around every light, but he could make out slick cobblestones, shoes paired with patterned stockings, and individual leaves on violent shrubberies.

"Your clarity, or the monster's?" Bodkins asked, interrupting his thoughts. Despite the chair's forward march, she leaned over her howling horror armrest to squint in his direction.

"I'm not sure," he said, confused by the question. "Perhaps the monster's, based on its actions. Last time, the movements felt desperate and driven by mindless hunger. Now, it's making calculated decisions. Stalking items in people's homes and waiting patiently for opportunities."

"Hmm."

Eddie tensed beside his elbow. "I don't like the sound of hmm. What's wrong?"

Bodkins leaned back and fidgeted with her armrest while the rest of the team marched in silence. The crunch of boots on gravel perfectly matched the motion of the monster's gnawing snout.

"I'm not sure I want to say . . . because I don't believe there's anyone alive who could pull off the stunt I'm imagining. Best not to speak it into the world."

Eddie waved his arms in the air and halted everyone beside a cabin selling adventuring souvenirs. The cute wooden building with cartoonish signage made Florian homesick for the complex architecture of Leechlief.

"You can't say something like that and expect us to ignore it," Eddie said. "What's the stunt, and which dead person could pull it off?"

Bodkins raised a hand to calm him but did not get a word out before he interrupted.

"It's Slugbeard, isn't it? I *knew* that tourist-haunting nonsense was a ruse. We have to stop him before this gets worse. But how do you even kill a ghost?"

"Quite easily," she said, stopping Eddie mid-rant. "But I doubt it's him. More likely, this is the work of a copycat or someone with access to similar spells. Hmm. I wish the spellbook in the castle was intact. Without it, there's no way of knowing if his techniques originated from ancient ruins or an otherworldly source."

Wardric raised a hand. "Sorry. I'm confused. What kind of creature did Peterman find?"

"Something brand-new, at least to me."

"Oh! That's good, right? That's what we asked for."

Bodkins exhaled. "I suppose time will tell. But if what I'm imagining is correct, it isn't simply feeding on magical items for sustenance. It's using the magic to assemble itself from nothing."

Eddie tried his best to follow. "So, it's like a sentient construct building itself from scrap?"

"Sort of. Only it's building with pure magic. Depending

on how much or what type it gets ahold of, that could be a big problem. It could easily become the largest threat to Naughtobelus since the Gart Splagosion."

"It's growing more powerful every day," Wardric whispered.

"It's chasing a squirrel," Florian said and collapsed to his knees with a moan. He dug his fingers into gravel and closed his eyes to stave off motion sickness while the creature gleefully bounded after a bushy tail.

Because of the monster's constant motion, he could not get a feel for its size, but based on how fast it climbed a tree, the thing must have been somewhere between a lanky dog and a pre-teen child on all fours. That did not bode well when examining the hooked claws that allowed it to scale rough bark. Hopefully, when they battled it, he would not have to watch from both points of view.

"No problem, though, right?" Wardric asked. "We're less than a day away. How bad could it get in a few hours?"

"It could find an arsenal of enchanted weapons," Florian offered.

He could almost feel as everyone turned to look at him, but held his gaze on the gravel road—and the monster's view of a strange outpost.

"There's a gate," he said, "with no wall. A lone stone gate with a moat-less drawbridge at the edge of the town. And behind it, there's a building that looks like an old schoolhouse. It's lit up like a bonfire with magic from within, and guards are patrolling the perimeter. The creature is interested."

"That settles it," Bodkins declared. "We're heading straight to Wontmoil. No more delays."

"Wontmoil?" a stranger asked.

Everyone jumped except Florian, who was still too dizzy from the monster's gallivanting to lift himself from the street. A middle-aged woman exited the souvenir cabin, arms full of odd trinkets, and approached the team.

"You don't want to go there," she said. "There's a raid on!"

"A bounty, you mean," Bodkins corrected. "We're aware."

The woman shook her head. She wore a black robe embroidered with books, giving the impression that she had walked from a bathhouse to the souvenir cabin.

Lucky her.

"A raid," she insisted, chin raised above her haul. "The theft of the Spoon of Glarblarkle and the destruction of the Shrine of the First Vessel shall not go unavenged!"

Florian groaned. There was a limit on how much weirdness he could digest in a single day, and "glarblarkle" was well beyond it. Unfortunately, Wardric misinterpreted the sound as a second round of motion sickness and helpfully hoisted him into the air.

The real world spun as the vision settled, causing a strange out-of-body sensation before he landed across Bodkins' lap. A shiver ran up his back and down his arms as he sank against the warm softness of her legs and the prickly claws of the limbs holding him in place. Fortunately, the mercenary was too distracted to notice.

"Thanks," Eddie said to the woman in a patronizing voice. "We'll keep that in mind."

Bodkins, however, was less hasty in dismissing the stranger. She shifted Florian's weight with her new howling horror arm and asked the woman, "Are you in a cult?"

The question was quite rude, but the woman perked up. "I am! As you should be if you wish to survive the coming of the second vessel. All who oppose their rule shall be eliminated! Also, we have mini pies."

"Ooh!" Wardric said.

Bodkins waved a dismissive hand at him and addressed the woman again. "You're in Sigeric Slugbeard's cult, then?"

"Pshaw. We do not claim the first vessel as our deity. We worship the consciousness within the source! As you should if you wish to—"

"So, do you still think his spellbook is out here somewhere? Because I saw one in Mooncalf-Pale that was pretty well destroyed."

The woman attempted to cross her arms, shifting objects to one elbow and the other before giving up and stomping a foot instead. "The shade in the castle has no memory of his final days. The wise do not trust his word or his so-called evidence."

"Hmm."

Eddie sighed and rolled his arms to indicate that Bodkins should extrapolate once again.

"The creature we're hunting *could* be the work of someone with Slugbeard's Spellbook. But why choose such a mundane spell when you have access to world-altering options?"

"Mundane?" Florian asked as he struggled to shift his rump toward the arm of the chair. The creature, for now, sat idly watching the gate, making it easier for him to orient himself. "You said it was a threat to Naughtobelus."

"Sure, sure. But what does that gain the spellcaster? They clearly aren't in control of it. I think, for now, all this tells me is that we'll have to avoid a cultist raid in addition to any penta-city competitors when we make it into town."

"Great," Eddie said with an exaggerated eye roll. "What else could go wrong?"

The cultist woman snorted. "My note bat said there's a protest blocking our route through the city. Citizens are arguing with adventurers in the streets."

"That was a rhetorical question!" he whined.

There was something oddly comforting about the knowledge that their team would not be alone. Adventurers, cultists, and angry citizens could join forces should the monster become too dangerous. At least, that was the hope. More importantly, however, there would be a wall of people for Florian to hide behind while the actual combatants handled the hard part. His share of the workload was almost over.

"Let's go," Bodkins said and directed the team back down the road.

Howling horror hands wrapped around Florian's waist and tugged him back into her lap, making it clear he would spend the next few hours cradled like an infant against her body. Heat prickled his cheeks, and he shifted his rump again only to receive a harsh glare. The message was clear—stop wriggling, relax, and do not make it awkward.

Three things he was incapable of while exploring an unfamiliar town through the eyes of a reckless beast.

The robed woman shouted as they moved. "Stay out of our way, or you'll regret it!"

"Don't worry!" Bodkins replied. "We've got a secret weapon!"

"We do?" Wardric asked as he followed the chair down the gravel road. "You mean the sword?"

"No, I mean Peterman. If he keeps eating collywobbles, he can lead us directly to the creature. We'll avoid all the crowds."

Wardric beamed like a proud parent. "You're a really useful merc, you know that? You should make this your fulltime job."

Florian forced a grimace despite his embarrassment and building horror, lest he insult the excited artist. "Yay."

Twenty-Two

Faux Crocodile

"I shouldn't have made it personal," Growina muttered as she shoved colorful bags, one at a time, onto a display shelf. "I should have said the shop had as much right to be here as anyone. Not *more* of a right than Lora. That was mean."

She paused, frowned at the tiny label on the shelf, and sighed.

"Balding mix. Not boldening mix. Focus."

She scooped the rose-scented bags off the shelf and hugged them to her chest with one arm. Then she bobbed up and down as she scanned each shelf to locate the cosmetics section. That was an unfamiliar experience for her. She could not remember the last time she had to search for a product's location by label.

"I should apologize to Lora . . . But she got nasty first! Shouldn't she apologize first?"

Red, blue, green, purple—each bag plopped onto the proper shelf with a crunch of leaves as she chucked them from a few inches away. Then she wandered back to the storage area, glanced at some jars filled with sky blue powder, and returned to the shelves to confirm she had set none out already.

"Yes. Lora told me to leave town. Or maybe she said she hoped I would leave? And I know she insulted my clients."

Growina sighed. "But that doesn't excuse my behavior. I should still apologize."

Before she realized what she had done, a glass jar slammed into the wall behind the shelf she had tossed it onto and shattered, spraying chunks of glass and cloudy powder onto the floor.

"Or maybe I should eat something to calm myself. Where is my broom?"

Growina checked the counter, kitchen, growing rooms, upstairs in her bedroom, and finally, out of complete desperation, inside the enchanted icebox in the cellar. She tended to be scatterbrained when recovering from a spat, so it was not unheard of to find non-food items there. Unfortunately, a search of the icebox and cellar yielded no broom. The luminous moss she found in the graveyard was doing nicely, though.

"What was the last place I used it? Hmm . . . There was a mess when the aliens read the first stone. Then later, I swept the dirt from the floor. Oh! But I got distracted when I found the pixie wing outside the door to the—fudgels! The garden!"

Growina hurried up the stairs, furious with herself for forgetting the one thing she had planned to do while the rest of Team Wontmoil freshened up. Sure enough, her broom leaned against the garden wall beside the windswept pile of dirt that once contained a pixie wing.

She set her hands to her dress and gasped.

The witches had failed to consider the garden when they set up their protective barrier, likely because of Growina's relative success in keeping them out of it. Unfortunately, someone or something had left a slimy vine as long as Growina's forearm in the dust by her door. Perhaps it was meant to send a message like the pixie wing—give up on the bounty, or your plants are next—but Growina could not believe her luck.

"Faux crocodile!" she shouted to the shrubs as she gingerly lifted the heavy vine. "My mother warned me away from these when I was little. I wonder if it will root in water."

Careful to remember her broom, she darted back into the house and hunted for an extra-large vase. It was not every day one stumbled upon cuttings from a plant mis-classified as a swamp monster. Time was of the essence if she hoped to revive it.

BOOM! BOOM! BOOM!

Growina jumped at the sound of fists on her door, toppling a pot and spilling fresh soil across a wooden potting bench. Instinctively, she scooped up the dirt and shoved it back into the pot. But she stopped when struck by a chilling thought. The person at the door might be Lora.

"Just a moment!" she shouted.

As quickly as possible, she righted the pot, shoved the vine into a watering can, and brushed her hands on a towel. Then she ran for the door.

Fists pounded again, and an icy wave of panic washed over her. What would she say? It was too soon. What if she made things worse or gave the impression that she was a pushover?

The door swung open before she made it to the curtains, and Margaret's voice called out, "You here?"

Growina's worry lifted, and a prickly sensation danced across her skin. She pushed through the wispy curtain to her storefront, grateful for the company should more drama find her. Her relief faded, however, when she witnessed the witches' behavior.

"Oh, there you are," Margaret said as she slammed the door shut and threw every latch. "Are all the doors closed and locked? All the windows too?"

"Even the ones upstairs?" Vivienne asked.

Growina blinked, unprepared for the barrage of questions.

"Uh . . ."

Margaret did not hesitate. "Go check," she ordered Vivienne, who did as instructed.

Yards of pastel fabric landed on Growina's counter, discarded by the witches who should have been wearing, not carrying, it. Something was wrong.

"Anyone going to fill me in?" Growina asked.

Margaret nodded. "Magwod's coming. Sylvie heard that loud mouth Chip kid talking about it."

"So? He's one of us, isn't he? An adventurer? What's the worry? Oh! Mind the glass on that side. I broke a jar."

Margaret made a sour face and lifted her skirt to examine her shoes. "Not the wriggleweed jar, right? That squirmy stuff bothers me."

"No, no. Just an herbal remedy for upset stomachs. Magwod?"

"Right. Magwod. He's not coming here to say hello and share baking recipes. He's coming here for business."

Growina grabbed a cloth and did her best to clear glass from the floor sans-broom. "I don't understand."

"I think the big guy is finally on to us," Margaret said with a scowl. "We cannot, under any circumstances, let him in here to find our clues. Is there any way to get in that we don't know of?"

"Well, I'm not sure if it counts as a way in, but I think you missed the garden last time. See, when I went to get my broom—"

"Sylvie, protect the garden," Margaret barked.

The silent witch nodded and turned toward the garden.

Growina shouted, "Wait!"

However, the concern was unnecessary. Sylvie held up a hand, palm flat, and stared hard in the garden's direction. Then she let her arm fall and returned to the conversation.

Vivienne burst in a moment later. "Everything's locked up," she said through heavy breaths. "Where are the clues?"

"Both stones are back in the cabinet," Growina assured her. "The hammer and chisel didn't fit, so I buried them beneath that plant. Do you need them?"

She gestured to a well-pruned tree in a decorative pot, and Vivienne scurried to it to examine the soil. Heavy fists again pounded on the door, prompting them all to turn, and a shrill squeak like a distant mouse filtered through. Margaret shook her head, then waved a finger in the air to remove the sound-proofing spell.

"The Penumbral Magwod demands immediate access to this establishment!"

She crossed her arms. "Maybe if he learned how to ask for things politely, he would be invited inside more often!"

A moment of silence passed, followed by a cacophonous boom that shook the floor and rattled jars. The team waited in silence for Chip's inevitable reaction.

"The Penumbral Magwod has noted your defensive barrier and has added it to his list of suspicious activity."

Vivienne rolled her eyes. "Security on a retail building is suspicious, but a mage attempting to break in isn't?"

"The Penumbral Magwod has observed dangerous levels of supernatural residue in and around this building that cannot be explained by the presence of local vegetation or amateur adventuring parties."

"Amateur?" Vivienne cried.

"Local?" Growina added.

Margaret remained calm. "The Penumbral Magwod needs to grow up and speak for himself. We're tired of hearing his name."

"The . . . he . . ." Chip sighed so loud it was audible through the door. "Please, just let him in to search the place. If you're not responsible for the magic he's detecting, you could be in danger."

"Let him in to size up the competition and check out our plans? Not happening!" Vivienne shouted. Then she lowered her voice and asked, "What is he talking about? What dangerous magic?"

Growina dug her nails into her skirt and bit her lip. She had a pretty good idea where dangerous magical residue might come from, but had no desire to spill the beans in front of Magwod. Margaret, maybe. Magwod? Never. He would call the gatekeepers right away—or worse.

Margaret thought for a moment. "Did we dispose of the pixie wing when we left to rest up?"

Sylvie nodded and flicked her fingers to indicate a fire.

"Hmm. That was my best guess. The wing might have residue from whatever spell our saboteur used to kill the pixie. Not to mention the pixie itself."

"Ah," Growina said, then shut her mouth tight.

"Ah?" Margaret asked with a brow raised.

"Well, there may have been a tiny piece of faux crocodile vine on the doorstep today."

Margaret came closer. "I'm not familiar. Is that bad?"

"Oh, no! It's wonderful! If I manage to root it, I can distill the vine into an allergy remedy, and the bark makes a lovely cruelty-free shoe leather!" Growina's smile faltered at the sight of Margaret's exasperated expression. "However, I suppose, in context, its sudden appearance could be bad. I thought maybe someone was threatening my plants."

"And you brought it inside?" Vivienne asked.

Growina pondered the remaining smears of sky blue powder on the floor. Now that they mentioned it, she may have been a smidge irresponsible. But to be fair, all the cloak-and-dagger nonsense was brand-new to her. No one ever threatened their local apothecary.

Except maybe Lora.

Her face prickled, and she realized she was getting worked up in front of her team. It was not the right time to stress about bullies—if a right time even existed. Focus.

"It's moot," Margaret said. "We need to deal with the matter at hand."

Vivienne nodded and turned back to the door. "Chip?"

The young man sighed again. "Please do not acknowledge me directly. I merely serve as the temporary voice of the glorious—"

"Yeah, yeah, whatever. We've discussed things and decided we don't need your buddy's help. We have plenty of potions to help us find the residual magic!"

It was a blatant lie. Theo downed the last bottle they had, and the process to brew up a new one took days. But if it got the giant to leave them alone long enough to solve the latest puzzle, he would have no chance to rechallenge them.

Everyone inside held their breath, eager to find out if the Penumbral Magwod would return to his hunt for the magic-eating creature or take another swipe at the door. Instead, he discussed the matter with Chip—a process which, presumably, was indistinguishable from a silent staring contest.

"The Penumbral Magwod," Chip shouted, "accepts your answer and will remain exactly where he is until the deed is done. He demands you inform him if you detect a threat."

Poo.

"Now what?" Vivienne asked, as if reading Growina's mind.

"Now," Margaret said with a deep breath, "we wait for our wizard."

Adventuring, it seemed, involved a lot of waiting.

TWENTY-THREE
Not-Phillip

"I DON'T FEEL right," Florian moaned as Bodkins' chair swerved around an embarrassed pedestrian and their panicked pooch.

No one was counting, at least not aloud, but the phrase had passed his lips more times on their journey than in the rest of his life combined. Bodkins did not shush him. Instead, she steadied her gait, slowed the chair, and tightened her grip on his trembling limbs as if squeezing him close to her lap might soothe his symptoms.

Perhaps the mercenary captain felt guilty for her role in the collywobble consumption that led to his queasiness. Maybe she had a tender and nurturing side that remained hidden until he fell ill. More likely, however, she simply hoped to avoid a lap full of soothsayer upchuck.

"We won't make it by sunset at this pace," she said, "and I'm not fighting that thing in the dark. Keep your eyes peeled for an inn."

Florian's eyebrows raised. An inn? After days of camping in woods and valleys?

His mood surged as he imagined heated baths and clean linens, then crashed when he realized how worried about him Bodkins must have been to suggest it. The mercs never explained why they avoided inns, nor did they humor his arguments for them, so the sudden change was concerning.

The team followed orders without question—also concerning—and three and a half *I don't feel rights* later, Eddie pointed to a four-story building with candles in each window.

"I think we found our place," he said.

Wardric stopped walking and inhaled. "Something smells amazing!"

The artist was right. Despite his discomfort, Florian's mouth watered at the smell of roast meat and seasoned vegetables. The inn Eddie had found provided more than rooms, it seemed. They were busy preparing a feast for supper.

Good work, Eddie.

Bodkins grumbled and made her way to the front entrance, which was narrow but passable if she crab-walked through. She grumbled again as a gentleman in a tailored suit scurried out of a side room to greet them. He had the poise of a stage-trained dancer but the expression of a parent whose toddler was holding a glass vase.

"Hello! Hi! Welcome," the man said in rapid succession, as if he had several rehearsed greetings to choose from but was too flustered to pick one. "If you're here for the night, we have an attached stable where you can store your . . . mount."

Bodkins sighed the heavy sigh of a person prepared for an unpleasant exchange. "The chair goes where I go. If there's a problem, we'll look for alternate lodging."

To emphasize her point, she reached into the bag at her hip and retrieved more silver fudgels than could possibly fit inside.

The greeter's eyes bulged before he regained composure and chewed his lip. "It's technically against policy, but . . . let me grab the manager and see if there's something we can do."

The man scurried off, and Bodkins sighed again. Her lower lip pressed against her front teeth in an involuntary expression of defiance that made Florian want to jump out of the chair and shout expletives after the departing greeter—or at least get sick on the inn's expensive-looking carpet.

He reminded himself that mercs did not need defending. If Bodkins felt it necessary, she could lift the scrawny greeter in one clawed hand and drop him in his own goldfish pond. But that fact did not make Florian feel better.

The manager, a gray-haired woman in a tight skirt and tighter corset, did not react to the chair. She had an all-business appearance, a confident posture, and a face that said, "I have seen it all, so don't try me."

"We have three rooms available at one-hundred, one-fifty, and two-hundred fudgels," she said before anyone else could open their mouths. "Maximum occupancy is two per room, sharing a bed. Each comes with a complimentary three-course supper and breakfast. No substitutions. Cleaning fees are typically thirty fudgels per person, but the legged chair, sand spirit, and obviously ill guest will raise that cost to one-hundred each."

It was a shakedown. It had to be. The manager's expression was placid, but her underlying message was clear. Pay up or get out.

Florian again felt the urge to leap from the chair and do unpleasant things to the carpet, but Bodkins simply reached into the bag to retrieve another handful of fudgels.

"We'll take all three. What time is dinner?"

To her credit, the woman did not flinch. She snapped her fingers to indicate the greeter should collect their keys and replied, "Supper will be ready in an hour. Feel free to join the other guests around the firepit in the meantime."

Eddie whooped, oblivious to the tension. "Fire pit! Story time!"

He burst into a swirling cloud of sand and breezed back

and forth in front of windows until he found the right path, then whisked toward a set of double doors.

Wardric set his hands on his hips and called after the sand man, "Hey! What about Peterman?"

"It's fine," Florian told him. "As long as I can hold still somewhere, I'll be okay."

He pushed himself up and slid out of Bodkins' chair with the help of the howling horror arms. She frowned as he wobbled and steadied himself.

"What, exactly, is the monster doing?" she asked.

Florian gripped her arm as they made their way toward the fire pit. "Swaying back and forth like a prowling animal while it watches people leave the armory. It's as if the thing understands business closing times."

"All afternoon? Swaying and watching that building?"

"It stopped for a bit to dig up a fancy weed and drop it on someone's doorstep, but otherwise, yeah." He pressed closer to avoid a pillar, and a horrible thought struck him. "Have I cost us our chance to stop it before it becomes too powerful?"

A range of expressions passed over Bodkins' face before she settled on one with a tiny frown and creased brows. "No. I underestimated the distance with two people on foot—not to mention the creature's intelligence. This one's on me. But there's no use worrying about it now. We'll do our best in the morning."

They approached the fire pit, where a circle of brawny adventurers sat enraptured by one of Eddie's stories. Florian slunk off to a corner bench where he could lie back and close his eyes. It felt amazing to have only one layer of vision in motion, even as the creature's swaying picked up. It watched one guard after another wander home for the night, proving Florian's growing suspicion that the armory and gate guards were more for show than actual use.

"Hey, Phillip!" a voice called over the rising and falling sounds of Eddie's adventuring story.

Florian ignored the shout until a second "Phillip!" sounded, far too close to his bench for comfort. He opened his eyes to see a tall mage in green robes standing over him.

The mage blinked and grimaced. "Oh! Sorry, mate. You look just like my cousin, Phillip."

Florian sat up, let a wave of nausea pass over him, and muttered, "No problem. I get that all the time."

"That you look like my cousin Phillip?"

He locked eyes with the mage, shook his head, and made a wobbly attempt to get to his feet. If hiding in a secluded corner was no more restful than sitting around the fire pit, he would rather be near friends who could shoo oddballs away. Unfortunately, the oddball noticed his instability.

"Whoa, you look rough. Want me to grab you something? The inn makes a great spiced cider."

Even the mention of cider made Florian dizzy. "No, thank you. The last thing I need is more to drink."

"Hah! I get you," the mage said with an obnoxious wink. "Cushion for your head, then?"

The oddball had no intention of shooing on their own, but fortunately, Florian was an actor. He plastered on his most grateful expression, leaned into his unsteadiness, and said, "Oh, could you? That would be amazing."

The mage's eyes lit up. They gave a thumbs-up and hurried off to find an unoccupied cushion while Florian wobbled over to Wardric.

"If an overly friendly mage in green robes shows up with a pillow, please tell them I'm asleep."

Eyes closed again, this time with orange firelight behind the creature's intensifying wobble, Florian set his head against Wardric's massive bicep and listened to Eddie's long-winded tale.

"The baby king dug a ditch for a moat," the sand man told his captivated audience, "thinking that would keep marauders out, but Slugbeard knew of an ancient crypt deep beneath the castle."

"Hold on," a woman interrupted. "Slugbeard? Like, *the* Slugbeard?"

In the deliberate silence that followed, fabric rustled against benches. Florian opened one eye to confirm that, yes, every one of the impressive adventurers around the crackling fire had shifted a few seats away from the smirking sand man.

Eddie ate the drama up. "Would you believe me if I told you he was once an archaeologist? That's where he got his name. Slug beard. Always pressing his cheek to the grass like he could feel the caverns beneath our feet. He wasn't even our best mage! Too distracted by bones and dusty artifacts. They say it was something he found in a cave that turned him into the wizard you know."

The adventurers all sucked in a breath, but Florian was already over the story. Surely, Eddie was interesting enough on his own that he did not need to lean on the infamy of—

Florian sat bolt upright and gripped Wardric's arm. "It's moving."

"You're telling me Slugbeard . . ." someone began, but Eddie shushed them.

"It's left its perch," Florian continued as Bodkins moved closer. "Leapt straight across the rooftop the minute the last guard was out of sight. There's a trapdoor on the roof, and it's pawing at the latch."

"Clumsy pawing or dexterous pawing?" Bodkins asked over the sound of fireside grumbling.

"Clumsy. If it were a person, I'd say it had numbed hands. It's relying on its claws to do most of the—okay, it's inside."

Florian held on to Wardric as the monster slid down a ladder into the armory. The top floor had bows and crossbows on display, and the creature went straight for a bin of enchanted arrows. Based on the glow, the arrowheads produced fire, frost, and lightning upon striking a target. The creature gnawed each one off like meat on a skewer.

"You were right," he said to Bodkins. "The more magic it eats, the less cloudy the visions."

The crowd around the fire quickly lost interest in Eddie's tale and turned their attention to Florian instead . . . which was unfortunate because he still felt dizzy and a little green. He probably looked like hot rubbish as well. It was not his proudest performance.

"Is that the monster with the bounty?" one asked. "Has your wizard got an eye on it?"

Florian frowned and snapped his mouth shut. He was not about to share all the mercs' secrets with the competition, especially if they called him a *wizard*. He watched in silence as the monster chomped every arrowhead and moved to a glittering crossbow, which it pried from a display shelf with one paw. Individual leathery pads were visible, as were fur-covered knuckles and deep black veins that ran through its hooked claws.

"Clarity and dexterity," he whispered to Bodkins. "That's bad, right?"

The creature finished the last magic item on the upper floor and ran to the staircase. Even through the hardwood, it could see the glow of dozens of enchanted polearms below, and it craved them like a child craved birthday pudding. Instead of running down the stairs, it leapt over the railing and dropped without concern for its safety.

Florian was not so lucky. Unable to differentiate between the creature's sudden descent and his own, he toppled face-first toward the stone barrier of the fire pit. His eyes squeezed shut as he instinctively prepared for a jarring and painful impact, but his forehead landed with a *floomf* on a soft cushion instead.

"I got ya, Not-Phillip," the oddball mage said before the creature sank its fangs into the head of an axe, and Florian passed out from a burst of light and intense elation.

The creature's vision was almost as clear as his own.

Twenty-Four
Company Calling

An excerpt from the Lazy Botanist's Guide to Naughtobelus.

***Capto Submersi* Faux Crocodile**

Habitat: Opaque wetlands with sufficient insect and animal life.

Appearance: Aquatic plant with coiled vines that react swiftly to nearby vibrations.

Characteristics: Plant grows fully submerged in opaque water, occasionally sending vines above to ensnare passing wildlife. Unlucky victims are dragged below the surface, where they decay and provide essential minerals.

Author's note: Legend has it the exploring botanists of Sucklesap Swamp strapped blades to their legs for rapid removal of the deadly vines. Sounds like a good way to stab yourself in the foot.

* * *

"Are you aware people are waiting outside?" Theo asked as he emerged from a solid shop wall.

Unlike the anxious witches, he looked like he had had a restful slumber—before he woke with a start and ran to the shop. His hat was crushed, his jacket rumpled, and his beard resembled a well-used bottle brush. His eyes, however, shone with a clarity that had not been present since his first sip of magic detection potion.

Margaret crossed her arms. "We tried to get Mugmug to leave—"

"Magwod," Theo corrected reflexively.

"Sure. We tried to convince him to go, but he swears there's some threatening magic looming over this place, and he refuses to leave until we get rid of it."

Vivienne's fingers curled like claws. "We have no idea what he's talking about! Or referring to. Whatever. We're in an apothecary shop. *Everything* is infused with magic."

Growina bit her lip. Not *everything* was infused—and certainly not with threatening magic—except, perhaps, the clues they had found. And maybe the summoning circle out back.

As much as she dreaded the repercussions, a confession was in order. She inhaled, then opened her mouth to speak.

Theo got there first. "It's probably all the cultists outside," he said.

Her mouth snapped shut.

The witches stared like puppies awaiting instruction. Then Margaret flicked a hand in the air to drop her sound-dampening spell again. Sure enough, voices filtered through the walls, some shouting, some wailing, and some bickering with an unprepared Chip.

"The Penumbral Magwod does *not* have poopy breeches!" he shrieked.

"And smelly tassets, too!" one cultist said in a sing-song voice.

"How *dare* you! Fools! The Penumbral Magwod will make you eat those words!"

The cultists hooted and snarled. "Eat our words? Like you and your friends eat from our spoon? Return it, stink bottom, or face the consequences!"

"I . . . he . . ." Chip paused, presumably to consult Magwod or take a calming breath. "Nobody knows what you're talking about!"

Margaret flicked her hand again, and the shop fell silent.

"How did they find us?" Vivienne asked.

Theo leaned against the counter. "Well, we weren't exactly stealthy, were we?"

She pointed dramatically to the floor. "No. Here. How did they find us *here* in this shop?"

"Erm," Growina said. "The young man outside the mansion—the one who said nobody ever noticed him—is it possible one of you failed to . . . notice him . . . on your journey through town today?"

"Fudge," Vivienne spat.

"Oh! And, um, speaking of town, how is the crowd? Does everyone still look angry out there?"

"They've dispersed," Theo said, as he punched a fist into his silly hat to round it out. "The desire for dinner quashed their rage."

Vivienne's stomach growled. "Food," she moaned. "I was hoping we'd go to a restaurant tonight."

"With whose funds?" Theo snapped.

Growina stepped in before a spat could break out. "I have plenty of vegetables in my garden, and . . ." She trailed off and glanced at the jar of fish sticks. There was no convincing the team to try them. "Beans to boil."

"Oh! That reminds me," Theo interrupted. "I patched the hole you witches left in the garden barrier. Not the wisest move, if you want my opinion. A cultist could have fit through there."

Sylvie, who until that point had been spinning silently in Growina's chair, stood abruptly and glanced toward the garden exit. Margaret also flinched at the words but regained her composure a split second later.

"There was no hole in that barrier when we created it."

"Well, there certainly was one when I arrived." Theo raised his chin defiantly. "And unless something ate straight through—"

The words were hardly out of his mouth before they ran for the garden door, Growina following close on their heels. She readied herself for a million questions as they barreled through and stormed into the too-quiet garden.

Theo raised an arm to point at a spot above the nearest wall. "There. You see it?"

Growina did not. When she squinted, a patch of sky seemed slightly pinker than the rest, but it could have been reflections from the still-setting sun. The witches, however, behaved as if they had seen a ghoul on the ancient brick wall.

"Was the creature in here when you sealed it?" Vivienne asked with a hint of panic. "Is it in here, now, watching us, or maybe already inside the shop?"

"No," Sylvie said—just that one word—and the others relaxed.

She bent down and moved her spiderweb skirt to reveal a weed with purple flowers. It was fuzzy with thorns, ripped up at the roots, and definitely did not belong in the garden.

"What is it?" Margaret asked Growina. "What does it mean?"

Growina shook her head and scooped up the plant. "It's only a weed. There are millions like it all around Wontmoil. Lovely, sure, but common as grass. I guess I could find it a vase?"

Margaret groaned. "What does it mean in the context of our creature? Why would it break in just to leave this for us?"

For the first time since she was very small, Growina lacked the answer to a plant-based question. She shrugged and spun the weed in her fingers. "Nothing I can think of. It's useless for potions and perfumes. Common, unthreatening, and not used in any rituals. There's nothing significant about it at all. Other than the flowers."

"Just say you don't know!" Vivienne snapped, but Margaret moved the pale witch aside.

Theo raised a hand. "If the monster brought the weed, it also brought the wing."

"And the vine she found on the doorstep earlier," Margaret agreed.

"So not a rival, but the creature itself?" he asked. "I don't understand what it's trying to tell us."

"Perhaps," Growina offered, "it wants to share pretty things it found?"

"That's that most ridiculous—" Vivienne began.

Margaret shushed her again. "Perhaps we're looking at things the wrong way. Maybe the question isn't *why this,* but *why us?*"

Theo pondered the question as he slid back into the shop, snagging his still-rumpled jacket on a coat peg. "Because we're the only ones following the clues on the artifacts? Everyone else is chasing the creature—or trying to build devices to capture it."

Margaret followed him in, but did not snag her cloak, which prompted Growina to wonder, briefly, if she had ever seen a witch snag on anything. With their layers of spiderweb fabric, one would think the witches would catch on every sharp corner. But even deep within the woods, they had effortlessly breezed past brambles and twigs.

She made a note to ask them their secret, perhaps a bit later when they were less stressed.

Vivienne was especially cranky and stomped her heels as she stormed inside. She preferred her mysteries less mysterious, based on her reaction to recent events. Either that, or she still held a grudge about supper. It really was a shame they were trapped in the shop.

"Three clues, three objects," Margaret said with a nod. "Two objects threatening, but one mundane. Is it trying to scare us away from the puzzle or congratulate us for getting it right?"

Theo wandered to the kitchen and checked the pantry, uninvited. "For the sake of argument, let's say the thing is an ancient evil, long ago banished and re-summoned this week. What's the thing it would fear the most right now?"

"Getting re-banished. But I don't get—"

"The monster showed up at all three locations. Worse, it arrived before we did, demonstrating a desire to uncover clues first. It's as if the clues lead to something it fears. So, perhaps, the weed is just a weed, and the point of the gifts is to lure competition. Bog us down with Magwod and cultists while it searches for the next clue on its own."

"That's more ridiculous than what she said!" Vivienne screeched.

It was time to prepare dinner. Growina politely nudged Theo from the pantry and dug around for dried beans and a pot. Normally, she soaked beans overnight, but a quick-soak potion was in the cabinet. When projects got exciting, she lost track of time. Beans-in-a-pinch were better than nothing.

"Viv has a point," Margaret said. "You're assigning a level of sophistication to the creature that it hasn't demonstrated."

"Hasn't demonstrated?" Theo shouted. "The thing released a cloud of magic that hid its trail from the average tracker.

It evaded every adventurer in the penta-city conurbation and located all three clues without reading the riddles. 'Hasn't demonstrated,' my hat."

"It located a lot of other stuff, too," Vivienne said with a sneer. "Doesn't mean it knew what it was chomping."

Growina dumped the beans into a pot with a satisfying *shh* and reached for her potions and tasty spices. Tomato vines filled one windowsill and cured onions hung in a crocheted net. It was enough to make a passable meal, though not the fancy one Vivienne likely hoped for.

"Let's say you're right, although I don't believe it," Margaret said to the wizard. "Who would summon an ancient evil with no way to control it?"

"And what will happen to that person if they're caught?" Growina added before she could stop herself.

Theo raised an eyebrow but nodded sagely. "The wizards likely did it in their quest for anti-magic. For all we know, they concocted this drama as an excuse to assemble their trap without pushback. When we link the summon to them, we'll call the gatekeepers. We're adventurers, not mercs. Human affairs are not our problem."

Growina gasped at the mention of the gatekeepers, and a rush of onion fumes tickled her nostrils. She sneezed three times into her sleeve, then looked up to see two hovering children.

"You know there's a buncha people outside?" Zemni asked.

"Ooh! Dinner!" Zizel added.

"We know," Margaret said with a twinge of annoyance. "The big guy is here for some kind of magic, and the cultists are mad that we broke their statue."

"And the wizards?"

Margaret blinked, narrowed her eyes, and removed the soundproof spell again.

"Theo—oof!" someone shouted outside the shop. "This is your last chance to—unhand me, you garbage goblin!"

"Replace what you pillaged, or I'll bite you again!" a brazen cultist shouted back.

"This is your last chance!" the wizard yelled, and at first, it sounded like he was warning the cultist. But he followed the statement up with, "We go forward without your help in the morning!"

The cultist howled, the wizard screamed, and Margaret quickly silenced the shop.

"You don't think they can do it, do you?" Growina asked the scowling Theo. "Build the AMM device?"

Theo pressed his hands to the counter. "They're AMMs, not AMM devices. *Anti-magic machine device* doesn't make any sense."

She waited for an actual answer and patiently stirred the pot of beans.

"To be honest, it's possible. They were bound to stumble close, eventually."

"We should split up," Margaret said. "Half of us will solve the puzzle, and the other half will stop the wizards."

Theo shook his head. "If there's nothing to catch, they've no reason to use it. We all study the clues together. Not like we can leave yet, anyway."

"To the clues!" Margaret said with a fist in the air.

Vivienne whined like a cat shut in a bedroom.

". . .After dinner," Margaret added.

Vivienne grinned.

TWENTY-FIVE

Printing Squiggles

SOMETHING ABOUT A morning with no birdsong felt foreboding, even when one expected the silence. Beyond the humble shop's walls, robins still searched for worms in the soil, and early risers shuffled the streets toward their jobs. However, the only noises inside the building were the hushed whispers of bickering adventurers.

Growina felt guilty for falling asleep in her fluffy bed while the rest kept working, but she reminded herself that the others had gotten naps.

She selected a dress with a tree blossom print and a crocheted shawl that featured floral vines. If the morning refused to come inside, she would construct her own from bright fabric and yarn. It was the closest thing to an act of defiance she was capable of before her first tea.

Downstairs, Team Wontmoil was as she had left them; hunched and arguing over the clues. The storefront floor was a mess of paper, and her counter was black with charcoal dust. It seemed the team had worked all night with nothing more than a mess to show for it.

"Oatmeal?" she asked the assembled party after remembering she was out of flour.

Everyone jumped, save for Sylvie.

Theo beckoned her toward the counter. "Solve an argument for us," he said with the volume of a person tired of whispers. "Does this spot on the chisel say shush or chuck?"

Growina leaned down to examine the chisel, which Theo held up between two fingers, and her brow furrowed. "It doesn't say anything. It just looks like a bunch of squiggly scratches to me. Is everyone well this morning?"

"No, we're not," snapped Vivienne. "We've squinted our eyes, copied the marks, and attempted to translate them into letters. There's no way to read whatever this is—no matter what the wizard says."

"We're stumped," Margaret agreed.

"That seems more complex than the previous ones," Growina said. "How about cinnamon?"

It took them a moment to realize she was asking about oatmeal, not the puzzle, but eventually, they nodded, and she rushed to start the kettle.

From the kitchen, she heard Theo ask, "Maybe it says shoe?"

The others groaned.

Nobody said another word until Growina returned with a tray of bowls and filled the room with the smell of warm cinnamon. She lowered the tray to a clean bit of the counter, careful not to disturb the clues or the dust.

Vivienne was the first to grab breakfast. "I can't think anymore," the pale witch declared. "My brain is like this." She lifted a spoonful of oatmeal to demonstrate, then let it drop back with a splat to the bowl.

"We're all tired," Theo said, "but we can't give up while the association threatens all of our magic."

Something shifted in the witch's face, and she slammed her bowl onto the counter. "Did I say I was giving up? No. I did not."

"Then keep thinking!" he said, perhaps to encourage her, but the words came out more like a command.

Vivienne snarled at the rude wizard and tried to snatch the chisel from his hand. She missed, but he released the tool, and it rolled through charcoal and off the counter.

Margaret bent down to retrieve it. "We won't get anywhere if we can't—" she began, but stopped when Sylvie gripped her arm.

Both witches gaped at the floor, and Growina craned her neck to look. On the layer of discarded paper, a printed charcoal rectangle sat exactly where the chisel had rolled, and within its borders, white lines took shape like a rubbing from an old gravestone.

It was a portion of a map.

Theo grabbed the hammer and rolled its handle into the dust without asking. He printed the result onto another sheet and whisked it down to the floor by the first. The two matched up with a bit of maneuvering, and Theo swore beneath his breath. Not only was it a complete map, but the location seemed familiar.

"How could I have missed this?" he asked.

"We all missed it," Margaret said, and set a hand on his shoulder.

"Yes, but—" he began, then thought harder about his phrasing. "I know exactly where this is. I can lead us there now if the crowds are gone."

Growina perked up. It had not yet occurred to her that the people outside might disperse to get rest and avoid the night chill. In her mind, Herbs and Vices was under siege, and nothing short of a blizzard would deter them.

"Magwod?" Margaret asked with a hand in the air to drop the soundproofing.

Everyone inside held their breath as the seconds ticked

without a response. Unfortunately, one eventually came, though it was higher-pitched than the one they expected.

"Your mighty warrior has abandoned you!" a cultist said with a slurred voice that sounded like they were sleeping with their face pressed up against the front door.

Margaret frowned but only said, "Wizards?"

"Your bearded friends have left you as well! Turn over the spoon and replace our statue, or suffer the wrath of the second vessel!"

Theo stepped in, already annoyed. "Pardon, are you threatening us with the wrath of someone in the future, or is your deity among us now?"

An awkward silence stretched between them, punctuated by whispers, followed by a cough.

"The vessel may well be on Naughtobelus, but the power has not yet merged with them. Woe is you when the two combine!"

"Indeed. But for now, do you have anything real to threaten us with?"

More whispers and coughing encircled the building, but no snarky reply came back from the door.

Margaret silenced the shop and set her hands on her hips. "Do we take a chance?"

Theo shook his head. "I'll go alone. I can pass through walls, and I know the spot."

"And what if the thing you find is dangerous?"

He thought for a moment. "I'll take the twins."

Zizel and Zemni shared a glance, and Zizel said, "As long as we don't go near the monster."

"They took our candy away after we visited the cult," Zemni added with a dramatic frown. "Said we got too close."

"Do you have any more of those teleporting beads?" Theo asked Growina, who shook her head.

"Just the one, but it won't get anyone out of the shop. Blasted Glassflower draws stuff to itself."

Sylvie rolled her eyes and slid toward the door. Nobody moved to stop her. It opened with a tiny squeak at her touch, and she slipped through the crack like morning mist. Margaret held her breath and raised a hand so they could all hear what happened next.

At first, it seemed like the soundproofing was still active. If not for the chirp of a frustrated blackbird trying to get inside the garden, nothing made a peep outside the shop.

Then the screams began.

Oddly, the sounds did not emit from only one spot. Voices howled on all sides of the shop as if Sylvie could be in four places at once. Then, as soon as the wailing reached a crescendo, it stopped, like the screamers had fallen asleep. Only the blackbird called after that.

Sylvie slipped back through the cracked door in silence and tugged it open to show them the way. Nobody dared to ask questions.

Before she followed Theo out, Growina threw on her bottle bandolier—which she had re-stocked after the previous adventure—and grabbed the hammer and chisel. One never knew when a potion might help or if the wizard's memory might fail him.

She followed them out into silent streets, despite the screams that must have carried. Perhaps, the townsfolk were all sleeping in after the excitement of the day before. It was possible, but something still felt off.

Unaware of the typical morning hubbub, the others marched through the empty streets and back to the Howling Woods again, this time venturing deeper within. Theo led them past a gnawed pillar that was once a part of his protective barrier and toward a strange hill among the trees. It looked like the earth pushed up and out to form the shape, revealing red mud and several enormous boulders.

"This is the place," he said through heavy breaths, and though they did not know the spot, the others had to agree with him.

One boulder, taller than Theo and half-sunken into the side of the hill, bore thousands of scrapes, as if something with massive teeth and claws was desperate to claw through its solid surface. It helped them identify the next location but left them with a bigger question.

"What are we meant to do?" asked Margaret.

Sylvie ran her hands along the surface. The white-eyed witch stood and presented a stone with only two words carved on a side.

Brek it.

"Well, yes, that seems obvious," Theo said, as if he could address the author. "But break it, how? It's bigger than me!"

"I've got a spell," Margaret said and lifted her hands toward the boulder.

Everyone else took a step back as lightning danced along her arms. Her braided hair lifted into the air, as did the layers of her dress. But when she released the building power, and bright lightning slammed into the stone, it did not leave so much as a scorch.

"That's odd," she said, squinting at the spot. "That one has leveled barns before."

Theo crossed his arms. "You might have warned us of that fact before you used it so close."

The witch shrugged.

"So, we're meant to do this the hard way?" Vivienne asked. "Smash the boulder with physical strength? How is that even possible?"

"It certainly reminds one why adventuring parties typically

contain a non-magic user," the wizard said, wriggling his thin arms to demonstrate.

Growina gingerly raised the hammer and chisel. "Would these help?"

He slapped his forehead so hard his hat jumped. "Of course! That's why they're tools and not stones! We're meant to *use* them."

He grabbed the tools and set the chisel to the boulder, then raised the hammer to strike the end. A chip flaked from the stone when it came down, leaving a divot the size of a thumbnail. It was not the most encouraging sign.

Not to be deterred, Growina searched the area for sturdy weeds. "Builders drill a line of holes to split a stone in two," she told the wizard, "lengthwise, across the rock. They stick thick reeds in the holes first to help them get the chisel back out."

"This something you learned from a skeleton?" Vivienne asked.

"Oh no, I sell the reeds. It's a sturdier kind, not like these, and they usually have more than one chisel."

"Great," Theo said with an eye roll.

He had a hole as deep as a finger, with some weeds already packed in, but stopped when Growina mentioned more chisels.

"No problem!" Zemni said with a smirk. "We can make you another . . . chisel."

Everyone dodged as the literal word appeared in the air and thudded to the ground, each letter formed of solid metal.

Zemni lowered himself, lifted the l, and handed it to the exhausted wizard. "That one might do," the alien said.

The look on Theo's face said otherwise.

He fitted the letter into the hole he had already carved and lifted the hammer to nail it in. The hammer struck with a reverberating clang that shook the tool and the wizard's hand, but it failed to sink into the rock.

Theo dropped the hammer and swore, then flapped his arm like a baby bird. "I think this boulder is resistant to magic," he muttered. "Which makes no sense, unless . . . but, no. There was only one person who . . . hmm. The timing is right, but the creature . . .?"

"You've stopped making sense," Margaret said. "In case you hadn't realized yet."

"The awful crunching noise doesn't help!" he snapped.

Everyone stopped talking. Margaret pursed her lips. Growina listened, and lo-and-behold, something was chewing behind the hill. The sound was more like grinding gears rasping and gnawing against hard metal, and it inspired everyone to look at the ground.

"*Hise*," Zizel read as she searched for letters. "Did anyone see where the c fell?"

"I'm thinking into the creature's mouth," Vivienne said.

"I'm thinking you're on your own now," Zemni added before both twins vanished in a puff of glitter.

Theo retrieved the tools and stepped away from the boulder. "Retreat or attack?"

"Both," said Margaret. "Let's see what it does when it thinks we're gone."

And so, Team Wontmoil ran away.

Twenty-Six

Don't Say It

Florian spun to take in all the nothing, then pursed his lips and faced his companions. None of them spoke as they trudged past buildings with shuttered windows and signs flipped to *closed*. Good thing the inn from the night before had served them breakfast before they departed. Otherwise, he would be in a terrible mood.

"This normal for a town besieged by bounty hunters?" he asked.

Bodkins rolled her eyes at his sarcasm. There was nothing typical about a town with empty streets after sunrise, but none of them knew what had happened to the people. The day before, all Wontmoil had been out on the very same street, at least based on Florian's monster-eye view. And other than the unguarded armory, he'd witnessed no disturbances since.

"You're sure the creature hasn't been through?" she asked for the third time since they arrived.

Based on his reports of increased dexterity and interactions with physical objects, Bodkins was obsessed with the idea that the monster they pursued was a larger threat than it had been the day before.

Florian, however, had seen no evidence to support that.

"I wasn't awake the entire night, but from what I saw, it

gorged itself on enchanted weapons and trotted off to the woods to nap."

"And now?"

"It's chewing on an iron letter C—like something from a shop sign—near a handful of weirdos who think they're hidden."

Wardric fidgeted with his brushes, infected by Bodkins' paranoia. "Are they in trouble? Do they need rescuing? Or are they like us?"

"Not sure," Florian said with a shrug. "But I'm not sensing aggression or fear from the creature. It's aware of their presence but seems unbothered."

Bodkins' chair crept over cobblestones as she shifted to examine door after door. "Hopefully not like us, then. We've got big problems if it's stopped fearing hunters."

The scent of fresh bread carried on the breeze, and a knot between Florian's shoulder blades eased. Wontmoil was far less modern than Leechleif, with compact buildings of stone and stained wood instead of multi-story mansions with columns and colorful paint. Between the old architecture and eerie silence, it felt like the setting of every ghost story. Most ghosts, however, did not need to bake.

"What's this?" Eddie asked and plucked a damp paper from the stones at his feet. "An ad for some kind of event today?"

Wardric's eyes lit up. "Is it a fair? I *love* fairs! That must be where everyone went! Can we go, too? Just for a minute?"

"It's not a fair," Eddie said with a huff. "It's a demonstration by some wizards. Something they call—"

A nearby door burst open with a crash, and a wild-haired woman sprinted out. She waved her hands in the air as she ran and shouted for the oblivious Eddie to shush. "Don't say it! Don't say the word!"

Eddie lowered the paper and blinked. "Eh?"

The woman caught up, skidded to a stop, and bent forward to breathe with her hands on her knees. She took several enormous gulps of air and straightened to face the confused sand man.

"I can answer whatever question you have. Just don't speak that word aloud."

"What word?"

Her eyes narrowed. "Are you more adventurers?"

"Mercenaries," Bodkins corrected.

The woman frowned, and her chin drew back as if she had caught a whiff of onions. But whatever was bothering her overcame her distaste for Leechleif's heroes.

"The rest of your lot are out in the woods watching the wizards set up their . . ." She flapped her hand at the pamphlet. " . . .thing. And those of us with common sense have locked our doors for safety. Apparently, the thing they built is so dangerous, even the banking constructs have fled!"

Eddie scoffed. "What exactly is—"

"Hold on," Bodkins interrupted. "If the constructs are gone, who's left to pay the bounty?"

"Not my problem!" the woman screeched.

Florian thought she could use a course in etiquette.

Eddie waved the pamphlet about. "I still don't understand what this is about."

"The wizard's association built a *thing*," the woman said slowly, as if re-explaining something he knew, "that makes a cage resistant to *stuff*. But there's a chance it may go very wrong. So, stop standing around and get out of here!"

Years of practice with nonverbal cues gave Florian an advantage over his still-perplexed sandy companion. The box shape the woman made with her hands and the wiggle in her fingers when she said the word *stuff* filled in the blanks left by her vague words.

He nodded along, then raised a hand. "You mean magic doesn't work on the cage?"

"Shhh!"

He lowered his voice. "It somehow traps the creature we're hunting, even though the thing eats metal?"

Eddie pointed to the pamphlet and blurted, "So, AMM is referring to magic?"

And that was when he figured out which word the woman was trying to shush.

A brilliant flash of crimson light left bright spots dancing in their eyes as a robed man with a drooping hat appeared before the mercs. He tossed wads of crushed confetti into the air and addressed the party with open arms.

"Did someone here say AMM?"

The woman groaned and the wizard yelped as he caught sight of the eccentric crew. Unfortunately, he quickly regained his composure. "Fellow adventurers, I see. No matter! All are welcome. For the first time in Naughtobelus, come and witness a live demonstration of an anti-magic machine!"

He whipped more pamphlets from his robes and stuffed one into Florian's hand. When he turned to the woman, she shot him a glare that made him pull his arm back to his chest.

"You mean the second time," Bodkins said, and the nervous wizard yelped again, as if suddenly realizing the chair had an owner. "Sigeric Slugbeard used anti-magic."

The wizard tugged at his scraggly beard, which was already a few hairs short of full. "Slugbeard. Yes. Of course. Are you a scholar or a hobbyist?"

"Neither. But I can't seem to escape folks who are."

Eddie puffed out his sandy cheeks and kicked at the cobblestones, but the wizard was too nervous to notice the gesture. Florian wondered if that was how he appeared the first time he set foot in Bodkins' doorway.

"Ah," the wizard said. "There's been a recent resurgence of . . . passionate fans."

"I've met the cult," Bodkins replied dryly.

"Ah."

His gaze flicked from Bodkins' intense stare to the wild-haired woman who was slowly edging to her front door.

"Just a moment! You forgot your invitation!"

Instead of responding, she slammed the door, leaving the party alone with the wizard. His beard swayed side to side as his mouth formed a silent complaint, but he did not have time to voice it.

Wardric stepped forward and puffed up his chest, staring down his nose at the man. Aside from Florian, the artist was the least threatening merc, but nobody else had to know that.

The wizard attempted an explanation. "In a short while, the association will activate a device and imbue a cage with anti-magic. Once inside, the magical creature will not be able to gnaw its way out, and the association will contain it permanently. No more banishments and eventual returns."

The man held his robed arms in the air as if he was rather proud of himself. They sagged slightly when Bodkins replied.

"And how will the creature get inside?"

"It, uh," the wizard said, then scowled and wiggled his whiskers. "That's confidential."

She cackled and turned to Florian. "Do you suppose the creature will be in attendance at this so-called demonstration?"

He screwed his eyes shut to look. The double vision was easier to stomach with a lower dosage of collywobbles, but it took some effort to get a clear view. Thankfully, the sun was shining in the woods, and the creature had not strayed too far. It was easy enough to get his bearings.

Curiously, the thing was still watching the strangers—a mismatched party comprising three grumpy witches, a wizard-like man in a three-piece suit, and a middle-aged woman with bottles on her chest. The five reminded Florian of amateur theater troupes that could not afford proper costumes. None seemed to act their part correctly, either.

One witch quietly bickered with the almost-wizard in the bushes, while another coaxed the bottle-woman into tossing an iron h. It was as if they thought the monster was a puppy, and throwing a treat would make it fetch. The third witch, the one with colorless eyes, stared at the creature and gave him goosebumps. It was as if she was looking straight at Florian, aware he could see her with soothsayer's magic. But that was impossible, wasn't it?

He blinked away the woman's image to stop his skin from crawling. "I don't believe the thing's going anywhere. It's preoccupied with something else."

The wizard's eyes bulged, prompting Florian to wonder if showing their hand was a bad idea.

"We'll pass on the demo," Bodkins said. "Our business is with the bounty, not with you."

That would have been the end of their chat if the man had any common sense, but wizards in Wontmoil lacked basic self-preservation instincts, it seemed. The wizard leapt in front of Bodkins' chair as if his tiny body could stop her and held his flimsy arms out wide.

"You have a soothsayer on your team!" he said, as if Florian could not speak for himself. "Would you consider joining forces?"

Bodkins said, "No," and gripped the man in a monster's fist, so his feet dangled helplessly above the street.

She deposited the wizard to the side—rather more gently than Florian thought he deserved—and began her march toward the woods. Everyone, including the pestering fellow, hurried to keep up with her massive footsteps.

"But if you could direct us to the thing, together, we could—"

Bodkins stopped and showed the man all her teeth. "Is it your intent to follow us to our destination? Because where we come from, in the city of Leechleif, there are rules against stealing another team's bounty. Rules that would go poorly for you."

It seemed impossible for the nervous wizard to appear more frightened than he already did, but his knees gave way beneath his robes like a half-filled sandbag left backstage. It took him no time to catch himself, but the former confidence was gone. "L—Leechleif? Then, that makes you—"

"Mercenaries, yes."

"Disgusting."

Bodkins raised her brows. "We perform exactly the same role as you."

His scraggly beard dipped as he scowled. "With one difference! We don't collect on living people."

"Then how do you deal with villains? Let them do whatever they like?"

He pointed at something in the distance. "We call the gatekeepers!"

Gatekeepers. The word snagged in Florian's mind, and before he could help himself, he asked, "Do they operate from a building with a gate and no wall?"

The pestering wizard's brows knit, confirming what Florian already suspected.

"You may have to do your own gatekeeping until they can replenish their stock."

The wizard tried to cross his arms but got them tangled in his oversized robes. Instead, he huffed and turned his back as if Florian's talents were suddenly offensive. "If you don't intend to collaborate, I must return to the association."

He headed for the nearest junction, but Bodkins called after, "When, exactly, is your demo?"

"Within the hour, and thanks to you, I'm running late!" he shouted before storming out of earshot.

Eddie sauntered over to Florian. "Can we find the monster before they start?"

Florian shrugged and closed his eyes in time to see the woman with bottles chuck the h. To his surprise, the monster pounced.

"I think, if we get close enough, I'll recognize the strange hill beside it."

Bodkins clapped her hands with delight and started down the street again. A genuine smile crossed her cheeks like a child readying for a game. And why wouldn't she be excited? Soon, the mercs would meet their monster.

Twenty-Seven

Myth and Monsters

Theo raised a hand and whispered, "Three, two, one, throw!"

On that command, Growina bit her lip, squinted, and tossed an iron letter e into distant foliage. Something shadowy darted after, tentacles rippling as it pounced. Its fangs snapped shut on the magical bait, and Theo bolted toward the boulder.

The wizard made no sound as he ran, save the rustle of leaves from their cover, yet Growina heard his mental swears with every footstep in the open. Theo, for all his pompous snark, was braver than most adventurers.

Then again, bravery often came into play when flawless planning went out the door.

The current plan, far from flawless, revolved around the realization that Theo *was* a powerful wizard. And as such, he had the power to bypass a barrier like this boulder with only a whispered wizard's spell. The plan made sense, provided his legs were faster than the monster's teeth, but the way he flinched and raised his hands cued Team Wontmoil in to his doubt before his noggin struck the rock.

To his credit, he did not shout, even as the thunk of his skull striking stone echoed in the morning silence. Instead, he fell into leaves and crawled, hat in hand, back to the team.

Margaret should have been sympathetic, but seemed too

fascinated by his failure. "What *happened?*" she snapped at the woozy wizard as she dragged him back to the shrubbery where the rest of the team crouched, concerned.

"M-magic," he stammered as he tried to sit up, "doesn't work. It's as I feared."

"What do you mean it doesn't work?" the witch hissed, as if he had told a fib. "Magic always works. That's what makes it magic."

"Well, it didn't."

Theo, regaining his temperament, pulled his hat back onto his head and winced as it brushed a growing goose egg. He shifted to a crouch and rejoined the witches, whose faces were still scrunched up in doubt.

"Perhaps you uttered the wrong gibberish spell?" Vivienne offered.

Theo scowled.

The scowl deepened when Growina shook her head and replied, "He knows that one well."

"I do use doors," he said, "occasionally."

Margaret crossed her arms, an act which appeared far less natural when huddled in a prickly shrub. "You knew it wasn't going to work, didn't you? What aren't you telling us?"

The wizard looked at the ground, the leaves, and anywhere but Margaret's face before he muttered, "I had a hunch."

"Which was?"

"Well, it's just that the clues are ancient, and the writing on them seems quite wrong. Also, the magic letter bounced when I struck it with the sculptor's hammer—a different sensation than the chisel itself."

The witch tried and failed to look more cross. "You have two minutes left to make some sense before I raise my voice."

"It's all tied to Slugbeard, somehow," Theo blurted like a bubbly bottle uncorked too quickly. "Spelling ruined by the

Gart Splagosion, a direct reference in the statue, and now, a stone resistant to magic? Only one person knew that spell."

"Before you," Margaret corrected.

"And the wizards," Growina offered.

Vivienne snorted. "I'll believe that when I see it."

"Well, hold on," Margaret said. "Perhaps this was the work of the wizards. Maybe they used this rock for practice."

Theo shook his head so hard it seemed in danger of flying free, hat, goose egg, and all. "They don't have the proper formula for perpetual anti-magic, for one. And according to Crowe, what they have now is far too expensive to waste on a stone. The more logical explanation is that Slugbeard himself cursed this boulder."

"I see," Vivienne declared with an expression that said she had no clue what he was talking about. "But where, exactly, does the creature come in?"

Theo took a shuddering breath. "It seems likely we won't know until we get inside that rock. But if the monster is of his design, and it took perpetual anti-magic to stop it initially, that doesn't bode well for the rest of us."

Vivienne's expression remained confused, and Growina could not blame the witch. She also had questions, the first of which was why no stories of the Gart Splagosion mentioned a magic-eating beast. True, no one knew how Slugbeard passed, and perhaps the monster was a missing clue, but the wretched wizard did not curse the stone and set clues out posthumously.

"What are the chances this is a trap?" she asked. "How do we know there aren't more monsters waiting for us if we break the boulder?"

Theo shuddered. "I guess we don't. Though I'd like to believe his evil summons were all banished when he died."

"Hmmm," Margaret said with a frown. "I've heard of people sacrificing witches to stop their summons, but it never works. Once a summon is fully present, its life isn't tied to the witch. Slugbeard would have known that, but with all the knowledge and power at his disposal, there's no reason he would anticipate death. He would have taken on rivals face-to-face, not built a puzzle to ensnare them. Right?"

She glanced at Theo for confirmation, but the wizard only shrugged in response. Growina found it comforting that a summoner's demise was proven unhelpful in stopping a summon, but the idea that folks might try anyhow raised goosebumps all over her shawl-covered arms.

Hopefully, Theo was on to something, and the mess tied back to the meddlesome wizards—not her botched garden spell.

"What if the monster ate his spellbook?" Vivienne asked. "What if the book was keeping him alive?"

"Oh, the book was most definitely keeping him alive," Theo confirmed. "There are seventeen separate accounts of his defeat at the hands of various assassins. But he wouldn't feed it to the creature deliberately. The answer is within or beneath that boulder, and speculating now won't change that fact. I think our next step is to get—"

"Shh."

Theo's mouth snapped shut.

Sylvie held a single finger in the air, then lowered it slowly and leaned toward the group. "The monster has a second set of eyes," she whispered, then sat back quietly to observe once more.

Margaret swore but kept her voice lowered as she explained the cryptic statement to the rest of the bewildered team. "She means one of the other groups has a soothsayer. Keep your voices down when discussing plans, unless you want our rivals to hear."

Theo's hands clenched and unclenched in a movement that

could only be described as a physical manifestation of academic curiosity. "There's only so many soothsayers on Naughtobelus who can link their minds with a non-humanoid. I hear the practice takes decades to master, and those who manage it are spies for powerful governors. How deep does this rabbit hole go?"

One would think no single expression could succinctly convey a command to calm down *and* a complete disinterest in the subject at hand, but Sylvie somehow managed both with the swipe of a hand.

To his credit, Theo understood. His fidgeting stopped, and he swallowed hard to clear the embarrassment from his voice. "I'm starting to sound like the cultists," he muttered.

Margaret, for once, was merciful. "You were saying something about the next step?"

"Right. I think we need to ally with Magwod."

"Magwod?" Vivienne screeched, loud enough to receive her own shushing.

Theo shook his head and whispered, "Let's be honest. None of us are bodybuilders, and cracking that rock will take physical strength. Magwod is a magic user, so he understands our predicament. But he's also built like an angry bull—or at least his armor gives that impression. Adding him gets us the muscle we need without splitting our bounty too many ways."

"It's a solid plan," Margaret agreed, "but where on Naughtobelus are Magwod and Chip?"

Growina thought about it. "I think they abandoned the door before the cultists left. Maybe the same time as the wizards?"

Vivienne snarled. "I swear to the stars . . . if they got mixed up in that AMM nonsense—"

A sound like a popping cork, followed by thrashing leaves, disturbed their huddle. Beside them, a pair of robed legs that were not previously present kicked to free themselves of brambles.

"Did someone here say—pthoo! Why are you in a shrubbery?" the spontaneous wizard demanded while crumpled confetti settled onto their heads.

Vivienne screamed. The wizard screamed.

Theo grabbed the wizard's robed arms and dragged him down like a vengeful merman taking revenge on fisherfolk. "Did it see you?" he demanded.

"Release me!" the wizard shouted and stumbled backward out of the bush.

Nothing swooped in to attack or crashed through the fallen leaves in the forest. Team Wontmoil shared a frown and sighed, then followed the fool out into the clearing. Sure enough, there was no sign of the creature, its snack, or recently disturbed foliage.

The wizard brushed himself off and smirked. "I see. You were stalking the creature," he said with the smug certainty of someone who had no idea what they had stumbled into.

"N—" Vivienne began, but a swift elbow from Margaret adjusted her response. "—one of your business."

The wizard's eyes narrowed, then widened again. "You're what the creature was preoccupied with! Now there's no reason it shouldn't show up!"

"What are you blathering about?" Theo snapped.

"You're what the mercenary soothsayer saw!"

"The what? There's a mercenary? Here? In Wontmoil?"

Vivienne wrinkled her nose. "Disgusting."

The scraggle-bearded wizard cackled, manic. "This is perfect! I must tell the others before they begin!"

He bolted for the trees and Theo took chase without consulting the team.

Left with no choice, the others pursued through forest and

swampland that was oddly unoccupied by the usual howling horrors and pixies.

When they finally stopped, exhausted to the point of imminent collapse, the sight before them was depressing and worrisome.

Every adventurer who had come to Wontmoil to banish the creature and collect the bounty stood near a sizable group of wizards who were gesturing toward a massive cage. Connected to the cage by tubes and gears was a complex machine of equal parts alchemy, herbology, and misused clockwork. It seemed unlikely to do much when turned on other than splatter the viewers with oil.

Nonetheless, the adventurers watched, some in defiance and others in awe. And there, directly beside the wizards, stood the famous Penumbral Magwod. His metal arms tensed as scraggle-beard parted the crowd and approached his colleagues to share his good news.

If she did not know better, Growina might say the armored man was poised to attack.

"Stay back," someone said as he peeled off from the crowd and made a beeline for their group. "I think this is going to go quite poorly."

It was the first time Chip had ever spoken for himself.

Twenty-Eight

A Spot of Midnight

THE PROBLEM WITH weak supernatural vision was that it required closing one's eyes to see things from the subject's perspective. That was fine when a soothsayer was free to pause and consider the inside of their eyelids but less helpful when running through a deadly forest, pursuing a creature that *would not hold still.*

As the mercs hurried toward the artificial hill and the monster bounded away from it, Florian considered additional collywobbles. Clearer vision would save him the humiliation of stopping mid-run like a puppy on a walk, but his chances of confusing his obstacles for the monster's were worse the closer they drew together.

"Er. Wait. Hold on," Florian sputtered as he stopped to search for a landmark for the hundredth time.

Were the thing dashing through the streets of Leechleif, particularly the sections close to the theater, Florian would know its precise location. However, in the Howling Woods, the trees and bogs were all so similar he could swear the creature was running laps.

In fact . . .

"I think it's going in circles. I've seen that same stump several times."

"Walk and talk," Bodkins commanded. "Is it frightened?"

"Not at all. If anything, I'd say it feels smug."

He was self-aware enough to understand why he had no trouble reading the emotion and made a note to confront that later.

"You sure you don't need me to carry you?" she asked as Eddie nudged Florian's shoulders to get him moving again.

"So you can bump my head straight into a branch? No, thank you. No offense," he added on hastily.

Bodkins chuckled and said, "That's fair."

"So . . . it's circling something, yeah? But what?" Wardric asked as one of his massive legs swung over a log with colorful mushrooms.

"It may be a who, not a what," Florian answered. "It's taken a rather obsessive interest in a particular adventuring party."

Eddie jogged ahead—which seemed unnecessary since he could just as easily drift on the breeze—and used his sword to clear vines from their path. "Describe the party. Maybe it'll give us a clue."

Florian exhaled and considered how to describe them, then settled on, "Three witches, a wizard, and a lady with bottles strapped to her chest. Plus, two fairy-like floating children, but I haven't seen them recently."

Bodkins stopped short, and Wardric pinwheeled to avoid plowing into her chair.

"Did the children have short-pants?" she asked, brows creased.

Florian tilted his head. "How did you know?"

"They're the bank's enforcers. Makes sense that they're here. Shouldn't be helping a single team, though, but, hmm . . . I guess there's no rule against it. Clever. Good for them."

"Good for who?" Wardric asked as he skirted her chair and took the lead.

"Our competition. This will be an exciting hunt."

"We have different definitions of exciting," Florian mumbled before glancing up and recognizing their location. "Oh! This is the place!"

The artificial hill loomed ahead, a strange mossy mound surrounded by boulders that seemed out of place in the swampy woods. He readied himself to give a tour of the bushes and the remnants of the iron letters.

Eddie straightened and gasped. "No," the sand man said in a manner usually accompanied by a paling face when the speaker still had blood in their body.

Eddie approached the hill and circled it, then stopped at the largest boulder. It was the same one the odd adventurers had attacked. His gaze traced every scratch and dent from the top of the rock to the mossy earth where he settled into a sandy half-puddle.

"There," he said, and pointed to a spot invisible from above. "You see the signature?"

Bodkins shook her head and sighed, but Florian humored him and crouched to examine the faint scratch. The mark on the stone was an s or an eight—or an s someone hastily made into an eight—assuming it was not a natural blemish.

In context, if he was being generous, he might say it was a sign from Eddie's old crew.

"Is it something to do with the Stealthy Eight?" he asked.

Eddie's face lit up. "Yes! It is! Someone here paid attention in school."

Wardric snorted. "They don't teach about stealthy eights in school."

"Well, they should. We did a lotta good for all of you. Except this—" He patted the stone as he spoke. "This is bad, depending on how it got here."

"You gonna tell us what it is, or just how to feel?" Bodkins snapped with a look that reminded everyone the creature had gotten away again.

Eddie crossed his arms and lifted himself up. "It's a tomb." When nobody challenged him, he relaxed and explained. "We gave up our families, homes, and names. And when we died, we buried each other. Sigeric was an archaeologist who had a knack for finding ancient tombs, so he taught us how to make them to last."

"Hold on," Florian interrupted. "You're saying one of your crew is buried here?"

It took all his willpower not to roll his eyes every time Eddie mentioned the wretched wizard. The ghost they had met in the Indited Castle was barely any good at haunting. If Florian had to rate the performance, it might outrank a street magician—if the magician in question wore a blindfold and someone swapped their hare for a skunk.

The guy did not deserve a cult and forty mentions per hour from mercs.

Eddie's mouth twisted sideways. "Well, that's the odd thing. None of us ever came out this far. No offense to anyone from these parts, but nothing interesting happens in Wontmoil."

"It's a stuffy place," Bodkins agreed.

"Maybe they came here after your time?" Florian suggested half-heartedly.

As interesting as the conversation was, it was hard to pay attention to while the monster ran circles in the woods, so he sought a comfortable-looking stump and sat down to watch the visions. Every so often, he spotted a patch of unusual color or the twinkle of polished metal in sunlight, but nothing that told him where it was.

Eddie shook his head. "I died in our final attempt to stop the Gart Splagosion. We agreed to disperse and hide if it failed. Which, obviously, it did."

"Well, there ya go!" Wardric said far too cheerfully. "Some folks ran off and hid here!"

Eddie set his hands on his hips like the artist had said something rude. "Last I checked, it takes two to bury a body; a dead person and a gravedigger. *And* the only surviving couple I knew wound up in Leechleif, not Wontmoil."

"There's no ghosts here, either" Bodkins added. "Since that's the next thing you're going to ask. Any clue on the location of our monster friend?"

Florian shook his head. "If I didn't know better, I'd say it's circling a crowd in the woods. The glimpses I get change every time, but I haven't seen any landmarks yet."

Wardric's massive torso, with all its paintbrushes, moved to block Florian's view of Bodkins. "There's another way to find out who's inside."

Eddie made a strangled noise as Wardric whipped out a brush and palette. The large man squinted at the stone and delicately swirled the brush with two fingers to mix dark brown and sky blue paint.

"We should let this person rest in peace," Eddie said with an uncharacteristic twinge of worry.

Wardric gestured with the pointy end of the brush back toward Florian. "*He* said the weird adventuring party was trying to break into this rock. I may not be as smart as the boss, but I'd say there's a good chance something inside will help us with our monster hunt."

Eddie's subsequent frown was so deeply carved, his sandy chin seemed in danger of detaching from his face, but he made no move to stop the artist.

Wardric raised the brush again and stroked the air before his face, painting the rock from his perspective. Then he did it again. And again.

"I don't get it," he muttered, crestfallen.

Despite the attempt to crack it with magic, the boulder remained exactly the same. Eddie grunted and unsheathed his sword.

Bodkins raised a hand to stop him. "Stop! The enchantment won't help."

Eddie's eyes narrowed before realization dawned, and his hand went limp on the sword's hilt. "Sigeric built this! What? Why?"

Bodkins nodded and then shrugged. "I don't know what the competition's thinking, but I'd bet a year's bounties that tomb should stay sealed."

Florian followed the conversation with all the attention of a doodling student as he watched the monster circle a crowd. The dynamic of the situation changed while the mercs debated grave robbing.

The monster's gait shifted from circling to stalking, its mood went from playfully smug to tense, and its gaze finally swiveled over the crowd.

Something inside Florian's chest, previously held together by willpower and spite, crumbled to bits as he watched the scene. Dozens of armored adventurers stood, ready to fight, in a man-made clearing. Sunlight glinted off armor and swords as banners and robes fluttered in the breeze. It was as if something had transported Florian home to an Ava Triumphant dress rehearsal with all his friends and colleagues present.

A sudden weakness flooded his limbs as he wondered, first, when he would see his friends again, and second, where he (as Ava) would be if the scene in the woods was in the theater. If the scene was a battle, he would lead the charge, colorful skirts whipping in the wind. If it was an ambush, he would be in the center, sword raised and poised to take on the lot.

Meanwhile, Florian, the famous actor, a pathetic shadow of Ava Triumphant, sat on a stump beside a tomb and watched the real adventurers prep. On the whole, he considered himself a good person who gave to charity and voted his conscience. But had he ever done anything worthy of Ava Triumphant's reputation? Had he raised a sword to anything meaner than a wooden dummy in his life?

Florian swallowed the thought like collywobble tea and refocused on the mercenaries' mission. He didn't have time for another crisis.

Not for the first time since the armory, he was struck by the clarity of the monster's sight. Before, he interpreted blurry shapes. Now he saw details on people's costumes. One mage's robes had a floral pattern. A man in armor with a massive sword snuck cookies through his half-raised visor. It was as if each time the creature devoured magic, a semi-transparent veil lifted, and few veils remained between it and Naughtobelus.

One thing remained constant, however. The monster saw magic like he saw light. Bright blobs of magenta and orangey pink dotted the crowd of adventurers and flared when one of them cast a spell.

He noted the woman with bottles strapped on, as each bottle glowed with a different color, before the monster's head swiveled back and forth. It was like watching a field of fireflies, except for one spot—a wizard-filled section—where something dark as midnight loomed.

Florian leapt from his stump so fast it felt like he hovered beside it for a moment. He caught his balance and blurted at the mercs, "Wizards! Adventurers! And a dark spot! I think they've turned on the machine. The monster is panicking."

He was also panicking, but, thankfully, Bodkins was calm as ever. She wrapped a monster arm around his waist and ordered, "Get on," as if he had a choice.

"Who has the flyer?" she demanded as she hoisted Florian into the air.

Eddie produced it from a sandy pocket.

Florian tried not to think too hard about Eddie stashing items on his sandy person.

"Looks like the wizards are giving a demonstration at a clearing in the woods. We're way off the path, but I'd say it's to the right of us," Eddie said.

"Lead the way," Bodkins said and took off while Florian curled on her lap and covered his head.

"Why are we running?" Wardric whined from behind. A wheeze in his voice indicated that the pause at the tomb had not been enough.

"Because now we have two urgent goals," she replied. "We have to banish the creature before the wizards catch it and stop those adventurers from opening this tomb!"

Twenty-Nine

Gears and Goose Eggs

"Is it supposed to make that noise?" Growina asked.

Theo grunted, not in answer to her question, but as an acknowledgment that one was asked—as if a tiny receptionist inside his head took a memo for his brain to re-read later. That was just as well. The answer was all over his face, from his grinding teeth to his furrowed brow, and it was not the one Growina hoped for.

From where Team Wontmoil huddled together at the back of the crowd of adventurers, it was hard to get a good look at the cage or the noisy AMM beside it. Forty or fifty shifting people, most tall, broad, and heavily armed, blocked every viewpoint from the ground. And Chip already occupied the nearest tree with branches low enough to climb.

Growina desperately hopped about, conscious of her sloshing bandolier, but only managed a peek at a time.

"Does it look like it's working?" she asked Margaret, who had the decency to nod.

"Sounds like a bog lizard gargling gravel!" Vivienne shouted over the racket.

Sylvie made no observations. Instead, she slipped back into the trees, prompting the rest to step back as well. That left Chip as the only one with a decent view of the rattling cage.

Fortunately, the role of middleman was one with which he was well accustomed.

"The machine is fully functional, if a bit low-tech," he called from above in his grating voice. "The wizards are manually pumping oil to keep components from overheating, but the clamps attached to the cage are red hot. Amateur work and unstable to boot. The incantation is far too advanced for the chosen materials—but never fear! The Penumbral Magwod will smite the vile miscreants if their incompetence threatens innocent people."

Vivienne mouthed, "Vile miscreants?" to Growina, who suppressed a grin.

Oblivious, Chip continued commentating. "The wizards are congratulating each other. Premature, in my opinion. Looks like that machine is about to—hmm."

"Hmm?" Margaret asked. "What's hmm?"

A branch snapped behind them, and Growina spun, expecting to see Sylvie retreating further. Instead, she glimpsed a blurry shadow as something nimble darted between the trees.

She chewed her lip and turned back to her team. "Pardon the interruption, but we have company. I think the creature followed us here."

Theo held his gaze on the machine, or what little he could see of it, but his already thin lips turned a bright white.

Vivienne was far less focused. "Great. The creature? What next? A hurricane?"

A low rumble interrupted the machine's constant clatter, and a tremor shook the earth. Everyone stepped back except Vivienne, who pouted so fiercely that her mouth resembled a thin horseshoe.

Chip wrapped his arms around his tree and continued his high-pitched play-by-play. "Looks like that thing's about to pop! The clamps are melting right off the bars. Only question is, will the spell stop if the machine shakes free?"

Theo rejoined the conversation with a shake of his head, as if waking up from an afternoon nap to find the whole party in his room. "Eh? Stop? Absolutely not. Those wizards couldn't gracefully exit a barn with the doors flung open, much less an ancient incantation."

Margaret opened her mouth and shut it again, as if thinking better of her typical snark.

"If that's true," Chip said, "the Penumbral Magwod will position himself between the device and onlookers to minimize potential casualties."

"Casualties?" Margaret asked while simultaneously shimmying back. "You think it's going to explode-explode?"

Growina frowned. "What about Magwod? Won't he be harmed if the AMM bursts?"

Chip stuck out his chin and shook his head. "His armor is enchanted steel and double-thick. A diamond-edged axe couldn't scratch the surface."

"It might when the enchantment's gone," Theo said. "That spell will strip magic from anything in the blast radius."

"What?" The young man jumped up so fast that his head struck a branch above his perch, but a sudden boom muffled his cry of pain.

For a moment, all sound was sucked from the air in the Howling Woods, then it all came crashing back with a bang and high-pitched ring that made them all wince. The ringing resolved into screams of panic as adventurers trampled each other to leave.

Every member of Team Wontmoil stopped to check Growina's bandolier, on which many potions still happily glowed. Their anxious faces relaxed at the sight of magic not extinguished by the blast, but the bottles did nothing to comfort Chip.

He leapt from his tree and scrambled for the crowd, desperate to find a way through the chaos. "Help me!" he shouted as he struggled against the flow. "Magwod saved them all, but he's down. And I think . . . I think the armor failed. I need to get a better look!"

It seemed to Growina that the young man meant to say he needed to help, not look, but she was not about to pick on his phrasing while he shouted in distress. She and the others moved to form a human barrier with their bodies, and step by step, they inched the young man through the dwindling assembly.

Chip's face twisted in anxious concern, which made sense if his partner was injured or worse, but his voice seemed lower than usual as he side-stepped along with Team Wontmoil and said, "I need to prepare you for what you might see. It looked like his armor may have come free, or possibly even split in two."

Growina's stomach dropped at the thought of a man split in half at the waist.

Margaret nodded and spoke sincerely. "We're older than we look, kiddo. We've seen our share of battle wounds. Well, most of us have, anyway. Perhaps not the apothecary."

Definitely not the apothecary.

Chip shook his head. "No, that's not it. He . . . wha?"

The crowd parted to reveal what remained of the cage and affected adventurers. Though black smoke bellowed from the AMM and mechanical parts littered the ground, Magwod himself looked entirely unharmed. He sat on his rear before the machine, at the center of a chaotic pile of parts, his head slowly swiveling left to right.

Chip broke free and ran to him as the rest took a moment to survey the scene.

"And who is replacing my un-enchanted axe?" someone

screamed at cowering wizards.

"And my useless potions!" another cried.

"And my talking duck!" someone said, and held up a disgruntled mallard.

The front rows had taken the bulk of the hit from the out-of-control incantation, though Magwod deflected the actual blast. For all of his pompous posturing, the armored man lived up to the reputation Theo claimed he had. Except for a few minor injuries, most folks were more concerned about gear, but none thanked Magwod for his help.

Vivienne, of all people, noticed the heroism and stomped past the whiners to address Chip. "Aren't you gonna ask the guy if he's okay?"

"A . . . ask him?" the young man muttered and glanced at the copper components strewn across the grass.

Chip was just as stunned as Magwod, who looked to be regaining consciousness. The armored man opened and closed his fists with his fingers pressed awkwardly together, then stared intently at the open palms. Perhaps the silent giant realized his enchantments were gone after the blast, but he was not about to say so aloud.

"Anyone got a working treatment for a head wound?" a familiar voice asked, and Growina scanned the remaining adventurers until she spotted a couple she recognized.

Of the two women—a healer and warrior—only the healer remained upright. The two were semi-regulars at Herbs and Vices, small-time heroes making their name, but Growina never forgot a face.

She broke free of Team Wontmoil and hurried to help. "Is it a bump or a bleed?" she asked as she checked the bottles strapped to her bandolier.

"A big ol' goose egg," the healer said. "Bits burst from the cage and flew off *that* guy, and she got knocked in the noggin with a bolt."

Growina picked a purple potion and wrestled the cork off with her teeth. "Magwod, you mean? The guy in the armor? Stuff bounced off him and hit your partner hard enough to knock her out?"

"Flew off. Bounced off. Hard to say. Was a mess of smoke and robes while the wizards ran like the greedy cowards they are. Gimme that."

She swiped the bottle from Growina's hand and massaged the goopy contents into the warrior's scalp. It sizzled a bit, which was expected.

"Don't know how you lucked out with this," the healer said as she handed it back. "Even in my enchanted satchel, all my medicines turned to sludge. My bandages are usable, at least, though instead of being saturated in fast-healing ointment, they're now just unnecessarily moist."

Growina grimaced. "A friend said the anti-magic spell had a limited radius. I think I was safe at the back of the crowd."

"Smart choice. Smarter than us."

"Oh, no. Just late to the party."

The healer nodded back to Team Wontmoil, who huddled around the toppled Magwod. He slowly stood on trembling legs, then straightened, proud and tall as ever.

"That guy your friend?"

Growina bit her lip, unable to fib. "Not yet, but I suppose he may be soon."

"Watch out for him. He was actin' weird."

She raised a brow and corked her empty bottle, returning it to the bandolier. "How so?"

"You ever try to shake a snake from your dress?"

"N-no?"

"Well, imagine it. That's what it looked like he was doing inside his armor after he dropped."

Growina frowned. "Maybe he got hurt when the AMM burst?"

The healer shook her head. "I've seen a lotta people hurt. Watch out for that guy, is all I'm saying. And thanks for the potion."

"No problem at all. Thank you!" Growina said, though she was unsure what to make of the warning.

If the explosion injured Magwod, he needed sympathy, not suspicion. Yet she could not help looking him up and down as she approached and rejoined their conversation. Chip's high-pitched voice and attitude had returned, though his eyes narrowed every time Magwod moved.

The armored man stretched his limbs one at a time, as if testing them for injury. Perhaps that was what the healer saw?

Theo crossed his arms and scowled at Chip, then the armored giant. "But is he up for manual labor? Because we need help, and we're willing to split the bounty, however necessary."

"Please address the Penumbral Magwod as if he is the only one present!" Chip reminded him.

Vivienne rolled her eyes. "That's flipping difficult to do, isn't it? We're not even positive he's fully conscious!"

"Neither am I!" Chip shouted back, much to everyone's surprise.

He caught himself quickly and slapped a hand over his mouth, but Magwod didn't seem too bothered. The armored man set a hand on his shoulder, then punched a fist into the air—a clear sign he understood the assignment. It lowered Chip's anxiety some.

"The Penumbral Magwod accepts your offer," he said. "What do you have that requires his strength?"

Theo gestured back the way they came. "It's this way, and you may want to watch your back. We think the creature trailed us here."

The young man shrugged. "As you said before the blast. The Penumbral Magwod is unsurprised. He noticed your presence thrice while following the creature's trail. And try not to take this the wrong way, but he suspected *you* weren't the ones tracking *it*."

Margaret folded her arms. "What, exactly, is the right way to take that?"

Chip's life was saved by an ear-splitting howl from somewhere outside the smoke-filled clearing. Another followed from nearby, then a third from deep within the woods. Theo picked up his pace and ushered the team, which now numbered seven, away from the explosion site.

"Between us," he said in a half-whisper, "we've been onto something big for a while and suspect the creature wants us to stop. It's a lot to explain, and unfortunately, we're going to have to do so at a run."

"A run?" Vivienne asked. "Do you think the creature will attack?"

Theo shook his head. "No. Well . . . possibly. But no. There's something I forgot to mention about the anti-magic spell. Something I just now remembered from my first attempt."

A shriek of surprise from the clearing behind them caused everyone to jump and turn, but Theo gripped his hat and prepared to flee.

"Howling horrors really hate it."

THIRTY
The Buff Muffin Man

"Asking what I see every thirty seconds does not make the visions clearer!" Florian snapped as he clung to Bodkins' chair with his eyes squeezed shut.

"Sorry," Wardric muttered, deflated.

Florian sighed. It was not the big guy's fault that the visions were more frustrating. Nor could he blame the artist for his excitement. One did not have to be a soothsayer to hear the AMM explode or witness the mass exodus of frightened forest critters. Unfortunately, the following events were shrouded by smoke and human chaos, leaving Florian with only the barest sense of where the creature ended up.

"Visions still dim, then?" Bodkins asked.

"Like I'm viewing the forest through a keyhole, yes. The creature's emotions are strange as well."

Bodkins shifted beneath him, gripping and tugging his shoulder as she did. By some miracle, they had made it most of the way without her cracking his head on a tree, but the position he took to avoid disaster made it difficult for her to remain in place. It was one more frustration to add to the limited sight and secondhand discomfort.

"Define strange," she said with a grunt as she wriggled.

"It's an unfamiliar feeling, like getting pinned or squeezed, but as an emotion. Perhaps it's something unique to the beast?"

Bodkins snorted. "Sounds normal to me. You think somebody has it trapped?"

"I thought that at first. But I'm not getting fear or worry from the creature, and it seems to be moving under its own power. My best guess is that it's concealing itself in or under something for safety."

For the first time since the tomb, Eddie shook himself out of his thoughts and spoke up. "Stowing away, maybe? Like when Bodkins stores me in a box?"

"It would have to be a pretty big box," Wardric said with a laugh. "Or a bag like the one the boss has for fudgels."

Bodkins shook her head hard enough that Florian felt it. "Unlikely. My bag stores money on another plane of existence, and the creature is assembling itself into this one. I doubt it could travel to another place and remain in one piece in its current state. Although . . . hmm. Now that I've put those thoughts together, I wonder if my original assumption was wrong."

"Oh?" Florian asked, opening an eye long enough to peek at the underside of her thoughtful frown. She was pretty, for a merc, when forming a plan.

"What if it isn't building itself out of magic? What if it's a living creature trapped between worlds and eating magic to pull itself through? We have otherworldly visitors all the time, but never any self-made monsters, so it seems more probable. I can't think of a time it's happened, though, and all my history books are several cities away."

"I'm like a history book," Eddie said. "Old, dusty, and super biased."

Florian snickered.

Bodkins did not. "Can you remember a time when something like this happened?" she asked. "When something nasty got stuck between worlds?"

The three mercs crunched through fallen leaves while Eddie pondered the question.

"Not in real life, no. But there was an old play with that theme. *Burning the Broomstick* or something like that."

"*The Burning of Dorothea Broomhandle!*" Florian exclaimed before he could think better of it.

He expected Bodkins to come to a halt and glare down at him in confusion, but instead, Eddie said, "That's the one! You go to the theater?"

Florian squeezed his eyes tighter to stop them from rolling and mumbled, "Often."

"Oh, yeah!" Eddie said. "I remember now. You tried to use it as an escape plan. Hah. Do you remember what happened in that Broomhandle one? It's been a while for me, but I remember laughing."

"It's a tragedy," Florian said. "Based on the true story of a witch killed by her coven after she lost control of a multi-world familiar. But the play doesn't explain what she did to cause it. It's all flash and wild dancing instead because she took that information to her grave."

Bodkins snorted. "So, what? She could be spirit-stitched and back for vengeance. Maybe that's where our creature came from!"

"No, Broomhandle wasn't the vengeance sort. You'd understand if you watched the play. It really is a gut-wrenching story."

She nudged his shoulder with an elbow. "Maybe you can take me when you get your share of the bounty."

Florian jerked his head back and opened his eyes to see her wink and smirk down at him. He blanched. Was that a tease or a torment? Had she seen him sneak a peek at her smile?

Mercifully, Wardric interrupted before he had a chance to respond. "Who's that guy?" the artist asked, prompting Florian to turn to see.

A shirtless man as large as Wardric, with a sword in one hand and a muffin in the other, came at them, full speed, from the opposite direction.

"Ammph pwodeh!" he shouted. When no one replied, he swallowed his bite and slowed to wave them down. "AMM's exploded. Might as well head back."

"We're aware," Bodkins replied with more composure than Florian could have mustered. "Do you know which direction the creature fled?"

It was the man's turn to wrinkle his nose. "The creature?"

"Yes. The creature. The bounty. The thing we're here for. At least, I assume that's what you're here for, and you're not some sort of sword-wielding muffin bandit."

"Oooh, right. The creature. It wasn't there."

"It sure was!" Florian shouted.

Bodkins held up a hand to silence him and addressed the buff muffin man. "Why are you running?"

"Howling horrors."

"Seriously?" she scoffed. "You're a mercenary!"

"Adventurer," Wardric quietly corrected.

"Whatever. Why would you run from howling horrors?"

As if on cue, a howl erupted from somewhere in the woods, and the man shoved his muffin back into his mouth. "Mby," he said in apology and took off again without explanation.

Bodkins grumbled but started again toward the rising plume of smoke ahead. Just in case, she angled their path away from the howl, and Eddie brandished his enchanted sword.

Between their rapid acceleration and the imminent threat of a banged noggin, Florian nearly missed a moment of monster vision that was surprisingly clear again.

"Wait!" he cried, but the word was lost in the racket of monster feet in leaves. "Hold on! Stop!"

Bodkins slowed enough to listen, and he tried again.

"I saw something in the vision. The monster turned its head, and I think I saw . . . us."

All three members of the mercenary crew spun, frantically scanning the woods for the creature.

"Where?" Bodkins demanded. "Which direction?"

"I don't know. It was only for a moment and we were traveling fast. But we have a unique silhouette."

"So, it's behind us?" Eddie asked.

"I don't know."

Wardric raised a hand like a schoolchild. "Is it moving with us or away?"

"I don't know."

Florian screwed his eyes shut and begged the vision to give him something other than hazy trees. And for once, it obliged.

"I see a wizard's hat," he said. "A big dollop of a hat scuffed up enough to spot the dirt through the keyhole view."

"The wizards," Bodkins hissed. "They captured the creature."

"Can't be," Eddie said, and lifted a hand to point to something through the woods ahead. "I can see their broken cage from here."

He was right. In the haste to discuss the latest vision, Florian failed to notice how close they had come to breaching the clearing with the AMM. Nobody had to say a word before they all ventured toward it for a peek.

"I thought there was a whole crowd of adventurers," Wardric said as they cleared the trees. "But I only count six armed people, three cowering wizards, and eight howling horrors total."

"I guess the rest fled?" Florian suggested, but even he was confused by the sight.

Before the chaos, explosion, and inexplicable haze, there had been several dozen adventurers or more, all armed to the teeth and ready to fight. A battle with only eight howling horrors should have taken them under ten minutes, but the remaining six were overwhelmed.

"Hop off. I'm going to help," Bodkins said.

Florian obliged, happy for the option to climb down on his own.

Eddie looked apologetic. "I'd let you join in, but we need you to keep an eye on the bounty."

Florian shrugged. He never expected Eddie to offer since their last practice session left him on his behind, but it was nice of the sand man to pretend he could help. The sparring still bothered him, not because he had thought his onstage skills were a match for an experienced mercenary, but because he knew in his heart that he could do better.

What had changed so drastically in only a few days that he had gone from sword fighting horseback in a puffy dress to off-balance in the mud at the end of a blade?

Eddie, meanwhile, was exceptional. Sure, he had a lifetime and a half of practice, but he also used every advantage. When the first howling horror spotted the mercs and moved to attack the sandy man, he let it get close enough to swipe, then burst into a cloud of irritating grit, obscuring its vision as his sword came down.

Bodkins charged a pair of howling horrors fighting a single adventurer and delivered a monster-fisted punch that sent the nearest one sprawling into the grass. It was the first time Florian was seeing her fight, not having witnessed the battle at the barn, and it struck him how impossible it was that she could coordinate so many limbs. While wandering the streets, the chair seemed more like a lumbering mule than an agile beast, but in battle, it was slick and fierce, like a living monster with a merc at its heart.

"You going to help them?" he asked Wardric, who stood beside him as still as a statue.

Wardric shook his head. "Naw. I'm not really a hands-on fighter."

"Can't you paint on a howling horror to stop it? Tie it up with ropes or something?"

Wardric shook his head even harder. "I don't paint on anything moving. If I mess up, well, I don't want to think about it."

Florian closed his eyes to watch the still-hazy creature vision for a moment. "You won't mess up. I've seen your precision."

"Nice of you to say," the big guy muttered, then quickly found a new topic of discussion. "What do you think those wizards are up to?"

Florian opened his eyes to watch the wizards shuffle around their burned-out device, hats lowered as they picked through parts in the grass. Now that Wardric pointed it out, something about them seemed suspicious, but he could not quite put his finger on it. Perhaps it was their hurried movements or the fact that they did not bother to fight when they were, in theory, adventurers.

Wardric seemed to read his mind. "It's like they're more concerned with fixing their thingy than helping other people survive, not that I'm really one to talk. And aren't there more than there were before?"

The artist was not wrong. There had been three wizards when they arrived, but six now hovered around the machine, three without their telltale hats. And oddly, not all of them wore robes. It was not until one of them spread their arms that Florian saw the embroidered books and staggered to his feet to warn the others.

"Those aren't wizards!" he shouted, but it was too late.

He could do nothing but watch, mouth agape, as cultists ran off with the AMM.

Thirty-One
Cracked Eggs and Cold Gruel

If Growina were the gossip-loving sort with zero sense of self-preservation, she might have assumed that Magwod and Sylvie were flirting as they searched for the boulder. Fortunately, she was oblivious to all but the most cringe-worthy courtship rituals, so she understood the situation as two silent adventurers unused to sharing the role who were now having a surreptitious spat.

Sylvie tilted her head enough to peek past her hood at the armored giant, pale eyes inadvertently alerting him to her scrutiny. In response, the large man looked down as if watching his step in treacherous mud. In his armored helmet with thin slits for eyes, that meant turning his entire face downward.

To Growina, who was watching it repeat ad nauseam from her place at the back of the group, it was clear the act was deliberate. Every ten to twenty steps, the witch chewed her lip, tried again, and failed to look the large man in the eyes.

But why?

The other four team members missed the exchange as they hustled along, squabbling. It had been ages since anyone heard a howl close enough to be a threat, but Margaret, Theo, and Chip were equally prone to bossing others about. Each was, therefore, determined to prove themselves the most capable leader.

Vivienne, being who she was, had no inclination for leadership but instigated, nonetheless. "Did I hear something scuttling by?" she asked, then waited to see what the others would do.

Chip took the bait. "The Penumbral Magwod—"

"Needs to save his energy for the task at hand!" Theo interrupted. "I have enough Fang Lock to deal with a measly howling horror."

Margaret groaned. "Nothing's howling. Viv is messing with you. Keep walking."

"Am not!" Vivienne insisted.

Theo turned to glare, caught his hat on a low-hanging branch, and had to double back for it. "I have Leadfeather for pixies as well. Not that we want to mess with pixies, but if we must."

"Nothing is there!" Margaret repeated.

"Okay," Chip said. "But, should something—"

Margaret spun and waved her arms. "Don't humor her."

"Oy!" Vivienne whined. "I'm serious. Something's scuttling out there."

Chip stopped walking, squinted, and pointed into the trees. "Is that the hill you're looking for? The one with the big rock on one side?"

Theo froze. "Hmm. Yes."

The team approached the boulder as one, disrupting Sylvie and Magwod's routine.

Chip leaned close to examine it. "Please tell me you didn't drag us here so the Penumbral Magwod can shift the rock."

"Of course not," Theo confirmed. "We need him to break it. Quickly, if possible."

Chip's lips twisted in an expression somewhere between smug superiority and pity for the wizard, as if he could not decide which reaction would cause the most emotional harm.

"None of you are powerful enough to split a boulder? Isn't that kid stuff?"

"Watch it, brat!" Vivienne snapped.

Margaret brushed her back with one arm. "Magic isn't effective on it. The running theory . . ." She met Theo's gaze to gauge his reaction before divulging the rest of their secret. " . . . is that the boulder is cursed with anti-magic."

"From all the way over there?" Chip tilted his head toward a thin curl of smoke above the trees. "Unlikely."

Theo winced and rubbed his bruised head. "It's nothing to do with those brainless weasels and their broken apparatus. We're looking at a spell cast long ago—possibly during the Gart Splagosion."

"Ahh," Chip said with a nod before reconsidering and shaking his head. "The what?"

Theo scoffed. "Did you learn a single scrap of world history in your travels, or were you too busy shouting at everyone?"

Growina thought the question a tad harsh.

Chip shrugged. "History is dull. Math and science are far more interesting. Let's see you take something complex apart and put it back together again. I'll count the parts left over when you're done."

"If we *must* take something apart," Margaret said with an artificial sweetness before holding up the chisel and hammer, "let's start with this rock."

The young man crossed his arms. "The Penumbral Magwod hasn't agreed to—"

His mouth snapped shut as the metal giant took the tools from the witch. It seemed even Magwod was tired of the bickering. That was a relief to Growina, who found confrontation about as comfortable as a woolen nightgown full of baby spiders.

Magwod searched the boulder for the optimal crevice to plant the chisel, wedged it with a hammer tap, and swung his arm back to deliver a blow.

It was important to note that everyone expected Magwod to be extremely strong. One does not spend one's life tromping across Naughtobelus in full armor and battling baddies without the musculature required to support said gear.

However, no one—including the Penumbral Magwod himself—expected to see the chisel disappear into the splintering stone on impact, followed by the hammer and the greater part of Magwod's forearm.

The entire party jumped in surprise, apart from Magwod, who, true to character, simply pulled his fist from the boulder with a horrible screech of steel-on-stone. He tilted his head to examine the hole he had inadvertently punched in the hollow rock, then shoved both hands into the crack. One tug split the thing like an egg, allowing him to roll the halves apart.

Beneath, a brick-encircled well with a rusted ladder descended into darkness.

"Nuh-uh," Vivienne said. "Nope. Not going down there. I'll stay up here and keep watch."

Theo made his way to the well and tested the sturdiness of the ladder. "Keep watch for what, exactly?"

"I'd imagine for them," Growina said, drawing everyone's attention to the semi-circle of singed wizards that emerged from the trees without warning.

"Told you I heard scuttling," Vivienne muttered.

"Theodore, my old friend!" the tallest, lankiest wizard declared as he broke away from the pointy-hatted pack. "I knew you were hiding something important!"

"No, you didn't," Theo shot back.

The response threw the lanky one off his stride. "Well, I had a hunch. After following you for a while. And watching the big one smash that rock."

"Brilliant."

Theo began his descent into the well as if the wizards were inconsequential.

The lanky one waved his robed arms. "Well?" he asked.

Theo harumphed. "What?"

"Aren't you going to explain yourself?"

"No."

The singed wizard balked again at the dismissal. "But . . . there's eight of us and only seven of you."

Theo took another step down. "That isn't the threat you think it is."

"But your seven includes a talentless teenager and . . . wait . . . is that the local apothecary?"

Growina gave a sheepish nod, embarrassed by the wizard's implication despite the assortment of defensive potions strapped in the bandolier over her chest.

Theo waved a hand dismissively. "I wasn't saying you would lose a fight. I mean, you would. But your threats are pointless anyway because the bank's constructs have pre-programmed scruples. They won't pay out if you rough us up to gain an advantage and claim the bounty. And no reward means no compensation for the angry shop owners caught up in your scam. So, go on. Shoo. Leave us alone. Come up with original ideas for once."

It was a good point and very well put, but the wizard's association was not famous for their rational and honorable behavior.

Lanky gave the argument a moment of thought, then crossed his arms and glared at Theo. "Who said anything about a fight, eh? Nobody here wants a fight. Certainly not us. But this is public land, is it not? You don't own that well over there. And you can't stop us from following you down to peek at whatever's hidden inside."

"Want to bet?" Vivienne snapped.

A piercing howl interrupted the violence she planned.

Theo moaned and rubbed his bruised head. "You brought the howling horrors *with you?*"

A shorter wizard with ruddy cheeks scratched his patchy beard and mumbled, "We thought they'd calm down when the machine shut off."

"They're howling horrors," Margaret said, "not howling perfectly reasonable gents!"

"Actually," Growina interrupted with a timid hand raised. "I don't think—and mind you, my field of expertise is flora, not fauna—but I don't think that was a howling horror. It sounded a bit cheeky for a beastie."

"Cheeky?" Margaret asked.

Another howl sounded from the woods. A high-pitched giggle followed it.

"Also, I don't believe howling horrors giggle," Growina said. "Though, again, I'm not an expert."

"Show yourselves!" Lanky demanded of the empty air.

A young man with a crossbow obliged, slipping silently from behind a tree.

Growina recognized him instantly. "It's the all-seeing one!" she said. "Hello."

"You," the young cultist replied. "Where's the spoon? And no tricks this time. I haven't forgotten your sleepy soup."

"Oh, dear. I'm afraid we really don't have your spoon. See, we're after this creature that eats magic—"

"I said no tricks! You're lucky I'm the one who found you first. I just want the Spoon of Glarblarkle back. Please? The cold gruel we're eating tastes like crushed gravel. I don't know how much longer I can take it."

Growina nodded to show sympathy. "That sounds terrible,

and I wish I could help. But I have to ask—is it necessary to eat cold gruel? Couldn't one of you learn to cook? I know a recipe for baked zucchini with herbs and a sprinkle of aged cheese."

"The spoon! Now! Or I let the others deal with you. They're pretty sore about the defacement of our sacred statue."

"Defacement!" Vivienne snorted. "Because we removed part of his face! I get it." When the young man did not respond, she grimaced. "You weren't making a joke, were you?"

He leveled his crossbow at her. "Tell me where the spoon is before the others arrive, and you *might* get out of this alive."

The lanky wizard cleared his throat as if suddenly realizing he was lumped in with Team Wontmoil and not watching the drama from afar. He crossed his arms over his chest and stuck his bearded chin toward the young man.

"Big words for a little guy. Do you think a few religious weirdos will scare the wizard's association and . . . whatever those folks consider themselves?"

Theo pursed his lips.

"Well, for starters," the young man said, "there are far more of us than you."

When Lanky opened his mouth, presumably to copy Theo's earlier insult, the young man held up a finger to silence him.

"And, perhaps more importantly . . . we have your exploding machine."

Thirty-Two

Wone Gess

IN THE PERIOD known as the Experimental Age, long before the events of the Gart Splagosion, there lived a fine artist who went by the name of Digby Slobberstone. Though best known for his elaborate renditions of rustic barns painted exclusively on the broadsides of rustic barns, Slobberstone was semi-famous as an inventor of useless objects.

His slotted soup spoons and inverse doorknobs remained staples of Naughtobelus novelty shops for centuries after his premature death. Still, no one had ever summoned the courage to fabricate, much less test, his bathrobe bat wings.

No one, that was, until Vivienne flicked an index finger toward a charging cultist and sent them flying like a wriggling discus, saved only by the wind trapped in their robes.

Vivienne found the results disappointing.

"Adrshkk!" the lanky wizard shouted at a butter knife-wielding attacker, who went rigid and toppled like a chopped pine.

Growina crept toward the center of the party, closer to the well where Theo stood, two rungs down and too flabbergasted to emerge. Her fingers drifted to her bandolier, brushing one bottle after another as she tried—and failed—to justify their use.

Perhaps the nasty wizards were right; she was not cut out

for adventuring. Maybe only genuine heroes could ignore the guilt of injuring a misguided opponent.

"This is preposterous," Theo muttered, as if reading her mind. "All this over a cursed utensil? They need to get their priorities straight."

Growina hefted her skirts and crouched beside him to make herself audible over the din and become a smaller target for the cultists.

"Could we promise to make them a new magic spoon?" she asked. "To replace the one the monster ate?"

He ground his teeth. "Maybe if I had a few months and access to an expert in inter-world conjuring."

He paused while a young wizard struggled through a spell that sounded like a draining bathtub. Based on the noise, Growina expected a spray of water from the wizard's hands or a sudden rain cloud overhead. But the spell caused bushy patches of indigo fur to sprout from one of the cultists' ears.

It certainly gave its victim a pause, but a sag in the little wizard's shoulders told her it was not the intended effect.

"I don't want to bore you with the specifics," Theo fibbed. "But as they say, matter produced is matter spent. Either a sacrifice of equal volume is necessary to fill the spoon every time they use it to eat, or it must transfer the food from another world. Which is, of course, the preferable method. I'm ashamed to say I've dabbled very little in the technique. I'm terrified of conjuring something unexpected."

Growina fought the urge to grimace.

"In any case, I suspect these fools lack the patience to wait that long for uncertain results."

He was right. Even as they spoke, another dozen malnourished cultists emerged from the woods, flushed with rage and hunger. Most clutched blades and makeshift staves, but a few gripped tomes that appeared to startle the handful of wizards who could read the titles.

Margaret swept past in a swirl of fabric. "The assailants have their own mages! Time to form a defensive circle!"

At her words, the witches joined hands in a triangle formation. Fortunately, everyone present was too busy or sensible to correct the name and earn their wrath. The wizards focused on the cultists, and the cultists focused on the wizards—who now formed an accidental barrier by arriving to harass Team Wontmoil first.

"Gninthgil eht nommus i!" a tome-bearing cultist screeched, and a bolt of blue lightning struck a wizard.

"Adrshkk!" the lanky wizard said again, with similar results to his previous spell.

"Sgorf fo niar!" another cultist cried.

"Meeozwaa!" Lanky shot back.

"Yeep!" Theo said.

It took Growina a moment to realize it was not a spell but the sound of the well-dressed wizard losing his footing on an antique ladder.

The subsequent thud was harder to confuse with a garbled wizard's curse.

She jumped to her feet and pointed in the well's direction. "Theo's fallen! He may be hurt! Theo, are you okay?"

As hard as she strained to hear a response over the sound of shouting battlers, none came from the darkness below. She desperately looked to Chip and Magwod, who drew closer at her call, but something in the way the metal man moved made her question his ability to help. The great Penumbral Magwod had not drawn his sword to defend the team and seemed incapable of doing so. His arms flexed spasmodically as he approached, fists clenching and unclenching as if the double damage from the AMM and smashed boulder had injured him more than he expressed.

Not that he expressed much, but the point stood.

Even Chip seemed deflated. Instead of declaring something brazen on behalf of his companion, he nodded at the well and wrung his hands.

"Er . . . how deep is it? Do you know? Can you see where he landed?"

Growina opened her mouth to inform him that the well was dark as a cloudy night, and unless he had matches hidden in his pockets, his guess was as good as hers. But a single glance inside the well silenced the thought.

Now that she was closer to the opening, it was not pitch black after all. The top section of stones glistened with reflected pinks, purples, and greens—illuminated by the potions on her bandolier.

She chewed her lip and swallowed her fear. "You know what? I'll go check."

Before she could talk herself out of it, she swung onto the ladder and descended. The journey took longer than she preferred on a ladder older than her shop, but was not as long as she had dreaded.

The bottom of the well was suspiciously devoid of injured wizards.

"Theo?" she called into a tunnel lit only by her potions and a smattering of the lichen.

"Hmm?" he responded from somewhere ahead, as if lost in concentration.

Her shoulders sagged with relief. Typical Theo.

"He's okay!" she called up the ladder.

"We're not!" Chip shouted back. "We're surrounded. The Penumbral Magwod and I are coming down!"

Magwod's shins clanged against the ladder as he climbed, but the injured man made it down without incident, followed by Chip and all three witches.

Once everyone was accounted for, Margaret pointed upward. "We need to seal it until the battle is over. Same as we did with the shop."

"Not without us, you don't!" someone called from above.

Everyone groaned as the lanky wizard and a single dazed companion thudded unceremoniously to the earth.

"Fine. Whatever," Vivienne snapped. "Get out of our way."

The witches held their hands toward the well's opening, only for Lanky to interrupt again.

"Halt! There are more of us up there!"

Margaret rolled her eyes. "And about fifty cultists looking to smash our heads over a missing spoon. Move aside."

"Make me!"

"Can do!" Vivienne cried, and before Margaret could stop her, she flicked both arms in the wizard's direction, sending him—and a concerning number of stones from the sides of the well—flying.

The results were horrifying and predictable at the same time. A crack echoed through the tunnel, alerting the adventurers to the well's imminent collapse just in time for everyone to retreat into the tunnel. Centuries of dust and loose dirt billowed in the seemingly eternal time it took for the stones to tumble inward, blocking their exit entirely.

Finally, when everything settled enough to see, Theo poked his head out from around a bend. "Not how I would have done it, but it'll keep them busy for a while."

Margaret rubbed her eyes.

"So," Lanky croaked, lungs still choked with dust and battered from Vivienne's semi-provoked attack. "What have we found?"

"*We?*" Vivienne began.

Theo hushed her with a wave. "Come along. We'll need all the eyes and brains we can get."

He led the party, now comprising three wizards, three witches, an apothecary, a teenager, and a limping armored giant, through a series of branched tunnels marked with arrows made of glowing lichen.

It took Growina a moment to realize Theo had made the marks himself by navigating the entire underground maze to its conclusion before the rest of them even entered the tunnels.

Rude but impressive.

However, the challenge that waited beyond the maze made it look amateurish.

Theo set his hands on his hips. "I'd like to get your initial impressions before I taint your ideas with my own."

Growina decided not to share her initial thought, as it was an uncouth word considered taboo in most professional environments.

Before them, a sleek marble wall displayed fifty medallions propped up on corroded pegs. Each bore unique pictograms with seemingly no relation between them. Beneath, six slots big enough for one medallion each formed a repeating mathematical equation:

(space) plus (space) minus (space)—twice.

Other than the cryptic equations, the only instruction for the puzzle was a single phrase carved into the marble:

WONE GESS.

Lanky refused to be outsmarted by Theo, who he considered an inferior dropout. He adopted a smug and unbothered posture that clashed with his singed and dusty appearance and waved a hand toward the puzzle wall.

"Clearly, it's some kind of letter scramble. We rearrange the letters to form a spell that will reveal which medals go in which slots."

Theo grunted but let the others speak, true to his word.

"Naw," Vivienne said. "It's more of that Gart Splagosion

babble. Won gess. One guess. We get one try at this thing, and no hints. We're doomed."

"I'm sorry," Lanky's otherwise timid companion said. "Did you say Gart Splagosion? What does this have to do with the Gart Splagosion?"

Margaret groaned. "There's too much to explain. All the clues leading up to this had terrible spelling. So that, combined with the age of this garbage, led us to believe it was all created during the Gart Splagosion—where, as they say, the sky erupted in flames, inanimate objects revolted, and everyone lost the ability to spell."

"I thought you were chasing the monster!" Lanky whined. "Are you telling me we're down here for no reason? You're on a mundane treasure hunt?"

Theo caved and broke his silence. "It's all linked. You see, we found the first clue while chasing the creature, hidden behind an invisible door it was trying to get into. And it beat us to all the other clue locations, too. The one in the stone with hidden pockets. The one in the cultist's lair, where it ate their disgusting spoon. Of course, now that I'm saying all this out loud, I can't help but think I've missed something obvious."

"Of course you have!" Lanky shouted. "It's a magic-eating monster, and you've followed it to locations with magic for it to eat. You're a flipping fool, and I'm an even bigger one for thinking you had a lead."

Theo paled and moved his mouth like a fish before straightening and raising a finger. "Except! This last location had anti-magic! Why would a magic-eating creature be here if not to stop us from reaching our goal?"

The timid wizard pointed to a dark corner where Chip was doting over Magwod like a nurse. "Is that why you had the brute smash the boulder instead of doing it yourself?

We figured you were too weak to cast the spell."

The implication that the wizards thought Theo was inept, and the additional implication that he might not be after all, set both Theo and Lanky off, sparking further arguments that deviated wildly from the puzzle before them.

But Growina's focus was on Magwod.

The man sat in the darkest part of the room, far from the glow of Growina's bottles. His limbs hung limp, and his head sank low against his chest. Even stranger, Chip hovered about with a tool in his hand, tapping and tinkering with Magwod's armor instead of checking his vital signs.

"Let me guess," Lanky shouted, drawing everyone's attention again. "This puzzle wall has anti-magic, too. So, there's no way through without solving it, is there?"

"Wish the well had some," Vivienne muttered.

Theo bristled. "You're welcome to try walking through. I believe the apothecary has a potion to re-set your teeth when you're done."

"Growina," said Growina, just in case Theo needed another reminder.

"You're welcome to try walking through my fist," said the lanky and very mature wizard. "How do we solve a puzzle with no clues?"

"Well," Sylvie said, silencing the room, "you haven't asked my opinion yet."

Everyone quieted, and the pale-eyed witch grinned.

THIRTY-THREE
Saving Faces

"THEY'RE TRAPPED IN there with it!" Florian blurted, to the surprise of his otherwise quiet companions.

He also attempted to sit upright, which was a terrible plan for someone laying across a spirit-stitcher's lap in a chair propelled by monster limbs. It earned him a smack and a stream of curses before Bodkins recovered from the scare.

"Don't *do* that!" she scolded. "What did you see?"

He sucked in a breath and readjusted his hips, then tried to recall everything from his visions. The monster's sight had remained blurry while the mercenaries bested the pack of howling horrors and headed back the way they came.

"There was a cave-in. Wait. Sorry. First, I think the mismatched adventurers moved the boulder tomb thing we saw earlier. I didn't see most of that because of the howling horror that tried to eat my face when you ignored it. In any case, there was a hole in the ground, and a cave-in happened inside the hole. Now the monster has the adventurers trapped, and it's hungry as ever."

"I don't follow," Wardric admitted. "How did they move the boulder? That thing was as tall as I am."

Florian craned his neck to look at the artist, who strode alongside Bodkins' chair like a paintbrush-covered bodyguard.

"I haven't a clue. I focused on my own vision to avoid losing my face to a beast with huge claws and horrible breath."

"Quit whining," Eddie said. "I took care of it, didn't I? 'Sides, that face of yours is too plain. A few scars might add some character!"

"I'm partial to my face as is, thank you very much."

Bodkins shushed them both. "This is the same mismatched group you saw when we were in Wontmoil? A wizard in a suit, a few witches, and an older lady with bottles?"

"Mostly. They picked up more wizards recently and I spotted a teenager with them, too. I swear, they're like the fearsome geese of the adventuring world."

"I'm lost again," Wardric said. "Fearsome geese?"

Florian sighed. "It's a children's play about a fake beeveball team made entirely of kids rejected by pro teams. None of them are born players, but they all have unique skills, etcetera, etcetera. Heartwarming show. Lots of physical comedy. Not very cerebral. But kids love it."

"Oh!" Wardric said. "Like us! We're fearsome geese!"

Florian thought about it, scowled, and reluctantly nodded his agreement.

"Assuming they won," Wardric corrected. He looked like he might burst into tears at any moment. "They won, right?"

"They won."

"Was it dirt or rock?" Bodkins asked.

"Pardon?"

"The cave-in. Was it dirt or rock that fell?"

"Uh . . ." He scrunched up his nose and tried to remember what little he had seen of the collapsing tunnel before clouds of debris extinguished the light. "I want to say rocks. Lots of them."

"That's gonna take some time to shift. Hope your geese have that much time."

"Not a problem!" Eddie said. "If it's rocks, I can sneak through the cracks between them!"

Bodkins tsked. "Magic holds your body together, and your opponent gobbles it up. How do you see *that* rescue going?"

"It's gotta get by my sword first."

"Your sword. Which is *also* enchanted and won't fit through rocks."

Eddie made a noise that was either an annoyed hiss or a fistful of his own sand thrown toward Bodkins. Either way, it was impressively immature. Bodkins was right, though. They would have to clear the debris before they reached the gee—the adventurers. And who knew if the odd little group had that much time?

Then again, if the monster meant to harm them, wouldn't it have done so already?

"Hold on," he said, closing his eyes. "Something isn't adding up. Let me get a look around."

Even after the dust settled, it was difficult to see through the monster's eyes. But glowing moss lit the scene well enough to pick out some details. The adventurers were in a heated discussion beside a wall covered in shimmering dots. They pointed to one after another before debating each selection.

"It's hiding in the dark," he said. "Watching them. Waiting. I think it's anticipating something."

"Waiting for them to separate?" Wardric asked with a slight tremor in his voice. "So it can eat them, one by one?"

"It eats magic, not people," Bodkins said. ". . . Assuming we aren't too late. I figure it's more likely to maul them in its current state."

"Can we please not discuss their gruesome demise while I'm trying to focus on their behavior?" Florian asked.

"Right. Sorry," Wardric mumbled. "You're the soothsayer."

Florian pressed his hands to his eyes and tried to decipher

the adventurers' conversation through their body language alone. One witch pointed to some words above the dots, then two dots in different rows. She brought her hands together as if smashing something between them, then made chopping motions in the air. It was an oddly familiar ritual, but not one he associated with magic.

Florian had made the same motions many times as a child.

"This is going to sound silly," he said, "but I think they're playing a game."

"Eh?" Bodkins asked.

"When I was a kid—"

"Here we go," Eddie groaned.

Florian ignored him. "My parents and I played a vocabulary-building card game. It had a deck of cards with words printed on them and several decks with only pictures. Someone flipped over a random word card, and everyone assembled a sequence of pictures that spelled a synonym for that word. For example, if you took the word 'booth' and added the word 'air,' then removed the word hair from 'boothair,' you got 'boot.' Winners received one point for finishing first, two for picking the most obscure synonym, and three for using the fewest picture cards. The fun was trying to accomplish all three, so you earned six points every turn."

"Doesn't sound very fun to me," Wardric said.

Eddie was even less enthused. "Ugh! That's a kids' game now? In my day, it was brilliant encryption. It stumped the king's smartest advisers. I feel so old I could crumble to dust."

Bodkins shook her head. "Let me get this straight—"

"Get it? To dust?"

She paused her chair, got her bearings in the woods, and continued without responding to Eddie. "The geese are in a hole. In the dark. With the monster. Playing a card game?"

Florian blanched. "Oh, no. They're solving a massive

puzzle on a wall at the end of a tunnel. It only reminded me of the card game."

She clucked her tongue and brushed vines away from her face. "You're a talented soothsayer, Peterman, but you need to work on your communication skills."

"I'll have you know, my communication skills are some of the best in—" He paused, took several deep breaths, and started over. "You're right. I could have been clearer in that specific instance."

Bodkins' chair halted so suddenly he was sure his outburst offended her. His stomach tightened, a sure sign that he cared enough to not want to.

When had that mental shift happened?

Florian glanced at Wardric, who was reaching for a pre-dipped paintbrush, and realized they had not stopped due to his accidental offense.

He glanced around at the large cluster of robed individuals and gulped.

"You could have mentioned there was an army between us and our target," Wardric said through the side of his mouth.

"What's that?" Eddie. "The great soothsayer Peterman failed to notice an army?"

"Again," Florian said. "Howling horror. Eating my face!"

Bodkins scowled and whispered, "Stealth time."

Eddie dispersed into a cloud, and the subtle sound of sand peppering leaves filled the silence around the mercs.

But not for long.

"State your business!" a young man declared.

Florian spun, heart pounding. Where on Naughtobelus had the young man come from? He certainly was not there a second before.

Bodkins, who lacked the social skills drilled into Florian by the theater, simply snapped, "How long have you been there?"

The fellow, who appeared to be one of the raiding cultists, sighed. "Two, maybe three minutes."

"Nonsense. I didn't see you."

"I get that a lot. They call me the all-seeing one because nobody pays attention to me, even when I'm right in front of them."

"Ah," Bodkins said.

The young man rolled his eyes and took on a mocking tone. "Why, yes. It is a terribly lonely life. Thank you for caring."

"Terribly sorry," Florian said, to smooth things over.

The young man raised a judgmental brow, reminding Florian that he was still lying across Bodkins' lap.

His cheeks warmed. "It's not what you think."

"I don't care," the young man replied. "Please, just state your business here. It's been a very long day, and we're all a bit hangry."

Bodkins looked to Wardric, who shrugged. She then turned to Florian with an expression that asked, "Do we tell him?"

It was nice to be consulted as a genuine team member, but real-time battle strategy was not the sort of improvisation Florian was accustomed to. He shook his head, nodded, and shook his head again, unsure which answer was the least likely to land them on the cultist's bad side.

"We already spoke to one of your colleagues," Bodkins said as she scanned the sea of mismatched cultists gathered a good distance ahead. "We're mercenaries from Leechleif hunting a local bounty. I assume this is the raid she mentioned?"

The young man visibly relaxed and nodded. "That it is. What's your destination? I can show you the best route around our battleground."

"I'm not sure how to describe it. We're looking for a hill in the woods ahead. It used to have a distinctive boulder, but now there's a caved in hole in the ground."

Something feral flashed in the young man's eyes, and his demeanor changed. "You need to leave. Right now."

Bodkins tightened her grip on her chair as if she had expected the reaction and was ready for an argument. "We don't have that luxury. We have a job to do."

"Then you need to wait here until our raid is over."

Her fingernails dug into the wood like talons, and her voice took on a low growl. "Waiting isn't an option, either. Our bounty grows more dangerous by the minute."

"Well, then. Your funeral." He abruptly reversed into the nearest cover.

Bodkins swore. "Wait! Kid!"

It was no use. Florian rolled off Bodkins' lap and took his place behind her chair. He did not need soothsayers' magic to know what would happen next.

Beside him, Eddie reassembled feet first and crossed his arms. "I think that went well," he said with a smirk. "Don't you?"

Thirty-Four

Sing Beetle Beet

"This is a waste of time!" the lanky wizard complained, voice echoing around the cave. "The wizard's association should charge you all for lost revenue, abduction, and . . . and . . ."

"Intellectual theft?" the ruddy wizard offered. "They've trapped us here and forced us to provide solutions for their puzzles."

"That they have!"

Vivienne assumed a mocking tone. "Oh, but remember? This is public land! We don't own the well. And we could hardly stop you from following us down to get a peek."

"Furthermore, your so-called solutions are rubbish," Theo added.

The lanky wizard gasped as if struck and gathered his robes around him. "We'll see what you say when we save your party and you're still playing picture games."

He stormed to where the ruddy wizard sat with a hovering flame in hand. The two had several crossed-out phrases scratched into the dusty ground, and Lanky deliberately positioned himself so the others could not see what they wrote. No one minded since the two were still convinced the puzzle's solution involved an uttered spell, which would deviate from the puzzle maker's established pattern thus far.

Theo took several calming breaths to prove the wizards' nitpicking could not get to him. It had the opposite effect.

"I've completely lost my place," he said. "Where were we? Oh! Yes. One guess. We're all in agreement that the first word—one—is solved, and we're moving on to guess?"

Everyone raised a hand in agreement except the grumpy wizards and Chip, who still hovered around Magwod like a persistent gnat.

Sylvie nodded and set three medallions on the ground before the equations. The first medallion depicted a human head with wavy lines and music notes emanating from the mouth. They were pretty sure the second was a beetle, though no one could agree on the type. And the final medallion had an illustration of a freshly plucked beet, leaves and all.

"As long as we're positive it's not a turnip," Margaret said, second-guessing her agreement.

Growina beamed. Of all the challenges the party faced, identifying root vegetables was the easiest. "Oh, yes. Absolutely. Notice how the bulb, root, and stem look darker than the leaves? A turnip would have lighter stems and roots and a squat shape to differentiate it from a rutabaga."

Margaret nodded. "You're giving the illustrator too much credit, but I believe you. So, we have the word sing plus beetle minus beet. Singbeetle becomes single, which is a synonym for one. Any guesses for the word guess?"

"Prediction?" Theo offered. "Conjecture? Postulation?"

"Slow down," Vivienne said. "You're making her dizzy."

It was true. Every synonym for guess sent Sylvie scurrying and plucking medallions from the wall. She paused to rub perspiration from her brow, frowned at the selected pictures, and put two back where they came from. Growina felt awful watching the witch pick all the pictograms, but Margaret insisted each team member had something unique to contribute—except the wizard's association members. They were useless as ballet slippers for snakes.

Theo's role was vocabulary, and he was perhaps a bit too skilled. Unlike the witches, who performed magic with emotion, wizards (and similar mages) crafted spells with words. They studied for years, translating and encoding, until they found a phrase to alter reality in demonstrable and repeatable ways.

If there was one thing Growina had learned in her lifetime, it was never to ask either which method was best.

Patience, on the other hand, was not one of Theo's skills. His lips tightened as he waited, straining to hold in additional guesses, but he remained quiet for Sylvie's sake. Only Chip's worried tinkering, the wizards' scribbling, and a persistent "pop-pop" interrupted the silence.

The pop-pop sound was a metaphorical ticking clock, reminding them that an army of cultists might dig their way through the collapsed well at any moment.

"Hypothesis!" Theo shrieked when Sylvie stopped searching and set medallions back on their pegs.

She chewed her lip and returned to the wall, plucking pictures faster than ever.

Everyone crowded close as she held up images of a hyphen and an otter, then sagged in defeat.

"It would require more pictograms than we have slots in the equation," Margaret interpreted. "We need a shorter word. Or a longer one made up of other long words."

"Guess *is* the short word!" Theo whined, but he already knew it was the wrong answer.

A clatter at the back of the room made them all jump.

Chip stood, over the slumped form of Magwod, shaking so severely that his tools slipped from his hands.

"Excuse me a moment," Growina said and made her way

to the teen.

He saw her coming and bent to retrieve his tools, slipping them into a pocket before she could get a look.

"How is he?" she asked.

His brows pinched in thought as if he could mask his concern. "Not good. He's unconscious, and I can't figure out why."

Growina's stomach sank at the recollection that she had used her only healing potion on a stranger in the woods. Why didn't she save it for her teammates like a sensible person? And why did she think a variety of potions would be more useful than extra healing? This was why no one invited her out.

Who wanted a team member they could easily replace with potions and the Lazy Botanist's Guide to Naughtobelus?

"I'm not a medical doctor," she said, "but it seems he's fairly badly injured."

"Yes, I know. But if he was this bad after the AMM explosion, why did he collapse *now* and not back then? It makes no sense."

She sighed. "Some stubborn people try to push through injuries, but it always catches up to them, eventually." She fumbled through her pockets until she found a glittering marble and offered it to Chip. "This is nectar from a Blasted Glassflower in my garden. If you hold on to him and smash it at your feet, the plant should drag both of you there. I'm afraid you'll have to remove his armor, though. Plants can only hold so much weight."

"No!" Chip shrieked. "We have to respect his privacy. And I won't let you cut us out of the bounty after all this."

She softened her expression, unsure if he was thinking clearly. "We wouldn't do that. And what good is his privacy if he, um . . . you know . . . from his wounds?"

"He won't. He can't. I'll figure this out."

Chip dusted his hands on his coat, balled them into fists, and marched over to where the two wizards sat, scrawling gibberish into the dirt.

Lanky attempted to cover his work when he saw movement from the corner of his eye, but he relaxed when he realized it was only the teen. "Yes?" He asked. "What do you want?"

"I want you to describe what your AMM does. In precise detail. Skipping nothing you think is irrelevant."

Lanky folded his arms. "That's proprietary information. If you require our services—"

"Not the mechanics," Chip said with a roll of his eyes. "The effects. What did it do to the things in the blast radius?"

The ruddy-cheeked wizard's lip twitched. "It's an anti-magic machine. Duh. The effect's in the name."

Chip's expression hardened. "I said in detail."

Lanky sensed another opportunity for unnecessary confrontation and stood to his full height, four inches above the teenager. Ten if you counted the hat.

Chip did not back down.

"Why are you asking?" Lanky demanded.

"The blast struck the Penumbral Magwod. I need to know what happened at that moment. Technical details. Limitations. Side effects. Even if you think I won't understand."

Lanky waved a hand in the air dismissively. "There's not a lot to understand. It stripped anything it hit of magic, and magic can never affect that stuff again. Thus, permanent anti-magic."

"Cow puddles," Theo said. "Your machine didn't achieve permanent anti-magic. I saw the fluid transfer system you hacked on to periodically refresh the spell. Best case, it stripped existing enchantments from the guy's armor. We can replace them later."

Lanky's cheeks flushed five shades darker than his

companion's, and he shot Theo a vicious glare. "It was a prototype. Which is more than you assembled, *Theo*."

Theo's eyes widened. "Theory! How did I miss that one? Witch, try the word theory."

Sylvie flew into motion, medallions in hand.

But Chip was not about to let the puzzle distract him. "So, you're saying there's a chance the device malfunctioned? I see. Could it have struck his armor without passing through?"

Margaret drew closer. "Why ask technical questions now?"

"It did *not* malfunction!" Lanky hollered. "It was a prototype! And it worked perfectly!"

"Until it exploded," Growina offered.

It turned out, though factually accurate, the helpful correction was not what the lanky wizard wanted to hear. He expressed this sentiment verbally, but not diplomatically. It turned out that insults hurt more when uttered as spells instead of taunts.

The snore-like sound Lanky expelled knocked Growina onto her backside in the dirt.

She was surprised by the wizard's sudden violence, but more so by Magwod's reaction to it. The previously unconscious man leapt to his feet as if to fight, then collapsed again with a terrible clatter. Chip howled and ran to help.

"You're gonna regret that," Vivienne snarled.

So much for thinly veiled threats. Lanky was many unpleasant things, but he was not foolish enough to fight Team Wontmoil with only one companion by his side. He grabbed his friend by the shoulder and backed toward Magwod and the exit to the maze.

"No," he said with far less confidence than a minute before. "You're going to regret this when you're stuck here forever, and we've negotiated our way past those mush-brained cultists."

"Don't be a fool. The way's blocked."

"We're wizards! We can walk straight through it!" Lanky reminded her before sticking out his tongue and backing into the darkness.

Growina dusted off her dress. "Will the cultists hurt them do you think?"

"We can only hope," Theo muttered.

"Theo."

He sighed. "Not. We can only hope not."

Sylvie gestured everyone back to the wall, then held out her palms to show them three pictures. She was excited about her selection, which was a good sign.

Margaret was not as easily impressed. "I don't get it. X marks the spot, a book, and a corpse? How does that spell theory?"

Sylvie shook her head and opened her mouth.

Vivienne interrupted. "It's not a corpse. It's a sleeping person. See the little snores? X, book, sleep."

"There, plus story, minus rest," Sylvie corrected in an exhausted whisper.

Theo shook his head. "I don't know how you got the word *there* from an arrow and an x at the top of a hill. That could be anything."

"I can see it," Growina said.

"I can't," Vivienne retorted.

"Aaaaaughhh!" Lanky's voice screamed from somewhere deep within the maze. "Don't eat me!"

Vivienne scrunched up her nose in confusion. "Was that a wizard's spell?"

"Oh, yes," Theo replied with a roll of his eyes. "You'll frequently hear me shout, 'Don't eat me!' before I pass through a wall of rubble."

She frowned. "Sarcasm?"

"I would never."

". . . Also sarcasm?"

"Everyone," Chip interrupted. They turned to see him standing beside them, eyes wet as if holding back tears. "There's something I have to tell you."

Growina's stomach sank. She glanced past Chip to the lightless corner where only one motionless boot was visible.

"It's about the Penumbral Magwod," he said. "The thing is. He's . . ."

A painful screech of metal on metal drew their attention in time to see Magwod sit up and shake his head. Growina sagged with relief.

Chip panicked. "What? That's . . . that's impossible! He was—"

"Clearly, he wasn't," Margaret said, as if talking to a babbling toddler. "And now that we know it, we should get a move on before the cultists catch up and eat us, too."

Growina shook her head. "I knew they were hungry, but I didn't think they were *that* hungry."

Chip stammered. "But—"

Margaret shushed him. "All in favor of using Sylvie's guesses, say, aye."

"Weren't you the one who thought her guesses were wrong?" Theo asked.

"I did. But I trust her and we don't have much time."

"And what if we fail?" Vivienne asked. "What if we have one guess, and we blow it?"

"Then we get creative."

"Aye," Growina said to move the conversation along.

"Aye," added Chip.

"Same," grumbled Theo.

"Whatever," said Sylvie.

Everyone looked to Magwod, who stumbled toward the team like a deer that had gotten into fermented apples.

An awkward silence settled over them before Chip remembered it was his job to speak.

"Uh . . . my aye was, of course, on behalf of the Penumbral Magwod. Pretend I'm not here."

The practiced words were the same as ever, but the nervous glances Chip shot Magwod suggested something was seriously wrong. And Growina spent enough time around spirit-stitched skeletons to know necromancy was not out of the question.

She shuffled to the other side of Theo, just to be safe.

Sylvie, meanwhile, darted to the first set of medallions and pushed them one at a time into corresponding slots. Then she moved on to the second set, doing the same before pausing at the last.

Team Wontmoil held their breath and crossed their fingers as it slid into the final slot, completing the two equations.

The results were, frankly, underwhelming.

Instead of a dramatic rumble and dust-stirring shift of the entire stone wall as expected, there was a pop like a bottle uncorking, followed by a tiny creak. An average, door-sized section of stone swung inward in the far-left corner of the wall, and all six medallions tumbled out of their slots.

Sylvie and Theo shared a knowing look. She scooped up the pictograms and placed them back while he opened the door and held it wide.

"Everybody in," he said, ushering them through. "We're resetting the medallions to buy some time."

Growina did as instructed but asked as she passed, "Why not take the medallions with us? Then they couldn't solve it at all."

"Because, A, the door may only latch when the coins are in place. And B, if we're walking into a trap, I'd rather take my chances with the cultists than an anti-magic cell that no one can open."

"Fair point."

Chip helped Magwod through the door, which required him to stoop like a wooden toy. Sylvie slunk after, prompting Theo to shove the door shut with another pop. After a test shove to ensure it was sealed, they all relaxed, happy to be on the other side. But something nagged at Growina's mind. Something she noticed but had not pondered before Team Wontmoil made it to safety.

Besides the wizard's scream, no sound indicated any cultists had made it past the initial cave-in.

So what, if not them, had tried to eat the wizards?

Thirty-Five
Stick Figure Army

FLORIAN KNEW WHERE the monster was. It had slipped out of hiding long enough to spook some wizards and return. And in that moment, he understood why his visions had been hazy for the past few hours. The beast was more intelligent than he thought, which spelled trouble—for everyone.

Of course, knowing a thing and saying it aloud were two completely different matters. The distant army of cranky cultists preoccupied the mercenary team, and he had to admit, that problem took priority. The mercs were outnumbered a hundred to one and seemed rather unprepared for the fight.

Eddie, at least, was eager for battle. He hopped from one sandy foot to the other, testing the weight of his enchanted sword as if performing for an audience. Meanwhile, Wardric fidgeted. His large hands moved over paintbrushes as if none were the size and style he needed for the task.

That left Bodkins to rein them in, but she was not offering any instructions. Instead, she gripped her chair with both hands as if it might buck her off at any moment. Her lips twitched with silent whispers, and her eyes darted from tree to tree.

This did nothing for Florian's confidence.

"Hey," he said, figuring it was as good a time as any to

bring up the monster's new behavior.

Bodkins shushed him and resumed her whispers.

"Best leave her be when she gets like this," Wardric said while messing with paintbrushes. "She can't focus on too many conversations."

"Conversations, plural? It's dead silent!"

As if to prove him wrong, a cultist shouted something garbled and swung a staff in their direction.

"True," Wardric said, "but it's also daylight in the woods, and you're watching people underground. You two are a lot alike, you know. Can see and hear things the rest of us can't."

Florian blinked. "You mean she's communing with spirits? Right now?"

Bodkins turned with such a sour expression; Florian felt like a chastised child in class. But she nodded in answer to his question.

"Something terrible happened here in the past," she said. "There was a secret battle for the fate of our world, where hundreds of warriors lost their lives—until one of them finally vanquished the evil and restored order. However, this act required a curse that resulted in the fallen being forgotten. Their loss, lives, and dreams were erased for all but those of us who listen to the dead. And something about those cultists over there has them scared it will be for nothing."

"Slugbeard's followers," Wardric hissed.

Florian gasped. "He's coming back for round two?"

"He's running a bed-and-breakfast in Mooncalf-Pale," Eddie said. "The cultists are searching for his old spellbook."

"Ahh. And these spirits don't want them to find it."

"Can't blame 'em."

"So what—" Florian began, but the words caught in his throat.

For the second time since the start of their journey, he witnessed the beauty of Bodkins' magic. Brilliant emerald threads of light floated through her fingers like spiderwebs on a breeze. Again, they twisted, forming the shape of a single human who stretched and rolled its head on its shoulders. But the stitched spirit was too little too late.

While ghosts and legends had distracted the mercs, the cultists charged. What Florian initially took for sticks and staves were swords and spears up close, and the mismatched costumes all bore the same image.

Slugbeard's missing spellbook.

Florian decided at that moment that, should he survive, he would never underestimate an angry mob—no matter how ridiculous their complaints were.

Perhaps he could fight for his life if he had Eddie's sword, but no. He would be no use, as inexplicably clumsy as he currently was in combat. It was best for the more experienced fighter to wield the weapon, even if it left him empty-handed.

Or did it?

He was a skilled improvisator, standing in the middle of an ancient wood. Surely there was something he could use as a weapon. A heavy log, perhaps. Or a pocket full of stones to—wait—did that branch move?

"Two minutes!" Eddie shouted, without turning to look back at them.

He was speaking to Bodkins, who sat stiffly in her chair, breath ragged and eyes glazed. Her hands danced and twirled threads about, weaving until the surrounding air was a universe of tiny figures. The emerald people paced as she worked, unbothered when she brushed them aside to make more space for additional spirits.

Remembering the friendly skeleton that Bodkins spirit-stitched back at the farmhouse, Florian spun to inspect the twitching branch. Sure enough, in the short time it had taken him to turn around, the branch had assembled itself into a makeshift femur. Thick reeds wrapped themselves around the wood, giving the stitched spirit strength and mobility while it grinned at him with pebble teeth.

Forget finding a weapon. Florian knew where he belonged.

He kneeled beside Bodkins' chair, one hand on the arm, and willed his strength into her. Hopefully, she could feel his support through proximity, without the distraction of direct touch.

"Fifty seconds!" Eddie shouted.

Florian set his forehead against the chair, closed his eyes, and whispered, "You can do this."

She snorted and replied, "I know."

The glow and spread of the emerald magic made Bodkins a tempting target for cultists. And so it made sense that the first to arrive went straight toward her without noticing Eddie. A short one in embroidered trousers charged at her with an impressive spear that put Florian's theatrical replicas to shame.

Unfortunately for the well-armed cultist, Eddie's sword was made for slicing steel armor, and he had a double lifetime of experience. One flick of his wrist severed the spear and left the holder gripping a stick. The shock of the change made them stumble and pause, giving them time to observe their victim.

"N—necromancer," the cultist stuttered. "They have a necrmmmphh!"

"Shh," Eddie whispered, one hand planted over the cultist's mouth. "We don't use that word."

Florian flicked his tongue over down-turned lips, imagining how much mouth-sand it took to stifle a scream. Apparently, the answer was "quite a lot" because the cultist spat thrice the second they broke free and continued spitting as they bolted away.

One enemy down. Only two, maybe three hundred to go? But that was a job for the stick figure army.

"Next one's mine!" a stick-witch said in a surprisingly high-pitched voice.

The stick-witch faced the oncoming army as they charged through the trees, her twig-fingers lifted toward a mage.

"LLAB—Oooo!" the fellow shouted, unable to cast as quickly as she could.

He flew into the air, feet first, and his book splatted into the mud beneath him. The stick-woman, who must have been a witch in her lifetime, flung him into a pack of five cultists charging with a wall of shields. The resulting confusion might have been funny to someone less invested than Florian.

"In my day," a moss-covered stick-man said, "we memorized lengthy incantations. Now they're reading first-year spells from a book on a battlefield. What, do they think we'll wait for them to finish?"

She shook her gnarled-bark head as if already tired of his words. "I don't think they're real mages. They're, like, normal people with a weird hobby."

"In my day, we didn't start apocalypses as a hobby. Ombtwab!"

Florian had not noticed the cultist with a dagger sneaking up on the stick figures, but he noticed when the dagger-sneak vanished with a yelp, leaving only a pair of well-worn shoes. Depending on what the stick-man's spell did, it might have been a breach of modern battle etiquette.

Hopefully, Bodkins knew what she was doing when she raised an army of long-dead adventurers.

The monster limb directly below Florian's hand twitched as if reading his thoughts. Another lifted and flexed its fingers. He glanced up to see Bodkins slumped in her chair, no longer surrounded by glowing lights.

"Get back," she ordered in a hoarse whisper.

"What for? You're not going out there like this. You're

exhausted!"

She opened her eyes. "Don't tell me how to do my job, Peterman. I don't tell you how to do yours."

"What? Yes, you do. All the time!"

"That's also my job. Get clear."

He crossed his arms and backed up several steps. "Fine."

The monster limbs lifted her chair off the earth, and several flexed as she prepared to fight. Before heading off, however, she gave him a wink. "Your concern has been noted, though."

He flushed. "What? I never—"

It was too late to save face. She took off, leaving him alone with Wardric, who had an expression like a tattling child.

"You, uh, into the boss?" he asked with a giddy smile.

Florian wanted to bury himself alive. "Oh, no. No. Hah. No. Of course not."

Wardric scratched his head. "I'm not good at romantic stuff. How many noes in a row means yes?"

A wave of stick fighters crashed from the woods and slammed into a mass of unprepared cultists, distracting Wardric and giving Florian much-needed time to breathe.

"I'm not in the market for a partner," he clarified. "I haven't been for quite some time. I guess you could say I have trust issues."

"Hah! She says the same. But she lets you ride around with her. That's pretty cozy by her standards."

"It's only practical. I've been sick. It's not like we're using the time to flirt."

"Why not?"

Florian paused to ponder the question despite the welling battle around them. Why not, indeed? Because she kidnapped him, dragged him into danger, and coerced him into consuming weird herbs? Or was it because she mistook his identity, reminding him of all the women who pursued him after watching his shows?

Or more likely, was it because she embodied everything he thought he was?

How long had he tied his identity to a recurring character on a stage? When did he stop living for himself to protect the reputation of a fictional woman? And what did it mean to be standing back and clutching to the fake identity of Ava Triumphant while a real, live female warrior took the stage? Was it a demotion or a promotion? And how could he reconcile all of that if he survived to re-don the wig?

"Hey buddy, we're gonna need you back with us."

Florian shook free of the mental spiral. "Right. Sorry. I tell you what, if the right circumstances ever arise, I'll ask *the boss* out on a date."

"Nice!"

Florian glanced around. Wardric was right. The stick figure army might have been adventurers, but they were also bundles of forest detritus. And twigs held up poorly to swords and spells, unlike Eddie's sand-based body. So, though the fight was already in their favor, the path was littered with twitching sticks.

Back to improvisation, then.

With the mess came a thousand new options for a make-shift blunt weapon, and Florian reached for the heftiest option in sight. It took more effort than expected to lift it, due to a strange wriggling bulb stuck to one end. The bulb turned slowly until Florian realized the stick he had grabbed was a length of wooden spine with a gnarly head still attached.

The head grinned so wide he heard a crack—and he immediately recognized the face. "Oh, good," the stick figure wizard said. "I needed a new pair of legs."

Wardric guffawed, held up his palette and brush, and nodded toward the battle. "Looks like we're all spellcasters now. Let's get in there and help the boss!"

ThIRTY-SIX

No Sudden Movements

"Okay," Theo said at a third of his normal volume, "that's a problem."

"Is it, though?" Vivienne asked. "It's not even moving. Maybe it's dead."

He made a show of extending patience. "That thing was never alive. Notice the faint glow in the empty eye sockets? Dead giveaway for a primitive construct."

The team collectively examined the monstrous thing in the center of the chamber between them and the exit. It resembled Magwod in head-to-toe historical armor but it was thrice as tall and impossibly proportioned. In one hand, it gripped a mace that could take out the entire party with a single swipe. In the other was a rectangular shield large enough to hide behind.

The shield had an engraved message with typical Gart Splagosion spelling: Too git bye, yoo most frst pazz tru mi.

Yikes.

Growina raised a hand. "Construct? Like the clockwork bank managers?"

Theo nodded, then shook his head. "Yes, and no. Advancements in copper work and machine enchanting give modern constructs more flexibility, whereas this rust bucket is likely single-purpose. Sit in a cave. Crush adventurers. Repeat. Then again, who knows what was possible at the end of the Gart Splagosion."

"How do you mean?" Margaret asked.

"From my understanding, things got very chaotic in the final days, and no one remembers any of it clearly. If you want my educated guess, I'd say they wiped people's minds to hide information that could have led to a recurrence. That might even explain the existence of our creature, here."

"Ah," Margaret said with a sage nod. "Like when Dorothea Broomhandle and her coven refused to reveal how she half-summoned a multi-world monster."

"That story is real? I thought they made it up for a play."

"Not at all. It was very serious. A witch lost her life!"

Growina squirmed and raised her hand again. "Does this mean no one is at fault? For the creature, I mean. If it's super old and no one's been down here, there's no one to turn in to the gatekeepers, right?"

"You worry too much about the gatekeepers," Theo said. "Mind you, I agree their methods deserve more scrutiny. But it isn't our place to interfere in the judiciary process. Ours is to put a stop to evil where we see it. And collect a fee, of course. To answer your question, though, I'm not sure. We won't know what we're dealing with until we reach this tunnel's end."

"And the end of the tunnel is through that thing," Margaret added, gesturing toward the construct.

Growina nodded in understanding, despite her apprehension. "So, what do we do?"

"We blast it," Vivienne suggested. "Constructs are enchanted, so it can't be anti-magic. We just—"

She raised a hand toward the thing, but Sylvie grabbed her wrist and lowered it to her side.

Theo grumbled. "Indeed, the construct isn't anti-magic, but we must assume the shield is. Let's not start this battle until we have a strategy, please."

"Can Magwod take care of it?" Margret asked. "Like he did the boulder?"

All eyes turned to the armored man, except Chip's, which darted nervously around the group.

Margaret added, "Well?"

The teen's face contorted like he accidentally drank a cup of tadpoles. "I . . . I don't know."

"You don't know?"

"I don't know."

Margaret raised a brow. "You have one job. You talk for that guy. What does he say?"

"I don't know!" he repeated, face turning crimson. "I don't know what he can do right now. I can't—"

Growina stepped in to save him from embarrassment. "Magwod is seriously injured. He blacked out several times in the last room."

"Then why is he standing there?" Theo demanded. "Tell him to sit this one out."

Chip's eyes widened. "Seriously? You don't mind?"

"What do you take us for, bandits? Go rest. We've got this."

Vivienne whined. "Have we, though? What's the plan?"

Growina ran a hand over her remaining bottles. "I have a single shot of distilled wisdom. It might help one of you think of something, but it tastes a teensy bit like burned licorice and earthworms."

As she probably could have predicted, Theo turned up his nose at the offer. "Don't require any. Plenty of wisdom in this old noggin."

"Same," Margaret said. "Minus the old. And the noggin. Who says noggin?"

"Don't look at me," Vivienne added. "You hate my ideas."

Sylvie also shook her head and gestured for Growina to take it.

"Why not?" she muttered, then uncorked the bottle, pinched her nose, and gulped it down. It burned like hot grease and caused her to burp up magenta bubbles, but it also produced an eerie sense of calm.

She made a note to double-market it as an anti-anxiety tincture.

"That's all I have that can help," she said, glancing down at the remaining bottles. "Unless constructs can sleep, float, or sneeze. Or if it's hungry!"

She pulled a fish stick from her pocket and made to crack it open, but the entire team waved for her to put it away. What *did* they have against fish-flavored tree marrow? It was delicious, nutritious, and cruelty-free! Their loss.

Theo straightened his hat and gestured for everyone to gather around. "Let's take stock of what we have on hand. Everyone turn out your pockets. Apothecary, I assume you have the most experience in this department. Help us keep this organized, so we don't miss anything."

"Growina," she said.

"Hmm?"

She sighed. "My name is Growina. Apothecary is my occupation."

Wow. Either the potion itself or the subsequent relaxation were making her a bit more brazen than usual. Perhaps the potion didn't make one wise so much as silence the voices that insisted one wasn't. It certainly raised questions about the person she could have been if she had taken a different path in life. But there was no point pondering the implications while underground in a deadly cavern.

"Oh, of course." Theo's mustache twitched in what might

have been embarrassment—if such a thing were possible. "Growina."

The wizard fumbled through his suit coat pockets, inside and out, followed by his trouser pockets. In doing so, he produced more trinkets and pouches than could reasonably fit in the well-tailored fabric without adding bulk.

"One portable copper plate with adhesive and engraving tool," he declared. "Enough fudgels for a decent room and board. Miniature caltrops in case of spies. Notebook to jot down new spells. Hat wash. Fang Lock. Leadfeather. And, um . . . this."

He sheepishly produced the sad remains of the bag of flour he'd purchased from Herbs and Vices. It felt like years had passed since that gloomy morning.

"Look at mister wealthy," Vivienne said with a sneer. "Fancy. All I've got is this."

She waved a hand and produced a spellbook from nowhere, prompting Growina to wonder if Margaret's old grimoire was truly surrendered as collateral, or if the witch could reclaim it from anywhere. Sylvie did the same as Vivienne.

Margaret repeated the trick with a few extra items to add in addition. "Insta-stake. Bandage-in-a-bottle. Various herbs. Scented candles."

Theo perked up. "Does the bandage have a salve? Could the young man use it?"

Chip shook his head vigorously from where he sat beside the crouched, but oddly not reclined, Magwod.

"He's still worried about Magwod's privacy," Growina explained. "Silly if you ask me."

Theo raised a brow, finally acknowledging the change in her attitude since swigging the wisdom potion.

"Well," Margaret said. "We have a whole lot of nothing. Everybody, open your grimoires, and let's put our heads together. Perhaps a chain of spells can circumvent the shield before we're hit with the mace."

The four of them sat in a circle, crossed their legs, and flipped through their books.

Lacking a book to search through, Growina examined the massive room. She had not noticed it before, but the cavern's walls were perfectly smooth, as if hewn from a massive block of stone. Yet glowing lichen clung to every surface in unnatural repeating patterns. This meant the room, if not the whole tunnel system, had been built with magic instead of through manual labor.

Growina had met her share of magic users in her shop and on various journeys to gather samples from remote locations. But none possessed the raw power to displace an entire cavern's worth of soil and replace the walls with solid stone. Not only did that make her wonder what kind of people created the tunnels, but it also made her second-guess all her assumptions about the room.

For example, the puzzle door they passed mechanically latched but otherwise resembled a regular door. Yet the one at the far side of the current cavern had giant gears all over the front and no discernible handle or knob. The construct's shield, on the other hand . . .

She inched forward. The rest of the party kept their heads down, focused on their plans and problems, so no one noticed as she crept toward the construct to get a look at its rectangular shield. The closer she got, the more convinced she became that one rivet was larger than the others, not to mention protruding from the surface.

"Who, whoa, whoa!" Theo called, finally noticing she was not with them. "What are you doing?"

"I think there's a knob," she said, pointing to the raised rivet.

"Get back here!" Vivienne demanded. "You'll ruin everything."

Growina held up a finger and drew closer to the construct, one tiptoe at a time. No one objected, perhaps out of fear of making too much noise—or morbid curiosity. She drew close enough that, if the massive, armored construct were a living metal monster, she would have felt its warm breath stirring the curls around her face.

Its head twitched, not enough to indicate an imminent attack, but enough to make her second-guess her choice to approach without a plan b. Should her guess be completely off, Team Wontmoil was nowhere near ready to jump in and stop her from getting squashed.

The construct's head raised painfully slowly with an echoing screech of rusted metal. It examined her with its glowing but otherwise empty eye sockets. She knew it was about as intelligent as the automated bank machines that collected her fudgels, but she could not shake the feeling she was being sized up—or at least judged—for her lack of tact.

Growina cleared her throat, far less confident than a moment before. "Um . . . excuse me. Your shield. It says, 'To get by, you must first pass through me.' Does it not?"

The construct did not answer. Its shoulders rolled in mechanical sockets, loosening rusted joints without shifting its stare. It unfurled and re-furled one finger at a time, gripping its weapons as if she might steal them.

She tried again, voice squeaking with stress. "If that is what it says, is it possible we—I mean, may we, please, pass through it?"

Whatever confidence the potion gave her was false or painfully short-lived. Growina held her breath and wrung her hands, hoping her assumption was correct. If not, she hoped her squashing was rapid and would not damage her skeleton too much. After all, she had promised the Wontmoil Dancing Band she would be their accordion player when she passed.

The construct dragged its mace upward with the painful screech of spikes on stone and, to Growina's exhausted relief, set the weapon off to the side. It stood to full height, stretching each metal leg, and gripped the shield with both hands. The earth trembled as the giant lumbered toward the door, pressing the shield into it with a click.

Finally, with unexpected precision, the construct pinched the doorknob in two fingers, tugged it open with the sound of grinding gears, and stepped aside to let the team pass. Its job complete, the giant stomped back to where Growina stood and collapsed, head lowered as if it had never moved.

Someone let loose a long whistle.

She turned, heart pounding, to see the entire party standing in awe.

"That was impressive," Margaret admitted.

Theo wrinkled his nose and brushed dirt from his sleeves. "I would have figured it out, eventually."

"No, you wouldn't."

"No," he admitted, "I wouldn't. Nice work, Growina."

She beamed.

Thirty-Seven

Like We Practiced

"Incoming—to the left!" shouted the wooden skull atop Florian's staff.

"My left, or yours?" he asked.

"What's the difference?"

Florian's brow knit. "Your head's spun backward."

"So?"

"It matters!"

The skull tsked. "Has anyone ever told you that you're difficult to work with?"

Florian's grip tightened around the staff as if he could strangle its ghostly occupant. "*Which left?*"

"Mine. Goodness."

He spun, muttering about stage directions, and the wooden skull spat out some nasty spells to dispose of two stealthy cultists. That out of the way, Florian scurried to catch back up with the fast-moving mercs. The team was close enough to their destination that he could see the mound of dirt against which the now-missing boulder had once sat.

"Having trouble with your weapon?" Eddie asked before gracefully parting a woman from her axe.

"It's not a weapon. It's a crotchety wizard at the end of a stick."

"Hah! Give it a rattle or two. Show 'em who's boss."

The spirit-stitched wizard gasped. "Try it, and I'll—"

"Nobody touches my soothsayer!" Bodkins interrupted. "Unless you want to be stitched to a bag at the back of a horse."

"Yes, ma'am."

One of Bodkins' monster arms, a blueish one with yellow spots, hoisted a stunned cultist into the air and brought them close enough for her to threaten.

"Get outta my way," she said with a snarl.

The cultist obliged the moment their flailing toes touched dirt, taking off at a run toward their companions.

Wardric, who was busy freshening his palette, chuckled to himself. "This fight's practically over," he muttered.

Florian groaned. If there was one thing he'd learned from years of live performance, it was to wait for the final curtain to fall before declaring the production a success. To do otherwise always ensured an unpredictable stroke of bad luck.

Lo-and-behold, Eddie froze a few steps ahead, waving to stop them from nearing. The group followed his gaze to a cluster of cultists tinkering with something in the grass.

"Tell me that's not what I think it is," he said.

"That's definitely what you think it is," Bodkins confirmed.

"Not so brave now, are you?" a cultist shouted in the exact voice Florian would give a villain if he were doing a children's puppet show.

Wardric frowned. "They're bluffing. That thing was in pieces a minute ago."

A cultist jumped back from the AMM, which clanked and thumped away in the grass as heated oil flowed through its copper tubes. Occasionally, a thin stream spurted from a crack, and someone rushed in to slap on a patch.

"Unfortunately, they aren't," Bodkins said. "But I doubt

they understand what they're doing. I'm betting they know the thing's dangerous but haven't a clue why."

Eddie nodded. "If they did, they wouldn't be that close."

The machine squeaked, burbled, and let out a sound like an opera singer with a chest cold. Spurred by the mercs' reaction to the noise, the villainous cultist pointed at them.

"This is your last chance! Go away!"

"You go away!" Eddie shouted and hefted his sword as if to charge.

Bodkins raised an enormous, clawed hand and set it gently against his shoulder. "Don't." Her chair took a step back, then another, forcing the rest of the mercs to retreat. Not far enough to count as surrender, but further from the whining device.

"What's the radius if it explodes again?" Florian asked.

The wooden skull at the end of his staff cleared its nonexistent throat. "Anyone going to tell me what *it* is?"

"Anti-magic machine," Florian answered, "and it's already exploded once."

The skull spat. Or, at least, it made a sound resembling spit. "That's Slugbeard magic. Let me at them."

The machine whistled like a teakettle as cultists danced around it, pleased by their apparent success.

Bodkins' scowl deepened. "Nobody's going anywhere. Stay back."

"Sure, but are we out of the radius?" Florian asked again.

A piece of the AMM popped off with a bang, and Florian's skull staff laughed aloud. "By my guess . . . absolutely not!"

Another piece of the device burst free and soared past Florian's ear with a whistle. He dropped to the ground, sure he had been hit, and lost his grip on the chatty staff. The soul-stitched mage pitched a fit as he rolled into a ditch, away from the party.

Florian was more concerned with his ear. He rubbed it to verify there was no injury, then ran his fingers through his hair.

Satisfied, he looked back toward the battle but found himself face-to-knees with Eddie.

"Take it," Eddie said, and handed him the enchanted sword. "You need a better weapon."

Florian took it reflexively and stammered. "But . . ."

"You can do it. Like we practiced."

The sand man's eyes were as sincere as they could be without moisture or realistic color, and something about that made Florian nervous.

Eddie was never that serious about anything.

"I fell over when we practiced. What are you—"

The AMM's whistle grew so loud, even Florian could not hear his final words, and the cultists scattered with their hands to their ears. Eddie strode toward it, calm as ever, with his arms wide as if to hug it.

Bodkins was not calm. Though the words were lost to the wail of machinery, she was obviously screaming at Eddie. Livid. Giving orders.

He turned and stuck out his tongue in true Eddie fashion before bursting apart into a curtain of sand.

The AMM didn't blow apart so much as pop, spraying a cloud of oil in the air and emitting a fast-moving burst of steam the color of slimy river algae. The Eddie curtain held long enough to block the blast and force it upward, where it dissipated rapidly. Then the curtain fell like shimmering silk, peppering Florian's clothes and face until he had to look away.

It was only when he heard Wardric cry, "That does it!" that he realized the squealing sound was gone.

He glanced up to see the big guy standing front-and-center for the first time, dabbing a brush with determined speed into a blob of white paint. Wardric's expression was pure rage as he lifted the brush and jabbed rapidly toward the flustered cultists.

Florian squinted to see what the merc had done, but all the cultists looked perfectly fine. Sore and disappointed, but fine.

The AMM, on the other hand, glinted in the afternoon sun as if made of diamonds or . . .

"Glass," he whispered, unable to stop himself. "You turned the AMM into glass."

With a few more brush strokes, a small boulder appeared above the glass machine, and gravity did what it did best. The sound was terrible.

It brought back memories of dropped trays in dinner theaters. Glassware turned into tiny shards. And then there was nothing. No whining, no bursting, no smashing, no screaming. Nothing.

Followed by the sound of cultists fleeing as fast as their robed legs could carry them, lest they also become glass.

Wardric waved his arms as if chasing crows from a garden. "Go! Flee!"

That marked the end of the battle. Florian wiped sand from his eyes, then stared at the tiny grains. They clung to his fingers and the crevices of his clothes and made no attempt to reassemble.

"Oh no," he whispered. "Eddie."

The dark cloud had not been burning oil. It was the anti-magic blast. Eddie, that stubborn sand man, had thrown himself before it to protect the rest of the mercenary gang. That was why he shared the sword.

He knew he would not come back from the blast.

"Eddie!" Florian cried again, and without thinking, he plunged his hands into the grass, grasping for as many grains as he could.

"Come on, get up," Bodkins commanded. "Take us to the cave before we run out of time."

Florian gripped fistfuls of dirty sand and looked up at her in disbelief. "But . . . Eddie's dead!"

"Yes. And he's laughing at you."

The sand slipped from Florian's hands. "He's here? He's okay?"

Bodkins sighed. "He's been haunting me for fifteen years. Why stop now?" She listened to something, then shook her head. "Absolutely not. You'll get the same type as last time, or you'll get street gravel. I'm not traveling north for fancy sand."

Florian forced himself to take a deep breath and exhale several times, as if warming up for a performance. He gripped the sword, which still felt strange, and stood to get his bearings. It was strange knowing his deceased companion was watching nearby, invisible.

"This way, I guess."

He led the remaining mercs to the cave-in, which, upon closer inspection, was more of a hole surrounded by extracted stones. A mangled ladder snaked through rubble at the bottom, lit by a glowing plant.

Bodkins eyed the collapsed well with dismay, realizing, as they all did, that her monster-powered chair would not fit.

Wardric stretched out the muscles in his back and selected a paintbrush without a second thought. "Step back. I'll take care of this."

They did, and he measured the well with a thumb, then wandered a bit and measured it again. He dotted his palette with earthy tones and swirled them together to match the scene. Then, meticulously, he painted a landscape.

What was initially a collapsed well became a tunnel wide enough to enter side-by-side. Freshly laid stones supported the walls, spotted with the glowing plants from below. Florian realized he had never given Wardric's skills enough credit—possibly because of the man's self-esteem. But the truth was, Wardric could reshape reality. Any reality. Any time he wanted.

Though the art was temporary, it was infinite in possibility.

"Would you—" he began, intending to ask if Wardric might be interested in a job in set design. But screams interrupted his words.

"Run away!" A lanky wizard shouted as he burst from the tunnel at full speed.

A ruddy wizard hustled behind him, gesturing back the way he came. "Monster! In the cave!"

They did not slow down to explain further, but continued toward the woods at full speed. Fortunately, Florian did not need an explanation. He had witnessed the monster spooking the wizards and was pleased to see they were still alive.

The thought inspired Florian to take a quick look at the inside of his eyelids before venturing inside. Unfortunately, the monster was in near-total darkness—or the collywobbles he ate needed a refresh. Few details of the cavern stood out, no matter how tightly Florian closed his eyes. Hopefully, the odd adventurers were fine, and the monster had not yet gobbled them up.

"We should go," he said, nodding toward the tunnel.

It was too late for second sight, anyway.

Time to see the bounty for himself.

Thirty-Eight

Construct

"That's a problem," Theo mumbled.

Vivienne glared. "Stop saying that!"

He was right, though. At some point in its life, the new puzzle wall had been directly beneath a bog or creek. It seemed even stone hewn with the aid of magic was susceptible to the whims of nature. Whatever instructions had been on the wall had been eroded by time and covered in minerals.

Worse, there were no other indications of what the puzzle once was. No coins, slots, aggressive constructs, hidden doors, or passages. Just one smooth rusted rectangle surrounded by indecipherable garbage.

Theo shook his head. "I'm open to suggestions."

"Blast it?" Vivienne offered with a wince, anticipating objections.

Her sheer excitement when Theo said, "Sure, have at it," could have taken the door down by itself. Fueled by their lack of condemnation, Vivienne struck a dramatic pose and flicked her fingers toward the door. Nothing happened—except for the team receiving confirmation that the door was anti-magic.

"I'm getting bored of anti-magic!" Vivienne whined. "You'd think they'd mix it up a bit. Give us a puzzle without it to throw us off, you know?"

"I don't imagine they had our entertainment in mind when they built this cavern," Theo countered.

Margaret nodded in agreement and brushed her dress, releasing a small cloud of dust in the process. The sheer amount of gray cavern dirt clinging to the hems of the witches' gowns made them look like pensive ghosts.

Growina supposed that, when they returned home, she should offer to stitch each a new outfit. There were ways to advertise witchiness without becoming a stereotype.

Sylvie, the ghostliest witch, slid to the wall and ran a hand over its surface. She scraped at the stains with painted nails, then pointed to Growina's bandolier with a questioning look.

Growina paled and shook her head. "Sorry. I might be able to make a solvent with some pine sap and a great deal of heat, but there aren't many conifers around at the moment."

"Are there underground trees at all?" Vivienne asked.

"Technically, most trees are underground. And above ground. But, unfortunately, not here." Growina's gaze slid once again to the witches' dusty dresses. "If we could combine some of the grit from the floor with water and scrub the wall with a thick rag, we might be able to polish the stains off."

Between the need for extra healing and a mineral solvent, Growina realized her potion selection was naive. She'd read too many story books where a person happened to have the right tool for every situation they encountered, and it turned out real life didn't work that way.

At least that was also true for the others, despite their greater experience.

Vivienne scoffed. "Raise your hand if you've got the stamina to polish a wall with spit dust."

Everyone looked at the ground, shuffled, and muttered, but no one raised a hand to volunteer.

"So," Theo said, exasperated, "is this it for us? We give up, go back, and face the cultists? Or do we attempt to polish the wall, even if it's futile?"

"This is where the old Chip would have told us fancy-pants Magwod could do it in seconds," Vivienne said.

Growina frowned. "That's not funny."

"I wasn't being funny. We could have used his help."

They glanced over their shoulders at Magwod and Chip, slumped against the back wall of the current room.

Chip raised his head from his chest to meet their gaze. "I'm sorry," he said and honestly looked it. "He's not even able to move at the moment."

The Penumbral Magwod felt otherwise. He pushed himself up, using the wall for support, and took a few wobbly steps toward the wall.

Chip leapt up as well, alarmed. "Hey, stop!"

Magwod did not stop. Instead, he picked up his pace, limping toward the wall with determination.

"Stop!" Chip cried aggressively while everyone else looked on, gobsmacked.

The armored man set his hands to the stone, then dragged them down with a horrible noise, crushing years of built-up deposits and the tips of his armored fingers in the process. The stains scraped free along with chunks of stone, further distorting the words beneath.

"The Penumbral Magwod will stop immediately!" Chip commanded the massive man. "You're not even helping! You're making it worse! Do what I say this instant!"

Team Wontmoil collectively gasped as Magwod ceased his attack on the stone and turned to stare at the teen quizzically. Their business relationship was unclear, but it seemed to all present that a line had been crossed. Chip was supposedly Magwod's voice, speaking for the man instead of himself. But, perhaps due to the day's events, the teen was coming across more like a parent.

Surprisingly, the big man did not seem to mind. He hobbled back to where he started and slid to a seat against the wall. Chip, meanwhile, collapsed in place, muttering something into his hands.

Growina's nurturing instincts kicked in. It would be horrible if those were the last words the teen ever spoke to his companion.

"I think you should apologize to your friend," she said gently.

Chip stared up with red-rimmed eyes. "No. That's not necessary."

It was an odd choice of words, and Theo noticed. "What's that supposed to mean? Not necessary? What's going on with you two?"

Chip took a deep breath, held it, and exhaled. Then he stood to full height to face the team. "The Penumbral Magwod . . . is not human."

Growina blinked, resetting all her preconceptions of the large man. "Oh! He's an alien? Like the twins?"

"He's not alive. He's mechanical."

Theo's jaw dropped. "No. Another construct? This whole time?"

Chip nodded. "I built him myself with funding from my father. And there's no way he's going to give me more. This is a disaster."

"So . . . he isn't injured?" Growina asked. "He's—"

"Damaged. Yes." The teen massaged his temples. "Decimated, even. As far as I can tell, he's missing some innards. But none of it makes any sense! He's only programmed to do what I say he's decided to do. Nothing more. *The Penumbral Magwod wants to stand up. The Penumbral Magwod wants to sit down.* Broken or not, there's no room for defiance. He's got no will to speak of. Yet, just look at him sitting there."

Growina thought sitting there sounded fantastic. She had a hard time accepting that the big man was not a man and not dying inside his armor. Though she supposed it explained Chip's hesitation to remove the helmet. What, exactly, did a construct have underneath?

Vivienne rolled her eyes. "That's Wontmoil for ya. Nothing ever goes how you think it will."

"This whole time?" Theo asked again, as if the conversation had not moved on. "You've been the magic user this whole time? That thing has been channeling your spells?"

Chip stuck out his chin in defiance. "What of it?"

"If you're that good at your job, what do you need a construct for?"

The teen spread his arms wide. "Look at me. Do I look threatening to you?"

"Well, no. But clearly—"

"Did any of you, even once, consider me a worthwhile target?"

"Every time you opened your mouth," Vivienne said. The look in her eyes suggested she was actively considering it.

Chip groaned. "Not personally. Professionally. I've yet to face a single opponent who viewed me as more than a disposable accessory. And when people see you as worth less than the effort it would take to spit out a spell, well . . . you might as well be invisible."

Theo nodded excitedly. "So, you're safe because you're small and malnourished. I see it now. Very clever."

"I don't need your approval. I need answers! What did that vile machine do to him?"

Theo took a step back. "Well, you said it yourself. It damaged his innards."

"Gutted them, more like. Half his body sounds hollow.

So how is it he can walk and scratch at a wall? And why is he doing it against my orders?"

"Better question," Vivienne said with a tone that suggested it would not be better. "Why did you stop him? If he's not alive and can't be hurt, why not let him dig straight through the wall?"

Chip flushed and attempted to make himself larger. "And who's gonna pay to replace the armor? Who's gonna help me rebuild the gears? You think a measly two-sevenths of this lousy bounty will pay for that?"

"One-sixth," Vivienne hissed, leaning forward to meet his eye.

Margaret stepped in. "Now, Viv. A deal is a deal."

"We were scammed!"

"You were saved!" Chip corrected. "You wouldn't even be here if it wasn't for me. You think the construct put itself in front of the machine? And who was it that told you to stay back, hmm?"

"It's true," Growina said, earning herself a nasty glare.

"What's the use of getting here if we can't get back out?" Vivienne shouted, temper rising. "You wanna count as two people while you take advantage of our compassion and sit on your rump at the back of the room? Not happening. Order that guy off the floor and get us through that wall."

"Make me!" Chip screamed, unafraid. Which made more sense now that everyone knew he was a capable mage.

"I don't have to make you. Apparently, I can just ask him!"

"Viv, calm down," Margaret said.

Growina sucked a breath through her teeth. *Calm down* was, in her opinion, right up there with *What could go wrong?* on the list of phrases no one should utter. That was because the person asked to calm down was, in most cases, provoked into a rage.

It was like ripping branches from a sentry shrub and trying

to smooth talk it out of a wallop. The faster some folks learned about consequences, the better.

"Me? Calm down?" Vivienne growled. "He's the one yelling. I'm perfectly calm!" She punctuated the last bit with a stomp of her heel and a magically charged swing of her arms that blew dust from the air.

Chunks of stone from the puzzle wall skittered across the room like rolled dice. Chip's eyes narrowed, and he raised his hands in warning, but Sylvie slithered between the two and held up something small and gray.

Both quieted out of curiosity. Why was Sylvie showing them a rock?

The answer dawned on them all at once, and they turned together to examine the wall.

"What was it you said," Margaret asked, "about them mixing things up to throw us off?"

The puzzle wall had an inch-deep crater where Vivienne's perfectly calm spell had struck it. Only the *door* was anti-magic.

"Do we blast the rest away?" she asked.

Margaret shook her head. "Only if you want to risk another cave-in. Luckily, we have a wizard."

"At your service!" Theo said. He muttered something under his breath and strode straight through the damaged wall.

A heavy silence fell over the room as everyone listened for sounds of distress. Excruciating seconds ticked by with no confirmation that the wizard was safe.

Finally, after what felt like ages, a latch clicked and the door creaked open. A wide-eyed Theo popped his head through the opening.

"This doesn't bode well," he said with a scowl.

Margaret stepped forward. "What? What is it?"

He pushed the door the rest of the way open. "I think it's best you see for yourselves."

Thirty-Nine
Bad Feelings

"I still don't get it," Wardric said. "How did you make words out of other words using pictures?"

He swerved around one of Bodkins' monster limbs, a sinewy thing with orange tufts of fur, and slid through the doorway on the puzzle wall.

Florian glanced around the medallion room before following them into a corridor. "Doesn't matter. It's a game meant to teach kids vocabulary. What's important is, we're through."

A memory of Eddie complaining about parents teaching young kids cryptography floated through his mind. Perhaps Eddie's ghost was complaining as well. Florian felt the sand man's absence in the cavern as much as he felt the weight of his sword.

"What I don't get is why the folks who built this place made the rooms two stories tall and the doors so narrow!" Bodkins growled.

She was in a bad mood and not bothering to hide it. If there was one thing Beatrix Bodkins hated more than anything, it was feeling useless, and her two primary skills—tearing things apart and stitching spirits—were of no use in an empty puzzle cave.

"If the architect still haunts this place, I'm gonna have a

few words with them."

"At least they left us these glowing plants!" Wardric said, ever cheerful.

Florian doubted they had left the fuzzy moss where it was deliberately, but he was not about to sour the man's mood when it was the only thing balancing Bodkins'.

Instead, he quirked his head and pointed down the corridor at a bright rectangle. "Looks like this opens up in a bit."

That inspired Bodkins to pick up the pace, and they soon found themselves in another large room—face to face with an armored giant. The frighteningly tall and oddly formed man held a tall shield and a spiked mace.

"Now, we're talkin'!" Bodkins said. "Wardric, add a few cracks to that thing, and I'll smash it up."

The painter pulled out a thin brush and mixed a couple shades of gray. But the moment he raised his brush to paint, the armored giant shifted its arms, blocking its body with the huge shield. Wardric took a few ineffective swipes.

"Fine," Bodkins said with a snarl. "We'll do this the old-fashioned way. Never met a construct I couldn't disassemble."

Several of her monster arms reared up, fingers spread and claws extended, making her look more like a crab than a spider. She lunged into the room, poised to circle the shield and reach the construct's body before it could react.

Unfortunately, the thing was quicker than it looked.

The construct's eyes flashed violet, and its mace swung round, landing close enough to Bodkins to spray her with chunks of the stone floor. She backed off slowly, then tried again, faking left and dodging right. The construct, being a single-purpose tool explicitly designed to thwart such tactics, countered and sent her leaping off to a corner of the room.

"You gotta get in there," Wardric said. "I can't do anything to get past that shield."

Florian knew that. Or, at least, his brain did. His legs were going to take some convincing. He took a deep breath and gripped the sword, pulling the blade from the sheath at his hip. Then he stood, frozen with indecision.

Flanking the construct made the most sense. The rectangular shield could only protect one side of the armored man at a time. If Florian could get behind the creature while Bodkins was on the other side, it significantly increased the chances of one of them landing a blow.

. . . Assuming the body was susceptible to magic, and Florian could survive long enough to reach it. His recent attempts to use the sword shattered his confidence, making it harder to take the first steps.

"Peterman," Wardric coaxed. "I believe in you."

Florian attempted to turn his grimace into a smile. Meanwhile, Bodkins charged the construct head-on, diving away only when it dragged the mace across the ground, clipping one of the outstretched paws. She howled as if injured and reared back, gripping the limb with another until she could stop and assess the damage.

It looked bad. The spiked mace had torn its green scaly skin, rendering the monster limb's clawed hand useless. Bodkins winced and fussed at some clips that held the now-broken arm to the chair, letting it fall with a thud to the ground. She motioned with one hand, gripping a green thread and tearing it free as if pulling the stitching from a botched hem.

She moaned and held her face in her hands as if hiding tears from the rest of the party.

"Did . . . did it hurt you?" Florian ventured, afraid of the answer.

She looked up. "I had some rough emotions stitched to that one, and now I've gotta deal with them like they're fresh. Just some body image stuff. I'll get over it."

Florian frowned. From where he stood, her body looked great. But he understood the sentiment, anyway. At least in Leechleif, folks criticized women's bodies far more than their male peers. It was even a problem for him when he got onstage and . . . wait.

Wait. That was it!

Florian waved excitedly to Wardric, even as Bodkins girded herself and stepped back into the construct's range.

"I need you to paint me!" he told the artist. "I need a dress, heeled boots, and a couple of bags of rice. About this size and hanging right here." Florian cupped his hands before his chest to demonstrate.

Wardric raised a brow. "You want me to paint you a pair of—"

"Don't say it. Just paint it."

"Right."

Wardric nodded and whipped out his palette, once again impressing Florian with his kindness by asking no further questions. 'Peterman' could never have explained his new theory about the clumsiness when practicing swordplay with Eddie. Specifically, that he had trained and performed day after day as Ava Triumphant, who had an impressively heavy bosom, heels, and tricky gowns. All his training was in a different body!

Wardric finished mixing his paint. "Hold very still. This makes me nervous."

Making Wardric nervous made Florian nervous. He held his breath and stiffened his body, refusing to flinch as the first icy stroke of paint slid along his arm.

In his head, he shrieked. The paint was cold! And wet! It felt like Wardric was tracing his arm with a brush as big and moist as a mop.

Just as quickly as it struck, the chill faded into the warm

softness of a silk sleeve, a tight bodice, and flowing skirts. Florian waited until the artist gave a thumbs-up before glancing at the handiwork.

It was flawless and far more detailed than Florian expected for the time it took.

He beamed and said, "Perfect! Thank you!" before brandishing the sword and testing a few lunges.

He was back.

Florian Honeybeard, the master swordsman who wowed audiences daily, was back and ready for his next performance. He dashed out into the open room, sword at the ready, and took off in the opposite direction of Bodkins. The construct's glowing gaze followed, and Bodkins took that opportunity. She dashed around the swinging mace and swiped at the construct's shoulder with gnarly looking howling horror claws. The swing tore off its pauldron and exposed the gears beneath.

It quickly switched targets back to her, spinning the shield to knock her aside, and Wardric painted a nasty crack across its other arm.

That was Florian's cue.

He sheathed the sword and rolled closer, then drew it and brought it down on the arm Wardric had weakened.

Were he holding a standard sword, the blow would have widened the crack at best while ruining the weapon. And were it a normally enchanted sword, perhaps it would have split the armor.

But Florian held an enchanted sword designed and purchased for wealthy schoolkids engaged in outlawed competitive sports, so, alarmingly, he sheared the arm off.

It hit the floor and took the shield with it, making as much ruckus as a sound artist recreating a thunderstorm. That got the construct's attention, and it lifted the mace to attack again.

Unfortunately for it, both Wardric and Bodkins were now

free of obstructions. She leapt and latched on to the exposed shoulder while Wardric slashed at its remaining fingers.

The arm went limp, and the mace crashed to the floor, leaving the construct defenseless against Florian. As he climbed onto its back and slashed at its helmeted head, it struck him how embarrassing it would be if the thing's brain was elsewhere. What would Bodkins stitch him to if the construct reared back, headless, and crushed him into a wall?

Fortunately, his instincts paid off, and the thing crashed to its knees, signaling the battle was over. Florian sheathed his sword, mopped his brow with a sleeve—a shame considering the lovely fabric—and met up with the mercs by the fallen shield.

Bodkins pointed to the shield. "The gears on the back of this thing look like they line up with the ones on the exit door. I'll need your help getting it over there to check. Each of you grab a corner and lift. Oh, and Peterman, what are you wearing?"

Wardric coughed. "He needed confidence, so I made him pretty."

She gripped the edge of the shield with scaly hands. "Good call. Remind me later to give you a promotion."

He beamed. "Thanks, boss!"

Florian struggled with his corner. "How about you? Are you doing okay?"

"Well, nobody gave *me* a dress, but I'm doing all right."

For a moment, Florian wondered if he should say something to make her feel better about her appearance. But, after a wobbly start with the three of them carting the shield to the door, he decided it probably was not the time. The three set the shield against the wall, then tilted it up to meet the door, where it clicked in place.

"Hope this works," Wardric muttered and turned the knob.

The door opened with a creak, large enough for everyone, and a surprising sound came from within.

"Is that . . . muffled talking?" Florian asked. His heart leapt at the sound, elated to finally be so close to his goal.

It plummeted to his stomach with the realization that the excitement he felt was not his own. The monster was nearing whatever it wanted, and its glee was enough for him to feel without trying.

"We need to move!" he said and ran.

The mercenaries did their best to keep up.

 Forty

Are You Sure?

Margaret inspected the wall as one might a plant infested with mites, then drew back and read the sign above the door. "Last door. Are you sure?"

"Well, I was," Theo replied as if she had asked him the question directly. "Now, not so much."

Vivienne crossed her arms. "Don't be a baby. It just has spooky decorations to scare us off."

"It's a wall of human skulls!" Theo exclaimed. "There must be hundreds of them!"

"One thousand, five hundred, and forty," Margaret corrected as she moved along the wall. "And they're real."

"Maybe this used to be a catacomb," Vivienne said with a shrug. "Let's go!"

Growina had no desire to get involved but could not resist sharing trivia. "Actually, the Wontmoil Cemetery holds every local dating back to the town's establishment, and they're all very much intact. The spirit-stitched skeletons keep an eye on things. Or . . . a socket, I guess. They're quite proud."

"Eugh," Theo replied. "If these aren't local skulls, who were these people? How did they get here? And more importantly—"

"Why is the sign spelled correctly?" Sylvie interrupted.

Theo spun to stare at the sign, looked back at Sylvie, and furrowed his brow. For once, he had nothing snarky to say.

Growina felt around her dress pockets until she located the first puzzle stone. *Wud mapl orng ruk beneet str*, it said on the bottom. The thing was almost indecipherable. Compared to that, the shield on the construct had seemed almost legible, at least to her.

She raised a timid hand and waited for the squabbling to stop.

"Yes? Apothe . . . wina?" Theo asked. It was somehow worse than apothecary. But at least the wizard made an attempt.

"It seems to me," she said, fidgeting with the stone, "the words have been getting easier to read all along."

"What words? What are you talking about?" Chip demanded.

Growina jumped, having forgotten the teen was there.

Margaret attempted to pry a gold tooth from a skull without success. "We've been following clues like the one on the first puzzle door for days. And Growina's right. The text is less cryptic down here than it was on the clues above ground."

Theo's eyes widened. "I have a theory! What if the building of this cavern coincided with the end of the Gart Splagosion? If the curse lifted as they worked, it would explain a slow recovery. It's only logical since it surely took them months to cart all these skulls down here."

"Actually," Growina said again, feeling like a bit of a pest, "I noticed the lichen growing here isn't spreading naturally. It, and the stone walls, seemed deliberately placed. Like they were magic'd here, somehow. Do you think maybe the skulls were, too?"

Theo waved a hand dismissively. "Preposterous. I've read every book in the Wizard Association's Library, and there's no record of an individual or team capable of transporting an entire wall."

"What makes you think it was a wizard?" Vivienne asked with a sneer.

Chip missed her implication entirely and chimed in with, "It could have been aliens. Like those children who work for the bank."

Theo shook his head instead of replying, and Growina did not blame him. It would take far too long to explain the twins, their otherworldly powers, and their . . . unique . . . drawbacks.

Though, now that Chip brought it up, where *were* Zizel and Zemni? They said they'd pitch in as long as the creature wasn't nearby, and she hadn't seen them in what felt like ages.

"Do we put it to a vote?" Theo asked. "Decide together if we should go in?"

"No," Vivienne insisted. She swished her lacy skirt for emphasis and spun toward the skull-flanked door. "No more votes. We came this far, and we're going in. Better us than someone else."

Margaret nodded. "I agree. Whatever's in there was well hidden until we uncovered it. Reward or punishment, we've earned it."

Chip reluctantly followed her toward the door with the sluggish Penumbral Magwod in tow. Growina shrugged and followed as well, leaving poor Theo without any choice. They huddled around Margaret, and she cautiously cracked the aging door open. When no traps sprung, she shoved it wide and stepped through.

Growina wasn't sure what she expected when she entered the last room of the cavern. A prison, perhaps, torn apart by the escaping creature. Or maybe a portal to another world. She definitely wasn't expecting an elaborately decorated room with a book on a pedestal at the center.

Half-columns of veined marble lined the walls, interrupting

crumbling frescos of a wizard-like character in various heroic acts.

"Who . . . was that?" Margaret whispered, nodding to a pile of charred bones and ashes at the pedestal's base.

Theo cleared his throat, then cleared it again as if suddenly unable to speak. "Well, I, for one, have never seen a spellbook hover so far above its pedestal. Nor have I witnessed one, in person, that warps the air around it like that."

"And laughs," Vivienne said.

Theo scowled. "You hear laughter?"

"Oh, yeah. This thing is noisy. I'm gonna touch it."

"Halt!" Margaret commanded, and Vivienne did, though she looked none too happy about it.

"I can't believe I'm saying this," Theo said, "but I think I know whose bones those are."

"There's a message!" Chip said, pointing to some words etched into a tile.

Growina crouched and dusted it off.

"If you're reading this," Theo read, "you survived. Bravo. I bet you think you're pretty clever. I bet you think you're above doing what you imagine I did wrong. But did you know I found the book underground, like you? Did you know I died when I tried to destroy it? Were you aware I was imprisoned inside my possessed corpse for years, watching that parasite slaughter my friends? It took patience, planning, and the sacrifice of strangers to spring my consciousness from that prison. And even now, with infinite power, I can't stop the decay of my body. Do you still think you're better than me? Best of luck, S. Slugbeard."

Theo's face scrunched up, and he leaned closer.

"P.S. I'll definitely be haunting something. Look me up later. Tell me how it went."

Margaret pursed her lips and rocked on booted heels. "Did

we just—"

"Accidentally uncover the hidden location of Sigeric Slugbeard's infamous spellbook?" Theo asked. "Indeed, and the cultists searching for his missing book are right behind us in this cave."

"We messed up," Margaret said.

"Absolutely."

"The wizards were right," she added.

Theo's nose crinkled. "Well, now. Hold on. Let's not jump to any conclusions."

Growina raised a hand. "What do we do next?"

"What can we do?" he said. "Touching it seems like a terrible plan and trying to destroy it didn't work for Slugbeard. But leaving it for the cultists is out of the question. I can't think of any viable options."

Chip stepped forward. The teen still seemed to be teetering on the edge of a meltdown, but his confession must have lifted some weight because his voice regained its irritating whine. "What an arrogant jerk! If he had the time to scratch all that into stone, you'd think he could have mentioned what didn't work, or at least what the strangers did to free him. But no, he's gotta prove his superiority by letting others make mistakes."

Growina sighed. "I know I give folks too much credit, but surely dying and merging with a book had a negative impact on his mental health. Though I will admit, he took the time to build a whole puzzle cave. Leaving us without details seems inconsistent."

"You're right!" Vivienne snapped. "You're giving him too much credit. I think he wanted to lure us here and sacrifice us to that—shut up, book! I can't hear myself talk over all your blabbing!"

Margaret and Theo shared a concerned look.

Theo tried to play peacemaker. "If what this message says is true, he used his power to undo the Gart Splagosion before his . . ." He gestured to the pile of bones. "Perhaps Growina is right, and the book took a toll. We can ask his ghost when we solve this last puzzle."

"There's no solution!" Vivienne snapped. "Either one of us becomes the next Slugbeard, or one of those cultists does. What's the difference? We might as well—"

"Look out!"

Team Wontmoil spun to see a man in a dress—or perhaps a very plain, short-haired woman?—barrel into the room behind them.

The newcomer set their hands on their knees and huffed, then raised their head and said, "It's not what you think it is."

Behind them, a woman in a spider-like chair propelled by inhuman arms and legs entered the chamber, followed by a bearded artist. None of them bore the telltale embroidered uniform of the hangry cultists.

"Who the fudge are you?" Vivienne asked.

The spider woman answered, "He's a soothsayer. You need to listen. You're in danger."

Theo crossed his arms. "We already know the book is Sigeric Slugbeard's. We aren't going to touch it or try to blow it up."

The man in the dress shook his head. "No, not from that. From the monster." He lifted a graceful finger and pointed directly at the hulking form of Magwod.

The construct burst apart into a thousand pieces that bounced and pinged around the room. A shadowy creature sprung from the torso, leaving a trail of colorful smoke that lingered like an oil slick in the air. With the grace of a ballerina, the creature bounced around the walls, looking like little more than a blur of claws and tentacles.

Vivienne crumpled to the floor with both hands pressed over her ears. "Stop screaming! Stop it! Shut up, book!" she howled.

The creature got its bearings and pounced, but not on Team Wontmoil or the strangers. Instead, it crashed into the podium and snatched up the spellbook, seemingly without consequence, then chewed it up in massive jaws with fangs visible even through the smoke. It gobbled the book like a dog with a treat and the colorful smoke became so intense it lit the cavern like a flared match.

"We *really* messed up," Theo said.

Vivienne stopped screaming and curled up on the floor.

"Yeah," the spider woman agreed. "You did."

Forty-One

Dorothea Broomhandle

"I'VE CHANGED MY mind," Vivienne moaned from the cavern floor. "I'd like to go back to voting, please. I vote Magwod stays the same thing for more than ten minutes."

Mercenaries and adventurers alike ignored the witch, focused as they were on the flailing creature. It thrashed and clawed at the air around it as if trapped in a monster-sized bubble, emitting bright puffs of color with every swipe of its terrifying paws. Hooked claws punctured an invisible film, drawing into sharp focus before sliding back into blurry shadow.

Theo tugged off his hat and thumped himself in the head. "Think, think, think. What are we looking at? It clearly tricked us into bringing it here to eat Slugbeard's Spellbook. But to what end? What's it doing now?"

"I know," Beatrix Bodkins said. She leaned back like an old sage. "It's using the magic of the spellbook to pierce the barrier between worlds. Tearing its way into this one. And if it gets through with that power intact, you're gonna wish the cultists had won."

"A half-summon," Margaret breathed. "Like Dorothea Broomhandle."

"Thank you!" Florian exclaimed. "Someone else remembers

the play."

She gave him a withering look. "It's not a play. It's our history."

"And I can't help but notice," Bodkins said, "that I came here hunting the nasty thing and found it in a room full of witches."

Growina fiddled with her shawl, simultaneously aware that such a move was stereotypical guilty behavior and that real criminals rarely did it. "Oh, I'm not actually a witch. I'm an apothecary, really. I've no idea how to cast spells."

Bodkins quirked a brow and examined her as if she were the bounty. "I can see that."

Vivienne picked herself off the floor, looking for a fight to pick. Whatever power the book had over her must have stopped when the creature consumed it. Fortunately for her, it was difficult to ruffle Bodkins' feathers.

"Are you accusing us?" she demanded. "Just cause we're witches, you think we all know how to half-summon, is that it? I don't even know how to whole-summon! Search my grimoires. I've got nothing!"

Sylvie pointed to her and nodded. It was not clear if the pale-eyed witch meant that she, too, lacked summoning spells or if she agreed Vivienne could not cast one.

Margaret thought longer about her response. "I've also never attempted a summon. But I took a rubbing of a summoning spell I found on an old gravestone—for laughs. Oh! But I don't even have that grimoire now. The other day, I gave it to . . ."

Her mouth snapped shut, and she turned to Growina, who could not bear to meet her eye.

"Growina," she said calmly, "where did you leave the grimoire I gave you?"

Growina found her mouth too dry to speak. "Ahh. Um . . ."

"Was it stolen from your shop or borrowed?"

"Oh, no. No. It's still there."

"I see. Did you . . . open it?"

"Er, a bit."

Theo's eyes widened. "Apothecary, what have you done?"

Growina winced. "Nothing! Really. Nothing happened. See, I tried the summoning spell, but—"

"Why?" Vivienne asked. "Do you know how dangerous those spells are?"

"No!" Growina cried. "I don't know anything at all! I saw the spell and thought, well, I don't have any friends. I thought I could summon someone here who wanted to go on adventures with me. But nothing happened! It didn't work."

Bodkins' mouth hardened into a line and she struck an authoritative posture. "We're not here to lay blame. We're here to stop a monster from eating this town. Sounds like we know what we're dealing with now. Anyone present know how to stop it?"

"There's the easy way," Margaret said.

"Kill the summoner," Florian added, but his hand did not move toward his sword.

Goosebumps traveled up Growina's arms.

"And there's the hard way," Margaret said. "We complete the summon and burn the magic away in the process. Then we banish or kill the monster if we can. But we have to recreate the spell *exactly* how it was before and lure the creature back into the circle. I have some candles on me, but I never found the right ingredients. What did you use?"

Growina's mind blanked. What had she used? "I remember berries. It might have been the ones from the collywobbles?"

"I have those," Florian volunteered.

"And some sticks. Maybe Skrabblin's Dagger? Or a cutting from my sentry shrub?"

"Which one?" Bodkins asked. "I have the former."

"Wait, no. It was neither. And—oh dear."

"What's *oh dear*?" Margaret asked.

"I just remembered. My kettle whistled, and I bumped into the candles. A few things on the ground caught on fire."

"What things?"

"Well, it was near where I prepare the pouches, so it was probably . . . anything? Everything? The entire contents of my garden could have been on the ground. I'm so sorry."

"We're doomed," Chip added unhelpfully.

"Yeah, we're not gonna recreate that, are we?" Vivienne agreed.

Growina squirmed and eyed the thrashing creature. Was it her imagination, or had it freed an entire arm? "If it helps, it's still set up in my garden."

Theo perked up. "The whole thing? You didn't clean it up when you were done?"

"I meant to, but things kept coming up."

"That's great!" he said. "We can use the original circle!"

Wardric raised a hand. "How will you lure the monster there? It's been tumbling around for five minutes. Look." He waved his arms and shouted, "Hello, monster! I'm gonna stop you! See? It's not interested in us."

"Hrm. We could entice it with something magical."

Florian gripped his sword's hilt defensively, giving the wizard a practiced glare. "I assure you, it's got all the magic it wants."

"Oh, yeah?" Theo asked. "How can you be so sure?"

"I have a connection to the creature. I can feel and see what it feels and sees. And it doesn't want magic anymore."

"Well, then, what does it want?"

"Proper food. It wants to come here and gorge itself."

Theo swallowed and replaced his hat. "On us?"

Florian shrugged. "I can't read its mind. I can only feel its emotions."

"Fine. We'll figure it out."

Growina scooched up beside Wardric. The large man had a gentleness to him that made her feel more secure in his presence. She reached into her pocket, pulled out a glowing pink marble, and held it up.

"I think I have a way to get it to my garden. But I don't want to send it into town alone. It could hurt someone there." She swallowed, unable to believe what she was saying. "I'll have to get close so I can go with it."

Chip perked up. "Hey! Right! Your blooming blastflower!"

"Blasted glassflower. I'll get close and smash this on the ground, and the plant will move me and the creature to my garden—assuming the creature is as light as it looks. Vines are only so strong."

"I'm coming, too," Margaret said. "You won't know what to do without me."

Growina finally met the witch's eye. Getting close to the creature was dangerous, but if Growina died, it would still stop the beast. There was no logic to Margaret putting herself in danger. And yet, the look on the woman's face quashed any thought of argument.

Was that how all heroes behaved? Risking their lives to save others, even when there was an easier option?

Margaret did not wait for a reply. "It's settled, then. Let's not waste time."

Everyone took a step back as Margaret and Growina sized up the creature. Every few moments, a furry arm shot out, presenting both a dangerous obstacle and a potential anchoring point for the vines.

"Wait for the arm to center itself," Margaret said. "Then you take the left, and I'll take the right."

Growina nodded and gripped the marble in sweaty fingers, gathering her nerves. She was pretty certain she had stopped breathing but couldn't spare the attention to check.

After what felt like days, the creature's arm flailed in their direction.

"Now!" Margaret shouted, and dove in.

Growina ran to keep up, taking her place to the creature's left, as close as she could safely get. She smashed the marble as hard as possible on the stone tile beneath the waving paw, hoping to create a large splash radius. Smoke curled from the released liquid, and a pool of inky nothingness opened beneath them. Vines shot out, encircling their boots and the creature's forearm, tugging them down.

They vanished with a whoosh into the closing portal.

Wardric approached the empty center of the suddenly much darker room and toed at the glass with a booted foot. "What *was* that?"

Theo shook his head. "I've never understood the potions. I've always relied on her to have all the answers. We all did. It'll be hard for everyone in Wontmoil if the worst happens." He fell silent and pretended to smooth his beard rather than express his emotions. "You know, I've been shopping with her for thirty years and only recently learned her name. What does that say about me?"

Bodkins ignored the question and eyed the door. "Peterman, did they make it safely?"

Florian closed his eyes and watched the monster battle a nasty shrub. Both women were already free of the plant and hurrying off behind a bountiful arbor. The monster's disposition was alarming. As expected, the plant frustrated it, but other emotions battled for dominance. There was a sense of longing or abandonment, and eagerness to sate the ever-present hunger. Who knew monsters were so complex?

"They're safe for now," he told Bodkins, "but the shrub trapping the monster won't hold it forever."

"Then we need to move," she said. "You, there. Wizard. Where did they go?"

Theo scowled. "Herbs and Vices. It's in the middle of town."

"You'll need us to get in," Vivienne added. "We put protections around the shop, and you're definitely not on the guest list."

Bodkins nodded before squeezing through the door. "All right," she said. "If you're all coming, try your best not to slow me down."

And with that, the mercenaries vanished into the hallway.

Forty-Two

Wriggleweed

FLORIAN COULD NOT remember the last time his legs ached so badly. But with his collywobbles nearly depleted after the hour-and-a-half journey to Wontmoil, there was no good reason for a grown man to hitch a ride on Bodkins' lap.

Or, at least, as Wardric pointed out, no reason if they were not intimate.

He skidded through the quiet streets, last in a parade of bounty hunters and trailed by paint flakes fluttering behind him. Seeing the gorgeous dress go was sad, but Wardric had warned him it was temporary. Besides, the chances of them needing his sword now that they numbered eight instead of three were about the same as them needing his acting.

"Hey!" a stranger called to him. "You there! Stop!"

He looked over his shoulder to see a put-together woman in the doorway of a building called Pollywog's Pampering Powders. When he did not stop—could not, really—she jogged to catch up.

"What's going on?" she demanded. "Where's everyone running?"

He inhaled, drawing upon his experience projecting his voice during action scenes. "The bounty is in Herbs and Vices, but don't worry. You're safe." He took another, larger breath as the distance between them grew. "We have a plan, but if it fails, we'll kill the apothecary, and the monster will vanish."

The woman came to an abrupt halt with a horrified expression. "*Our* apothecary?"

Florian put his hands in the air apologetically. She was too far away now to hear him, and he did not honestly know the answer. But the woman did not wait for one. She hurried down a parallel street and out of sight before he rounded a bend.

A bell broke the relative silence.

"This is it!" Theo shouted, stopping before a cottage-like building with a high-walled backyard.

Florian considered collapsing in the street and curling up in a ball like a sleepy toddler. Fortunately, the part of his brain that remembered he should walk off the pain still functioned. He compromised by wobbling in place while the witches made silly hand motions at the door.

Theo did not reach for the knob. He sneezed—or said something close to a sneeze—and walked straight through the solid wood. Behind him, the witches made more odd gestures, and the door flew open without touching it.

Apparently, adventurers did not use doors?

"A rudimentary spell," Chip complained. "Irresponsible security measures. Even I could thwart that with minimal effort."

"Prove it or shut it!" Vivienne sang.

Chip pouted and begrudgingly followed them inside. Bodkins took a moment to appraise the entrance and, satisfied with what she saw, stepped into the shop with Wardric and Florian on her heels.

They passed through an eerily sparse storefront, pausing only long enough for Bodkins to eye a jar of wriggleweed living up to its name. The stuff gave Florian terrible flashbacks of his first encounter with the mercenaries before he got to know them well. Then, they were through the building and into the backyard, which was, as promised, a fantastic garden.

"Don't get close! Circle 'round again!" Margaret's voice called through a maze of trees and trellises.

Everyone dashed toward the sound, only to come to a comical halt when they discovered the reason behind it. The monster had gotten loose, free of the sentry shrub for who knew how long, and was now slashing at the barrier between worlds with precision. Claws, paws, and vicious fangs pierced through the fog as the thing pounced, narrowly missing the circle of flame Margaret maintained with her palms outstretched.

"Eep!" Growina shouted and dodged.

The routine felt oddly practiced, as if the two had been dancing around the circle the whole time the mercs ran from the caves.

"Finally, you made it," Margaret said as if they had strolled to catch up with her and not rushed so quickly their legs fell off. "We can't get the creature into the circle. It's more interested in Growina than food."

Florian examined their progress thus far and was unsurprised by their lack of success. "Is that a frozen spinach quiche?"

He pointed to a pale pie-shaped object in the center of the toppled candle circle. It sat beside a bubbling cauldron—not exactly the most appealing bait.

"Is it a carnivore?" Margaret asked, distress evident in her voice. "I thought it might be a carnivore."

"I don't have any meat!" Growina whined. "I only do plants!"

The monster shot a paw in her direction, claws thankfully retracted, resulting in another yelp.

Wardric tugged a narrow brush from a band around his

thigh. "I might be able to paint a roast turkey."

Theo's eyebrows shot up so high it was a wonder his hat stayed on his head. "Paint-based imaginative matter creation? I've never seen anyone do that before! Incredible! By all means."

Margaret shook her head. "No good. Magic is magic, and food is food, and this thing can tell the difference between them."

"What's your suggestion?" he asked, perturbed that she denied him a show. "Do we hit the market to buy a porkchop?"

"No time. Perhaps we can push it in now that everyone's here?"

Bodkins leaned forward to get a better look as the thing leapt for Growina again. Its paws struck bare soil with a puff of rainbow smoke, and otherworldly plants curled from between its furry toes. Then the legs pulled back into blurriness, leaving behind a massive paw-print of lavender leaves and silver berries.

"Anyone that thing touches now is risking a face full of Slugbeard's magic. Any volunteers?"

The mercs and adventurers looked at each other and, one at a time, down at their feet. Death in battle was one thing, but the atrocities Slugbeard—or his controlled corpse—committed during the Gart Splagosion were potentially far worse than death.

Growina released a pent-up breath and grabbed her puffy skirts in both hands. She hoisted them up, exposing stockinged calves, and trained her gaze on the flaming circle.

"Wait, don't!" Margaret shouted.

Growina ignored her. With a running hop, she cleared the flames and landed beside the frozen quiche.

"You won't be able to dodge it in there!" Margaret said in a panic.

"That's the idea," Growina replied, releasing her skirts and squeezing her eyes shut.

It was a plan. Not the best one, as it relied on two assumptions: first, that the circle would deplete the monster's magic before it landed on top of her, and second, that it could not eat her faster than her friends could act.

Everyone struck a nervous pose, ready to strike one way or another depending on the outcome of the gamble. But, to their surprise, the draw of the new bait was still not enough to entice the creature beyond the flames.

Bodkins watched it toe at the circle, swishing paws above the flame and drawing them back as if burned. "Peterman, why is it after the summoner?"

He was unsure he could answer the question without consuming more collywobbles, but he closed his eyes and pushed his mind toward the monster, anyway. "I'm sorry. I'm very— wait. No. *It's* very confused. I don't think this is helping."

Bodkins drummed her fingers on her chair, said, "I have an idea," and vanished into the garden.

"Whoa!" Chip shouted as the monster extended an entire arm through the barrier and flailed in Growina's direction.

The thing was black and furry with lean muscle and deadly looking, retractable claws. The rainbow smoke released with each swipe was so intense it flashed like lightning and fired in the direction of the movement, billowing off everything it touched and causing tiny mutations in the surrounding plants.

"Retreat!" Margaret commanded, and everyone, including the grumbling Theo, complied.

"Are you kidding me?" Vivienne asked. "Now we can't get close enough to . . . you know . . . if this doesn't work."

She, like everyone else present, seemed hesitant to say aloud that they might have to murder one of their team. Growina winced and cowered to avoid blasts of smoke.

Florian held his breath as he watched. Then he shrieked as Bodkins slapped an iron frying pan into his hands.

"Think of a solution and tell us what you see!" she demanded before dumping a cup of salt and a fistful of wriggleweed into the pan.

Florian broke out in a sweat. "I faked this last time!" he admitted. "It doesn't—huh."

"Out with it! What do you see?"

He examined the shape left by the wriggleweed as it shoved a pattern through the salt. It was unmistakable.

"A fish."

"A fish?" Bodkins said. "Where do we get a fish in a forest town?"

But Growina suddenly perked up. She grinned and rummaged through her pockets, then pulled out a handful of dry sticks.

"Fish sticks!" she declared, and snapped them in two.

A pungent aroma filled the garden as foamy marrow spewed from the sticks in the exact shape of fileted fish.

The monster drew back, tentacled rear shoved in the air, and leapt directly into the circle.

For a moment, no one could make out a thing. The blast of smoke that filled the air as the monster flew into the circle obfuscated everything. But eventually, a breeze picked it up and carried it into the clouds, giving them a hazy view of the circle.

The monster, still black and furry but no longer hazy, head-butted Growina's cheek, twirled in her lap despite its size, and settled down, gnawing on fish sticks.

Theo narrowed his eyes. "Am I hearing this right? Is the creature . . . purring?"

"It's got three tails!" Chip said, excitedly pointing to the assumed tentacles.

Vivienne was not excited. "You summoned an alien housecat?"

Growina looked up, already stroking the creature between the eyes. It was more like a small jungle animal than a housecat, honestly. "Oh. Hmm. I suppose I did, accidentally."

"Why didn't you adopt an actual cat?"

"Oh, goodness, no. I couldn't do that! Many of my plants are poisonous!"

The beast looked up from its meal and around the garden, then nodded its furry head in agreement.

Florian pointed. "I knew it! I knew that thing was intelligent!"

It grinned.

"What will happen to it?" Growina asked, dancing around a much larger question.

Margaret extinguished the flames with a push of her palms and leaned forward to stare the cat in the eye. "That depends. Do you plan to continue menacing this town?"

It shook its head and innocently nibbled on its snacks. Florian was unsure he believed it, as menace was default cat behavior. But at least the former monster seemed bright enough to cover its tracks.

"Well," Margaret said, but she did not continue. Instead, she listened to a sound that had been inaudible while they were shouting.

Someone was banging on the shop door.

Forty-Three

Bounty

Bodkins burst into laughter so loud it made everyone around the circle flinch. "A cat! I can't believe it. Honeybeard, they told me you'd come up with something, but this is the best adventure of my life. Bravo! Now, let's go home. We've earned a nice meal and a rest. Then I'll get Eddie reassembled."

"But, but, but the bounty!" Florian stammered as he trailed her through the garden. "The money! Do we not get any of it? You promised—" He paused. "Wait. Did you just call me Honeybeard?"

She turned, a sly grin on her face. "That is your name, is it not?"

Florian went white and bright red, as if he had been doused with ice water and thrown into a forge. "You've known this whole time?"

Wardric covered his mouth, apparently aware it was not time to laugh but unable to contain one anyhow.

Florian shot him a glare, as well. "You knew, too?"

Wardric nodded sheepishly. "I figured Eddie gave it away when he blabbed about his old crew's fake names ending in beard."

"The Stealthy Eight. Honeybeard. Were my ancestors in his crew? And that's why I can do what I do?"

"You got it!" Bodkins said with applause. "We're big fans of your work on stage, but we noticed you read the audience a little *too* well. That, plus your surname, made us curious. And when the Spherule managers showed up on my doorstep begging me for donations . . ."

"Those rats already have your money, don't they?"

"They do."

"Those filthy creeps! They're getting a piece of my mind when we return. This is no way to treat an employee."

Bodkins brushed a vine away from her face. "And why is that? Did you have a bad time with us?"

He crossed his arms and pursed his lips, mulling it over. "I suppose not."

She beamed, moving back into the shop. "Want to do it again sometime?"

Another moment of thought passed.

"Professionally or privately?"

"Whichever you prefer."

He passed through a wispy curtain and into the storefront. "In that case, there's something I've been meaning to ask you."

Wardric pulled a face and inched backward, giving them relative privacy.

"Chicken Trug," Bodkins said.

"E-excuse me?"

"It's my favorite restaurant. I don't enjoy fancy dates. Snobbish people irritate me."

He flushed. "Chicken Trug, it is!"

With that, he opened the shop door and stepped out into an angry mob pointing various implements at his face. A butcher held a cleaver in each hand, and a baker gripped equally intimidating bread knives. The put-together woman he saw earlier gripped what appeared to be a makeup brush with the handle end sharpened to a point, and someone beside her had a nasty-looking set of hairpins pointed his way.

He blinked, shocked, before instinct took over, and he fell into the role of a more confident human. "The deed is done, and your apothecary is fine," he said, leaving off the details. "You're welcome."

"Prove it, or you're going nowhere!" Pollywog demanded with a jab of her brush.

Wardric, overhearing the commotion, returned to the backyard herbary, where Growina stood with her new cat. It circled her skirts and looked up at her with golden eyes that still contained a hint of the rainbow smoke.

To his surprise, two identical children in short-pants appeared in the air beside her.

"Witches! Silly hat man!" Zizel cried while stretching her limbs. "I thought you'd never sort that out."

"I was *so* bored waiting!" Zemni agreed. "So, what is that thing?"

"A cat," Vivienne said. "A plain old cat with too many tails. It was a half-summon all along."

"I don't know what that means, but good work!" Zizel said. "Let's get down to business, shall we? Clipboard!"

A laundry peg and a wooden plank appeared in the air and fell to the ground, much to the alien's dismay.

"Never mind. I'll remember it. Who here is claiming the bounty?"

"We *were* planning to split it among us. But we've decided instead to share it with the town, in hopes that it will reduce the sentence. See, one of us accidentally caused the half-summon." Theo glanced around the circle, meeting everyone's eyes to confirm they were all still okay with the answer he gave.

"One of you?" Zemni asked. "Which one?"

Growina raised a shaking hand.

"Wow, lady!" Zizel said. "I did not see that one coming!"

"I did," Sylvie whispered, earning a side-eye from Margaret.

"Am I in trouble?" Growina asked, voice catching in her throat.

Zizel shrugged. "Couldn't say, we're not the law. But we'll have to report it. That thing did a lot of damage."

"Hold on!" Theo interrupted. "Tell them the entire story."

Growina glanced up, mind blank with terror.

"Tell them how the monster you summoned ate *the* Sigeric Slugbeard's Spellbook. The creature obliterated it, saving the entire planet from a second Gart Splagosion—or worse! Nobody else could have done that! We would be in an apocalypse right now if not for that summon."

Zemni turned upside-down and asked Growina, "Is that true?"

"Sort of, yes. But—"

Zemni spun again. "Great! Then there's no need to report you! Damages caused by heroic acts fall into a different category. You'll need to file some paperwork itemizing the objects consumed by the creature versus the estimated value of saving the planet. And get it notarized, of course."

"And register your cat!" Zizel added. "It'll save you a lot of paperwork next time!"

Growina nodded, holding back tears of relief, and the twins waved their goodbyes before zipping off to notify the bank.

Wardric took the opportunity to interject. "Excuse me, ma'am. The entire city is outside your door demanding we prove you're still alive. Would you mind coming with me and giving them a wave, so they don't chop my friends' heads off?"

Growina gripped her shawl. "The whole city? For me?"

"Yeah. They're really, very mad."

"Oh!"

She started after him, then stopped when she realized the rest were not coming. It struck her, then, that the adventure was over. And yet, somehow, she could not let them go. The comfort of returning to her old routine warred with the fear of being alone. True, she had her new cat—which was what she must have subconsciously desired on the dark night when she cast her spell—and the creature was guaranteed to join her on adventures, if not cause them itself.

. . . But one friend no longer felt like enough.

She wanted more.

She wanted a community.

"Are you not coming?" she asked the group formerly known as Team Wontmoil.

Margaret shook her head. "We don't do crowds."

"And besides," Theo said with a nod toward Chip. "We need to help this one gather bits of Magwod before someone discovers him in that cave. The big guy's not going to reassemble himself . . . I hope."

"We'll come back around when things die down," Vivienne added. "Your shop makes for a nice base."

Growina's heart did a somersault. "You mean we're still a team?"

"Fearsome geese," Wardric muttered.

"What's that?" Vivienne asked with a hint of challenge in her voice.

"Means you're an odd combo, but you win anyway!" He counted each of them off while pointing. "Three witches, a wizard, a mage with a construct, and—hmm." He eyed Growina, bottle bandolier and all, clearly uncertain what her title was.

Theo stepped forward and puffed up his chest. The dapper wizard tugged off his hat and gestured to her with a proud smile. "A soon-to-be world-famous summoner," he said.

Growina glanced down at the tiny tug from carefully-placed claws on her skirt.

She grinned. "And don't forget—her new best friend."

Acknowledgements

Writing a book takes time and focus, two things in short supply for full-time working parents. Nonetheless, my patient spouse put up with my habit and acted as my beta reader. Many thanks for responding to calls of, "Want to read this?" even in the middle of the night.

Similarly, I would never have made it to the finish line without the experienced eye of my copy editor, Chelsea Beam, who went above and beyond to make this book shine. Thank you so much for making sense of my nonsense.

I would also like to thank Despina Karras, who provided invaluable feedback for the character of Beatrix Bodkins, and caught some typos along the way. I am so grateful.

Terri Lambert cheered me on as I wrote, and I carried her kind words with me through the end.

The Loons kept me on the rails, not only through many drafts, but through the production of the cover and book layout as well. Their feedback (and the occasional emoji newspaper swat) steered me in the right direction as I navigated the complex world of publishing.

Last but not least, thanks to my mother for sharing my story and artwork with her friends, rather than judging the subject matter. I hope they enjoy the witches and wizards, or, at least, have a good sense of humor.

About the Author

L. N. Clarke is a video game producer by day and word nerd by night. In the past, she designed comic books and studied computer science. She is a total sucker for strange old books, antique lockpicks, and pen and paper cryptography. She lives in the Eastern U.S. with her equally nerdy spouse, cool kiddo, dog, cat, and a flock of chickens.

9 798986 246604